WHERE CROWS WOULD DIE

ON MARY GRIESE'S PREVIOUS WORK

Beryl Bainbridge:
'I get many manuscripts – many – and most are so dreary I hesitate to turn the page. Yours is immediately different... I think it terrific: I really mean that. You use language like paint, with an attention to light and shade... You have a very individual slant on life, and that is what makes a novelist. You're bloody good.'

Samuel Hodder of Blake Friedmann, judge of Bath Short Story Award 2019 (shortlisted):
'Another atmospheric story set in rural Wales.'

Vanessa Gebbie, judge of The Fish Publishing Short Memoir, Ireland (3rd prize):
'A very atmospheric, beautifully written account of a young family buying a Welsh hill farm, something from another era, and the neighbours – everything superbly evoked, drawing me in, bringing a lost generation into striking view. The characters in this piece are marvellously alive – this piece was much enjoyed.'

Euan Thorneycroft, judge of Bath Short Story Award 2017 (2nd prize):
'One of the most individual of all I read, with a totally authentic depiction of life in rural mid Wales.'

WHERE CROWS WOULD DIE

MARY GRIESE

For my family
and in memory of my dear friends,
Ruth Cook and Sue Stoner

First impression: 2020
© Mary Griese & Y Lolfa Cyf., 2020

Cover design: Y Lolfa
Cover image: Mary Griese

ISBN: 978 1 78461 828 5

Published and printed in Wales
on paper from well-maintained forests by
Y Lolfa Cyf., Talybont, Ceredigion SY24 5HE
e-mail ylolfa@ylolfa.com
website www.ylolfa.com
tel 01970 832 304
fax 832 782

PART ONE

ONE

1960

A BELL RANG. The ominous clang echoing up through the mountains sounded more like a Dickensian warning of escaped convicts than the end of a playtime. The sky had lightened to pale grey; only the hilltops were still shrouded in cloud.

The playground had emptied, leaving two small girls: one waif-like, the other well-nourished. The urchin girl was holding court, dangling a coiled worm above her open mouth. With dark eyes flashing from her prey to her audience, she dropped it between her neglected needle teeth and made a big show: chewing slowly, savouring the taste, swallowing and licking her lips. She rubbed a hand across her mouth, down her thin cotton dress and gave a loopy wink to the new girl, who vomited into the roots of a hefty oak. The only tree to split the playground concrete.

The second bell rang and the worm-eater ran into the grim Victorian building. Bethan Pritchard stood mesmerised. Still queasy, she wiped her mouth with her handkerchief, stuffed the mess into a hole in the tree trunk and willed movement into her leaden lace-ups, rooted to the spot. She checked the front of her dress was clean. This was her first playtime without a mac. It had rained continuously since their move and the view from her new bedroom window hadn't altered: sheep statues with their backsides to the weather under slate skies.

She saw a boy standing in the long grass on the other side of the railings. He was wearing stained green overalls and workboots and was past school age. It was unlikely he'd witnessed the worm performance as he was intent on watching a cat play with a bird, cruelly batting it about as cats do. The bird hopped and flapped hopelessly and Bethan resigned herself to more death.

The boy dived to the ground and his hair, black as the cat, slithered through the undergrowth like another creature. The cat was concentrating on the bird, unaware of its stalker until grabbed by a hind leg. It spun round in fury and sank its claws into the boy's arm. Without a wince he unhooked them and held the cat in a vice-like grip, stroking violently hard down its back, over and over until at last the yowling and hissing stopped. With a flat hand he smothered its face and whiskers, the pressure squashing its ears inside out. The cat forgot the bird, clung to the boy's clothes and began to purr loudly. The boy tucked it under his arm. He finished off the dying bird with his boot then, cradling the cat like a baby, strolled to the school railings and fixed his eyes on Bethan. A shiver tingled her spine.

He had huge hands, quite out of proportion to his scrawny body, thick farmery fingers travelling roughly down the cat's throat and overlapping its neck. Still the animal purred. It was upright now. The boy had propped his foot on the school wall and the cat was doing its best to balance on his bony knee. The boy's eyes bored into Bethan's making them water. She sensed his grip tighten on the cat's throat, and it gave a loud pleading mew as if sensing its perch was about to collapse.

He spoke fast in Welsh. Bethan's grasp of the language was still tenuous, but she knew enough to learn he hated cats for the cruelty of their nature and in those few sentences could tell his Welsh was as pure as her father's. He turned to English to pronounce with piercing clarity "I love birds see," glaring at Bethan as if it were her fault. He lifted his right hand, turned it palm upwards and made a sharp slice through the air. Just how her uncle killed a rabbit, his massive hand stretched flat, sideways on, the single movement of a sharp chop behind the long ears breaking its neck. The flip of fluffy white legs, then still. A twitch. She held her breath with the memory. The cat gave a hideous yowl.

Up the hill from the school Mr Williams hovered outside the village shop. Had he not heard the name of his farm mentioned, he'd have entered the shop and the women would have stepped aside. All men jumped the queue, they only ever bought tobacco or chocolate and the women wanted them off their territory as quickly as possible; the cramped shop was the front room of a cottage. He sat on the wall by the open door out of sight and settled to eavesdrop.

"My Joss went fishing up there Sunday. He was at the bridge and the branches start shaking, no wind mind. *Duw* there's wild they are. Like bloody monkeys."

"*Iesu mawr*, I haven't been up there since I was a child."

"Hell hole."

Mr Williams smiled; the women spoke as though Cwmgwrach were on the edge of the world and his children reared in trees. He shook his tobacco tin and decided to make the bits last rather than face those birdbrains. He was climbing back on to the tractor when he spotted the green overalls of his eldest son. He was standing at the school railings staring in at the new girl, who was alone in the playground. She was easy to recognise: most of the children had black hair, a few would blend with his dark bay stallion. Hers would match a fresh conker. He presumed Nia would have confronted her: she was the most feral of his offspring, after Morgan. He put two fingers in his mouth and whistled piercingly, but the boy ignored him.

The Pritchards were the talk of the village. The new people at The Plas, big house for three people. Strange to see the girl here, he thought, when they could have sent her somewhere posh. Her father was the newly-appointed headmaster at a Swansea grammar school. Mr Williams knew nothing about schools, other than that this one managed to hold most of the children captive for six hours a day. His own included, apart from haymaking and shearing times when the headmaster (fair play to him) turned a blind eye. He whistled again then made his way down and shouted, "Morgan, get my tobacco." Without a word, the boy held out a hand for money and started up the hill. At the same time a teacher called out for Bethan.

At each whistle Morgan shuddered. His hand went to his neck to feel for his dog whistle. It was there, as always, the small square of flat metal on a cord against his skin. Had his father used a whistle, it would no doubt be on the outside of his shirt rubbing on filthy overalls. He had no qualms about sticking dirty fingers in his mouth.

Bethan was breathing again. The boy's hand had ended an inch from the cat's neck; he'd sniggered and chucked the animal into the longer grass where it shot off between a row of tin sheds.

The teacher trotted across the empty playground and found Bethan rigid, teeth clattering together as if spring had reversed to mid-winter. The young woman, assuming new school nerves, put an arm round her and walked her inside. That night during her marking and on her second sherry, the teacher remembered that little sod Nia Williams coming in after playtime and sitting down tidily. 'Butter wouldn't melt' tidily.

Bethan's mother yukked and clasped her throat at the worm-eating story (though bright-eyed with fascination) and tightened her grip on Bethan's hand as they walked home from school that afternoon. Bethan stayed quiet about the cat-boy, but began to keep strict vigil on her own two cats in case he targeted The Plas.

In her English primary school her best friend had been a tiny bruised boy who drank ink, now to be replaced by a small Welsh worm-eater. She and Nia became wary friends: to each the other's life held an air of mystery. Ten years old, they were in the same class and though there was a mile, a derelict cottage and a river in between them, they were direct neighbours. The cottage, midway on the riverbank, had been abandoned years ago, fully furnished. Unfazed by dank rooms and a piano that occasionally played itself, children sneaked in to bash out 'Chopsticks', sit in the antimacassared armchairs and drink cider.

Way above the ruin the rough, unmade track to Cwmgwrach ran parallel with the river. One vehicle wide, it dipped, rose and turned sharply with sheer drops and, according to the postman, was so bloody high you could count the eggs in the crows' nests. With five gates between the lane and the farm, the journey made alone was tedious, in bad weather an ordeal. The track ended in a cobbled yard of rundown barns, barely enough to serve the flock at lambing time, and a ramshackle farmhouse. The meagre grazing ranged from thin yellow grass to bowling-green smooth, mushroomed with mottled grey boulders exposing a tenth of their size to the world. Out of the hundred acres barely thirty, bordering the river, were worthy of haymaking.

The Plas on the opposite side of the river was a detached Victorian house built for a mine-owner and hidden at the end of a tree-arched drive. Mr Pritchard was overly proud of the entrance, always keen to refer to The Vestibule: a pair of solid wooden doors opening to a wonky hat stand and half-glazed inner door with a fern design on bluish glass. A slight shabbiness to the house and the unkempt garden gave a welcoming air; manicured it might have appeared austere.

The Plas was remote. Cwmgwrach was isolated.

Nia suggested visiting the whirlpool one evening after school, meeting at the footbridge below Cwmgwrach. Bethan was on red alert. Dusk was falling early with the drizzle and her route to the bridge was tough going. A constant rush of water had worn deep gullies in the riverbanks. In many places the narrow path fizzled out altogether and she was forced to edge round on a few inches of mud, clinging to any growth that held firm, the twisted trees keeping her in shadow. She badly needed a dog for company. Her father thought cats independent and dogs a tie, as if they were always jaunting off on holiday. Now his father was dead there would be no more trips to Aberystwyth. She knew Grandpa's legacy had bought The Plas and he'd have wanted her to have a dog.

She expected the bridge to appear round every bend; when it did and there was no sign of Nia, her spirits sank. The planks bounced as she crossed and at the loud squeak of metal gates at both ends Nia emerged from a roofless pigsty on the top of the hill and glided diagonally down the slope. No greeting. Bethan followed her to the end of the Cwmgwrach land where she barged open the kissing gate to open mountain, ran through the rushes to the edge of the riverbank then raised her arms and leaned forward like the figurehead on a ship's bow. Bethan caught up, saw the precipice and immediately sat down.

Nia made a little mocking snort and pointed down to a black pool encircled by rocks. "The whirlpool." She clasped her hands in the air and hula-hooped her body. "The doctor was sucked under in seconds before his family's very eyes. There's shelves of sharp rocks just under the water. Land wrong, you're dead." She spoke with casual pride as if she'd dammed the river to shape the pool herself.

She kicked a clod of dirt over the edge. Bethan quickly squirmed back into the bracken.

The opposite bank was a knobble of roots welded together by moss and ivy, ending in scrub oaks and a sprinkling of mature trees. A thick rope tied to one of the sturdier branches shimmied gently above the water. A sudden movement in the trees startled her and she jumped in alarm as a skinny figure charged out: a boy, possibly the cat boy. She froze as he hurled himself at the rope and flew off the bank into mid-air, his long legs entwining the rope as it soared out above the pool. She glanced at Nia, who was standing arms crossed, grinning. The daredevil swung back and forth five or six times, flung his arms out wide then dropped into the water with barely a splash and disappeared. Blue bubbles broke the black surface.

Nia looked as though she'd ordered the timely display.

"It's getting dark," said Bethan. "I think I should go."

"I'll go home from here," said Nia. "Go on then."

A matted head rose from the water and shook itself, dog-like, and Bethan took off. Tears clouded her eyes and her throat burned at the impatient crack in her new friend's voice. She far preferred Nia to the neat, skipping, hopscotch girls. Wild farm girl, always in possession of two penknives: one delicate, inlaid with mother of pearl (stolen), one for sheep's feet.

Moving fast through strangulated undergrowth was impossible, and an embedded bramble trip-wired her flat on her face (out of Nia's sight she hoped). She crunched through the grey ash of an old fire to the kissing gate back on to Cwmgwrach land, where the closely grazed slopes made running easier. A rising moon flickered. She skidded on black bullet sheep droppings.

Another figure. This time of small stature with mad hair. Her father, motionless on the footbridge, showed no surprise at seeing her, merely lifted a finger to his lips to shush her and pointed up the hill towards Cwmgwrach. No house or buildings to be seen, just the silhouette of the roofless pigsty, a feathering of trees and sparkling dots.

"Cats' eyes?" Bethan whispered. Had her father actually been up to the farm? A keen walker, he covered miles in gumboots a size too big, convinced air should circulate the feet. His flappy scuffing drove her mother mad.

"I'm not sure. It's rather a mystery. I've been here for quite some time."

His penchant for the supernatural occasionally unnerved her. She'd have quite liked him to show a little concern for her, but her tear-stained face was hidden in the gloom and he knew she'd no fear of the dark. Her breathing was often fast from running everywhere; at least she'd stopped shaking. Neither parent fussed; they inhabited separate worlds from each other, let alone hers.

"I presume you've been to the pool," he said. "I take my hat off to the miners, shifting boulders to make a wash-pool, all those years ago. Imagine washing in freezing river water."

Imagine is what he did, thought Bethan.

"Then the walk home to the hills, way above Cwmgwrach. Your mother still has a job pronouncing it. 'Coomgrac' is near enough, I suppose. 'Valley of the Witch', strange: 'valley' for a farm on the mountain, though it does nestle in a bit of a dip."

To Bethan, the 'witch' part was stranger.

A squeak similar to the bridge gates came from above, growing to a loud whine.

"Ah." Her father lifted a finger to the air knowingly, as if expecting such a noise. "The Italian-looking postman told me the farm was named by a shepherd. At dawn every day during lambing, he saw three thick plumes of smoke rising from the woods surrounding the farmhouse."

"Why would smoke mean witches?"

"Quite. It was pale blue, puffing up into eerie rings. He convinced the entire village it came from boiling cauldrons, spell-making, that sort of thing. Good story."

A dark shape flashed down through the branches and landed in a tree at the bottom, quite close to them. A rusty wheeze moaned back up to the top and another shape shot down. After four or five times, all went quiet apart from the rustle of leaves as the bottom tree shook. She stared into black branches and saw eyes in the moonlight.

TWO

Alice Pritchard was quick to snatch at any name her daughter mentioned more than once and invite them to tea, never mind they were usually the maddest in the class. The emaciated boy who'd slugged back their black Quink ink and the dreamy girl who wore a hat whenever she ate; but that was England.

Nia had never been invited anywhere, let alone stayed a night away from home. When The Plas had been empty, her older siblings used her to break in through the larder window. Now inside officially, she was astonished. The house was stuffed: books, paintings, photographs, plastic daffodils free with Daz, an enormous dark sideboard with china animals reflected in multiple side mirrors. On the windowsills, plaster of Paris moulds of cats and goblins, balanced on ice-lolly sticks over jam-jars. Two real cats snoozed on a lumpy velvet sofa alongside Mr Pritchard, his eyes closed. A lady was warbling on the wireless. When called for supper, he took a toothbrush from his top pocket and brushed his eyebrows.

The octagonal dining table wore two cloths: checked seersucker cotton over bottle green chenille. The table was quite the wrong shape for the stack of books at Mr Pritchard's fork side, Mrs Pritchard's collection of knitting patterns and magazines, a tortoiseshell dustpan and crumb brush and large walnut veneer wireless. The family of three could have been there for twenty years rather than weeks.

Nia rocked backwards and forwards on the high-backed dining chair, hands tucked under her little thighs, wanting to say she wasn't hungry. She was starving. Bethan sat next to her, a multi-coloured guinea pig tucked up her jumper. Mrs Pritchard paraded in with a glass bowl of red jelly. Giving the 'wait for it' wink of a magician she dug in with a silver serving spoon, the jelly made a loud squelch and she and Bethan fell about giggling. The suggestive squelch meant nothing to Nia who lived in a house of uncouth brothers. Bryn Pritchard smiled to himself like a long-suffering warden in an asylum and didn't look up; he assumed his wife made jelly daily for that purpose.

Clutter was nudged aside to make space for cutlery, glasses of pink Nesquik, plates of fish fingers, peas and mashed potato blobbed with butter. The jelly was topped with butterscotch Instant Whip. Bryn tried to avert his gaze. As fiercely as he embraced healthy eating, so his wife had fallen under the spell of convenience food. Once, in a rare moment of flippancy, he'd called her Angel Delight.

"No reading at the table," he said, head in a book, as Bethan passed Nia a copy of *Bunty*. Bethan counted his pyramid of books. Perhaps she'd said fourteen out loud: without looking up, he said, "Comics are too large."

"Reading at the table is terribly rude anyway, what will Nia think of us?" Alice dragged the bewildered girl onto her lap. "Hells bells, what's all this?"

Bethan had already noticed the bruises, but she was used to her little inkpot friend being daubed in purple and yellow. These were dark and fresh. Her mother's face fell as she held their small guest tightly, rubbed gently at her arms and asked, "Who did this, Nia dear?"

"Some's the trees, some's my brother."

Alice squeezed her in closer, rubbed harder and found nothing else to say.

Later, at bedtime, Nia carefully positioned her clothes and shoes close to her head as if expecting them to disappear in the night.

Halfway through reading the girls a story, Alice called "Train please, Bryn." Doors opened and closed before her husband strode into the room.

"I thought Bethan slept in the back bedroom," he said.

"She's forever changing, dear, you know that. She hasn't quite settled yet."

"Why doesn't she ask?" He began to whistle.

Nia sat up. An uncanny double whistling trilled from Mr Pritchard's pursed lips, grew steadily louder as the invisible train approached, gave a toot as it swept through the bedroom station and softened as it faded into the distance. She stared in amazement at the small man. Suitably satisfied with his extraordinary display, he nonchalantly saluted the girls goodnight and left. Nia was barely aware of the story's ending, Mrs Pritchard tucking her in under weighty blankets, the paisley eiderdown or pink glow of the bedside lamp.

"Whatever does your brother do to you?" asked Bethan from the next bed, once her mother had gone downstairs.

"Half-brother. Gets mad, really mad. He's not right in the head." Already bereft of her sisters' warm, unwashed bodies, Nia had no desire to revisit her life. "He hates everyone, even his dogs sometimes."

"God that's terrible, I'd love a dog."

"Why?" Under the sheets she counted on her fingers the stinking collies in the disused railway carriages. "Have one of ours, must be ten there."

Bethan wondered if she was lying. Halfway through the night she felt a sleepy body creep in beside her. Nia had wet the bed.

In the morning Bryn did his best to be magnanimous about the brand new divan bed, one of a pair.

"It's too bad, really it is." He'd no wish to get the accident out of proportion, but they so rarely invested in new things.

Once he realised Alice was fretting more over the bruises, he decided to take a walk. The minute he left the breakfast room Alice slid his molasses, yeast tablets and literary matter to one side then shook the Fru-Grains tin she was eyeing-up for knitting needles, one of her daily habits. Rearranging the knitting in her marsupial pinny pocket to avoid stabbing her bosom with needles, she trotted to the sitting room window to watch him stride down the drive in his usual Groucho Marx fashion. He passed her papier-mâché people without a second glance, which she found a little hurtful. As if he couldn't acknowledge the creation of her trouble-free guests: four life-size lumpy women she'd built from wire mesh after giving up hens. They sat in striped deckchairs at the edge of the lawn where the grass went wild into the trees and occasionally Alice took another deckchair from the summerhouse to join them. Sadly their flamboyant hats had begun to droop; no doubt this endless Welsh rain would finish them off.

Bryn reached the lane and turned right and she returned to the breakfast room. The girls were sitting at the table. Alice replaced the cold toast with white. To her, wholemeal seemed halfway to toast anyway.

"And tell me, Nia dear," she said. "How many brothers and sisters do you have?"

Nia looked puzzled by the interest shown in her life. "Two sisters and three brothers." She paused and added quietly, "And another."

Bethan was aghast with envy: a multitude of dogs and siblings. She'd already heard the odd name of a sister, but now her mother was getting Nia to name them all.

"And the other?" she asked kindly. "What about this other one?"

Nia screwed her face and rubbed at her arms, "Half-brother. Morgan."

When Bethan went to Cwmgwrach she wondered whether she'd actually been invited, until she saw the children gawping with delight at tins of mandarin oranges and Carnation milk. Mrs Williams, small and bony, hugged a loaf of bread and sawed inwards to her flat chest, thin slices snatched up before they hit the breadboard. She was pouring tea the colour of burnt oranges when Mr Williams burst through the door muttering, "Bastard, filthy bloody bastard." He filled a chipped enamel bowl with hot water from the range, snatched a bar of green soap and stormed out, drenching the flagstones.

"My father stands his crook by the door for when he goes back out to check the ewes," Nia told Bethan in a normal voice. "I saw Morgan stick it upside down in the shit bucket then put it back."

No one said a word. Bethan thought she might be sick. The younger children snuggled up to her on the bench and stroked her white arms as if calming a nervy pet and when Mr Williams stamped back in, they stroked harder. To wash, he'd flipped frayed braces down over filthy trousers and stripped to a grey vest. The dark crimson V on his chest matched his face and forearms; the rest of his exposed skin was lily-white. Bethan already knew no self-respecting farmer removed his shirt in the sun, nevertheless the sight of all that red and white flesh came as a shock. She'd never seen her father in anything less a three-piece suit, apart from the odd glimpse of white ankle when he was changing from shoes to wellingtons.

Mr Williams reeked of diesel, sweat and lanolin. Her father reeked of ink and nylon shirts. Neither pleasant. She almost sighed with relief when Nia gathered a cluster of full feeding bottles and took her from the steamy kitchen.

The long sheep shed was haphazardly divided into pens, all occupied: sick ewes, lambs being adopted (wearing dead lambs' skins) and orphans. Someone was working at the far end of the building. Nia showed Bethan what to do, then got on with feeding two lambs at once: bottle in each hand while expertly holding back the others with her foot. After the testing teatime, Bethan was delighted to see to the little Welsh Mountain lambs who barged and jostled until picked up. Her lamb wriggled and fought her grip till he found the teat, sucked manically and finished in seconds. He pushed on for more.

"Little and often," Nia said. "Otherwise they bloat, get pop-bellied."

Bethan put him down and picked up the next, heart won.

The figure in the shed was working his way up through the pens towards them. She knew Nia's Morgan would be the boy of the cat incident and this was going to be him. Her neck tingled as he grew closer and she couldn't bring herself to look up. Her lamb buffeted the bottle until it was sucking air.

"Bethan! It's finished," said Nia. *Twpsyn.*

"Sorry," Bethan prised the persistent little mouth from the flattened teat and stood up. Morgan had reached the adjoining pen and was clipping a severe notch into a lamb's ear, his brown coat plastered in blood. The gory task of earmarking lambs for the mountain. He turned the lamb round to cut the other ear and hit a vein. A spurt of blood showered Bethan in red spots and she wet herself a little. She forced herself to look at him. He grinned as if he knew, glowering eyes black as his hair. Catboy.

"Bastard," said Nia. She pushed her to the door and dipped an unsavoury rag in a water bucket. "See how he aimed that? Here, clean your face."

"It must hurt the lambs."

"Only for a second, then that's them marked for life. Our earmark's bad, but the worse the earmark, the harder it is for thieves."

Bethan shuddered. As they ran off, she noticed Morgan had come to the door.

The lavatory was a galvanised hut in the yard. Nia's idea of standing guard was not Bethan's. The door had rotted down to a vertical plank with two horizontal lengths of split wood hanging on rusted hinges, but even those could have provided some privacy. She kept quiet about her damp knickers. Nia, still cursing Morgan, kicked the plank and it swung round. Afterwards they headed for the top fields and found the two brothers around Morgan's age in the trees.

"They'll be checking for sabotage," Nia pointed to a rusty bicycle frame balanced on a thick wire disappearing into the trees. One of the boys shouted "Ready". Nia looked at Bethan and nodded to the pedals as Morgan appeared at their side.

"Be our guest, Bethan," he said quietly. "Take firm hold of the pedals and hold tight." He clasped her round the waist and lifted her up into the leaves.

Suspended like a puppet, she looked down at her cardigan. One of her mother's complicated Fair Isles; rows of dancers dotted with lambs' blood. Three stripes fanned the back of Morgan's massive weathered hand, scars immune to the sun. He was holding her effortlessly. Mid-air, she thought she might be sick and only just gripped the pedals properly as he shoved her off. The bony fingers poking her in the back had to be Nia's. He was using both hands.

Her arms were weak compared to Nia's. Taking her full body weight, they felt wrenched from their sockets. Eyes flung back into head and impossible to breathe, she clung on, picturing the inevitable: smashing against a tree and death. Landing in a pile of tractor tyres and straw, she wet her knickers properly – terror and strong tea made it gush from her, soaking her cotton skirt. She lay in a damp ball and sobbed.

THREE

MR WILLIAMS SLUMPED against the long bar of the Llwyn Celyn, pondering unrequited love over a warm pint and watching the landlady pad up and down the worn lino. The dimly-lit pub hadn't changed; ochre walls, mud-brown floors and the all-pervading odour of shitty boots, unwashed overalls, stale beer, Old Holborn and boys crowding the off-licence for money back on stolen empties.

He tried to visualise the barmaid of his past. It was eighteen years since he lost his heart in the Celyn and Mrs Williams was made cruelly aware he had one.

Bryn Pritchard was sitting at a nearby table with his pipe and a dry sherry, trying not to obsess over the ruined mattress. The overpowering stench of his herbal tobacco couldn't help but instigate a conversation and Mr Williams, quite out of character, offered to buy him a drink. Bryn took a drag on his pipe, puffed out the dreadful aroma of bonfire and contemplated his empty schooner. "No, I don't think so thank you, I'm no longer thirsty."

Somewhat thrown, Mr Williams ordered his fifth pint.

The two men had first met on the river path. Bryn's fluency in Welsh and his knowledge of farming, for a headmaster, was a pleasant surprise for Mr Williams and they'd managed a worthwhile discussion. Born in Aberystwyth, Bryn considered himself South Walian, though he sounded like a Gog to Mr Williams, who spoke in such strong local dialect that it wasn't long before they'd made a mutual decision to converse in English. Mr Williams drained his glass. "I'll be walking home past The Plas, I check the ewes from across the river, so as not to disturb them."

"Ah, splendid," said Bryn. "Do you have many left to lamb?"

"Just a few, but the weather's with us now: cold at night still, but dry."

"I daresay your lads are a great help."

Mr Williams shoved his cap to the back of his head to consider. "Morgan can be when he's willing. It's all but over now." He reached for his crook. Two stiff-coated collies got to their feet in the porch and slunk in behind.

It was the first warmish evening of the spring. Alice Pritchard was flitting round the garden rearranging her papier-mâché people and planting plastic Daz daffodils among the real ones in bud. She'd little interest in gardening, but did harbour a sense of duty towards lawns, and occasionally attacked weeds. Unfortunately her efforts were few and far between and all their gardens soon turned to jungles. Bryn had no interest.

"Ah, Mr Williams," she swirled round on the grass and came to the gate. "Isn't it lovely how our daughters have made friends? We're thrilled, aren't we dear?"

Bryn gave a curt nod and pictured the mattress.

Thrilled? All sorts flooded Mr Williams' mind: this lively woman in her mad garden in contrast to his sour-mooded wife and scatty daughters flashing past him like hares. He nodded, "Better move on or it'll be too dark to see if anything's lambing."

"Oh heavens yes, goodnight then. *Nos da,*" she said proudly. Alice Pritchard was originally from London. She and Bryn stood at the gate to watch their new friend start along the river footpath, the collies glued to his heels.

When he came level with his best field and the bulk of the flock, Mr Williams plonked down on the riverbank and pictured the Pritchards sitting down for supper. He'd noticed some scruffy women in deckchairs and hadn't liked to stare past Mrs Pritchard too much, but with all that socialising at the gate he realised they hadn't moved and were some sort of horrible models.

The ewes were calling in their lambs for the night. He'd missed the twilight races, not that he would have admitted to watching them. Every evening, fifty or so lambs ganged up and, as if someone had fired a starting pistol, they shot off in a mad bunch charging the length of the field and back again. He often spotted Morgan behind a hedge, no doubt willing a good pile-up. He scraped his pipe clean of Mr Pritchard's gift of herbal tobacco and refilled it with Old Holborn. Striking match after match he thought again of Mrs Pritchard in her full skirt and pale blue cardigan, skitting round the overgrown garden.

Two lambs bleated for their mothers, who replied half-heartedly but clearly enough. How could lambs be so dense? He was always reluctant to leave the fields until they all had paired up and were tucked under walls, though all ewes got serious about the last call, with udders full to bursting.

It was dark when he saw a small glow bobbing across the mountain. The piercing scream of a vixen doused him in ice; he shuddered and quickly got up from the damp grass.

Morgan called in his lurcher, kicked a battered enamel saucepan into the brambles and took a breather against the only wall of a cottage left standing. He thought of all the feuds and revenge hovering in the mountain air – air so pure that lichen flourished, and he sniggered at the irony. The pale green plant covered stone and shattered roof slates everywhere, like miniature trees.

He was young when the people left the hills for good. The smallholdings couldn't wait to collapse and fell derelict weeks after they were abandoned, worn as ragged as their owners. The land told a different story. Though every fence had disintegrated or been trampled, the once-cultivated fields still grew emerald against the dark mountain and in sunshine seemed to hum with iridescence. Morgan saw this perpetual green as the heralding of hard labour, honouring the stalwart farmers. He could still picture the families; as a small boy he'd delivered their provisions. It was at this chimney wall, with a wood fire blazing, he'd learned the story of his early years.

Tonight there was no moon and a chill had now fallen. He rubbed his hands together more for the morbid pleasure of feeling his ridged scars than to generate heat. Whenever he crossed this piece of land he felt the shape and thickness of the threepenny bits, one placed in each hand by the farmer who usually paid him sixpence, and the big man's look suggesting "Keep one for yourself". Morgan had clenched his hand round the extra coin so tightly it pressed into the blisters that ran along the base of his fingers.

Mrs Williams' jagged nails came at him like the claws of a crane, gouging three lines down the back of his small dirty hand, leaving scars as prominent as the cross on hot cross buns and as evident after nine years as the emerald fields. All teeth and venom, her ugly look of triumph had almost made him smile through the pain as he handed over the second coin. He'd owned it for twenty minutes, the time it took to run down the mountain.

He stood up effortlessly through a squat. His best lurcher bitch was there at the ready and they set off: she at a loping canter, he leaping lightly across tussocks of damp moss. It wasn't long before his flashlight beam picked up a hare weaving elegantly through the rushes. The lurcher was fast. Morgan regularly tested her against his father's old ex-post office van. It was risky, the Cwmgwrach track was one vehicle wide and she flew behind as he drove crazily over the stones, one eye on the speedometer the other on the mirror, keeping his speed up in case she tried to overtake and went under the wheels.

The grasses swished back into place after she'd cut through in chase of the hare. Then out of the blackness came a single hollow 'thwack' and silence. Something unfamiliar shone up in his light and Morgan ran faster. The ground squelched under him, the flashlight bounced and landed on a thick post. Brand new, pale wood, planted in one of the boggier patches of mountain, an area he was accustomed to skirting round and his dogs knew to skim at speed.

The lurcher was next to the post, her eyes shining luminous green in the beam of light. Morgan sank into the quagmire over his boots and dragged himself heavily towards her. She was submerged to her fine head and her slender neck was doubled back on her body like a snoozing swan. He reached her too late. Though he was all too familiar with death, he'd never lost a dog in such a way. For support he gripped the post that had mangled her and slammed his boot on her body, forcing her down into the swallowing slime till the surface spluttered with soap bubbles. He had so little to call his own and for a second he was overcome with spite for her, leaving him in such a ridiculously pointless manner. Her accusatory eye met his. As she disappeared he threw back his head and screeched the eerie cry of a vixen.

The rust-coloured peat took his right boot. When he hauled himself up by the post he felt the fresh mallet marks that bruised the wood on the top. He knew not to turn back, but keep going to the firmer ground a little to the right.

FOUR

THE SHEEP WERE hanging round the perimeter fences bashing at gates with their hard little feet, eager to return to the mountain. All flocks were restless by June. After shearing and once the lambs had had time to recognise their naked mothers, they were turned back to their natural environment, not to be gathered again until weaning and the sales, when they'd come in wide-backed as donkeys.

As always, Mr Williams rode up round his ewes at the end of the first week to check everything was paired off and enjoy a day away from his disturbing family. It was early afternoon when his pony returned to the yard with her head down, broken reins and empty saddle. Morgan was the one to see her standing there, lifting her feet one at a time, nose nuzzling the ground. He tied baler twine to the bit, threw himself across her back and turned her back to the hill. He rode armchair-fashion like his father: reins in one hand, stirrups so long his legs were virtually straight. The little mare found her second wind and took him straight to the spot.

Fly lay poised alongside her prostrate master, ears flat to her head. High above them a skylark fluttered, beside herself, her little nest squashed beneath Mr Williams's cumbersome body. His crook was stabbed upright into the earth. The loop of baler twine was still tied round the narrowest part of the handle, his habit to keep the wood from opening out in the rain. He was particular about his crook.

Fly stood up, lay down and cringed flat as Morgan knelt to feel his father's thick wrist for a pulse. Then she circled the body twice, lay down in the same place and blinked fast and desperate back and forth at the two men. Morgan had seen plenty of dead livestock, never a human. His father's face shone mustard yellow against the deep plum V of his chest. Coarse stubble sprouted from his cheeks. His shaving time was early evening before a session in the Celyn.

Morgan had brought many a sickly ewe down from the mountain, dangled across the pony's shoulders; he'd never expected to bring his dead father home in the same way. With a rare touch of tenderness, he lifted his body onto the mare's back and led her quietly down, with Fly worrying and weaving from side to side behind them.

Mrs Williams saw them from the yard. By the time Morgan carried her husband into the house, she'd swept everything from the kitchen table and she and most of the children were lined up in silence. Straightening his limbs and laying him out on the scrubbed wood reminded him of the rough post-mortems he and his father had carried out on sheep in the poor light of the barn. A caesarean once when they were snowed in, an old door on straw bales their operating table. One year they'd slit open nine dead ewes, each one stuffed with acorns and every eye gone. Thank God he'd reached his father's body before a magpie spotted the glitter of eyeballs, vile, bloodthirsty birds. His father called them the devil in evening dress. Everything now would evoke a memory.

Morgan took in the shocked members of the family, statues round the table staring at the corpse, all with their own thoughts. He was hardly ever inside among them. Nia was the only one missing; he presumed she was at The Plas. His gut reaction was to leave the house and run for it.

He tore to the rugby club in his father's van, driving like an idiot. The doctor was holding up the bar in his usual place. Morgan dragged him outside, pushed him into the van and drove him back up to the farm. The doctor, well used to being accosted at the rugby club, ran his unfocused eyes over the body and with hot whisky breath, pronounced the man dead from a heart attack.

"How the bloody hell do you know that, man?" said Morgan. "You can't fucking see straight." He knocked the doctor across the floor then grabbed his father and shook him violently by the shoulders. "Talk man. Talk." The body in its patched overalls slumped up and down on the table like a giant rag doll.

The village revered the doctor, however inebriated. He had never been physically attacked. Mrs Williams stood white-faced, hand frozen over her mouth and the younger children began to whimper. Morgan left the mumbling doctor to find his own way home, staggered out to his dog sheds at the far end of the buildings and shut himself in with his remaining lurcher. He'd fixed a bolt to the inside for times of necessary isolation, and he shot it across and collapsed in the wood shavings, the dog trembling at his side.

It was evening when he returned to the house. The body on the table was shrouded in an old sheet with everyone huddled in corners. No sign of food. He passed through the kitchen at speed and began to search the rooms like a madman looking for something of his father's, anything, some sort of memento. Finally, upstairs in a drawer jammed with papers, he came across the sepia photograph of a young Mr Williams in meticulous dress and posture, astride a handsome Welsh Cob. A horse far too well-covered, glossy and immaculately tacked-up, to be seen on Cwmgwrach. This fine pair was not about to gather sheep on the hill. He slipped the photo into his pocket, went downstairs and in an uncharacteristic moment of compassion, announced he would collect Nia from The Plas.

He half-ran, half-staggered along the riverbank, running his fingers round and round the serrated edge of the old photograph – unaware he was puffing and blowing, as he did after a particularly long stint of chasing livestock. He approached The Plas as furtively as he approached everywhere, another habit inherited from his father, along with innate knowledge of the land. He knew every inch for miles. Creeping through a gap in the hedge and across the vegetable garden, he circled the house, picking up the acrid scent of a fox on the same route with similar suspicion. It was twilight, lights on, curtains still open, easy to dodge between the mature trees and peer in windows unseen. He moved from trunk to trunk, keeping each window in sight then settled in the base of a wide old cedar to prepare his message of doom.

His position allowed a good view of Mr Pritchard sitting at his piled-up desk in his study. His eyes were closed, a large cream candle was burning and Morgan wondered whether he'd already heard the news and lit it for his father, like they did in church. He knew the two men had become good companions, which seemed more unlikely than their daughters' friendship. He edged round to the sitting room window and saw a green mermaid lying on her stomach, talking on a black telephone. Mrs Pritchard was sitting in an armchair smiling, a lump of knitting on her lap and wine glass at her side. He shuddered at the sight of a cat on another chair, asleep on a pile of papers.

Every wall was filled with books, plants on little tables, lamps glowing gold, faded red rugs.

There was no sign of the girls and Morgan remembered Nia returning home after her first visit to The Plas, announcing with huge drama that "Bethan had a bedtime!" At Cwmgwrach the young ones fell asleep where they were, though they woke in their beds in the mornings. He could only assume his father carried them up. He pressed his face against the cold stone wall. If they thought he was going to carry anyone to bed, they had another think coming. The mermaid rolled onto her back, brought up her knees and crossed her legs. It was a dress; all that inflated green. He walked to the front porch and clanged the bell. Mrs Pritchard opened the door. He couldn't speak, just blew out his breath involuntarily. Seeing his agitated state she quickly led him through the vestibule and into the sitting room. He started to mutter and Mrs Pritchard could have sworn he'd said his father was dead. She was completely unable to determine the boy's age; being so slight he could have been anything from thirteen to twenty. Chancing it, she poured him a whisky and guided him to the sofa. Morgan took too large a gulp, stinging his throat and nostrils, but managed not to cough and choke. It was his first taste of whisky. The girl in green threw herself into an armchair opposite him.

"This is my niece, Veronica," said Mrs Pritchard. "And what's your name?"

"My father died on the mountain. This afternoon. Morgan Williams."

"Good God." Mrs Pritchard instantly pictured Nia's bruises. "Veronica dear, could you fetch your uncle, please? He's in his study. This is devastating news. Oh, Nia! Poor love. The girls have gone to bed."

The whisky burnt into the pit of Morgan's small empty stomach and took its effect. Soon his words were arriving effortlessly and he was conversing with these weird people, even found himself describing the vivid colours of his father's skin against the bleakness of the mountain, which seemed to upset them all over again. Mrs Pritchard did nothing but stand up and sit down like Fly at the scene, and gasp. Mr Pritchard sighed and twirled his hair into bizarre shapes. The niece watched in silence, pivoted on the edge of her chair, the balloon skirt allowing her little comfort.

"Do you think we ought to leave telling little Nia until the morning?" said Mrs Pritchard. "This might be the last good night's sleep she'll have for a while."

"It's up to Morgan, he might want to tell her himself, now," said her husband.

"No," Morgan lifted himself from the sofa and made for the door; it made no difference to him who told her or when. "That'll be alright."

But the sound of the doorbell had brought the girls to the landing and they'd huddled on the stairs pressed against the banisters staring at each other, knowing everything. The sitting room door was ajar. Hearing Morgan make a move, they froze.

"I'll see you out," said the niece.

Morgan glared at her. See him out? He wasn't an imbecile, he'd just come in. But she was there at his side, teetering on stupid shoes and him teetering from the whisky. She led the way through the front door out into the garden and headed for the driveway. When he turned to cross the grass, she followed. He bent low to slip through the gap in the hedge.

"You poor, poor boy. Were you very close to your father?"

He had no idea of the answer. His body swayed. She was terribly close and there was a strange familiarity in her thick perfume. Then Nia was at his side. The niece turned back and Morgan watched the peculiar green ball flounce across the half-tamed grass.

"I'm coming home with you," said Nia and, brave in her confusion, slipped her hand into his. "Where is Daddy now?"

"Kitchen. I'll go round and open the front door so you don't have to see him." They walked silently hand in hand; it was the first time they'd touched. When the dogs heard the creak of the footbridge gate they started to bark in their sheds. "Help me feed them," said Morgan.

The pair moved with the instinct of foxes. He mixed chunks of slimy tripe with stale bread. She ran fresh water into battered saucepans with tidemarks of green slime and resolved to scrub them in the morning. Fly backed into the corner of the railway carriage, the others skulked unsettled.

The untouched food had turned crusty by morning.

FIVE

B RYN WAS SITTING at the breakfast table thinking of Mr Williams's sudden death when "Fuuck-kiiing hell" resonated through the hallway. He did admire the Welsh for pronouncing every syllable; it was the first thing he noticed coming from England to teach in his homeland: "Pleee-aaazz, Sir". Though this expletive was a bit much.

"Time you sent your daughter to a good convent school," said Veronica. "Away from bad company."

Bryn had assumed the expletives were Nia's, then remembered she'd gone home with Morgan twelve hours earlier. Alice stifled a splutter; she and her niece had attended the same draconian convent, at different times.

Bethan burst in, rubbing her arm. "Bashed it on the banisters. Why do they call it a funny bone?"

"I've never known, dear." Her mother wasn't one for making a thing of language. "Poor you, come here."

Veronica, on her second coffee, was dressed in smart riding kit, hair lacquered into a hard dome, eyelids bright blue, lips pale peach. Recommending a convent was rich coming from her, thought Bryn. He'd noticed her concentrated observation of Morgan last night and suspected the young man would soon be subjected to those tight jodhpurs and long black boots. Still, might take his mind off his dead father. What a shock. He'd miss old Williams, their odd drink at the Celyn, the walk home sharing tobacco. He smiled sadly at Bethan, sitting opposite him next to her mother. She gave a little jump, or maybe it was his imagination.

Dead Mr Williams lay in the Cwmgwrach parlour with two household candles casting a yellow glow to his sunken cheeks. Morgan had sat at his side on a hard dining chair and talked to him on and off all through the night, well aware of the absurdity of the one-sided conversation, especially with himself as the instigator. When his father was alive, they'd barely exchanged more than a couple of coherent sentences a day. He imagined it all to be a mistake: his father waking, sitting up and the two of them able to speak at length. By morning he had no inclination to deal politely with anyone.

The funeral director hadn't ventured up to Cwmgwrach for years and clumped round bemoaning the state of the track and potential damage to his fine cars until Morgan agreed to order a lorry-load of scalpings to fill the holes. They settled on a date for the funeral and the small man went inside to measure the body. Morgan wandered off. Apart from a strong urge to inform people of his father's death, he was at a loss. He'd have liked to announce to the world that his life would not be continuing as usual; the fact that few cared was immaterial. He leaned against the old pigsty feeling furious, even more so when he spotted the Pritchards' weird niece mincing over the footbridge. He quickly slid behind the sty wall.

Veronica retied the gate and came wiggling up the bank. She reached the farmyard as Mrs Williams came out of the house with the funeral director who, feeling he'd scrubbed up unnecessarily for the state of the place, was eager to leave and hurrying to his car. At the sight of the glamorous girl his feet almost left the ground and Mrs Williams gave a little shriek. Used to all sorts in his line of work, the undertaker quickly recovered his composure and drove away with great care, his mind back on his sleek cars and the appalling track.

Morgan moved closer to watch the two women edge round the yard like sparring partners. When his stepmother reached the back door she scurried in without a word, slammed it and crept to the window to peer out at the stranger. Not put off, Veronica looked round the yard and nosed into every barn. When it seemed she was about to leave, Morgan emerged.

"Ah, Morgan," she said. "I thought you might need some help today – perhaps your horses need exercising or something. You must be busy with other things."

He looked her up and down, imagining her on a polished thoroughbred. "Maybe." Their small Welsh ponies were ridden half to death then turned out on the hill with white sweat marks and manes matted with burrs. He came from the cowshed with an old saddle and bridle, tossed his head and walked off. She half-ran to keep up.

Bethan ducked down. She'd followed her cousin along the river path and now Morgan's attention was glued to Veronica, she managed to reach the tree-lined ridge above Cwmgwrach unnoticed. He was helping her on to his father's stallion, who was so narrow her feet came down below his belly. Bethan couldn't hear what they were saying. Veronica was smoothing her jodhpurs as he adjusted the stirrup leathers and as the stallion took off up the mountain track Morgan shouted, "He's a trotter. Sit to the trot."

Bethan could see the animal had no intention of responding; he'd probably never experienced a conventional rider. There was no fast walk or canter, just trotting at tremendous speed. Veronica was tight in the saddle and had no choice but to go with it, up into the white mist with the sun streaking through and Morgan keeping up in a casual run, smiling to himself. Bethan was dodging along the ridge behind them, moving carefully between the trees, when half a dozen ponies came galloping towards the fence.

With a pig-like squeal the stallion stopped dead. Veronica fell forward, the animal's head shot up almost knocking her out, he jumped forward as fast as he'd stopped and she was thrown back in the saddle. Bethan held her breath. He veered sharply to the left and by the time his manic step reached the gate, his head was rotating, neck vertical and nostrils flared to twice their size. Two mares, obviously in season, bashed against the gate screaming and dancing in reply to his snorts and stamps, stretching out their necks to touch noses. At the mere tickle of whiskers the stallion gave an ear-piercing screech and leapt back, all four feet left the ground and Veronica fell off.

Morgan was there instantly, yelling abuse at him in Welsh and English as he threw himself across his back. The stallion froze for a second and tried to turn his head to meet his eye. Veronica stood up. Morgan, still cursing, leant down and grabbed her hand. He slid back behind the saddle and pulled her up to sit in front of him. Bethan quivered behind her tree. His mouth appeared to be lost in her cousin's hair; his left arm wrapped round her waist, reins held in his right hand. They turned for home, squashed together on the prancing bay stallion with the mares shrieking and galloping up and down alongside the fence.

Once they were out of sight, Bethan ran down across the hill and under a few fences to come out halfway along the

Cwmgwrach track, where no one would be surprised to see her. She was almost into the wooded part when she heard a vehicle thundering down the stony road and before she had time to think about hiding, the old post office van stopped at her side. Veronica sat in the front seat, flushed and dishevelled. Morgan lowered his window, "Get in, if you like." He got out, opened the back doors and Bethan climbed in. He slammed the doors and tore down the track as if he couldn't wait to be rid of them both. The dark inside smelled of dogs, old carpets and diesel. No one spoke. Bethan clung to a rope looped along the inside of the van and watched hairpins fall from Veronica's stiff hair like dead stick insects. Tiny black and white birds led the way, swooping and swerving in front of the wheels, ducking and diving and circling so low the girls cried out when Morgan didn't alter his speed.

"They're attracted to the chrome around the lights. I haven't killed one yet." He stared hard at Veronica. "Anything flashy excites them." He slowed when he saw Mrs Pritchard in The Plas driveway, but the tyres still threw up dirt and small stones.

Alice Pritchard was busy removing the most disintegrated of her papier-mâché people and pulling the deckchairs of the remaining trio closer together. She did like them to appear in conversation. Seeing the Cwmgwrach van, she dropped a shrivelled paper arm into the grass and guiltily stood to attention. It seemed horribly flippant to be dealing with her barmy sculptures the day after Mr Williams's death. A deformed leg fell off and she kicked it backwards into the shrubbery without looking.

Veronica opened the door before the van stopped and got out. Bethan climbed over into the passenger seat and followed suit as the van was still crawling round the drive. Morgan leant across to grab the passenger door, slammed it and drove off. Bethan went over to join her mother. Veronica swept into the house patting her haystack hair and didn't appear for supper. The next day she returned to London. No one broached the subject of her black mood or mentioned her sudden unexplained departure.

Bethan's father was unflinchingly old-fashioned, with no doubts about the superiority of his Riley over the powder blue Jaguar parked alongside them. Following Veronica's suggestion, Bethan was to sit an interview at a convent in Herefordshire. They sat in the car in the shadowy school drive while he did his best to put a date to the building. Bethan tried to see his expression. She could see her mother's mouth open very slightly, not wide enough to catch flies. The foreboding manor house was built in a light, plum-coloured stone without emanating the usual warmth associated with red. Castellated towers stood at both ends and every window was black and curtainless.

When it was time to leave the comfort of the car, Bethan and her mother dawdled across the gravel driveway to the arched entrance. A peacock, withholding its plumage, screamed hideously and his out-of-sight compatriots replied. Mr Pritchard strode ahead, disappeared into a dark lobby and tugged on a bell rope. As they followed him inside, a small door in the wall shot open to reveal a wire grid. In the blackness behind the metal squares came a slash of white brow-band, a set of yellow teeth and squinting pink eyes. Mr Pritchard announced their name. The trapdoor slammed shut and they waited for two or three minutes before a full-size door opened and a low Irish voice commanded them into a dismal room and told them to sit. Bethan perched next to her mother on the edge of a hard tapestry sofa, knees and heels neatly together as, according to Mrs Pritchard's nuns (her mother rolled her eyes), "You never saw the Virgin Mary cross her legs." Her father scanned the bookshelves, until he realised every book was on Catholicism and sat down.

A tall, hefty nun entered. Her florid complexion could have been mistaken for a happy disposition, but she stood there cold as the convent stone and Bethan realised her puffed-up red cheeks were the result of an over-tight wimple. Colourless lips set in a leer, arms folded under the top layer of her black bell tent and pale grey eyes framed by wire spectacles. An ironmongery of gaoler's keys clunked against the rosary beads at her waist and a cloying stench of camphor hung in the grey haze of the room. Outside was startlingly bright.

Bethan's white gloves stuck to her clammy palms. She was saving every detail to relate to Nia later. She pictured the nun born in her black garb, waddling round with no one thinking to enlarge the veil and her squashed face growing increasingly crimson. She was asked few questions. Her father seemed unperturbed by his interrogation of their circumstances. She wondered if the nun realised he was a headmaster, be just like him to keep it quiet. Her mother was sitting straight-backed and Bethan knew from the look on her face she wouldn't entertain the idea of her daughter coming to this dreadful place. At her convent they'd had to sew pockets into their knickers – the nuns were thieves.

Surely she would go to the local school with Nia.

SIX

Mrs Williams stabbed the smouldering broom handle into the base of her bonfire to lift the mass of rubbish and stir the ashes. New air surged in and flashed out tiny sparks. It had been on the go for two days, feed sacks, papers, toys, rags, shoes, a pram, tyres, anything that would burn and stuff that wouldn't. She loved a good bonfire, but this beat the lot, black smoke belched through the trees and could be seen from the village. It wasn't over yet. She was saving the best till last: her dead husband's clothes.

Morgan had watched the small, nasty woman for a while. Haloed in smoke she circled her pyre, poking and coughing while papery smuts drifted and caught in her straggled hair. He came out of hiding and moved closer until there were a few yards between them. Her expression was crazed, but liberated.

"I'm going to buy an old caravan to put on my field," he said. "I'll live there."

"Your field?"

"The nine acres. It'll be in my father's will."

She laughed. "Do you honestly think a man like that would make a will? We could go to hell for all he cared. You don't own any field, Morgan."

He'd never heard her say his name out loud like that.

"My father promised to leave me the top field," he said. "It needs grazing, fencing properly, mowing… you can't. I'll live there and farm it."

Though Cwmgwrach was rented, Mr Williams had somehow managed to buy the nine acres at the top of the track. Just last year, he'd told Morgan in a voice puffed up with pride, though it killed him to say, "That field will be yours when I've gone; you're the only one who will farm it." Morgan's heart sank. The damn woman was right; he would never have put it in writing.

"I'll be keeping sheep there. It'll be an income and the boys will help," Mrs Williams smiled. For once in her life she felt calm. Though Morgan was quite capable of throwing her into the bonfire, somehow she didn't think he would. Things would be different from now on. She'd been offered a cottage in the village, a job in the fish and chip shop and a hint of optimism. No more fist-thumping the table when supper wasn't ready on the dot; no dirty body huffing next to her in bed and now the perfect opportunity to rid herself of this weasel.

"Pack what's yours," she said. "We're out in two weeks."

"The witch of Cwmgwrach: it's true then."

"The witch that took you in. Reared you." Her eyes were bright with new life.

The Pritchards were on their way home after buying Bethan's school uniform when they saw black smoke rising from Cwmgwrach. For a headmaster Bryn was not a worldly man, but insurance fraud did enter his mind

"The farm's rented," said Alice, reading his thoughts. "There's no point."

"I think I might go and offer the Williamses a hand," he said, pensively.

Bethan paused in her rhythmic kick of the shoebox at her feet and studied her father's narrow back and white hands on the steering wheel. They were delicate for a man, the first two fingers on his right hand ink-stained black as always, and she wondered what physical use he could be.

Mrs Pritchard felt too exhausted to be included and asked to be dropped off. Bethan stayed in the back of the car and pressed her face against the rear window. Her mother was walking slowly to the house, ignoring her papier-mâché ladies – which was unusual: she always acknowledged them, if only to adjust their deckchairs an inch. Bethan slit open the brown paper package on the back seat and dragged her fingers across the scratchy school coat. The shocking decision of sending her to a convent remained a mystery, especially considering her father's atheism. It must have been down to her mother's father. Grandpa was a staunch Catholic.

When they pulled up to the yard and she saw Mrs Williams' look of horror, she stayed put in the car. Bryn got out and closed the door gently. For a small man, he was made of stern stuff – or maybe he hadn't noticed Mrs Williams' expression. She abandoned her raging bonfire and scuttled into the windowless cowshed. He followed and quietly enquired into the dark space whether there was anything at all he could do to help, anything at all. When his eyes settled to the gloom, he saw her backed up against a pile of bulging woolsacks as if he'd pulled a gun on her. After a while she edged out, arms tightly wrapped round her stretched old cardigan. Soot and flakes of lime-wash from the wall had stuck in her hair. She tried to straighten up and move with some decorum and he stepped away from the door to allow her escape, but it was another scuttle out into the yard and away to the farmhouse. He called after her in Welsh to put her at ease. A door slammed.

"Well, I think they'll be all right," he said to himself, turning in case Bethan was in earshot. He saw her in the distance running with Nia across the fields. He paced to and fro for a while then pulled a sketchpad from his pocket and perched on a wall to capture the view, thinking an oil painting of the surrounding landscape would make a good house-warming present for Mrs Williams. He smiled to himself, pleased with his brainwave, but after a moment laid the sketchbook and pencils on the wall. An abstract of purple mountains wasn't to everyone's taste.

Morgan came out from one of the railway carriages, his father's sheepdog at his side. "She'll be fine when I've gone," he said.

"Ah, Morgan. Gone? Who, your mother or this dog? And gone where?"

"Her." He nodded towards the house. "Fly's coming with me. I'm going to work on the other side of the mountain. Davies Tŷ Newydd needs a servant boy."

"Servant boy? Good Lord, that sounds terribly outdated, will you be happy there?" Bryn immediately realised happiness was hardly an issue in the Williamses' lives, least of all Morgan's. No answer came. Bryn began to twirl his hair madly then pack his pipe. He lit up. The herbal tobacco actually smelt sweet against the toxic bonfire. After a few puffs he put down the pipe and grasped Morgan's hand. "Good luck, Morgan," he said, shaking it firmly, his own soft hand lost under the broad palm and thick rough fingers. "All the very best for your future."

Morgan had never had his hand shaken. He smarted with the same warmth as the night of his father's death when Mrs Pritchard had put her arm round his shoulders and poured him a whisky. He nodded and managed a brief smile. He was tempted to confide in Mr Pritchard about his nine-acre field problem, then predicted his stepmother's reaction and thought better of it. He shoved his hands back in his pockets to preserve the handshake and with another little nod, left Mr Pritchard by the yard gate.

He was taking the van. He hadn't announced this or asked, but no one else could drive. It was packed ready: a bag of clothes, a few bits and his father's crook slid between the torn old seats. Fly jumped into the back, Morgan got into the driving seat, started the engine and slammed the door.

Bryn felt the second door of the afternoon to slam on him held less distaste, perhaps a little reluctance. He watched the dog's nose smudge the rear window as the van bumped up the slope and he remained there long after the dust had settled, hands clasped in mid-air as though Morgan had cast a spell between them. "Servant boy, I ask you," he said to himself, wondering what on earth would become of him.

He'd learnt Morgan's history in stages. First from the postman, a pleasant Italian-looking fellow who kept tobacco and whisky behind a loose stone under the bridge halfway on his round, wrote poetry and took his lambs to the Thursday mart in his post office van and hosed it out on Friday mornings. Friday letters were always damp. Bryn liked him a lot.

He sat down on the wall, hands still together. There was no hurry. Mrs Williams might reconsider and venture out.

He replayed the night he'd walked home from the Celyn with old Williams inebriated and swaying about on the river bank, but confirming the postman's story and confessing to a barmaid being his one true love. How she'd cruelly abandoned him and their baby son Morgan and how he'd stupidly presented that baby to his wife as casually as he would a rabbit or a hare, when they already had two baby boys of their own, even younger than Morgan – all three of them ridiculously close in age.

The previous landlady of the Celyn had been on a par with the postman for embellishing stories. She had come searching for her errant barmaid in the rented hovel and discovered the eighteen-month-old Morgan wedged between a dresser and meat-safe, propped upright, crumpled arms hanging over his body like a pot-bound plant. She reckoned a black cat had kept him alive, licking tears from his face, cheeks all raw. She'd pummelled his razor-like ribs, spoon-fed him her special concoctions, and when he opened his black eyes and fixed hers with what she could only describe as fury, she was the first to look away.

That night instead of a pint she handed the baby over the bar to his father. There were no endearments over the tragedy because of what Morgan had become. Everyone was astonished he'd survived at all.

Bethan skipped round the corner, saw her father's hands together and thought he was praying, then remembered he was an atheist. Nia skipped behind her. They'd taken this time to discuss schools. Nia had never seen a nun. Bethan hoped her curiosity was masking some sort of sorrow at their enforced parting.

"Married to God, are you joking?"

"No," said Bethan. "They wear a ring. I have to be a weekly boarder. I may write, but I'll see you every weekend."

Horror, envy, something dramatic flashed across Nia's face; pure shock, maybe. "*Iesu mawr.* Yes, write. I'd like a letter."

Bethan had rather liked the idea of the long walk to the local secondary school together.

Her father was musing about Morgan's hands. "Quite disproportionate to his body, absolutely huge, extraordinary." He rubbed his palms, still aware of the line of sandpaper calluses at the base of Morgan's fingers, gnarled from walling, fencing and tractor engines. Although in that handshake with the lad's leathery skin, he'd somehow felt the sort of sensitivity required for lambing.

"Maybe he'll grow into them," said Bethan. "Like with guinea pigs."

"What do you mean, dear?"

"His body may catch up with his hands, like baby guinea pigs catching up with their ears." She stared at him. Surely he knew guinea pigs were born with full-size ears?

He opened his steepled hands and held out his pinky-white palms, studying them sadly before sliding them deep into his pockets. "Huge, huge hands. Ah well, I do hope he'll be alright."

"Don't worry about him, Mr Pritchard," Nia said brightly. "My mother always says, '*Duw*, that one would live where crows would die'."

SEVEN

Seven bare, dead turkeys hung from the beam by their knobbled feet. Morgan was more than halfway through plucking the eighth when it lifted its neck and looked him in the eye. He ran from the barn and bounced across the thin tin sheet balanced from the door to the garden wall, twenty feet above a passageway of muck. The makeshift bridge twanged as he leapt off into the garden.

Elin Davies was gouging weeds from the path below the lawn with an old kitchen knife.

"Fuck it. Fuck it," he said. He loathed plucking turkeys; their skin ripped so easily, though ducks were worse. But to pluck a bird alive! Livid at his incompetence, he stamped out a circle, took out his knife and turned back to the barn. "Fuck it."

"Coffee in ten minutes?" called Mrs Davies, her hat now visible above the wall.

He swung round. "Oh. Thank you, yes." Damn, had she heard his language? He couldn't bear her to think badly of him. He admired and liked the woman and it was obvious his feelings were reciprocated, how she was with him. He occasionally thought of Veronica: snooty, arrogant, that day on his father's stallion. She'd always be there for the taking.

He slithered the eight or nine steps back across the slimy tin sheet, years of rain and men's weight had reduced it to a flimsy ice rink. The upside-down turkey faced him with its beady eye and Morgan had a fleeting vision of his beautiful lurcher sucked into the quagmire, her eye meeting his with similar disdain. He sliced his knife cleanly through the bird's throat and watched crimson blood pool on the blade and drip into the heap of feathers and old saucepan. He was about to wipe his knife on his thigh until he remembered who washed his overalls. He cleaned it with straw.

He took off his boots at the door and entered the kitchen so quietly she dropped a duck egg. The thin blue shell smashed in the sink. She inclined her head for Morgan to sit at the table. She was balancing on the arm of a worn leather armchair pulled tight to the sink, an elderly collie occupying the seat. She took another filthy egg from a bucket, powdered it with Vim and began to scrub.

Morgan sat down. The kitchen reeked of straw and hot ironing. In place of an ironing board she'd laid two blankets and a sheet across the dining table and it was one of his work shirts spread out ready. He noticed the frayed cuffs and missing buttons and had to look away. The old mother Manx cat with her needle claws leapt onto his knees. He pushed her off and caught Mrs Davies' reproachful glance. Her husband padded in with an empty egg tray, silent socks embedded with hayseeds and large parts of his waxed jacket hanging in shreds. Mr Davies leaned against the Aga rail. His wife dried her hands in a scrap of flannelette sheet, re-pinned her hair away from her face and brought a colander of clean eggs to the table to dry and slot into the tray. No one spoke. Morgan knew Davies could have saved the milk from boiling over, sizzling across the hot plate and turning the flavour of the kitchen rancid. As Mrs Davies ran across to save it and her husband left the kitchen, Morgan slid the worn-out shirt from the table and stuffed it into his overalls.

She pushed back the ironing blankets to make space and sat down opposite him. He'd never tasted Camp coffee until he came to Tŷ Newydd. A mug of Camp with full cream Guernsey milk was a meal in itself. She sliced two pieces of fruitcake and asked if he liked Christmas. "Your family, all those brothers and sisters, the meals and everything: what's it like?" Her tone was wistful. She was forever asking him confusing questions and like now, often had to wait an age for his answer.

He fought for an appropriate word. "Dismal."

She looked mortified and pushed his plate closer to him.

"Eat your cake."

His full mouth offered a slight reprieve. He'd hated Christmas at Cwmgwrach for many reasons, and couldn't stand being inside with all the animals outside, not that he was ever in for long. He swallowed and said there was very little money rather than reveal the family's loathing for him.

"Cut enough holly and mistletoe to take home and I'll make you a cake," she smiled generously as if all that would cure everything. She was assuming he'd been invited to his family's home in the village. He'd had no contact with his stepmother or half-siblings since he'd left for Tŷ Newydd.

Davies allowed Morgan two days' holiday for Christmas. He drove to Cwmgwrach, knowing it was still unoccupied since their eviction. He had nowhere else to go. His only home was falling further into disrepair. They'd left many things at the end: old pots, pans, the kitchen table, which was too large for the Williamses' new cottage. His stepmother wanted a fresh start. It was as if he'd been expected. The table was in the same position with chipped tin mugs, plates, half-burnt candles in jam jars and a tiny arrangement of holly. No doubt Nia and Bethan were responsible for this festive touch, still playing house at their age. He smiled; they wouldn't have bothered had they known he'd reap the benefits.

He imagined taking the old place on and had considered making enquiries, he knew every inch of the land, didn't care about the house. He had no money as yet. His job and life at Tŷ Newydd would give him the opportunity to save. A farm, even rented, was his one aim. He lit the candles, which almost brought cosiness to the place – or at least more so than when it had heaved with his family. The very thought of them here, he'd do better to start elsewhere. Ten minutes after the tiny black wicks had caught and a glow flickered through the kitchen, there was a knock on the door and it opened.

"Good heavens, man!" Mr Pritchard's eyes flashed round the room and landed on a pile of old blankets. "Please don't say you're living here. Please. It's Christmas."

Morgan shrugged indifference. "It's just another day."

"Well yes, I have to agree. I left my wife and Bethan decorating the tree: the minute they finish, Bethan removes everything and starts again so I decided a good walk wouldn't go amiss." He paced the kitchen then settled into a rickety chair and took out his pipe. "As I left, she was balancing a hideous cloth witch in the branches. It belonged to my wife's mother, Bethan's always been fascinated by it and was given it on the condition she stopped going cross-eyed. Her grandmother told her she'd be stuck like it if the wind changed. I ask you."

Morgan pictured the cross-eyed family who had lived high on the mountain where the wind was always changing. He felt something akin to honour that Mr Pritchard should come in and sit without commenting on the state of things, merely start on his ramblings. He looked round the kitchen for anything dry and burnable. "I'll have a fire going soon, for some tea."

"Splendid," Mr Pritchard smiled. "Well now, tell me how it's all going."

Morgan tried to compare his six months at Tŷ Newydd with his old life here, his stepmother dishing out double the amount of food to her real sons, his father silent or shouting.

"Good," he said.

"And do they just keep sheep?"

"No, I'm milking."

His visitor sat forward in the old chair, "Ah, marvellous, how many? Friesians?"

"No, Guernseys. Only thirty."

"Guernseys, really? Well, well, there can't be that many over here. Lovely cows, those chestnut and white coats and yellow milk."

This headmaster's agricultural knowledge always took Morgan aback.

"Mrs Davies is keen on the cows; Mr Davies, the sheep."

"And how are they treating you?"

Morgan found a crunched saucepan at the sink. He turned on the tap, watched orange water gush out and considered the benefits: there were meals, his clothes washed, ironed and mended and the small caravan he'd made home. Before he could construct a reasonable answer, Mr Pritchard stood up and the chair fell apart. "Look," he said. "Come and have a meal at The Plas or at least a Christmas drink. Alice would be awfully pleased to see you, hear how you're getting on."

"No, no, I have everything I need here. But thank you."

"Come on, man," he insisted, re-buttoning his coat. "It's Christmas Eve; they'll be off to bally midnight mass. I need company, Morgan – I'd really appreciate it."

Morgan was well aware if anyone enjoyed solitude it was Mr Pritchard. An hour or two without his wife and daughter would be no hardship for a man like him in a house overflowing with books and music. His invitation was a big-hearted gesture. He caught Mr Pritchard's eye. Without a word their gaze travelled the derelict kitchen and when their eyes met they laughed at the absurdity of it all. Morgan picked up his coat. They closed the door on the terrible old farmhouse, slithered down the hill to the footbridge then walked at a smart pace along the narrow river path in single file and companionable silence.

At The Plas, Mr Pritchard led Morgan on round to the drive, passing the hole in the laurel hedge as if he didn't know of it. They left their boots in the vestibule and went through to the sitting room.

"We have a visitor!" He clamped his hand to Morgan's shoulder as though he were a rare species on the verge of escape. "Would you believe it? I found Morgan at Cwmgwrach."

"Oh lovely, how good to see you!" Mrs Pritchard stabbed her needles into a ball of wool and jumped up. "What would you like, dear?" She hadn't forgotten little Nia's bruises, but her husband had related Morgan's gruelling history in detail. Bryn believed he was a decent fellow at heart and he was usually a good judge of character.

Bethan was on her knees sorting a tangle of tinsel and baubles. The Christmas tree was bare apart from the cloth witch poking from the middle branches.

Morgan would have appreciated a strong cup of tea, but Mrs Pritchard was opening a bottle. It was almost seven months since his father's death and that first taste of whisky at The Plas. As he sipped tentatively at his second, Mr Pritchard handed him a small blue book. "You'd better borrow this, old chap, if you will insist on camping at Cwmgwrach. This has heartened me in adverse conditions." His jacket swung open like a weighty office shelf, the inside pockets bulging with sketch pads, pens and pencils. He took out a navy marbled fountain pen and small notebook and wrote inside: 'Palgrave's Golden Treasury, Christmas Eve, 1960. Morgan Williams.'

Morgan heard a tut from the Christmas tree. Mr Pritchard replaced the lid of his pen and slid a pencil from the worn satin lining of his jacket. He rooted in another pocket for a pencil sharpener and circled the lead to a thin point. "Fountain pens should only be used by the owner," he said, handing the pencil to Morgan. "Would you mind just signing here, please?"

At more tuts, Morgan looked round. Bethan was balancing on a chair with a silver bauble, glowering at her father. Her mother, pink-faced, rolled her eyes and raised her glass. "Chin-chin," she said, taking a huge mouthful.

"They think I'm obsessive, but I do like to know the whereabouts of my books," he explained. "You may keep it for as long as you like. Even good friends can be unreliable. It's a good system, please don't be offended."

"I'm not," said Morgan and quickly signed his name. He wasn't in the slightest. Flashing his dark eyes at Bethan and her mother he raised his glass. "Chin-chin," he said, for the first time in his life. The little signing ceremony had pleased him. It gave the lending of the book great significance and borrowing a valued possession felt far superior to the gift of a cast-off, which could easily have happened, it being Christmas and he an unexpected guest.

A gift did appear just before Mrs Pritchard and Bethan left for midnight mass: a balaclava helmet. One of the many knitted by Alice in tweedy four-ply. Whether she was misreading the pattern or misjudging the height of her husband's head, each hat rose at least six inches too high.

"Marvellous things, I always wear one in bed in winter," said Mr Pritchard. "And perfect for Cwmgwrach. Always keep your head and feet warm."

Alice prayed he wouldn't mention the miners' lamp contraption he also wore in bed on top of the distorted balaclava, swearing it "essential for night reading without disturbing anyone". Anyone? She'd never told her sister of her husband's cranky night attire. Cecily would kill herself laughing, then pull herself together and look concerned.

EIGHT

BETHAN PRAYED FOR snow and six-foot drifts to engulf the house. However, the rain just turned cold and the ancient school coach never failed to collect her at the end of the lane, rattle her out through the woods and past the rows of cottages and grey primary school. The steamed-up windows dripped with condensation; sometimes she wiped a spy hole and sometimes she didn't. The route had become all too familiar. Still in a state of shock at being sent to a convent, she spent hours picturing Nia in her normal school. Was it a ploy to separate her from her dear crazy friend?

Half a mile from school they regularly clashed with the abattoir lorry, parked outside the butcher's. On a road built for a horse and cart, the coach had to inch past the open truck overflowing with a tangle of severed limbs, sheepskins and bloodied wool. The girls sitting on the driver's side of the coach had a bird's-eye view and those in the farther seats clambered over to reach the window and scream. Blood oozed from the corners of the lorry and trickled down the gutter.

Not much about the sheep world fazed Bethan after her harsh initiation at Cwmgwrach. She had no qualms about meeting the bulbous eyes of a decapitated ram stuffed in the mess with a stray sheepskin draped round his horns like a shawl. The other girls were too hysterical to notice her quiet composure. When the coach moved on, they returned to their seats to unfinished homework, magazines, knitting and Bethan to relive her bloody encounter with Morgan, eartagging the lambs.

They disembarked at the convent church. She loathed the sight of the bile-green corrugated iron hut. No heating and instead of the traditional pitch-black confessional box (grappling for the hassock and kidding yourself the priest didn't recognise anyone) here the sinner knelt before a flimsy folding screen. The priest sat behind it on the floor, his legs sticking out sideways. It did dispel her father's theory that "these fellows arm themselves with a comfortable chair and bottle of Scotch to wallow in the misery of others' lives". Bethan cribbed her sins from *Examples of Venial Sin* and page 31 in her missal (disobedience and the odd lie) and always forgot her assigned penance. To cover herself, she'd recite a dozen Our Fathers and Hail Marys.

There were bearable moments. For half a term, a plainclothes English teacher was wafted before them, a brief warning. Short skirts, fishnet stockings, stilettos, she wiggled onto the desk, crossing her long legs and the girls breathed her in like an illegal drug. They mimicked her devil-may-care mincing strut long after she'd been sacked. Had the nuns stalked her with admiration, disgust or jealousy? But then, thought Bethan, what normal woman marries an invisible man and wears his wedding ring? Her mother. Her father was never in the same room or on the same holiday.

What would he make of an art room with no north light? Their class took place in a dark basement as if hiding something untoward when their most sensual subject was an anemone. Sister Ursula was wide as a wall, her large black back an invitation for constant flicks of orange paint. One afternoon a sharp blow between Bethan's shoulder blades took her breath away, her shoulders shot back in reflex action, hands slipped something round the nape of her neck, down her front, under both armpits and tied it tightly at her back.

"Our girls must not slouch when they start developing," Sister Ursula glared at Bethan's flat chest. "This will ensure proper deportment. And keep it up on your retreat tomorrow."

It was a silk stocking. Bethan broke two fingernails picking at the knot before resorting to the dressmaking scissors.

The retreat was two days of prayer and contemplation in the woods where the sun couldn't reach them. Sister Margaret was entrusting them with vows of silence, they assumed she had a rendezvous with the gardener. Bethan imagined Nia's reaction to a ban on talking.

Not daring to speak, they hopscotched to the devil with music in their heads until a quiet serious girl glided to a clearing and began to pirouette. She leapt and twirled as if floating or attached to a wire in the trees. Every girl sat cross-legged, hearts pounding in adoration and fear: ethereal beauty spelled danger. If questioned, Bethan would say they'd been chosen for a vision, like Saint Bernadette. No nun could argue with that.

At the end of the first day Sister Margaret swept round a tree in her Dracula outfit to take the Angelus or blood, or both. Their head music died. The nun's duchess face was prepared and eager for trouble. To her disappointment the dancer and the other girls were kneeling in the grass; heads reverently bowed over prayer books.

The quiet girl danced the following day, in her navy skirt and long wool socks, leaping through the trees. When her performance and the retreat were over she was heard to say, "Next time the bitches will see just how long we can go without food."

Bethan was chosen for an investigation in the needlework room. Beside the Adam fireplace (desecrated by the nuns nailing leather skirts over Adam and Eve's bits) was a store cupboard reputed to lead to a priests' hole. Pushed through fabrics, wool, sewing machines and tailors' dummies, she squeezed through a small square door into a mile-long tunnel where men of the cloth had hidden or escaped to the village. She was a yard into the suffocating stink of stale priests and mice when the girls' whispered encouragement stopped, their hands on her ankles were replaced by rough clamping paws and a jubilant Sister Margaret dragged her back through the rolls of calico and tartan.

Her punishment was to sweep the tower steps every lunchtime for a week, until four prefects insisted she shared a smoke on the tower roof, a small patch of bobbled roofing-felt the nuns were either too decrepit or colossal to reach. Sister Margaret must have smelt her cigarette breath (she did get dreadfully close) and on the third day her punishment took a different turn. Bethan had influenced her class so drastically she was to join the kindergarten for a week, taking her own desk, which she'd damaged by carving her initials on the lid. Surely, she thought, she'd be a worse influence on the little ones. Nuns were illogical.

As if manoeuvring the desk up two flights of stairs in near darkness with the iron runners bashing into the steps and the weight killing her arms wasn't enough, four sharp whacks stung the back of her legs. There had to be a stick or ruler among the nun's cache of glass rosary beads and crashing keys, to cause the perfect red lines Bethan discovered when she peeled off her socks that night.

Two days later she was sent home to The Plas. Her mother was seriously ill.

Bethan had had no experience of hospitals. At the sight of her mother lost under white sheets, coupled with the dry heat and overwhelming smell of disinfectant, she fainted. She came round with her father looming above her, his hand hovering over her shoulder.

"Are you all right now, dear?"

Head swimming, she checked her socks were pulled up; she couldn't bear her mother to see the red stripes on her legs.

"Has Mummy got her wool here?" She'd never seen her without some knitting on the go.

Her mother opened her eyes a fraction, "Just look at me, dear. I ask you?" she said, only her face and weak smile visible above the starched sheet. "You mustn't worry; I'll be home in a few days to everything." Her eyes closed.

Bethan tried to attract the attention of two large nurses who were diving in perfect synchronisation round the next bed, expertly flapping and tucking in clean sheets. They'd tell her what was wrong; they'd only have to look at her father to see he was unlikely to divulge much. They smoothed the finished bed, smiled kindly at her and left. One returned with a glass of warm orange squash but by then Bethan couldn't speak.

Driving home, she and her father spent the first couple of miles in silence. At last he spoke. "You've been allowed time off school, dear, provided we do a little studying. If you don't have any books, we'll improvise. Finding anything difficult?"

"French," she lied. She had good marks despite the nun's dislike of her.

"Ah, jolly good." He burst into a minute of fluent French. "In the war, I was coming home late from the Bath French Circle, just crossing Pulteney Bridge, when an ARP warden stepped out of the dark. 'Halt, who goes there, friend or foe?' he said. He must have mistaken me for a German. That was just before I met your mother."

The last time Bethan had been on Pulteney Bridge was in a café with her mother, who was relating how she'd gone right over the weir in a reckless boyfriend's boat. Bethan glanced at her father and knew it wasn't him. Why weren't they discussing her mother now? He asked her a question in French and, confident she'd answered correctly, she turned proudly to see his reaction. He was wearing the same pained expression as when her mother requested *The Mikado* (she and Bethan weren't to touch the record player).

"We'll work on your accent," he said after a moment, with another faraway look.

Bethan stared at the road. Arriving at The Plas, she leapt from the car and ran straight to the back garden. The guinea pigs squeaked alarmingly the minute they heard her and she imagined her bookworm father forgetting to feed them. The cats could meow to remind him – not that they needed to: he liked cats. She opened the hutch door to find clean hay, a barely touched food dish and full water bottle. Her mother had seen to the guineas before her journey to hospital.

The house felt different. Though her mother was hardly one for domesticity, the atmosphere had changed and Bethan was aware of a strange stuffiness as if nothing was moving, the smell of settled dust and a heavier reek of herbal tobacco.

Even less of the tablecloth could be seen under notebooks, letters, pens, pencils, twirled ribbons of orange peel, cake and breadcrumbs.

Her father was often on the phone to Auntie Cecily. The times she wasn't with Nia, Bethan would creep along the hallway, listen to his serious tone and learn nothing. There were no medical books in the house; no one had ever been interested.

For the three weeks her mother was in hospital, Bethan and her father lived on oranges and crumpets, interspersed with fish and chips brought to The Plas by Nia. Mrs Williams was working in the village fish and chip shop.

PART TWO

ONE

1965

Towers of books filled every corner of the caravan; Morgan's collection had long overtaken the few shelves. In that first winter he'd installed a wood stove and begun to cook. He fixed an alkathene pipe to a spring on the hillside to bring water to the small sink, hung a clothes line between the trees and did his own washing. Insofar as any man reared without direction or warmth was able, Morgan had made the small caravan his home. At each stage of independence, Elin Davies appeared slightly put out. He had been at Tŷ Newydd for five years.

It was a mart morning. He'd just loaded a batch of old brokers onto the trailer when Davies asked him to take a sack of rabbit pellets from the Land Rover to the top shed. The shed Davies never entered. It was the worst on the farm: a patchwork of planks and tin sheets, high cracked windows opaque with black cobwebs, split drainpipes swaying on baler twine and a roof held down by concrete blocks and tyres.

The interior was quite the reverse. Morgan paused at the door. Mrs Davies was sitting on a bale of hay in the middle of the shed, miles away. Half her long dark hair was pinned up with combs and the rest curtained a large white rabbit on her lap, another two hundred lolloped peacefully around her.

At first it appeared the whole lot ran loose, but she'd divided the shed into open-topped wire mesh runs for various groups. The huge runs were the reason Davies ignored his wife's venture. She knew well enough that meat rabbits confined to small hutches fattened quicker and mesh floors made easy cleaning, but wouldn't have it: she thought it cruel. She did all the killing herself – she wouldn't trust anyone else. Once Morgan knew her better, he wasn't surprised.

"This feed was in the Land Rover," he said. "We're off to mart in a minute."

"Oh thanks, didn't know I'd missed one." She stayed on the hay bale stroking the snowy rabbit draped over her knees, stretched out, in heaven. He slid the bag from his shoulders, cut the string and poured the pellets into the bin just inside the door. Emptied in seconds, he folded the bag and turned to go.

"Morgan, could you just help me for a minute? Please."

His boots slid towards her through knee-deep straw, a strange sensation. Such thick bedding; no wonder Davies couldn't be doing with it.

"I need to clean a little cut," she said. "It keeps going wild."

He crouched beside her, took the rabbit, holding it flat across his knees and saw a wound near the rectum. She dipped a small wad of cotton wool into a jug of water. For all their manual work her slender fingers didn't resemble farmers' hands. The rabbit stayed stock-still while she plastered the cut with yellow Battles ointment, as if spreading butter.

"Shall I put him back?" he asked.

"Her," she washed her hands in a bucket and shook them, accidentally splashing a few rabbits. They leapt twisting into the air, thumped their hind feet silently into the straw and sat up to dry their snuffly faces with their fast little front paws.

"Talk about over-reaction," she laughed, taking the rabbit.

"Are you coming to mart?" He didn't call her anything unless he had to attract her attention from a distance, then it was Mrs Davies.

She occasionally had a lift, squashed between them in the front of the Land Rover, knees tightly together to one side of the gear stick. But mostly she went to Swansea on her own. He'd seen her tramping down the long track in her wellies, shoes swinging in a bag. She'd change her footwear at the roadside, tuck her boots underneath the milk churn stand and wait for the bus. On her return at five o'clock, he'd often see her secrete a few bags in her rabbit shed.

"Not today. Thanks for your help, some of these blessed rabbits will struggle." She brushed the rabbit against Morgan's arm. "Daft things."

In the Land Rover he could smell the yellow ointment and found a little splodge on the arm of his jacket.

"God knows why she forgot that last sack of feed," said Davies as they bumped down to the road. "She'd already unloaded nine. Bloody rabbits. She's mad."

Morgan didn't answer. He covered that part of his sleeve with his hand and stared out of the window. Davies didn't deserve her.

"The hours she spends in that shed!" said Davies. "Still, with any luck, the place'll fall down soon."

Morgan slid the window open. Thank God he had a rare day off tomorrow. He'd get away; go fishing, maybe bring her back a trout.

He always drove to Cwmgwrach to fish; saw it as his divine right. Still no one lived in the farmhouse: the three stupid old sisters who owned the farm couldn't agree on a sale price. They'd let the land to a neighbour – must have started negotiations before Mr Williams was cold in his grave. The neighbour, a lawyer who played at farming, already owned a hundred and twenty acres. He bought the sheep from Mrs Williams and as his name was William John, she threw in their marking iron and tin of green paint. Morgan was as incensed about the marking iron as he was about his field. His stepmother had kept ownership of the nine acres; he'd seen his father's trotting stallion there and a handful of ewes. It was the land that had the pull.

He tried to control his eagle eyes and keep tunnel vision, passing through sheep still marked with green Ws on their sides. The ewes barely moved. He could travel through any livestock without disturbing them. He liked to imagine they might recognise him, though five years was a long time and there were only a few old ewes he knew himself. Coming to the river he quietly settled himself on the bank.

In seconds he fixed on a large trout calmly circling a little inlet, gliding in and out of shadows thrown by a canopy of trees. He cut a long piece of hazel, leaned over and began to run it lightly along the length of the fish, before carefully lowering himself into the water. The fish slowed. Ten minutes passed with it moving more and more languorously and Morgan also, for once, at peace. When the shadow of a figure fell across the water he didn't move or look up, merely lifted a finger to his lips for silence. He kept his eye glued to the fish which had begun to drift to the edge of the inlet and the main flow of the river.

Bethan slid in with barely a ripple. She was on her way home when she saw the fisherman bent double over a trout plotting its escape. As expected, ice-cold water filled her boots, the spate river gushed from the mountain without a moment's pause for the sun to take effect. The trout waved its tail lazily and turned. Morgan looked round from the corner of his eye. They hadn't seen each other close-up for a couple of years. They couldn't speak now and alert the trout. Both remained silent and motionless: Bethan poised half-bent over the water, Morgan stroked the stick against the speckled scales. When the trout appeared to be eyeing its escape again, Bethan crossed imperceptibly to the next stone to block its route. Though her movements appeared instinctive, Nia had taught her the fine art of trout tickling last summer. The fish was barely stirring.

Morgan reached for the forked stick he'd thrown into the grass. A shower of water shot from the river like a firework. Hurled into the air by the stick, the fish spun in a stardust of water beads and landed on the bank. To Bethan's relief, Morgan splashed quickly from the river and knocked it on the head with a battered old priest, none of that desperate tail flapping and slow suffocation. It lay there shining. They stared down at it and then at each other. The deep trance had been contagious. Their smiles broke the tension; it was a huge achievement, mesmerising a substantial fish to its death.

"Thanks," said Morgan, still grinning. "I've been watching him for weeks."

"How do you know it's the same one?"

"I know."

She tipped the water from her boots and rubbed her feet with ferns. "Want to come back to the house and dry off?" She couldn't look at him for long. His black eyes bored into her, made her shiver. He would always be slim, some would say thin, but he'd sort of muscled up. Boy to manhood. She guessed he must be 22.

He shook a bag from his pocket, dropped the fish inside and lifted it up and down to guess the weight. He wasn't bothered about being wet, but the possibility of a bookish conversation with Mr Pritchard appealed. "Yes. Thank you, I will." They started off along the footpath, Bethan in front.

"I suppose your father taught you all how to do that."

"My earliest memory. I think." His abandonment was more a retold story than a physical memory, though he swore he could remember a cat licking his face till his cheeks smarted. "We lived on fish, mutton, rabbit, hare."

"My father couldn't have taught me anything half as useful. My first memory was finding a dead sheep in the sand dunes at Ynyslas, heaving with maggots."

"*Ych â fi.*"

She decided against telling him the whole story. Farmers never went on holiday and however grim their wet week in a tiny caravan, it was a holiday. On their one fine day she and her mother had been on the beach, her mother bolt upright in her deckchair to allow room for her knitting needles to shoot in and out; her father had disappeared with his paints and easel to capture a nearby stubble field. She remembered wandering off, her little feet sinking in the sugary sand and coming across the heaving mound of filthy grey wool (even at three she knew about wool) squirming with fat white grubs. She told him of the patch of raw flesh, bony head, empty eye sockets full of flies and one yellow tooth ready to bite her. She'd run for it, a small fireball yelling, "Daddy, Daddy, thing in sand!" Busy daubing purple across an abstract landscape, he'd raised his left hand and said, "Not now, dear." Her mother had charged up from the beach. Half the time her father could have worn a 'Do Not Disturb' sign.

"Funny really," she said. "I've felt a strange affinity with sheep ever since. I loved bottle-feeding the *swcis* at Cwmgwrach, couldn't believe you all hated it."

"We'd had to feed them since we could stand. How's your school then?"

"Awful, spend most of the time on our knees. Just been praying for Ruth Ellis's soul. She killed her lover, remember: last woman in Britain to be hanged. It's some anniversary of her death. Nuns adore that sort of thing. Sadists."

He stopped dead and Fly ran into his boots. He knew a certain type of spider ate her mate after intercourse, but had never heard of Ruth Ellis. He'd look her up in his encyclopaedia the minute he got home. As for nuns, he'd never encountered one.

"Nia seems okay at her school," said Bethan.

He couldn't remember when he'd last seen Nia. It came as a bit of a shock to realise the two of them had to be about sixteen. They squeezed through The Plas hedge and crossed the grass to the back porch, where they peeled off their sodden boots and socks against the doorstep, dripping water everywhere.

"My grandparents are here," said Bethan.

"You should have told me," he retrieved a boot. "I wouldn't have come."

"Oh, they're fine, and look at the state of us. You can't drive home like that."

He could, but too curious, he threw down the boot again and followed her into the kitchen and along the hall. They squelched into the sitting room barefoot and sopping wet to the thigh. Mr Pritchard was standing by the window and his wife at the sideboard, pouring out pale sherry for her parents, who were half-swallowed in the old sofa.

Bethan took the bag from Morgan and opened it under her grandmother's nose. "We tickled this trout to death."

"Good God!" The elderly matriarch shot as upright as her dowager's hump and the lumpy sofa would allow. She fanned herself with the *Radio Times* and held out a hand for a sherry.

"Good gracious," said Mrs Pritchard, also taken aback. "Oh dear, the poor thing."

"Morgan, old chap!" said Mr Pritchard, oblivious of their appearance and pools of river water spreading across the rug. "Good to see you. How are you?"

"Wet, dear," said his wife. "Do you have a pair of trousers he could borrow? Or Pop, yours would fit better. I'll fetch some towels."

"Don't worry," said Morgan quickly. "I have to be back for milking anyway."

Bethan's grandfather, tall and still handsome, gently lifted a cat from his knees and extricated himself from the sofa to peer in at the fish.

"I'd love to paint it," he said. "Make a wonderful jigsaw."

"Oh Lord," said his wife. "But how soon will it stink?"

Morgan thrust the bag at the silver-haired man. "Have it, keep it," he said, imagining him dicing and carving it into jigsaw shapes.

"We must have a literary evening, Morgan," said Mr Pritchard. "How are you for reading matter at the moment?"

"Yes, alright thank you: I've quite a book collection now." He began walking backwards. They were all mad.

"Splendid. Well, do come again soon."

Bethan walked him to the back door; Mrs Pritchard chased them with towels. "My father owns a jigsaw factory. He's a brilliant artist and your trout will appear as a watercolour on a double-sided wooden jigsaw. Dry your hair at least. Anyhow, thank you for giving it to him, Morgan. His jigsaws are the most intricate ever seen; you're bound to have one for your generosity. I doubt he's seen such a beautiful fish."

Morgan gave his hair a quick rub, handed back the towel and nodded. Bethan accompanied him to the hedge.

"Where were you off to today, anyway?" he asked.

"Just walking. Don't forget I've just been released from prison for the summer. My life isn't like yours." She turned to walk away. "Thanks for the trout, s'long."

She went back in and straight upstairs, gathered some clothes and turned on the bath taps. The Ascot whooshed into life and grudgingly rattled out half a bath of hot water. She dipped in a toe and climbed in, the water turning peaty around her. She dunked her head back and closed her eyes. Through the open window, she could hear voices in the garden: her father and grandfather off to her father's studio in an old shed to discuss the painting of the trout. They'd be delving about for pots and jugs to create an interesting still life around the fish. Her father was intensely possessive over his brushes and paints, but she knew her grandfather had carte blanche to use anything that took his fancy. Their companionable conversation faded as they disappeared into the trees, leaving the clink of her mother's and grandmother's glasses just below the window.

There was no electricity in the shed; her grandfather would be unable to paint through the night as he did in London. Bethan often wondered how her mother and aunt were conceived unless her grandparents did it on the stairs. Her father painted in the morning and insisted on north light.

Her skin was as crumpled by the hot soaking as by the freezing river. When the last swirls of bathwater had gurgled away and she was drying herself, her mother's voice rose up the stairs, unusually high and insistent. Bethan crept halfway down to hear better.

"He is not a gypsy or a vagrant, Mother. He's hard-working and has had a truly awful time: deserted by his mother as a baby – it doesn't bear thinking about. Morgan is an unusual young man who lives close to nature, sort of hefted to the hill like the sheep. We're actually rather fond of him."

TWO

A MILLION STARLINGS filled the sky. Morgan was watching from his caravan window as the black mass swirled high above the rabbit shed in ever-changing patterns. He stepped outside for a better view, wandering the yard, head in the air in admiration. Impeccable synchronisation: swooping down as though compelled to visit a spectacle then soaring away.

Tap, tap on glass: he hadn't noticed Elin Davies, hazy behind her cobwebbed window. She was beckoning him. They met at the door. "Could you give me a hand?"

"Seen the show?" he asked.

"How they don't crash."

At an invisible signal, the birds changed direction and were away and the empty sky went quiet. Morgan followed her into the shed. Sacks of rabbit pellets were propped against the feed bins. "Want these emptied?" He knew she was capable.

She shook her head and kept going. As he followed, the rabbits danger-thumped their hind legs on the thick straw. She stopped in the windowless corner, where stretched skins of white fur had been crucified with thin brass nails on to a display board. "I've something strange to tell you," she said.

Hell, he thought, what now? She smiled coyly. He'd made the mistake of sharing Bethan's stories of hangings and nuns with her. Sensing his morbid fascination, she was collecting macabre tales of her own, relating them in an overtly intense manner. Taunting him.

"I've just read that in the eighteenth century a woman claimed to have given birth to seventeen fully grown rabbits. People believed her for a few years, then she was convicted of deception and thrown into Newgate gaol."

He made the mistake of laughing. She grabbed a rabbit skin from an old table, plastered her fingers in salt and began to rub away at the underside. Head down, hair flopped over her face; he couldn't see her expression. Sinewy ribbons of skin formed small lumps that she ripped off and flung to the floor.

"Abernant has come up for rent," he said. "I've applied." He was going to add that he'd stay at Tŷ Newydd until they found a replacement, but he'd had enough of her ways, staring at him until his entire being filled with heat; deliberately blocking doorways so he was forced to squash past her.

She looked up and flicked back her hair. "You won't get it."

"I have." He would: no one else would take on such desolate farmland. In places it was only distinguishable from the mountain by the odd bedstead and a few strands of rusty barbed wire. "It's my chance, probably the only one I'll get."

From the moment he left Cwmgwrach, he'd been on the prowl for a farm. Women came second. He related his patience and self-discipline to that of an older man, but in fact took a masochistic relish in biding his time.

She began to dart desperate glances round the shed as if willing a miracle to burst through the wall and persuade him to stay. "I know that," her face crumpled.

He doubted they'd find a replacement; even the term 'servant boy' was hardly used now.

"What was it you wanted me to do?" he asked, more kindly.

She smoothed the rabbit skin flat to the table, washed her hands and dried them on a ripped square of candy-striped sheet. Eyes down, she whispered. "Me."

Speechless, he stood stock-still as she un-popped her drab blue overalls. Underneath she wore a flimsy cream blouse. He counted ten small pearl buttons as she undid them in slow motion then wrapped her arms around his neck. This was to be savoured. She'd flirted cruelly for the last few years, now he'd leave everything to her. She could get on with it. Having thought rabbits made no noise, snuffles like little sneezes broke the silence. Hundreds of beady pink eyes were on her graceful descent and he was vaguely aware of their sparkle as she dragged him down into bedding laid for them, her rabbits. She smelt of fur and sandalwood soap, he knew it was sandalwood from the little Bronnley boxes on the kitchen dresser used for buttons and pins. Wisps of fluff floated in the dust motes from the disturbed barley straw, as she got on with it. A soft nuzzling into his neck, gentle as a little rabbit in fact, then she held his head in her hands and kissed him carefully. Long drawn-out kisses. Her hands sticky with salt.

A single woof of abandonment came from outside: Fly waiting loyally by the shed door. A perfect giveaway, but he didn't care. His stomach tightened as she slid a hand into his jeans, stroking his skin, circling his navel. Davies could burst in and blow his brains out as those long delicate fingers went squirming down. The threat of death was intoxicating. His flesh barely noticed any sharp stalks of straw; it could have been a feather bed. She burrowed under him warmly, naked apart from a black silk scarf tied at her throat. At first her need seemed more desperate than his; she'd played too many unspoken games. He tried to remind himself that he was totally sick of her. Her eyes closed and she was gone, a breathless sweet sighing, kisses frenzied, almost making love to herself. He took a second to look at her before he matched her frenzy. Davies could have a shotgun pressed to his temple.

Afterwards, he experienced a supreme satisfaction, far more to do with arrogance than any form of love. He was pleased with his performance. She said he'd watched too many rams at it and was like a bull in a china shop. She ran a risk saying that with his temperament, but he laughed, knowing she'd enjoyed him. Anyhow, it appealed to him, associating the act to livestock. 'Be a good animal, true to your instincts', he remembered from D H Lawrence: it portrayed the appropriate earthiness.

"Where is Davies anyway?" he asked.

"I trained those starlings to entice you to my shed," she said, with a self-satisfied smile.

Her habit of ignoring questions drove him mad. "I'm sure you did." Most women were witches. He twisted her scarf until the knot was at the front. "Can I keep this?"

"If you like." She lifted her arms to untie it and he cupped her breasts in his grazed hands. The knot had tightened and she struggled, digging her nails into the black silk. He bit her nipples too hard and she shrieked but kept her arms raised, trying unsuccessfully to work the scarf loose.

Fly barked again and they heard the engine. Her eyes flashed. Morgan hissed an order through the thin tin wall for the dog to be quiet and lie down. Now it was all over, he had no intention of being discovered. "Get dressed," he said, sliding on the straw as he leapt up. "You go out, I'll wait here." He shook out her overalls. She pulled them over her naked body and popped the press-studs up to her neck.

The Land Rover came round the corner of the farmhouse and stopped. Fly gave a short yelp to announce it. Morgan unearthed his jeans and took a knife from the pocket. She smoothed down her hair while he picked out strands of straw. He held her, felt her heart thumping into his body and pulled her closer by the scarf, like dragging Fly by the collar. He sliced his knife through the black silk next to the knot, threw the scarf behind him and led her through the rabbits to the door. She closed it behind her and calmly crossed the yard. He cleaned a tiny circle in a window opaque from grime and watched her enter the farmhouse a second behind Davies.

Their clothes lay in the flattened bedding. He kicked them together, making his shirt, her blouse, his pants and jeans into a small intimate pile. It seemed she'd worn nothing else under her overalls apart from the scarf, which lay curled in the straw like a newly shed snake skin, the knot as its head. The silk was dotted with pinprick holes from her nails. He threw it into the air to land on his upturned face like a feathery parachute, inhaled and rubbed it over his body. A silken towel. Then he dressed, stuffed her blouse into an empty feed sack and pushed the scarf deep into his jeans pocket.

Fly was waiting below the minuscule back window, guessing it to be her master's exit. Clever dog. Morgan squeezed through in a diving position, jammed the window shut and sneaked off between the buildings, up and away to the fields out of sight of the farmhouse, Fly tight to his heels. He'd walk for a while, turn at a suitable distance then come into view as if returning from checking the ewes on the mountain. Davies owned a shotgun and rifle. It wasn't long before Morgan was out of range of both. Several old bomb craters dented the hill. He dropped into the first and lay spreadeagled.

The abrupt ending suited him, Davies appearing when he did. Morgan had not only deceived the old bastard, but lost his virginity in extraordinary circumstances. It felt perfect, taken to his heights by an older married woman in a sea of white rabbits, gun-toting husband at large. Some men would be unable to eat rabbit again, but he'd continue lamping and devour their small roasted bodies even more voraciously. He left the crater with the sudden notion he could keep going, leave Tŷ Newydd for good, now this minute. The thought of his books filling the caravan stopped him.

Another deterrent waylaid him: a ewe and lamb on their own. The huge lamb had somehow missed weaning and was butting for milk so roughly its mother's back legs were bouncing off the ground. The old hat-rack ewe, drained dry by her child, seemed to be balancing on her nose, which was touching the ground, and was in danger of tipping right over. She looked at death's door. Her earmark was Tŷ Newydd. He had no choice but to return.

Fly was eager to drive the pair down off the hill, but the ewe collapsed, too weak to walk a step. Morgan pulled up his shirt collar and swung her up on to his shoulders. She was a feather. With her head lolling and all four thin legs clamped to his chest, her mournful bleats kept her lamb trotting anxiously at his feet until it tired and he scooped it up. It was almost dark when he arrived in the yard, wearing the dead ewe like a scarf and the lamb under his arm, ready for the orphan pen.

The next day he made arrangements to meet the owner of Abernant.

Abernant was terrible and beautiful, a rambling farmhouse weather-beaten and bleak from every direction, and two hundred acres of rough grazing, mostly unfenced. The house stood way higher than Cwmgwrach on The Plas's side of the river and much of the land bordered the riverbank. Some broken windows bore shards of glass welded like daggers into the frames and roof slates were missing, but the big old kitchen was intact and that's where the old farmer lived and slept.

They met on a day thick with grey mist. The old man came through the stark landscape wearing a hessian sack as a cloak, a billhook on baler twine dangling from his wrist like a handbag. Morgan carried his father's crook. The pair stood with their accessories in the weed-choked yard. The old man was months away from moving down to his daughter in the village. He would have had no plans other than walking away from his life, leaving his home to rot like the smallholdings above Cwmgwrach, had she not persuaded him to try and let the farm. Morgan's interest had come out of the blue. They signed scraps of papers. When the old man threw in the sheep, with no idea of the number, Morgan thought of Mr Pritchard and instigated a good handshake.

On his last night at Tŷ Newydd a full moon drove them to the darkest corner of the rabbit shed. They'd watched Davies leave without lights, crashing down the track, fluorescent by moonlight, to the pub. The shed was cold; they'd removed as few clothes as possible. She showed mock outrage at Morgan still in his boots.

"Chosen my replacement yet?" he asked. "Or am I irreplaceable?"

"He's selling the cows and we'll be able to manage the sheep on our own."

"Selling your cows, so you can devote yourself to his needs? That's why he's strutting round like a damn cock pheasant."

She shrugged. He untied her scarf. He had seven in his collection: all silk, one with a silver thread running through it. Exotic keepsakes from the times Davies had arrived home unexpectedly, the Land Rover engine alerting them to a mad dash for clothes. "You'll have to ride near Abernant to check the sheep. They wander that far."

She looked down and shook her head.

"But it's a perfect excuse: you have to check the ones on the mountain."

"I have to make some sort of life with him, Morgan. I hadn't been near him for years – now I have to, in case I got pregnant." She blushed and gave a cold laugh. "It's a blessing the three of us are dark-haired, I've thought that since we started. I've no feelings for him."

Morgan pulled the scarf taut across his chest.

"Feel what you like." He bent over and lifted her face with his finger under her chin as if he was going to kiss her, and she closed her eyes. He slipped the scarf back around her neck, smiling as he tied it, and pulling on the knot, dragged her to her feet.

"Don't you ever come checking for stragglers round Abernant." His smile gone, he twisted his hand to tighten the scarf and for a second held her close to his face before pushing her down into the straw. He left her spluttering and made his last walk through the rabbits. They scuttled away, the moonbeams illuminating their transparent ears with the red mapping of veins. They thumped their hind legs in vain; his silent standing ovation, and he bowed and thanked them as he closed the shed door.

His van was already packed with his books and clothes and two crystal glasses wrapped carefully in a lambswool jumper.

As for her other gifts of food, china and towels, they were still spread across the flimsy folding table and could stay there. He had planned to clean the caravan the next morning and end his Tŷ Newydd days in the kitchen with a Camp coffee and slice of her fruitcake.

The moon lit the puddles and the thin strips of chrome on the caravan. Fly worked her way through the boxes and settled behind the driver's seat. "We're off. Fuck the lot of it," Morgan said aloud. A minute passed and he felt a consoling paw land softly on his shoulder.

He opened and closed two gates without any ewes darting through from the mountain, though that rarely happened at night. Davies had replaced the last gate with a cattle grid, which a few sheep had immediately worked out how to cross. Not to be beaten, he'd tied a tin lid to the tail of the ringleader and as soon as metal hit metal the startled ewe tottered into reverse. He'd chained an elderly collie to an oil drum at the edge of the grid. As the van rattled over the iron rails she flew to the end of her chain and barked crazily at the wheels. Morgan kept to his usual speed; it was when vehicles slowed and dithered that collies got hit. She slunk back to the scattering of damp straw in her metal home. He couldn't remember ever seeing her off the chain.

At the road he switched on the headlights and steered with his knee to gouge whatever was annoying him from under his fingernails. Threads of black silk fell unseen into dried mud on the van floor.

From Tŷ Newydd to Abernant a crow would have flown a simple journey. The wild lonely road was three times as long, steep and twisting with hairpin bends over precipitous drops, on and on above fields of good pasture and yellow lights flickering from the odd farm building. The bend on the summit marked a dramatic change in the landscape. The van clanked over an ancient cattle grid and began the descent through rocky, coarser pasture. Here sheep roamed everywhere in search of anything edible sprouting between boulders on the verges. Streams rushed down through narrow cracks in the hills and the froth of water shone white in the headlights.

Few travelled this mountain road. There wasn't a dwelling for ten miles. Morgan knew it by heart and would close his eyes for mad personal dares, once opening them to a curly-horned old ram phosphorescent in the van's headlights and once coming perilously close to the edge. The usual plume of smoke rose from one precarious bend where old vehicles were pushed over for insurance claims.

At last the lights of his old village and he was passing the Celyn. The pony was waiting on adjoining waste ground to take the drunken coalman home as he had done every night for years, with one flick of the worn reins.

The Abernant track was longer and rougher than the way to Cwmgwrach, but fairly straight, passing through fields a little inland from the river. As Morgan prepared for the shape of the moonlit farmhouse, her pathetic excuse came to him. To resurrect her dead marriage in case she got pregnant; when she'd trained him, for God's sake. He remembered his acute embarrassment when she'd flippantly referred to their method as "getting out at Llansamlet instead of going all the way to Swansea". He couldn't stand vulgarity in a woman.

THREE

This time a nun hadn't inflicted her bruises; though, as with all incidents, it was nun-related. Sister Margaret had allowed a record to be played ridiculously quietly in the dinner hall. Such privilege was unheard of and the stunned girls were straining to hear the Beatles until a prefect marched across to Bethan and ordered her to turn it up to full volume. She obeyed, the record player was immediately confiscated and she was dragged behind the hall by the same prefect who kicked her legs and punched her in the stomach. Bethan would remain in lifelong confusion over the minds of nuns and the girls they brainwashed, and eternally grateful for long socks.

The Plas, with its old trees and mess of brambles, was a welcome sight and so was Nia, who always appeared within the hour. They sat at the kitchen table with her mother flitting round with tea, cake and excitable questions and Bethan poised, both desperate to hear about Nia's new life. She'd left school and home and lived in an annexe of a Swansea mansion owned by an elderly gentleman.

"But first," Nia opened her bag, whipped out a white card, frilled yellow blouse, short grey skirt, Bluegrass perfume and peered inside. "No white rabbits. Invitation to the Young Farmers' cheese and wine do at the Celyn and stuff to wear, in case."

"God, Nia, thanks," said Bethan, grateful and worried about the blouse.

"Do tell us about your gentleman landlord, Nia dear," said Mrs Pritchard. "How elderly is he exactly and where are you working?"

"He's a magician and I'm his glamorous young assistant. Every Saturday night I wear a long pink dress over an itchy swimsuit, feather boa and long kid gloves and we tour the working men's clubs. When I've risen through the ranks, I shall star at the Palladium and wear a man's dinner suit."

"What!" She clapped and left her hands together in the air like a toddler.

"You're joking, Nia," said Bethan. "Whatever gave you the idea of doing that?"

"You! You Pritchards coming to The Plas with your paper people, squelching jelly, guinea pigs up your jumper, your father's incredible train impression. I'd never met anyone like you; well, I'd never really been anywhere. Ten years old and your father insisting on my first visit I entered through The Vestibule, like the Narnia wardrobe. The spell was cast." She dropped her shoulders and beamed. "Anyway, what are you going to do?"

Bethan hadn't dared think seriously about her future. "Sheep farming, from the spell of Cwmgwrach!" They all laughed and she believed herself.

"I must go and tell Bryn," said her mother. "A magician! He'll absolutely love it."

The kitchen went quiet without her. Bethan stared at Nia across the table in awe.

"You didn't think I'd eaten a real worm? That time in the playground."

"Course I did," said Bethan. "But about your gentleman, is he a gentleman?"

"Perfect. He's lovely. It's a proper apprenticeship. What are you going to do after your expensive education?"

"Education? You're joking, I don't think the nuns were even qualified to teach. I'll shock the career adviser: sheep farming. Yes, that's actually what I'd like to do. Farming."

Nia rolled her eyes. "You're mad."

Bethan's mother drove them to the Celyn. She'd never taken a driving test and they were relieved to jump from the old car and flee from her ten-point turn, which threw up the dust storm of a helicopter landing. A girl who'd been away to agricultural college had transformed the drab function room at the back with tissue paper flowers, tablecloths and candles in Chianti bottles. The landlord banned the candles for fear of fire and insisted the harsh strip lighting stayed on for fear of any funny business, but once his Friday-night regulars crowded the main bar the Young Farmers were forgotten and the lights went out. The girls sat in a stiff row along one side with the boys opposite.

Bethan wore Nia's blouse; she'd never have chosen yellow or frills, which made it all the more thrilling. She gulped white wine too fast and kept her eyes from the boys. Nia hadn't mentioned there'd be music. A few couples were jiving. Bethan would die if anyone asked her, having never danced outside her bedroom – a disjointed effort to the Supremes' *Baby Love*. The minute an agricultural student dragged Nia on to the floor, Bethan made a beeline for the freezing outside lavatory, the thought of sitting alone too unbearable. Her exit was unsteady; she felt queasy after two glasses of wine and not a sign of cheese.

Two boys, too scruffy to be part of the do, were leaning across the wall in the waste-ground car park, messing with cigarette lighters. She could just make out their gormless faces in the glow of the lighters. A procession of woodlice was fleeing from an upturned stone where a pile of little grey bodies had shrivelled to black balls.

"What the hell are you doing?" she said.

They turned and looked her up and down, fags wobbling between thick lips, their thumbs pressed down on the lighters to keep the flames flickering. "Listen, can you hear them crackle? He's next, we'll have a good flare-up with that tail."

The coalman's pony was waiting patiently against the opposite wall, eyes closed, head low, a back leg resting on the tip of its hoof. His iron-grey tail reached the ground.

"Bastards," said Bethan. "You bloody dare."

"Fuck off. None of your business."

The boys' shirtsleeves were rolled up. Bethan took two steps forward and sank her teeth into the nearest arm, just above the elbow, then spat. The boy screamed and clasped his arm. "You fucking little bitch!" He took his hand away and all three stared at the circle of bloody red teeth marks.

"I'm poisonous. You'll die slowly." She spat out more of his vile taste and, swaying badly, grabbed his lighter from the ground and flung it far into the bushes. She fell on her knees and vomited onto the gravel. The boys stood there, rooted to the spot.

Morgan could have reached out and touched them but he'd kept out of sight, flattened against the wall of the Gents, enjoying the spectacle of her feisty attack. He guessed this was her first encounter with alcohol. He came out, told the boys to clear off and picked her up. She was light as a child.

The moment he put her in the van she began to moan that she wanted to die and he must let her die, please, for God's sake. He asked a lad crossing the car park to tell Nia Williams that Bethan had gone home and for the coalman to come out to his pony, then he drove to The Plas at a steady speed with her curling and uncurling on the passenger seat. Mrs Pritchard opened the front door to see her daughter limp and white in his arms. "Wine and no cheese," he said quietly.

"Oh goodness me, Bethan love!" She shot a look round the hall and up the stairs. "Can you bring her into the kitchen, please, Morgan?"

He lowered her into the armchair by the Rayburn and she slid to the floor and began retching. Her mother leapt across the room and threw open the door to a tiny cloakroom.

"In here."

In between jackets, boots and shoes, there was just enough space for Bethan to kneel with her head over the lavatory. Her mother knelt behind her and wrapped both arms round her chest to keep her upright. "Try to be sick quietly, dear, so your father doesn't hear. You go, Morgan dear, we'll manage. And thank you."

Highly relieved, Morgan retraced his steps along the hall. He couldn't cope with vomiting. In the vestibule he turned to close the inner door. He assumed the figure crossing the landing was Mr Pritchard in his night-time balaclava.

The next morning Bethan waited forever for the room to stop rotating. Eventually she eased herself from bed and dressed in the bathroom close to the paraffin heater. She could hear the guinea pigs' hunger squeaks quietening to a greeting burr – they'd become as much her mother's pets. She walked gingerly downstairs. Her father's concerned questioning was slightly unnerving as the previous evening was a blur. Her mother loyally reinforced the idea of rancid butter or mouldy cheese causing her tummy upset, but all Bethan could remember was biting into dirty flesh and watching woodlice run for their lives. She said nothing.

"Anyhow, very kind of Morgan to give her a lift home," said her mother, not adding that he'd carried her inside practically unconscious. "Lucky he was passing."

"Why on earth would he be passing the Celyn when he lives the other side of the mountain?" asked her father.

"He doesn't now. I heard in the shop, he's on this side again. Lights are seen on in Abernant in the early hours – they think he's hiding out there."

"Bally nonsense, gossip," he said, intrigued. "The place is derelict."

A wave of dizziness hit Bethan. "Think I'll get some fresh air," she said and left the room. She removed her thick jumper, put on a mac and boots, slipped through the hedge and headed for the river footpath. She took long walks to prove she'd exercise a dog should her father relent (not that he noticed), treks verging on the obsessive.

She crossed the bridge below Cwmgwrach. It was hard work going up on to the mountain, the soggy ground sucking at her boots. Whenever she stopped to catch her breath, a chattering continued around her feet like thousands of peat-living creatures egging her on. She closed her eyes, saw the bloody circle of teeth marks and imagined biting the school prefect who'd attacked her. Nia would be proud of her, though the importance of rescuing woodlice might pass her by. She walked a fair way, lost in thought.

Her head improved. She wanted a destination. The haunted lake would suit her mood, regardless of what the weather decided to do. She didn't pause again until well past the tree line and on a level with Abernant.

The dilapidated farmhouse was clearly visible on the other side of the river, a view unimpeded by a splattering of naked trees, planted years ago for shelter on land too high and exposed for them to thrive. She was familiar with the layout of the yard and buildings from childhood, Nia had insisted they explore the place every time the old man was taken to hospital with some ailment or other. Once they'd found the back door kicked in, lukewarm ashes in the grate and a ripped sleeping bag. That night the wireless announced a police search for a farmer who'd murdered his father and was thought to be living rough in the hills. "Do not approach him." The girls made their next visit armed with sticks and shaking with trepidation.

Apart from a few scraggy sheep, there was no sign of life. Morgan could be peering out from a glassless window, if the gossip about him living there was correct. She shuddered and rushed on, now crossing more stone than grass. Here and there leftover dollops of snow sat on rock platters like ice-cream.

She reached the lakeside with relief and no thought in her head of the journey home. The cliffs cupping the bowl of black water way below were devoid of birds, no sheep or cattle grazed the steep banks, no ripple of fish broke the glassy surface and no movement stirred the air. She slithered down on her bottom, sending an echoing cascade of rubble to the little pebble beach, where she wriggled to form a dip and sat, chin on knees, arms round legs, contemplating the flat water in the eerie hush.

Nia had brought her here first. She'd taken her everywhere: two small girls running wild, Bethan captivated by her friend's stories. Nia had waited till they reached the dark water before relating The Lady of the Lake legend, how a maiden of supreme beauty had taken revenge on her farmer husband by enticing his magnificent cattle, noble stallions, fine sheep, goats and every other animal into the remote lake to drown. She'd timed her storytelling for twilight, afterwards grabbing Bethan's hand and dragging her down the dusky mountain through indigo into blackness. Bethan had never moved so fast, frenetic running for her life, arms flapping like a mad bird, then Nia veering off at Cwmgwrach, leaving Bethan the last lap in pitch black. She'd burst into The Plas kitchen and collapsed with a violent stitch. No one had heard her come in, so no questions. Again she was grateful for her parents living in a parallel world. The way Nia had acted out the story, Bethan should have known she was destined for the stage. She pictured her sewing on sequins and layering on stage make-up for that night. Today was Saturday.

When Bethan returned to school it would be her final year, the prefect would be bullying elsewhere. She sat on her stone beach until she guessed by the light it was time to start for home. She never wore a watch. The temperature had dropped dramatically.

Her scrambling ascent sent down another shower of stones. At the top of the cliff she met an extraordinary scene: the mountain rose at a gentle incline to a horizon lost in a thick *Doctor Zhivago* blizzard (they'd seen the film twice; her mother would die for Omar Sharif), and below her the land was a sheet of grey rain.

She could just make out a black dot in the snow. It was moving down the mountain, and before long she could see it was the silhouette of a pony and huddled rider, heads down against the weather. They appeared to be heading for Craig Siglo, a standing stone a hundred yards or so from the lake. The tall flat rock leant at an impossible angle on its narrow base – a giant's sword, according to Nia, cast into the earth to mark the convergence of two rivers, where it had pivoted precariously for a thousand years.

As the pony drew closer, Bethan ducked out of sight.

FOUR

M ORGAN HAD INHERITED two horses with Abernant, a corpse in the yard and a live dark bay mare who appeared the day after he moved in. Having thought herself abandoned, she'd rushed to the gate of a side field with a loud urgent wicker, beside herself at being discovered. The old man hadn't mentioned a horse and Morgan was damned if he was going to. He named her Ness and from loneliness or desperation she responded immediately. She stood about fifteen hands, his father would have said too large for the mountain, he favoured a thirteen two, for hauling sick ewes up across the saddle without dismounting. Morgan filed her overgrown hooves. Feeling her pick her way across the rocky scree with confidence, his father would have agreed she was a grand mare for shepherding.

No shepherding today: he was riding up through the rain to meet Elin Davies. She'd sent him a note: two scrawled lines suggesting a rendezvous at Craig Siglo. He almost couldn't be bothered, but no one had replaced her and he was too intrigued to let it pass. At one time he'd done nothing but obsess about their high times in the rabbit shed, but lately it was Veronica mincing about in her skin-tight riding get-up.

He veered the mare away from the river and on up towards the giant rock, the thunder of the waterfall gradually fading.

All was quiet. The speck of a pony came into view in the distance; if they both kept this pace they'd reach the rock together. It was impossible to distinguish the sex of a person camouflaged in waterproofs, but as they grew closer he saw the hooded shape was too large, even accounting for layers. A flash of something appeared beyond the pony. The apparition materialised into a solitary figure on foot, vanishing from sight every so often, testing Morgan's concentration. Before he knew it he'd reached Craig Siglo.

Afterwards he'd relive the following few minutes as some kind of 'pistols at dawn' scene, except it was afternoon and there were no guns. Davies Tŷ Newydd leapt off his pony before it stopped, chucked his cap into the air, dragged Morgan from Ness and smashed a big fist into his face. There was a loud crack and Morgan's hands shot to his nose, streams of warm blood pouring down his coat cuffs. He made no attempt to retaliate; despite his strength, his furtive nature had never led him into battle. He'd clouted his sisters, never a man. Davies hit like a professional boxer. With the next punch, Morgan's head flipped back and he began to anticipate the following blows with an odd perversity, nothing to do with shame or remorse. He didn't consider himself to blame. She had started their brief torrid affair.

Davies grabbed him by the collar and like a terrier with a rat, yanked him backwards and forwards, crashing his spine into Craig Siglo. It was the final attack. Davies stopped as instantly as he'd begun. He shoved Morgan to the ground, settled down against a boulder and took a pipe from his coat pocket, calmly, as if they'd merely shaken hands.

Morgan rolled on to his side to watch from his good eye; the other had swollen shut and the blood from his nose had slowed to a trickle. He'd never smoked, pipe or cigarettes, and couldn't stand either. The pipe routine was all too familiar from his father: scraping out the residue of the last smoke with a small penknife, tap out, scrape, tap then pack and press the bowl with fresh tobacco and light match after match with hands cupped against the wind.

Davies zipped his coat higher and leaned back in silence. Unperturbed, Ness and the pony pawed and nibbled at the earth, lips waffling in search of a blade of grass, side by side like old friends even though they'd never met before today. Morgan turned his head painfully for a glimpse of the hazy figure on foot. The follower might have been her – racing to warn him. The bare mountain offered few hiding places, but there was no one in sight. Smoke wafted into the wet air and he prepared to breathe in Old Holborn through nostrils clogged with blood.

"She flirted," he said. "All the time, I couldn't move for her, brushing past me…"

"Don't speak about my wife." Davies stood up.

"It's true, it was always her…" before Morgan could elaborate about her enticing ways, the rabbit shed, small enclosed corners, a boot hit his stomach. He doubled up.

Davies kicked him again then caught his pony.

"I will always have my eye on you."

The fizzy pony, unschooled in manners, danced circles with Davies attached: one foot in the stirrup, the other hopping. He belted a fist into the animal's ribs. As he swung his leg over his back, the pony spun round and broke into a canter from standstill. Davies sat rock solid in the saddle staring back until they were out of sight. Morgan pushed his thumping forehead into an icy pool of slush. The fight (or rather, his beating) had intoxicated him. Davies being a man of few words somehow created more drama.

Morgan imagined returning to a woman installed at Abernant, a wife to whom he would describe a "violent fight". How would that be: a woman at the window, the sort of woman who would slaughter half a cow for his safe return? The entire house would have to be seen to: kitchen, proper bed, bathroom, pantry, the range blackened, coats on hangers, boots outside. He thought of Mr Pritchard forever quoting from *Under Milk Wood* and pictured pyjamas in a drawer marked pyjamas. He didn't own any. No, he couldn't bear it, even Elin Davies wouldn't be welcome.

Slowly, he lifted his head to scan the empty mountain again. If it was her, maybe Davies had forgiven her adultery and swooped her up on to his charger as he galloped for home, from bastard to chivalrous knight. He peeled her damp scrappy note from his pocket. He'd no idea of her handwriting. She'd never had cause to write a love letter or suggest a meeting place; from his caravan to the rabbit shed was less than thirty paces. The blue ink lettering had smudged. Morgan sniggered. Fuck the pair of them.

He lay on his back for a while. Ness, having lost her new companion, drew closer and nudged his foot. The brief contact brought him solace and he struggled upright, brushed himself down and dragged himself up into the saddle. He left the homeward route to her and she criss-crossed down the hill, negotiating slippery sheep paths no more than a foot wide high above the river, assuming Morgan (like her previous owner) was up here to check the sheep.

Slumped and aching, he didn't see the approach of a low-flying jet. It swept overhead and he waited for her to take fright and hurl him from the cliff. The roar of the engine came with the power to suck up man and horse and spit them on to the rocks below. Ness didn't flinch until he leaned forward to give her a grateful pat on the neck; affection in her life was rare. He turned his damaged face to the sky, envying the pilot courting danger in so spectacular a manner. He tried to flare his blocked nostrils to inhale the lingering fumes and tasted blood. Punishment indeed.

He had no cause to kick the mare on; she was keen to reach home. As the square shape of the farmhouse formed in the near-darkness he could smell the sulphur of coal smoke. Small mercy: he'd banked up the range before he left, so there would be hot water for a good wash.

With Ness settled in the barn, eating hay, he crossed the yard and opened the kitchen to a wave of heat, going straight to move the kettle across to the hotplate. He assumed his nose was broken. Harbouring a morbid fascination for injuries inflicted by a human (as opposed to a farming accident), he postponed examining his body until it would display a satisfying array of blacks and blues. He wasn't disappointed.

The usual house noises continued long after he sank into bed. His footsteps on the bare floorboards had set off a groaning that died down to a constant tick-tick moving round the room. The window was open, the rain hammering down, the clicks and knockings might have been outside noises. Davies wouldn't waste time and come to the house; he'd done the necessary. He was a busy man.

His breathing wasn't right. Whether that was down to a broken nose or broken ribs he couldn't tell, but he'd heard nothing could be done for either. He pulled the blankets up to his chin and tried again to visualise the lone figure in the snow.

It would be quite a journey on foot from Tŷ Newydd. Other people walked the mountain – the Pritchard girl wandered miles alone.

The incident barred Bethan's way home: that's how it was on the open mountain. She'd changed directions, wriggled along on her stomach, crawled on all fours and by the time the two men parted she was well out of their sight and plastered in mud. She didn't recognise the man galloping off up the mountain, but knew Morgan from his thick black hair and chosen route down the hill.

Even witnessing the beating from a distance had shaken her; she'd never seen anything like it. The stranger's brutal behaviour had tainted her mountain; any future walks there would have a very different feel. Never had her need for a dog felt greater.

Both riders had long gone from the barren landscape. It was almost dark when she reached The Plas unseen. She came in through the back way and hung her filthy mac in the cluttered cloakroom next to the kitchen. There was every chance no one would enquire where she'd been. The house was as quiet as ever: somewhere the tap of her father's typewriter, no sign of her mother. She got halfway up the stairs when the seventh tread gave its usual noisy creak.

"Bethan, that you?" called her mother. "Guess what!"

"They've invented steam," said her father from somewhere, unable to resist.

Bethan turned and came back down. Her mother was in the sitting room poised over a roaring fire, pink-faced, wearing a cat as a scarf. Her needles lay idle in a heap of cream wool on her lap. "What do you think, dear? Veronica has an art gallery!

In Bath of all places, I ask you. Bath. What on earth would that cost? Well, Cecily must have helped out."

"Does Veronica know about art then?" asked Bethan.

"I've no idea, but won't she look the part? Your jeans are soaking, dear. How are you feeling? Headache gone?"

"Yes, I'm better thanks, walked miles." All the way home she'd been weighing up the pros and cons of telling her parents about the fight: they might allow her a dog for protection or ban her from walking the mountain altogether. They were both horrified by violence.

"The gallery needs renovating apparently – should be ready in the spring. No doubt she'll have some sort of launch. Maybe she'll want your father's paintings," she smiled. "Or maybe not. You should paint more, dear. Do you know what you'd like to do yet? Goodness me, what with Nia a magician and Veronica an art dealer."

Bethan sighed. "A nun or sheep farmer."

Alice clapped and laughed, "You are joking."

"Yes. Well, about the nun." She decided then to keep the mountain fiasco to herself; her mother was far too enthralled by Veronica's revelation to bring her news of a sordid brawl.

She often suspected her mother's high colour was more down to quality anthracite than the bloom of good health; away from the fire she could look quite pale.

FIVE

Bᴇᴛʜᴀɴ ᴀɴᴅ ʜᴇʀ mother always gave up chocolate for Lent. No great hardship: they preferred coconut mushrooms. They were getting the last of a box of Milk Tray out of the way when Veronica rang to say she'd be in Swansea at the weekend collecting paintings and would call in on her way home.

It was the Saturday after Ash Wednesday, three days since the priest pressed a lump of grey ash onto Bethan's forehead with his fat white thumb. It took another damaged convent girl to notice the fading stain she'd meticulously circled with her face flannel to avoid hell and damnation. She was picking mint at the front of the house when her cousin pulled up.

Veronica ducked her beehive (a tangled mound the size of a top hat) out of the car and grabbed her. "Christ's sake, you're 17 – wash that bloody muck off."

"And go straight to hell?" said Bethan.

"Bloody nuns, brainwashing." She glanced at the mint. "Lamb for dinner?"

"No, Dad's mint tea. It was you who suggested I went to a damn convent."

"Come here." Veronica whipped out a hankie from her long black coat, held it out for Bethan's spit and wiped off the ash. "Now I'll go to hell." They linked arms. "Not before the grand opening of my gallery, I hope. I've brought invitations for you,

Nia, maybe her weird brother – shouldn't think he has many social engagements."

"Morgan? You're joking; he only ventures off the hill for food and the mart."

"Freak. How can anyone be happy with all that solitude? Ask him though."

Bethan stopped at the front door. "I saw him being beaten up on the mountain. I haven't told anyone. It was horrible, really shocking. I didn't tell Mum."

"No, don't. How bad?"

"He rode home. I expect he deserved it, but I've got no idea what it was about."

"Take him an invitation and find out!"

Mrs Pritchard opened the front door. Veronica's visit was fleeting: barely time for a high-speed description of her gallery, two black coffees and four menthol cigarettes. When she'd left, Bethan's mother poked the fire into flames a foot high and sat rubbing her mottled legs.

"Lovely isn't it, dear, this opening? Shame it's a Saturday, Nia will probably be performing magic somewhere. Your father's a bit put out about Veronica suggesting saving his paintings for a purple period exhibition, so it might be just you and me. What would I wear?" She beamed with a tight mouth and a look of despondency. "I can't see Morgan coming, can you?"

"Veronica asked me to deliver an invitation."

"She knows how far you walk, dear. I'll come, or we could always drive."

She pictured her mother crashing along, trying to dodge oceans of potholes and the car ending up in the river.

"I don't know his track well enough. We'd better walk."

Brambles, bracken and no path. Fortunately Bethan remembered the way she and Nia had forged up to Abernant as little girls, negotiating the narrow streams pouring off the mountain over slimy rocks. She went first, stamping out paths through undergrowth and bending back branches for her mother to grasp for support, desperate for her to manage it all. Halfway up the incline they were crossing a foam pool made by a small waterfall when Bethan stopped, clasped her mother's arm and tried to turn her away.

A pyramid of dead ewes had been built alongside the water. Alice fastened the top button of her mac and pulled it tight round her neck. White skeletons of lambs' heads protruded from soaking layers of filthy caked wool, limbs stuck out at all angles. Old blood had stained the river boulders like pools of dark tar. Dislodged by the rushing water, a severed leg knocked against her mother's wellie and sailed on.

"We'll go back," said Bethan. "Damn the invitation."

"No. No, heavens, we've come this far. That's farming for you, I daresay you've seen it all before, dear." Alice forced brightness to her face, her eyes wide.

"Not this. Wait till I see Veronica." She looked at her mother, a foot of damp tweed skirt stuck to her legs in the gap between her green PVC mac and short wellies. Bethan took her arm. They climbed up past the bubbling water with a fleeting last glance at the mangled bodies, and then continued on their way in silence.

Once out of the woods on to flat fields there was a little more light, though dusk was coming in with the drizzle. Beyond a strip of haphazard fencing, the greener green of managed pasture then the hazy outline of the large square farmhouse. In the yard a young collie rose slowly, stretched and shuffled towards them in a sideways waddle, wearing a crooked grin. Coming to the end of his chain, his tail swept back and forth in welcome; he hadn't been tied up long enough to turn savage.

The house wore the sad cloak of dereliction. Most windows were patched with hardboard and ragged strips of woolsacks. The front door was closed. Moss-green wood, warped, veined with black mould and no letterbox.

"Morgan?" Bethan called softly at first, shouting felt inappropriate in the stillness. A little louder, her voice echoing round the barns bordering the square yard. There were enough ruined outbuildings for his van to be hidden from view. Alice turned the handle of the front door and gave a tentative push with her foot. Locked. She plonked down on an old bench within the reach of the dog, who came to her in a friendly manner. Ignoring his rank smell, she began to stroke him. He fell against her legs with delight.

The daylight was going. Bethan wandered round, calling out. Fresh sheep droppings flattened softly beneath her boots and she followed their trail to a high Dutch barn with sides covered in rusty corrugated sheets. Inside on an earth floor, she waited for her eyes to adjust to the gloom. Lambing pens roughly constructed from hurdles zigzagged across and down the length of the dank building. Ripped, empty feed sacks, trodden-on cans of antiseptic spray, baler twine, fusty matted hay being used for bedding. She stepped over a heap of woolsacks, tripped on a hammerhead and hissed his name. Pitchforks and scythes dangled from hooks, oily frayed towing ropes lay coiled like snakes, flapping cloths had been nailed over draughts. A peppering of holes in the tin sheets captured an eerie cocktail of pale new moon and the final trickles of daylight.

Something was moving against the back wall. She squinted for clearer vision, crept forward and stopped breathing: a thick rope tied to a beam. Swinging gently from the rope was a long coat and battered hat. The body of the coat looked flimsy, not quite filled to capacity and the sleeves were either empty or hiding stick thin arms. The shoulders however, were occupied. It was a dull brown gabardine coat, the kind Mr Williams wore and, strangely, called a smock.

She ordered her jelly knees to move her legs forward, imagining Morgan shrivelled to nothing underneath. It was plastered in old blood, mud and shit. Her teeth began to chatter uncontrollably. She focused on the bottom half of the coat and kept going. Body shaking, she grabbed the hem, flapped it open and leapt back. An ancient shearing machine was rusting away under the inadequate protection of the fabric. The hat was nailed to the beam behind it.

She ran from the barn with an ear-piercing "Morgan!" A ewe bleated. The collie barked and shot to the end of his chain, wrenching his neck. He yelped and skulked back to her mother, still sitting on the bench.

"No sign of him?" she called, fussing the dog.

"Nope, we'll go in a sec," Bethan took her penknife to a square of cardboard jammed in a window frame, stabbed a slit and worked it bigger with the blade. She peeled the damp invitation from her wet fingers and flicked it through the gap, "That's it, Mum – come on, we're off."

"This is a lovely dog," Alice said, reluctantly taking her hand from his back and standing up. He immediately gave a short yowl like a pleading 'no' and stared at them until they left the yard. "He wasn't thin and he had a nice coat." She sniffed her hand. "Bit smelly, poor thing."

"Let's get a move on," said Bethan. "It's almost dark." She had no intention of confronting Morgan now, not after all that. The very idea of inviting him to a civilised social gathering was laughable. She remembered the sheep corpses in time to make a wide berth. "Wait till I see Veronica," she said for distraction. "Why the hell she couldn't have posted it. I suppose her idea of delivering something would be crossing a few streets and stopping at a nice teashop on the way. I could kill her."

Her mother was quiet. The minute they arrived home, she washed her hands in steaming hot water. The completed parts of an Arran jumper were laid out on the kitchen table, ready to be stitched together; she buried her face in the thick ivory wool. "Were they Morgan's, d'you think, the sheep?"

Bethan shrugged. "Maybe. He probably thought he'd get away with it. No one but us would be mad enough to walk that way."

He'd told her of a farmer who had a large hole dug out at the beginning of every lambing and filled in at the end. Ewes died in plenty at that time of year.

"Think I'll get on with this." Her mother stuck a row of pins in her mouth, gathered the front and back of the jumper and began to match up the shoulder seams. Head down, instantly immersed – more so than usual – needle flashing in and out manically as if compensating for the waste of life and wool by the waterfall.

Bethan ran her finger down the immaculate cable stitch, stuck her face in a sleeve and breathed in the cloying smell of lanolin.

SIX

NIA WAS DELIGHTED with her invitation. She accepted immediately: there were no bookings for that Saturday. Her gentleman magician was off on a quest for new supplies of doves and white rabbits.

Bethan's mother was persuaded to try on her one posh frock. Bethan could see her discomfort, whereas Nia was fired up with compliments, saying how her own mother wouldn't have a clue about what to wear or do at such an event. Bethan wasn't sure that helped. The dress was a shade lighter than the brown coat in the sheep shed, with a fitted bodice and full skirt of lace over satin. The scooped neck was entirely modest, but Bethan felt funny seeing a little more of her mother's white skin. She usually wore polo necks and scarves.

They caught the train to Bath and arrived at midday. They were to stay the night with Veronica, whose flat was ten minutes' walk from the station.

"I spent hours here," Alice smiled as they passed the Parade Gardens. "I ask you, Veronica living within spitting distance of Great Pulteney Street."

Nia had been to Bath once, for a magic show at the Pavilion, there and back in a day. She enjoyed the running commentary; she loved Mrs Pritchard.

Veronica rented the top flat in a large Georgian house. Her reclusive landlord lived on the ground floor with dead pot plants squashed between the closed curtains and grimy windows. Alice counted seventy-two stairs; it was the sort of detail her husband would ask about. Nearing the top landing, the pictures changed from gilt-framed landscapes to frameless Modiglianis. Bethan heard a piano and smelled coffee and cigarettes. A door was ajar and there was Veronica sitting at a shining black piano, her hair scrunched up into a sun visor, scarlet nails on white keys. She was playing beautifully. Bethan had no idea of the composer; her father kept his music knowledge to himself. She knew her mother would be emotional, but Nia was near tears.

Veronica saw them and leapt up. "Practising for tonight. Excuse my gambling hat: just opened an account at the bookies. I need to buy a music hat. Coffee's on."

"I'd die to play like that," said Nia.

"I hadn't touched a piano for years, till a month ago," said Veronica. "Memories of that bloody school speech day. I had to play a complicated Chopin piece. I went wrong and the nuns were spitting feathers. It finished me off."

"According to Cecily, you played brilliantly," said her aunt.

"Damn nuns glaring death wishes at me; Mummy in a hairy purple hat; me pretending not to know her; Daddy showing off about nothing." She closed the lid, stroked it and swivelled round. "We thought the school piano was haunted by dead nuns fluttering round inside – sadly it was moths. They taint your life. Nuns, not moths. It's wonderful of you all to come."

"We're very excited," Alice said and clapped.

Bethan imagined her father admiring "rooms of charming proportions", if only he'd deigned to come. She imagined writing letters at her cousin's lovely old desk in the bedroom, gazing out over the city, her convent a distant memory; though even Veronica seemed haunted by nuns at 28. The rooms were huge with high ceilings, picture rails, wide dark floorboards and oriental rugs. Even the bathroom had a fireplace and armchair, and a cloudy glass dome high in the roof.

To their surprise, Veronica had prepared plates of jam sandwiches and angel cake. The sort of old-ladyish tea Bethan's maiden aunt would offer in her Bath attic flat. Even her mother had anticipated cocktail hour. As they finished and were about to go to their respective bedrooms to change, there was a shuffling noise and two tortoises appeared from under the sideboard. Nia shrieked, never having had an animal in the house, let alone a reptile.

"I have to have something breathing in here besides me," said Veronica. The tortoises lifted their dinosaur heads to eye up the strangers then tapped across the floorboards on big grey claws, wolfed down some crumbs and returned to the dark. "They're 48 and 52. I was given them by an old lady."

"What an age!" said Alice, delighted. "I thought they were a marvellous size."

Bethan left to get ready before Nia declared her entire family insane. She was borrowing one of Veronica's black, clinging frocks. Nia had brought her long pink gown that on every other Saturday night pinged open to expose her itchy swimsuit, and cerise feather boa. Bethan's mother had brought sensible shoes for the walk to the gallery, with kitten-heeled shoes in a bag. But when everyone was ready and out on the street, Veronica took them along a few yards of black pointy railings, through a gate and down ten uneven stone steps. The gallery was in the basement of the house.

Rough stone walls painted white, dark flagstone floor and just two small windows at the front and back, her husband wouldn't approve of the lack of natural light. Alice counted the light bulbs to reassure him the paintings were perfectly well lit, and he was bound to ask the number and style of pictures and whether they were hanging absolutely straight. To mask the smell of damp and fresh paint, Veronica had bought pots of electric-blue hyacinths. Their scent was overwhelming.

"It's all wonderful. Bryn should see it," said her aunt. "Honestly, staying home to look after the cats! He could have pretended to have a pile of schoolwork. Why did your mother and I marry men that have to show off?"

"I should have had his purple paintings," said Veronica. She lit six tall cream candles on the mantelpiece and went to an older piano. Elegant in long black crepe, she sat poised, fingers fluttering over the keys. "I feel like Sadie Thompson in this dress." Her three guests looked blank. "An old floozy pianist who played on the cargo ships."

Cecily burst through the door carrying gin and daffodils, her cheeks sealing-wax red. Gold Eiffel Tower earrings swung in rhythm with her straight auburn hair.

"Goodness what hyacinths, it's like a chapel of rest in here. Nervous, V darling?"

"Little bit. Would be if they were my paintings."

Alice visibly relaxed at the sight of her sister. People arrived. Bethan and Nia sashayed round offering wine and canapés, studying everyone as subtly as possible. Veronica began to play slow sensuous jazz.

An enormous abstract landscape caught Bethan's eye: ochre mountains, indigo forest, ultramarine river, lemon diagonal rain and in the foreground two dead trees deformed by relentless wind, all outlined in black. In the unlikely event of Veronica enquiring about Morgan's invitation, Bethan could say, "Add a pile of stinking dead sheep and it illustrates our horrendous journey to Abernant."

Nia started going on about power and strength. "I've never seen so many together, I almost can't breathe."

"But mountains are the one place you can breathe, you know that."

"No, these hyacinths. Veronica will suffocate any prospective clients, on top of the perfume, cigarettes, cigars…"

"The painting, Nia. It has to be our mountain, doesn't it?"

"Could be. Good God, look what the cat's dragged in."

Bethan looked over to the door and saw her father. She'd just been thinking how nice it was without him; he was always calling out 'hear-hear' at do's, embarrassing her and her mother. She didn't know about speeches tonight – maybe Auntie Cecily would say something, having put up the money. Her father was wearing his tweedy 'going-out' suit. He owned no casual clothes and wore a three-piece suit every day. The oldest he referred to as his gardening suit (he never gardened), there were two in between and the one he wore now.

"I didn't mean your father."

"No. No, I see that now," said Bethan. Morgan was standing behind him.

"What the hell's he doing here?" said Nia. "Please don't say he was invited."

Bethan nodded. "I kept quiet. I didn't think for one moment he'd accept."

"Good grief," said her mother. "What a transformation, and from such dire living conditions. Did you magic him from frog to prince, Nia?"

He was wearing an immaculate dark grey suit, black brogues and an air of sophistication completely foreign to Bethan and (she presumed) to himself. His hair had been well cut and his swarthy complexion accentuated by a white shirt. She wondered whether his sheepdog whistle was on its cord underneath the crisp cotton. He was polished up fit for a wedding.

She watched him step into the throng of skinny women with hennaed hair and long patchwork skirts gliding round as though on wheels, men in creased trousers and paint-splattered boots. He was so ridiculously overdressed that for a second her heart went out to him. Her father came over to them with an expression of pride as if he'd captured Morgan to put on show and was the only one to get the measure of him.

"Spur of the moment," he said. "Bumped into him this morning. He said he'd never been to a gallery opening or indeed Bath and I made a snap decision, which I know isn't like me. We're driving home tonight though; he's busy lambing."

Morgan was heading for the piano. He smiled across at Bethan and Nia and showed no indication of surprise at their glamorous get-ups. Nia glared. Bethan slipped through the crowd until she was close enough to eavesdrop. Veronica stopped playing, shook Morgan's hand and he kissed her on the cheek.

"Isn't that what you do at these things?" he said formally, their hands still clasped. "Thank you for the invitation."

"You made it! I'm so pleased." Veronica beamed as if she'd burst. She hadn't seen him for a couple of years and he was the first guest that she'd stopped playing to greet. When he strolled away, Bethan could see her cousin was stirred. He stood in front of each painting in turn. What a great actor he was.

"Don't tell me he's my daughter's latest," said Auntie Cecily, curiously.

"God no," said Bethan. What could she say? Part-recluse, abandoned as a baby, half-starved by wicked stepmother, passionate about literature, speaks pure unadulterated Welsh, devious – or be as generous spirited as her mother? "He's our neighbour, Morgan Williams; a farmer."

"Ah, not the trout tickler, the jigsaw man?"

"Yes." Bethan could have used the description on her grandfather's jigsaw boxes, 'Double-sided with deceptively intricate pieces', except Morgan had more than two sides. "He looks good tonight. I've never seen him out of wellies."

"Hmm, wonder if Veronica has," said her aunt.

Bethan watched him carefully. He appeared at ease. As comfortable hugely overdressed, talking art and sipping red wine as crossing the river with a sick ewe flung over his shoulders. He joined her father and they moved slowly from picture to picture in deep discussion, with Morgan also managing to subtly scrutinise every female in the room. Bethan could see her father was enjoying his company.

She returned her attention to the abstract mountain and Veronica began to play one of her mother's favourite songs. Morgan stopped in his tracks, walked over to the piano and sort of stood to attention. He lifted his head and began to sing. Conversation stopped and the crowd froze, wine glasses and cigarettes mid-air. *You Are My Heart's Delight*. Every face lit up as he sang in a breathtakingly clear tenor. Veronica smiled up at him as if they'd performed together all their lives.

Bethan moved across to Nia, "My God, I didn't know he could sing like that."

Nia rolled her eyes and hissed "Show-off" loudly.

A girl swirled into the tiny space in front of the piano, a moth to his flame, and performed a lone waltz, quiet floaty movements, reminding Bethan of the ethereal dancer on the gruelling school retreat. She compared the nuns' monochrome life to tonight. She overheard someone say "Terribly sexy man" and shivered.

By her father's shocked expression, he also knew nothing of Morgan's extraordinary voice. She could see he was put out.

SEVEN

IT WAS WELL after midnight and the roads were completely empty. Out of the blue, Mr Pritchard sounded the Riley's horn. "The horn of a Rolls," he said proudly. "I want to remember the mellow resonance in case it comes to selling the car. She's getting on."

Morgan assumed he was merely likening the horn to a Rolls Royce, not that he had stolen it. He'd enjoyed the evening and now the homeward journey. Despite the invitation for seven till nine-thirty, no one had left the gallery before eleven. Mr Pritchard had congratulated him on his voice then gone on about bally hyacinths stinking the place out. Elin Davies liked hyacinths. Morgan had watched her tap out bulbs from the pots on the sideboard to plant alongside the garden path. She wouldn't have looked out of place tonight in her overalls and silk scarf, fluff-balls of white rabbit fur in her hair.

"How about stopping for a bite to eat?" said Mr Pritchard. "Can't say I go in for these blessed canapés."

"I could eat something." Morgan hadn't touched those small morsels of unrecognisable food and a wafting dizziness lingered. He wasn't used to wine.

Spotting an all-night transport café, Mr Pritchard sounded the horn again. Having never eaten out in the early hours, he entered the tin shack with anticipation. An elderly woman wearily whacked out cod and chips and they took their plates to a sticky Formica table. She brought a pot of tea.

Several fellow night-travellers sat dotted round the soulless place, heads in newspapers or books. A slumped woman smoked and ate alternately, her lined skin tinted violet by cruel fluorescent lighting. Guessing Mr Pritchard had never been in such a place, Morgan fought a sudden urge to order her to sit up straight and stop smoking, as if she were responsible for the startling comedown from their evening of culture. After all that singing his lips felt thick, and the chunks of battered cod rose like a cliff of brown coral around the plate. Afterwards he bought a packet of wine gums to take the taste away. He wanted to say that he'd never frequented such a depressing café, but was doing his utmost not to lie to Mr Pritchard.

"Good substantial meal," said Mr Pritchard contentedly, as if rather taken by the seediness. "Better get going. Will you look round your ewes tonight?"

"Probably wait till daylight now." His father hadn't believed in disturbing the ewes at night, flashing a torch about could part lambs from mothers. He checked them just before pitch dark then again at dawn.

A spitty rain predicted the bleakness of the day ahead. Nearing the end of their journey, the car swayed towards the hedge a couple of times and Mr Pritchard's head jerked up. He opened the window and started whistling. "I should have asked you to sing to me, Morgan, to keep me awake. Any other talents or mysteries up your sleeve?"

"No," he smiled.

"You're as bad as your magician sister!" They turned into The Plas drive and pulled up alongside Morgan's van. They shook hands before they parted.

Morgan drove to the start of the Abernant track, switched off the engine and closed his eyes. He woke to grey daylight and heavy rain. Halfway up the track he met disaster: a littering of tiny limbs in the wet stones, further on a lamb's head and a couple of tails like giant catkins dropped from a child's collection.

A shining blue-black magpie sat on a fence post, a spectator. Morgan slammed on the brakes. Below the devil bird a lamb dangled lifelessly from a ewe, half-in, half-out, head engorged and swollen tongue protruding stiff and grey. The exhausted ewe struggled to her feet, the lamb's head swinging at her rear like a pendulum; she scraped at the mud only to collapse again. The magpie fluttered to the ground, strutted round them, his head tilted to one side anticipating a tasty eyeball, then flew back to his post. The ewe began to heave herself up again. A bang, the bird's body shattered into a cascade of feathers. The morbid ritual was over.

Morgan slid the twelve-bore back in the van and ran to the ewe. He worked the lamb's distorted head back inside her and searched for its legs while the ewe rolled her eyes and ground her teeth on hardened gums. Finally the lamb came out in the right order, let down by its enormity, it had stuck at the shoulders. He poked a rush up its nostrils to clear any muck and get it going then gripped its slimy back legs and swung the inert body in circles. He pumped its chest, felt air huff out over the huge tongue and imagined it huffed in once. Eventually he gave up and flung it into the rushes, the ewe grappled to her feet and stumbled across to fuss and rough it up, bully it into life. Morgan left her gobbling the yellow mucus from its mouth, she'd clean every inch of the body as if preparing for a decent burial.

He shouldn't be losing lives when he didn't have that many ewes to lamb. It was anyone's guess how many sheep he'd inherited with the farm, as more ewes with the Abernant earmark wandered in off the mountain. Many toothless and wearing two years' wool tottered in like grannies in loosely hanging shawls.

He grabbed a bitten-off leg from the ground, caking his fingernails with mud. The thin limb felt like his gun-cleaning brush: a sponge with a rod running through it. He squashed the wet wool and bent the fragile bone, steadily increasing the pressure until the tiny knee joint broke, then hurled the sodden mess high into the trees. His boot fell against a lamb's head; he stamped it into a puddle to watch water gurgle from the empty eye sockets. He mimicked a screech owl, yelled obscenities into the rain then returned to the van and drove on up the track.

Just before the yard was an old broker proudly showing off her dinky twins. Another ancient was nuzzling a new lamb to her udder hidden under a curtain of wool. A ewe close to lambing was coveting a twin, until the mother stamped her away. The rain stopped. Ness whinnied to him as he crossed the yard and his heart lightened slightly. He'd get changed and take out the iodine to dab their navels. A memory came: five years old, watching his father chuck a dead lamb into a ditch with "Keep livestock, you'll have deadstock".

What would his father have made of last night's do? His daughter a picture of glamour in pink, his son singing to an audience riveted to the spot. According to Veronica no one wanted him to stop, she said he had them eating out of his hand and she'd kept playing, sitting straight-backed at the piano in her slinky black dress.

The kitchen still felt warm from yesterday's fire. He removed his jacket, slipped the hanger neatly into the shoulders and stepped out of his trousers. The suit was creased from his sleep in the van. He hung it on the door and standing in his shirt and pants imagined unzipping Veronica's black dress and watching it slide to the floor. It was silk, he was sure, like Elin Davies' scarves. Elin: naked in the straw apart from her black scarf. His old trousers and overalls were thrown over the back of a chair; he put them on, took the dog whistle from a cup hook and went out to feed.

The sack of sheep cake disappeared as it hit the ground, even the oldest ewes barged their way through. He threw a wad of hay to Ness then stole one of the new twins to adopt on to the bereaved ewe. His father never turned twins to the mountain, hard enough for a ewe to protect one lamb from the fox.

He brought the ewes to the fields nearest the house and the rest of the morning passed with general farm work. He went inside for a mug of tea and bread and cheese, eating the plain food with relish, sneering inwardly at the gallery's snooty offerings. With the fire built up, he kicked his chair round to rest his feet on the hearth, doze and think of Veronica. Now he knew where she lived. He fell into a deep sleep for an hour, legs outstretched. Sparks shot from the fire onto the cold flagstones, some burning pinholes in his trousers.

The light was fading when he woke. He put on his boots and took his second gun from behind the kitchen cabinet.

A large dog fox lay curled up in the middle of the flock. It didn't sense or hear Morgan's approach; the cheeky bastard was sound asleep. The ewes, seemingly oblivious to any danger, had settled against the remains of stone walls, lambs tucked in behind them. A bucolic scene too tranquil to disturb. If he shot the fox now, he'd unsettle everything and the dozier lambs could mis-mother. Besides, a live fox could replace the dead one; the mountain was crawling with them.

He left quietly to collect a warmer coat from the house and a woolsack from the sheep shed then headed for the broken-down barn in the corner of the field. The parts still standing offered enough shelter for the night. He'd scorned afternoon naps, but after his lack of sleep the night before he was grateful for his brief siesta. Determined to stay awake, he swaddled himself in the musty hessian and settled into a corner. The fox slept soundly all night.

It was dawn when he shot him. The minute he stirred Morgan took aim. The fox stood up to stretch then tumble-tossed into the air, falling in slow motion into contorted limbs, guts spilling across the mud. Morgan used both barrels. He returned to the house and slept in the chair for a few hours.

This time he woke to sunshine. After weeks of rain and wind whipping through the rushes and bracken, the sun had come out to toast the ground. After the feeding, he washed to go down to the village. His diet was frugal. He lived mostly on what he caught and wasn't bothered about proper meals. His shopping habits varied with his mood. If feeling secretive and in need of new books, he drove to Swansea, away from the village spies. In a "Fuck the lot of them" mood, he strutted into the village shop, all bolshie and glaring at anyone who dared look at him.

He didn't wear a watch, and judged time by the sky. It was early afternoon when he parked his tractor outside the shop. The headmaster was coming out with a bag of Mint Imperials to disguise his lunchtime pint. A group of women in crimplene tabards fell silent as Morgan walked past them without a word, damned if he was going to mention weather. Pessimistic lot, after months of rain the only comment on unexpected sunshine was *"Duw, we'll pay for this."*

He entered the tiny shop and weaselled his eyes round the shelves, ignoring the few inside women. The outside women resumed their loud chat and he wondered whether they turned to lambing because of his presence, though most of their collier husbands kept a few sheep. Someone mentioned his half-brothers. So, the conversation was for his benefit. He studied a packet of tea and listened to them praising the idiots, how well they were doing on just nine acres. Served with antipathy he bought tea, cheese, a loaf and left with the feeling of an invisible stiff broom nabbing at his heels to sweep him from the shop.

"Duw, what did he want then?" said one, with Morgan still in earshot.

"Bread, cheese and tea," said another.

"No, really. I mean, when did we last see him?"

Out-staring the old bats, he walked backwards till he reached the tractor. He drove straight to the Cwmgwrach track and the nine-acre field.

A couple of ponies heard his approach and cantered down at the slim chance of hay. One backed up to scratch on the enormous padlock and chain securing the gate. The sheep looked up. Morgan bounced the tractor up the outside of the field to the top fence, jumped off and kicked his steel toecap into a rotten post. It split. He took a pair of wire cutters from the tractor toolbox, snipped away at the old sheep-netting embedded in the grass, uprooted a good stretch along to a small iron bedstead and peeled it back. Fly circled off quietly to bring the small flock to the gap.

The sheep were well-covered, better than his old girls. Some Abernant ewes had udders like screwed-up leather pouches and should have long been culled; consequently he had too many *swcis*. Then there were ewes with a single tooth in their heads. Like his father he took pliers to the last remaining tooth, they could graze with no teeth, their gums soon toughened. But it was too late to improve their condition this year.

He whistled for Fly to lie down. The young ewes charged out through the gap, leaping high at imaginary fences, the older trotted through with their lambs, followed by the ponies. Confused lambs bleated as their mothers marched off. Pregnant ewes waddled behind. The liberated sheep fanned out, heads down to snatch at any new grass, but the mountain stretched away in blocks of purple, blue and brown. No green showing yet. Morgan climbed back onto the tractor and lifted his leg for Fly to jump up, turn and sit in her usual place beneath the steering wheel.

Jolting down the rough terrain he saw a green van coming from the wooded part of the track. A vehicle he didn't recognise. Their paths grew closer and when it stopped, blocking his way, he recognised his half-brothers. An inch from the passenger's door he knocked the tractor out of gear and roared the engine; almost pleased to be caught. He'd hate them to think he'd grown complacent.

Though this was two to one, it was a similar attack to Davies'. Tomos jumped from the driver's seat, ran round, dragged Morgan to the ground and punched him full in the face. Steffan, the younger brother, unable to open the passenger door, slithered across the seats and was also out in seconds. Their oily overalls were dotted with holes from battery acid and their deadpan eyes were encircled in dark shadows, a single gold earring showing beneath lank greasy hair.

Steffan punched Morgan on the side of his head. "Do this again, I'll kill you."

"My father left this field to me. You've no rights to it."

"Your father? You were a stray our father brought home. And what about your mother, gypsy boy, where's she?" He flung back his head as if to laugh, but no sound came out. He whistled to send their scrawny dog up round the escapees while Tomos moved the van, opening the gap for Morgan's escape. "*Iesu mawr*, bugger off before we really damage you."

Two hard punches. Morgan thought Steffan might have shattered an eardrum; standing to pump the useless brakes on the last steep incline, he thought his head would split open. Once onto the lane he fell back in his seat, swung the tractor down over the bridge, up past The Plas entrance and onto the hill. It began to rain heavily. Every pothole filled instantly as if in waiting for their more familiar roles as puddles. On the Abernant track he rammed the throttle open. Rain stung his face as he hurtled along.

Apart from in the distance or at mart he hadn't seen those two bastards up close since the family left Cwmgwrach. He replayed his father's promise. He'd given up assuming they believed him, and didn't particularly care.

The majority of his two hundred acres was rough hill land. He knew he was fortunate to be renting Abernant, but there was probably more grass on the nine acres.

His revenge would be constant.

EIGHT

Bethan next saw Morgan when his black eyes were two days old.

She was out walking and found him trying to drive six ewes, all heavy in lamb, through the shallow part of the river. Each time he almost got them to the opposite bank, the same stubborn ewe shot back past the younger, inexperienced dog, who then set off on a wild, hopeless chase. The exasperated older dog tore back and forth trying to gather the five back to the single.

"Dogs are being idiots today," he said, showing no surprise at Bethan's sudden appearance. "It's this one old bitch. Could you come behind with the young dog?"

"Bloody hell, Morgan, who did that?"

He sniggered and cocked his head to the side. His eyes were outlined in dark purple and the whites were yellow. "Those tidy young farmers on my nine acres." He whistled the dogs and made a face.

She knew not to pursue it. Nia had told her, somewhat gleefully, about the dispute and Morgan only inheriting a faded photo of their father on horseback.

The six sheep were panting hard enough to show they were stressed. Bethan moved slowly, holding the younger dog on a length of baler twine. Finally, Morgan had them through the water and struggling up the bank. They stopped at the top and shook like dogs.

"Stragglers, are they?" she said. "You're moving them close to lambing."

He didn't answer, just stepped up the pace. It seemed she was in for the full journey. In the Abernant yard he drove them into the 'hanged man' sheep shed, slammed the doors and fell against them.

"Thank you," he said. "Let me make you a drink."

"Okay, thanks." She couldn't wait to see inside the house. He kicked open the warped front door and she followed him down the brown hallway into the kitchen. Thin shafts of sunlight fought the grimy glass but thick stone walls and lack of daylight ensured the rooms remained cold. No fire. A bed of dead ashes. He took a bottle of whisky and two glasses from the old kitchen cabinet, set them on the table and dragged back a tall wooden chair with singed legs.

"Sit here. I'll get the wood." He disappeared.

She heard the front door creak and went to the clouded window. The view was of mist. She'd never drunk whisky and didn't think he was keen on alcohol. Maybe because her mother had forced it on him, he thought it was the regular tipple of the Pritchards. She sniffed the bottle and poured two good measures into surprisingly spotless glasses. A noise took her to the front door, where she found a handful of kindling which she took to the kitchen and piled by the grate.

The mantelpiece was crammed with papers and brown envelopes stuffed behind jugs and bang in the middle, in pride of place, the sepia photograph of the young Mr Williams astride his handsome Welsh Cob. Though torn in several places, it had been carefully pressed into a small frame and was the only thing not coated in dust. She sighed at the poignancy then shuddered at certain memories of the uncouth man.

She looked round for paper to light the fire. A door at the far end of the kitchen opened to a long corridor of invisible scurryings leading to a small stark room with long stone sinks and a Baby Burco boiler. Beyond that was an abandoned dairy littered with empty paper feed sacks. One was enough to get the fire going. White flames matured to orange and the kitchen shed a little of its bleakness.

There was no sink or tap, just an enamel bowl on the windowsill half full of water mottled silver from melting soap. She washed her hands, wiped them down her jeans and held them in front of the fire. A gulp of whisky burnt her throat.

Morgan's suit was in a plastic cover, hanging on a nail. She looked towards the door and listened, then quickly pulled down the zip of the cover and slid her hand inside. The fabric felt as good as it looked.

A box of cartridges had spilled open into breadcrumbs on the metal flap of the old kitchen cabinet and a shotgun was poking out from behind. The one food shelf was crammed solid with books. Curious to read the titles, she looked round the lumpy walls for a light switch. She couldn't think what was keeping him. She lit a match and ran it along the books in the cabinet. If he came in now, he'd think she was setting fire to them. They were mostly poetry. Then she noticed cardboard boxes in dark corners, also bulging with books. No wonder her father had taken to him.

She sat in the tall burnt carver and propped her stockinged feet on the hearth rail. The silence was broken by the crackle of fire and odd spit of damp log. There didn't seem to be a fireguard, so she couldn't leave to go and look for him: her father was always going on about the danger of open fires. Not that there was much in this miserable place to catch fire. She moved the chair back to the table; any sparks would fizzle out on the flagstones. She had three more sips of whisky then ventured outside to the sheep shed.

A few of the lambing pens were occupied. Morgan was bending over at the back of the building and, for once, didn't appear to see her until she was at his side.

"I thought something had happened, you were so long," she said to him.

He was in a pen with the exhausted ewes. Five were pulling hay from a rack. He was straddling the other; her head was pinned between his knees, covered in blood. The scissors looked small in his big hand, and a metal hole-punch was jammed in his belt. His face was splattered with blood, complementing the red bruises outlining his nose. He looked stricken by smallpox.

Then she saw the Cwmgwrach earmark. "Morgan, what the hell are you doing?" Blood was gushing from a mangled stump that ten minutes ago had been the ewe's ear. The other five ewes were untouched. "Stop! These don't belong to you."

He looked at her, bewildered; his eyes watering, most likely from a squirt of blood. "There's not enough ear."

"Christ, you've risked them losing their lambs with that terrible journey and I actually helped you! Course there's not enough ear, you knew that. Your father went on about it enough."

Bethan had been ten when Nia flipped through the directory of earmarks showing diagrams of ears with various chunks and holes punched out of them, opposite the address of each farm. It was the day Morgan had showered her with lamb's blood in the sheep shed. The Cwmgwrach earmark was the most severe on the mountain, virtually impossible for a thief to alter unless they cut off most of the ear.

"Stop now. Come to the house." She put her hand on his arm and to her astonishment he followed.

She stoked the fire back into life, dragged two chairs to the hearth and handed him the glass of whisky. The heat of the room was no different from The Plas: front burning, back freezing. He threw back the drink and slumped forward. Never having seen this side of him, she waited. They watched the flames.

"You won't get away with this," she said at last. "I suggest you return them."

"What! We'd kill them," he snapped out of his daze and stared at her.

To her disgust, the 'we' didn't displease her. She was in it now. "Not on foot, in your trailer. We'll do it tonight."

"Tonight, are you mad?"

"It's you who's mad, Morgan. Keep the ewe you've already mutilated, decide what to do with her later. When do your brothers feed, you'll know that?"

"Mornings. At night they go straight to the pub from the garage. They might come up at dusk to check them since they're lambing, but they wouldn't count them."

Bethan got up and pulled her chair back to the table. "I'm off. I'll be back just before dark. I'll say I'm going to the pictures with Nia tonight."

"Why? Why are you helping me, Bethan?"

"God knows," she risked a small smile. "I make mistakes, heat of the moment stuff. Wouldn't like to see you hanged for sheep stealing."

"Wouldn't your nuns pray for me?"

"No."

Nia had said that everyone knows the faces of sheep, their own and others. Each flock has a certain stamp; the earmark's the final proof. 'Knowing the faces of sheep' had stuck in Bethan's mind.

The heavy old tractor hit the road with a thump. Morgan turned down the hill with Bethan squashed to his side on the wheel arch. Fortunately the lane was hardly used. At the sharp turning up to Cwmgwrach, he was forced to reverse once when the trailer threatened to jack-knife. They'd driven without lights and the engine on the lowest revs. On the steepest part of the hill the steering wheel wobbled from the weight of the old trailer. Bethan didn't need daylight to know they were at the worst sheer drop down to the river.

The sky lightened a little as they came out of the trees and she held her breath and scanned the land. He stopped the tractor at the corner of the field to keep any telltale tyre marks off the grass. They hadn't discussed this part. He jumped the gate neatly without clanking the massive padlock and chain. Bethan stood by the trailer. The ewes began to jostle about inside, unsettled now they were stationary. She could just see him moving like a wildcat up through the sheep across the field to the fence. He stamped about on posts and netting then ran back to her. "Get the trailer open."

They bashed up the catches with the heels of their hands and the ewes charged out as the ramp hit the ground. Up in the field the first of the sheep were picking their way across the broken fence, calling to their lambs to keep up. The five released ewes trotted up to join them. Morgan closed the ramp.

Bethan watched the white dots reunite and begin another nocturnal escapade.

The empty trailer crashed down the Cwmgwrach track spitting up stones. Her heart thudded. A mile left to go with no escape if a vehicle came towards them unless you risked the few feet of grass verge before the sheer drop, she wouldn't put that past him, even without headlights, especially without headlights. She didn't breathe properly until they'd rumbled down the steep incline and crossed the bridge.

"I'll walk home from here." She squeezed out to the top step, he stopped and she jumped down.

"Thank you, *cariad*," he said.

She whispered "Bastard" as she ran. The house was quiet. She slid in unnoticed and went straight upstairs. The bathroom mirror dotted with black age spots and shaving soap reflected a chaotic image: the mud-streaked face and tangled hair of a sheep-rustler's accomplice. Something inside her lit up. *Cariad?*

She washed and went downstairs. Her mother was gazing at a vase of daffodils in her usual post-visitor daze, as if she'd been abandoned in favour of real life. Auntie Cecily had given the house a good going-over just before she left and her perfume still hung in the air.

"Auntie Cecily's kindly tidied. I don't seem to have much energy and your father's stomping around in a mood, saying he can't find a bally thing."

"He couldn't before," said Bethan.

"She thought Morgan's performance at the preview was planned. She thinks Veronica may have her eye on him, said she wouldn't blame her if she had. Well, why ask him to the opening?"

"What?" Bethan laughed. "What on earth would Veronica see in him?"

"Cecily brought us a couple of the trout jigsaws, knew all about you standing in the river and everything. Your grandfather wants Morgan to have one. Maybe you could take it up to him, and find out what he thinks of Veronica!"

"I'm not mentioning Veronica."

She walked up to Abernant the following day, sneaked behind the house and went straight to the sheep shed, anxious to see what he'd done with the ewe. She was lying rigid in the pen, nothing remaining of one ear but a small encrusted wedge; he'd sliced it off barely an inch from her head. The straw was stiff with black blood where her throat had been slit. The shed felt more forbidding than the day she and her mother had delivered the invitation.

"I had no choice," he said, at her side from nowhere.

"Shooting would have been more humane," said Bethan.

"Too risky, someone may have heard."

"Oh yes, what, a passer-by? You'd better be quick and bury her then."

He nodded. She'd never seen him dirty – his clothes, yes, but never in himself. Still blood-splattered, hair unwashed and black eyes sunken, he looked years older. The only colour to his face was the rainbow bruising.

"My grandfather sent this for you." she pulled the jigsaw from a bag.

He wiped his hands down his overalls and before accepting it, studied every inch of the painting. Then he carefully ran his hands down over the trout, took the box, turned it over and read the back.

"*Duw*, it's grand," he said reverently rotating it. "Please thank him for me and tell him I'll value it."

"I will. I'll leave you to bury the ewe. I only came up to bring you the jigsaw." Crossing the yard, she was struck by a gory thought. Those six ewes were all heavily in-lamb. The straw was stained all around the ewe, not just by her throat. Maybe Morgan cut a live lamb from the mother's carcass then turned her over to hide the gaping stomach. One more orphan lamb to rear, but worth it. She ran down through the woods and met her father striding out in his gumboots.

"I've just taken the trout jigsaw to Morgan."

"Ah, and did he appreciate it? Probably never had a jigsaw of such quality."

"Probably never had a jigsaw." Bethan pictured him slicing the throats of stolen ewes, coming in plastered in blood and sitting down to do a nice jigsaw.

"And tell me about the film you and Nia saw last night." He took a step closer.

Bethan smelled hot nylon shirt. "We stayed in and watched telly instead."

"Ah." He took off his glasses to clean them and blinked mole-like. She looked away from his red-rimmed eyes. When he replaced them, he checked his pocket watch. "I'll come back with you, there's a concert on the third." They walked to the babble of the river and the slap of his over-sized boots. "So what's the man doing up there for heaven's sake, some sort of self-imposed exile? Is it as derelict as they say?"

"He's busy lambing. He doesn't care about the house, he only eats and sleeps there."

"I'm jolly glad we got him to Veronica's do. To think I knew nothing about his voice."

133

NINE

THE FOLLOWING YEAR was Bethan's last at school. The season of boaters, white gloves and glib-faced nuns gliding round the car park, checking the girls piling in and out of the coaches.

Sister Margaret was quick to pounce. "Bethan Pritchard. The rules are: the boater stays on your head on the coach and until you enter school or home."

"Sorry Sister, but I'm too short. If I sit properly, it hits the back of the seat, flips over and bashes the girl behind. It almost had her eye out. They're so hard." She bashed the brim on the tarmac. Sister Margaret simmered. Bethan went on, "I've seen them in the river perfectly intact after weeks, even stamped on, sailing down to the village losing flakes of straw, like confetti." She lowered her voice. "And what's a bloody boater in the great scheme of things?"

Sister Margaret's hand shot up and slapped her hard across the face. The girls gasped: they'd been whacked on the legs with rosary beads, rulers, shoes and sticks – never on the face.

Sister Margaret was caving in like a feed-sack kneed in the middle, her breath whooshed out as she crumpled to the ground. Bethan withdrew her clenched fist. The balloon of black robes settled round the winded nun like a collapsing parachute and everyone stood there waiting for the Wicked

Witch of the West to sizzle away to nothing. Bethan thought the onlooking nuns might have reacted more quickly, but shock had rooted everyone to the spot.

She was summoned a few days later. Her father was sitting opposite the Mother Superior, twirling his Brillo-pad hair with the air of someone who'd just given a satisfactory performance. The head nun looked equally smug.

"Your father and I have had a long discussion," she said, pleased to the point of salivating, spit frothing at the edge of her mouth. "You are obviously expelled, Bethan Pritchard. It won't make much difference, you'd be leaving school in a few months anyway, but your father will be paying until the end of the term. Good afternoon."

"She's delighted," thought Bethan, ridding her precious convent of the obstreperous pupil and the erudite father, always too relaxed in the company of nuns. She looked at him. He nodded seriously, not particularly perturbed, but he loathed nuns as much as she did. The nun slammed shut a black folder and swept away.

"That's that then," he said. "Have you had chance to think about a career?"

"I'm going to be a farmer," she said.

"Oh, for heaven's sake. You shouldn't have thumped her."

"I'm sorry about the school fees."

"Oh, worse things to worry about."

And that was it; he didn't demand an explanation. Bethan collected her belongings and they drove away in silence.

"Your mother's not too well again," he said, a few miles on. "She's in hospital. We'll keep this from her; just say you've been allowed home to visit her."

"Sorry, Dad."

"Well, you can't punch nuns, but what's done is done. We'll go straight to the hospital; maybe get fish and chips on the way home. Be prepared, your mother doesn't look too good."

Alice Pritchard had unusual eyes. One hazel flecked with green, the other green flecked with grey: pretty eyes. Now they looked black as coal, staring up at the ceiling above her little pointy nose and bright white nightdress, like a snowman, but her face had lost its roundness and thin yellow skin draped over her cheekbones.

Bethan was incredulous such a horror could happen so quickly; her mother was barely recognisable. Her father sat at the side of the bed with his hand resting on the cotton bedspread, cupping what looked like pale blue twigs but which was actually her mother's hand. No one spoke. After a few minutes, Bethan left the room. She paced up and down the length of the corridor. They were in an annexe to the main hospital: a row of green Nissan huts bashed into one like the convent kindergarten.

A nurse came marching along the tiled floor. Bethan ran to ask if her mother was dying. The nurse stopped and gently put her arm round her. "Yes she is, my love. She's not in any pain. Talk to her, hearing is the last thing to go."

Bethan sat opposite her father on the other side of the bed.

"I'm sorry, dear," he said. "This has happened so quickly. I was about to ring the convent when they rang me."

"Sssshh, she'll hear," Bethan stood up. She tucked back her hair, carefully bent low over her mother and talked quietly straight into her ear, saying everything would be alright and she'd soon be home. She wanted to say she loved her but no one in her family spoke that intimately. Whenever Veronica ended her phone calls to Auntie Cecily with "Love you, Mummy", Bethan and her mother rolled their eyes, Veronica could be quite off-hand to her mother in real life.

The nurse had left a damp flannel to cool her mother's forehead. Bethan patted and soothed and took her other hand, saying, "Squeeze my fingers if you can hear me." One finger twitched. Bethan gasped as if the tiny movement inferred full recovery. She looked across at her father and saw tears rolling out from his steamed-up glasses.

Her mother's breath was coming in throaty groans with longer and longer intervals. Then a little mew like a kitten and her lips stirred. It seemed the tremendous effort to say something might kill her and Bethan told her to leave it till later. Alice knew there was no later. Bethan bent low until her ear brushed her mother's mouth and though the faraway whisper came in a gurgle, she heard. "Good luck, dear."

She died at five in the morning. Bethan buried her face in the white counterpane, crying in that heaving sob that eventually forced people to slap you. Her father, crumpled into a large plastic armchair, rocked back and forth. When they left the room, he hugged her to him, a stiff embrace like the winding down of clockwork toy soldiers.

"White rabbits!" he said. "Your mother always said 'white rabbits' on the first day of the month, remember how cross she'd get if she forgot? Today's the first of May."

Auntie Cecily implored Bryn to bury her dear sister in London, beside their beautiful young brother shot down in the war. But Bryn wanted his wife close by and he chose the remote mountain chapel on the other side of the village. Bethan couldn't bear to think of her buried at all.

The tall thin chapel was the colour of wet plaster and stood encased in spiked iron railings, the only building on the vast wilderness of bogs and rushes. A nearby pile of stones had once been the TB hospital. As small girls, she and Nia had cycled up there to frighten themselves silly and steal the small glittery stones from graves to sell at school. When her father talked of the dramatic views Alice would have from the mountain, Bethan stared at him. He also thought it would appeal to Alice's sense of the macabre. She was about to ask what sense of the macabre, then remembered her mother switching off the main light and bringing a torch to read aloud the most terrifying parts of *Jamaica Inn*.

Had anyone mentioned a Catholic funeral, Bethan would have told them her mother was well and truly lapsed. She'd been voicing her doubts for years. The two of them huddled in the back pew, giggling when their tummies rumbled from fasting and agreed a mass without Latin held no mystery. The day her mother suggested no longer bothering with such nonsense Bethan was overjoyed. With her mother's penchant for intrigue, maybe the austere, isolated chapel was appropriate. Her father believed she drew her spiritual needs from nature rather than any Catholic church.

At the last minute he invited the local priest to add a little something to the proceedings as a gesture of goodwill to the family. Bethan hoped she could stomach his contribution.

The funeral morning dawned with that fine devious rain that soaked to the skin. Bethan's new black PVC mac stuck to the leather car seat and crackled at every move. She'd turned away with her face pressed to the window and her back to her father and Veronica. The cars had climbed the hill and started winding their way to the chapel, a small speck in the distance.

The road was one vehicle wide and their driver was forced to park on the grass verge. As he pulled on the handbrake, the car very slowly turned sideways and slid majestically into the back of the hearse. The driver, the epitome of a sedate funeral director in his top hat, turned crimson and said, "Fuck it."

Veronica beamed at Bethan, "Wouldn't Auntie Alice have adored that?"

Bethan nodded fiercely, her mouth clamped tight.

The coffin was already out of the hearse and onto the shoulders of the pallbearers. A small Dickensian character squelched nimbly through the mud towards them, carrying a large black umbrella. Veronica tucked her arm firmly through Mr Pritchard's and nodded at Bethan to take his other arm. She hadn't walked attached to her father since she was little. With the umbrella man weaving behind, they followed the coffin through the iron gates, past the four tall windows behind their heavy iron grids, earth-coloured gravestones and drunken angels sunk to wild angles. Two black trees whipped naked by mountain gales bent double over the railings.

"Emaciated nuns begging for expiation," said Veronica.

Bethan nodded. The only live flowers in the whole place were her mother's wreaths, placed by the stone steps at the back. The men carried the coffin through a huge oak door and started up well-worn stone stairs. Veronica looked confused.

"I know," said Bethan quietly. "Weird, but this is the entrance. We go up, then down."

They came to a dark landing. An arched doorway on the right led to the old schoolroom, while the men turned left down another set of stairs into the chapel. Veronica's heels clattered down the steps into more gloom. "We're the only women here," she whispered. An ancient crone sprang to life

to pump the pedals of a terrible old organ. "Apart from her."
Men loosened their collars and began to sing.

"In Wales the men go to funerals and the women do the
teas," said Bethan. "Maybe they made an exception because
Mum's English."

"Sounds medieval. How do you live in such a godforsaken
place?" The singing began. "God, goose bumps. Morgan?"

Bethan quivered as tenor and bass took the dismal building
to cathedral heights and tears flooded her cheeks. Veronica
slipped an arm round her shoulders as the priest stepped up
and said something about "for whatever sin Alice Pritchard
may have committed". Bethan glared at him, Veronica
tightened her grip and they hissed "Bastard". Alice Pritchard
hadn't committed a sin in her life.

Outside, the umbrella man leapt forward to escort them to
the graveside before the rain could add its mark. Both were
black-eyed from tears and mascara. When the men sang
again, a tenor could be heard well above the others, his voice
lingering at the end of each line. Veronica looked around.
Bethan kept her attention on the ground.

Her mother would have loved the tea, though might have
felt awkward seeing her flamboyant sister and imperious
mother floating round The Plas while the village women cut
pyramids of sandwiches. Not that either side seemed to mind.
Veronica sobbed and repeated "Dear Auntie Alice" over and
over. Somehow Bethan managed to hold herself together,
though she felt peculiar surrounded by friends of her mother's
she and her father knew nothing about. The hours Alice had
spent away from The Plas had gone largely unnoticed by
Bryn. She'd walked or cycled to the village shop then called at
various houses for tea.

Bethan felt she might expire. Her grandmother stood aloof by the fireplace with Auntie Cecily in a little black cocktail dress snivelling into her gin. Most mourners were drinking tea. Everyone was talking in high praise of Alice. An elderly man described her exemplarily calm approach to his escaped bees, raging round Bethan's pram when she was a baby. A woman bringing a tray of brimming teacups told Bryn everyone was the better for having known her. Bethan overheard. It was the perfect inscription for her mother's headstone, which they'd already failed to discuss.

Her father just stared out of the window until Veronica persuaded him to the table to eat something. Bethan and Nia took his place, looking out at the papier-mâché women.

"She was a funny one, wasn't she?" said Bethan.

"She was lovely. A scream," said Nia. "All that Angel Delight and farting jelly. I adored her."

"I don't even know what was wrong with her. No one's said."

"Cancer," Nia scuffed the carpet and increased the pressure of her hug. "Bloody cancer, Bethan. My mum told me."

Perhaps in her heart, Bethan had known.

"Brave of you, Nia, saying it out loud."

"Morgan sent his regards. He was lurking around outside."

"Why didn't he come in?"

"My mother's here. They haven't spoken since he left to work at Tŷ Newydd."

"I guess it was his amazing voice we heard above all the rest. He was really fond of my mum, I know that." Bethan looked at Mrs Williams in the corner, eating a triangular sandwich and talking to the apiarist.

"I hope your mum knows you punched a nun. That's right up her street."

TEN

As if the papier-mâché women had lost their raison d'être without their dotty creator to amuse, they began to fall apart. Bethan patched and filled various body parts then moved them in their deckchairs to an old outbuilding behind the house, to reduce their disintegration. She placed them as if in conversation exactly as her mother had, and a few days later her father sneaked in and adjusted them slightly. A week later Bethan moved them one behind the other as if on a bus excursion. The next week her father rearranged them. And so a pattern evolved and their solitary visits became routine, as if something of Alice Pritchard's spirit lived on in her wonky sculptures.

The house felt stale and unloved, the atmosphere melancholic. Months passed. The table piled up. The china sheep cruet was buried under old *Radio Times*, *The New Statesman*, bills, letters, condolence cards and breadcrumbs. They forgot to burn incense and candles, to fling open the windows on rainy days to catch the aroma of iron, arrange the closed curtains nicely, keep crisps in the airtight tin and rinse the cat-food knife. A can of clock oil took up residence on the mantelpiece. Alice must have done something on the domestic front after all. Bethan removed the oil. Her mother might have turned a blind eye to the film of dust, but a can of oil on the mantelpiece would certainly have offended her aesthetic eye.

Her father came out with extraordinary statements. Bethan assumed he'd be content with solitude and muddle, but he missed the clatter of saucepans and cutlery as if hot meals were always on the go, whereas nothing would please her mother more than her small family agreeing to bread, cheese and fruit for supper. He left Bethan to sort her mother's bedroom things and popped in at intervals with cups of tea and unnecessary comments.

He'd no need to mention her bedside table. To build a pile that high of nothing much, Bethan saw as quite an achievement: paper bags, stockings packets, *Woman's Weekly*, recipes, used wrapping paper, birthday cards, circulars, knitting patterns, photographs, postcards, tissue packets, notebooks. When he noticed Jean Paul Sartre in her books and said, "Ah, your mother was full of surprises," Bethan said she'd rather get on with it alone and he went downstairs.

At the bottom of the pile were two yellowing sheets of paper in her mother's handwriting. A backwards slope was supposed to indicate lack of confidence, another reason for Bethan's feelings for her father to fluctuate. He alternated between condescension and endearment when they talked of her.

She unfolded the papers, recognised the first few sentences and remembered her mother asking whether she'd like to hear the beginning of a story she was trying to write, laughing away, expecting her nine-year-old daughter to say no. It began with an overgrown driveway, a white-haired woman and an old house with red squirrels leaping through branches and on and off a dilapidated car. The woman faded into the trees. Bethan had been captivated.

Her father was right, her mother was full of surprises, it was just the way he said it. Sadly the ghost story was never completed. Bethan re-read it; her mother had described the tree-tunnel driveway to The Plas. They had been living in Bath at the time.

In the chest of drawers she found a small, battered portfolio with 'To dear Alice from Bryn' written diagonally across the top corner in his dramatic flourish. She untied the three lots of faded cord, sorry now for sending him away so sharply. It was a small collection of ink sketches: people outside cafés, labelled 'Paris, 1936'. She didn't know he'd been to Paris. The last was a pencil drawing of her and her mother in a caravan. Bethan painting at the flimsy foldaway table, her mother bowed over her knitting. Borth 1955. Another wet holiday with her father continually declaring "Only April showers" in August, thinking himself so witty. In contrast to Paris in deft, economic ink lines, Borth in soft pencil did seem touched with love.

Next drawer down there were twenty-three knitted hats, seventeen tea cosies and three teeth on a pinkish grey plastic gum in a tin. The teeth made her weepy. The hats made her cry. She kept expecting someone to appear and snap her out of it, but she'd dismissed her father and Nia was working, though she came whenever she could.

In the months that followed they kept their own counsel even after a drop of whisky, which neither really liked, but didn't say.

Nia rang one evening. "Come and stay," she said. "You've never seen my flat and I'll teach you to drive – Mr Gentleman's willing to lend us his old car."

Bethan was taken aback. Nia had driven tractors since she was ten and passed her test at 17.

"That would be good. Is that what you call him: 'Mr Gentleman'?"

"That's his name. I told him about you and where you live and he said driving is an essential string to your bow and we can use the fields without sheep to practise."

Nia lived in the annexe of a shabby mansion overlooking green parkland grazed by a small flock of fat Jacob sheep. Bethan felt guilty for not having taken the time to picture her friend's home beforehand. The grandeur of the rooms brought Veronica's flat to mind.

Nia greeted her, wearing a pink cardigan with two-inch lengths of beige wool poking from wide brown cuffs, like bracelets of worms. Her sitting room was packed and colourful, in contrast to her drab childhood: vases everywhere, with assortments of wands. Bethan wondered whether a glass bowl of marbles had belonged to her brothers, but couldn't imagine them playing anything as innocent, playing anything in fact. They were the kind of boys with serious intent on their minds the minute they could crawl, like Tomos and Steffan inventing that death-defying contraption. She still remembered it vividly: hurtling down through the trees, clinging to that flimsy bicycle wheel on a wire, landing in a pile of tractor tyres and then wetting herself.

Nia shook two packets of crisps into a wooden bowl and poured two glasses of Dubonnet and lemonade, adding ice cubes and flipping in slices of lemon straight from the knife. They clinked glasses, said "chin-chin" in tribute to Bethan's mum, then talked about her for most of the evening, a great relief to Bethan.

Nia had prepared her spare bedroom so thoughtfully. When Bethan saw the tissues and plant on the dressing table, two elderly towels and a face flannel neatly folded on the eiderdown and a hot water bottle in her bed, she was reduced to tears that developed into mild hysterics. She pushed her face into the pillow so there was no chance of Nia hearing.

Fortunately the following morning was dry; Mr Gentleman wouldn't have wanted them poaching his fields with a car. Nia took her to the stables first, a row of looseboxes with half-doors built for the height of a thoroughbred. Bethan stood on tiptoes to see ten or twelve white rabbits bobbing around in pale straw.

"New Zealand Whites," said Nia. "And believe it or not, they came from Tŷ Newydd, where Morgan went to work."

"How weird. They're beautiful."

"I didn't mention him, obviously. Funny set-up: supposed to be meat rabbits, but not an ounce of fat on them. Didn't see the husband at all and the wife didn't relax until we were in the rabbit shed; Mr Gentleman noticed that too. By the way, he's invited you to our show on Saturday night, in a working men's club not that far away. It makes the Celyn look like the Ritz."

Bethan felt a slight panic.

"Thank you, that sounds great – to see your act at last."

"Good, now to driving." Nia opened more barn doors, jumped into an old Morris Oxford, crashed it into reverse and shot out. "It's all about clutch control." After Bethan had lurched round the spacious courtyard for twenty minutes, they ventured into the fields.

"Now into third," said Nia. "Duck to water – look at you!"

Bethan beamed. Last night's hysteria had unstuck her grief and she was laughing, the first proper laugh since her mother died. She circled the field, her head full of new images: driving to mart in her own Land Rover towing a trailer of sheep, collie at her side. She put her lightening of spirit down to Nia's magical powers.

"We'll do the same this afternoon and tomorrow," said Nia, smiling.

"You've snapped me out of my bloody misery, Nia. Thank you. Honestly, the moods Dad and I have been in for months. I can get a job now."

"Hasn't he mentioned work? God, imagine my father if we hadn't worked. What on earth do you when he goes to work, and for money?"

"I sort Mum's things, walk, try to cook, read, draw – a bit like a spinster in a Victorian novel. I live on a little pocket money frrom Dad."

"I spoke to your mother just before she died. She knew you wanted to farm."

Mr Gentleman was elusive. Bethan saw his tall thin figure in the courtyard and met him properly in the club on the Saturday night. He had a neatly-trimmed dark brown moustache and prominent cheekbones. He spoke in quiet cut-glass and when she thanked him for his generosity regarding his car and fields he smiled charmingly and waved an invisible wand. He showed her to a small table right next to the stage where, had it not been for the pre-show drinks, dense cigarette smoke and poor lighting, she'd have felt horribly conspicuous. She sat alone in her privileged position.

Mr Gentleman had had a new top hat made to accommodate the larger breed of rabbit and Nia had chosen a simple long black dress in favour of her pink, knowing this particular club.

They were to have a fifteen-minute slot after a small dance troupe and a few members of a male voice choir. Bethan tried to assess the audience in the gloom and couldn't imagine them simmering down. Another drink appeared by magic on her table, then a shadow.

"Anyone sitting here?" asked a woman, already pulling out the other chair.

Bethan shook her head and the woman sat down. After the last dancer had high-kicked off the stage there was a drum roll and Mr Gentleman appeared in a dinner suit with the top hat, looking far too big for his head, tucked under his arm. He introduced his glamorous assistant and Nia came sashaying out through a swish of crimson velvet curtains, wearing black patent stilettos and pushing what looked like a large tea trolley across the stage. A table on wheels covered with a white cloth.

Bethan stole a glance at the woman next to her, who'd flipped her hair forward. When she turned slightly Bethan saw a handsome woman in her early thirties, sitting up straight, arms folded, with no drink in front of her and looking as out of place as Bethan. They smiled awkwardly and returned their attention to the stage. Nia vanished behind various scarves and curtains to emerge in different places, people were invited to participate in card tricks, Mr Gentleman pulled an egg from a woman's ear and then came the grand finale: rabbits popping up through the tea trolley in and out of the top hat until six were lolloping calmly round the stage.

The woman leant forward keenly and whispered. "Do you think it's cruel?"

"God no," said Bethan, who'd had her own doubts before seeing the rabbits' lifestyle.

"They're mine, you see: my rabbits, or were. They assured me there was no cruelty involved, but I wanted to see for myself, to make sure."

"No," Bethan drained her glass to conceal her shock. "No, she's my closest friend, she wouldn't dream of doing anything unkind. She's from a farming family."

"She didn't say that when they bought them. Some farmers can be cruel."

"She isn't."

The audience were applauding, the stage was empty; with no focus the woman unfolded her arms and slumped. "Someone worked for us for five years. He could be barbaric." Her eyes were watering. "He sang beautifully."

She hasn't bought a drink, thought Bethan, because she's already had a few.

"I saw the advertisement for the show and came to see my rabbits, of course, but I did wonder about the singing – if he might be here, it being in the Swansea Valley. I knew really that it wouldn't be his thing."

"No. No, it wouldn't," said Bethan.

The woman jolted and refolded her arms to keep herself upright.

"Do you know him, then?" The chair tipped backwards and teetered on its rear legs.

"No. I just meant it wouldn't be everyone's choice. Some singers can be shy."

"We owed him some wages. He did a moonlight flit," she laughed, and flopped forwards. "Hah, literally! The moon was amazing that night." She heaved herself up and staggered away. Somehow Bethan had the feeling she wasn't a habitual drunk.

Nia came down the side steps of the stage and over to Bethan's table.

"That looked just like Elin Davies, the rabbit woman."

"It was. She came to check your act wasn't cruel and to see if Morgan was singing."

"What! You didn't say he's my brother, did you?"

"Of course not."

"Thank God for that, we may need to buy more rabbits. They're so placid and easy to train. What did you think of the show, then?"

"It was great, and the rabbits seem quite willing." Bethan was cross with herself; she'd lost concentration at the final illusion because of the rabbit woman. "She owes Morgan money apparently. Wages."

"Bugger that," said Nia.

ELEVEN

At Veronica's suggestion, Bethan took and passed her driving test the following year in Bath. Veronica gave her the huge oil painting of ochre mountains. Seeing Bethan fixated by it at the gallery opening, she'd kept it back for such an occasion.

Whether her father had been inspired by Veronica's kind attention and generous gift, on Bethan's triumphant return to The Plas he suggested a day sketching at the mart. It would be heaving with wonderful characters. He was trying his best. She wondered if the mart would be his cup of tea, even with an artist's eye, having been there with Nia.

The pens were set up in the field opposite the Llwyn Celyn, every blade of grass flattened to mud and crammed with dark figures in cumbersome oilskins, stocky, broad-shouldered men instantly recognisable to each other despite the camouflage. A plethora of donkey jackets with NCB emblazoned across plastic shoulders, some belonging to genuine colliers running a few sheep on the hill, most inveigled from mining relatives or friends. The sheep men walked the pens, prodding and poking the damp ewes, examining teeth, squeezing backs to judge condition; then a stick in the ribs to scare her across a pen, to check she could move and had four good legs.

Every mart brought busybodies out of the woodwork, eyes sharp and ears finely tuned to the auctioneer's hammer. Sheep prices revealed income and status.

Bethan and her father were suitably dressed in waterproof trousers and boots ingrained with mud. She had made a flask, but for their first drink they chose the already well-trodden trail to the refreshment table to buy mugs of tea from the elderly woman who owned the village shop. It was tradition for her to serve hot drinks, sandwiches and cake until the last animal was sold and the men retired to the Celyn for ten pints, a brawl and loss of memory. Pens of forlorn sheep were often discovered the next day. Some were stolen overnight.

They took their tea to the edge of the field. Bethan sat on a straw bale softened by days of rain. Her father strolled away; he usually sketched standing. On the small pencil drawings he intended to enlarge and paint in the future, he wrote the colours of each part of the landscape for reference, though most ended up Prussian blue or violet.

She watched him cross the field and pause at the sheep pens to speak to Morgan. He inclined his head to point out Bethan and Morgan raised his hand to her in curt salute. No farmer waved. She watched them shake hands and thought about drawing the unlikely pair: her small animated father in his over-sized boots and the tall slender man moving swiftly through his sheep. Every other farmer lumbered, weighed down by layers of wet garments.

She returned to the table to buy a rock cake then went over to the pens. The bedraggled sheep looked pitiful, the older ewes skidded on the mud and wild-eyed lambs leapt high as they were driven into the ring. The auctioneer leaned over his makeshift stand as meagre bids were offered and asked the owners, "How we doing, Mr Jones (/Thomas/Griffith)? Are we getting there?" He made sure he gave each vendor enough stage time to shake his head and mutter "Slowly, slowly" to the ground in despair.

Bethan smiled to herself; most farmers deserved awards for drama. She moved closer to the ring with her sketchpad to try and capture someone, if only for her father's sake. The dark, weathered skin, cracked brown lips and grim expressions, knowing they'd have to sell whatever the price. Her father joined her, pleased to see her drawing. He held out damp black hands. "I stupidly chose charcoal today for some reason. Never mind. Well, Morgan has had some good prices for his sheep."

"That's good. You look tired, Dad – you go on home whenever you like. I'm quite happy to walk back later."

"If you're sure. I'll get some pies from the Celyn for us for supper."

"Okay." They disliked pies as much as whisky.

She drew on for a while, drank more tea and watched the sheep until the sale drew to an end. Once the auctioneer's banter had sold the last animal, every lorry wanted to be first on and off the mud. Eventually the field was deserted apart from Bethan and fourteen forgotten ewes. Eight in one pen, six in another; hungry and stressed after blatant exposure to hoards of rustling men with hurtful sticks.

She watched them watching her, this lone girl packing away her flutter of white paper, sitting close by in the grass. Though weary, they still had it in them to leap and bunch together in fright, but their orangey lemon eyes were no longer rolling. Each black oblong pupil was fixed on her. She stood up. The ewes jumped then. Not wishing to scare them further, but keen to practise the techniques of a buyer while no one was looking, she climbed into the pen of eight. She felt their backs and peeled back their lips (not a tooth among them) and they stood for her examination with quiet tolerance. They'd given up the ghost.

She considered waiting until their transport arrived or confronting the drunks in the Celyn: someone must have bought them. She sat back down and fished in her rucksack for the flask, then couldn't bring herself to drink in front of them. They wouldn't have had water all day. She waited for half an hour then walked away, choosing the field way home rather than the road. She was imagining stealing both pens of ewes as a potential base for her own flock when the sheep rustler extraordinaire appeared at her side, smiling. She hadn't heard or seen his approach. Close to his side, but not touching, stood a small solemn child.

"I was miles away," said Bethan. "Who's this?"

"I'm taking him up to Abernant to see my sheep dog pups. Are you willing to come with us?"

The boy beamed at the mention of pups. Bethan smiled at him and asked his name. He shuffled his feet and stared at her, so she crouched down to squat at his level.

"He's shy," said Morgan. "Come too. He'll be alright then."

He was walking on. She bumped her rucksack higher on to her back. The boy's cold little hand slotted into hers and she was involved.

"Morgan, hang on, I can't. I was on my way home. And surely Abernant's too far for his little legs."

He pretended not to hear when he'd have heard a pin drop in grass. Then he called back, "We'll carry him if necessary."

The boy looked up at her. He was dressed head to foot in waterproofs, with red wellies. Dark curls sprouted from the front of his hood. He looked about two or three, she didn't know, but too small and vulnerable to be subjected to the care of Morgan, who was practically out of sight.

"We'll give you piggybacks," she said. "Would you like to see the pups?"

He nodded frantically and began to walk faster. She squeezed his little hand.

They walked across the mountain, skirting above Cwmgwrach with Morgan well in front and Bethan carrying the boy on her back, rucksack moved to her front. He was surprisingly light. When they reached the river, she saw Morgan had already crossed the pool below Abernant. That made her wild when they could easily have gone down to the footbridge. If he had to come the most difficult way, he should wait to help them.

She put the boy down. It was drizzling and the river was already flowing fast from previous storms. The semi-circle of stones would be an ice rink. She fixed the boy to her hip. At the sight of the swirling water, he clamped his legs round her thigh and half-strangled her. As she was choosing her first stepping-stones, Morgan launched himself back across the river, climbing the swinging rope like a monkey. Showing off. He sailed through the air towards them and Bethan was suddenly ten again, standing with Nia as the scrawny figure ran from the trees, grasped the same rope and dropped into the black water.

He landed on the bank beside them.

"Let me help you across," he said, all gentlemanly, and tried to take the boy, but the child clung vice-like to Bethan.

"Take my bag instead," she said and shook off her rucksack. "It's not heavy, just awkward – my art stuff."

Her hood had fallen back. He lifted a chunk of her hair and flipped the straps from her shoulder. "Probably worth seeing," he said quietly, his eyes black as the river water. "The pups. I could keep one for you."

"You know very well my father's feelings on dogs." She jerked the boy higher on her hip.

Morgan grabbed her free hand and walked backwards, leading them over the wet stones, wobbling skilfully, pretending to slip. His eyes held her. If he was hoping to make her laugh, he was disappointed. She didn't trust him. Nothing to do with drowning: she was confident he'd hold on to her and if she slipped, his arms would be round her in an instant. The boy was watching him with equal suspicion, still not uttering a word. It was Morgan's motives she couldn't fathom. The boy: who was he? Who in their right mind would allow their dear little chap to be in this man's charge? He pulled them up the bank on to flat land. It was still a fair walk to Abernant.

They were now on The Plas side of the river. She'd leave them to it; get down to the footpath then home. Her father might be wondering where she was, maybe not.

"So what is his name?" she asked.

"Ask him," said Morgan.

The boy was close to tears. Bethan tightened her hold on him and made little leaps across the grass. "Gallopy, gallopy," she smiled. "You a horsey?"

"No, I not a horse." He squeezed his legs. "I a Rhodri."

"Rhodri? Ah, that's a good name. I'll have to put you down, Rhodri, you're getting heavy." She lowered him to the ground and he stood tight to her leg, clutching her waterproof trousers. She turned to Morgan. "Why didn't you tell me his name?"

"To get him to talk," he laughed. "It worked."

She was too wary to smile. "Who are his parents?"

"Friends of mine. May I see your drawings? It's not raining very hard."

"If you must. They'll be soaked anyway. And his parents know you have him?"

"Course." He opened the rucksack, took out the damp sheets of paper and peeled them apart. The boy stayed close to Bethan, but rose on his toes in an attempt to see the drawings.

"*Iesu mawr*, is that how you see us? Come and look at these, Rhodri *bach*, pictures of farmers and their sheep."

The little boy stepped away from Bethan and took a piece of the wet paper. "*Dadi!*" he pointed to one hooded figure after another. "*Dadi. See Dadi.*"

"You must take him back," said Bethan. "It's too far. Can't his parents drive him up to Abernant to see the pups another time? And I don't want to see them, I'd only want one."

"You're right," Morgan laughed without smiling. Maybe to make a game out of the situation, he made a strange whooping noise, grabbed Rhodri, threw him into the air and caught him in both arms. He ended up horizontal like a baby. The boy screamed and shot out his arms for Bethan. Morgan began to walk away with him.

"Wait," she said. "He's scared, I'll come."

"He'll be fine, Bethan. You can go home from here."

Hearing her name, the boy screeched. "Want Bethan!"

She wanted him. This was appalling. What was in Morgan's head? Rhodri's fear was leaving him cold.

"Morgan, wait for me for God's sake," Bethan called. "I'll come with you."

He was already crossing the river, expertly skimming the slimy stones on the toes of his boots. Each stone acted like a starting block to send him on to the next, leaving no time to slip. She stood there helplessly, arms still outstretched to take the boy. The rush of water muffled his cries.

Morgan set the boy upright as he climbed the opposite bank and took off at a run, little legs swinging from the knees down with each bounce.

"Let's go back to *Dadi*," he said. "See the pups another day."

Rhodri's little face was flushed with confusion. He kept screaming for Bethan.

"Come on, good boy. We'll be back with *Dadi* now." Morgan slowed to a walk. Apart from his singing, he was used to quiet; a pen of *swcis* bleating for milk could drive him mad. Still Rhodri screamed.

"Stop it, stop. Stop it now." He gave the boy a little shake; Rhodri jumped, stared up at him in fright and the screaming turned to crying.

Morgan tried a smile "Come on now, good boy." He tucked him closer into his chest, the first small child he'd ever held.

The sale field would soon be within sight. The light was fading. It was unheard of for him to walk rather than run when time was of the essence, but the boy was sagging in his arms from exhaustion and didn't need jolting. His head lolled forwards, an intermittent snivel jerked it back. Morgan tipped him into the cradle hold of a baby again and within minutes his eyes closed. His body was limp. Though so light, he was suddenly a dead weight. Morgan lifted him to brush his ear against his mouth and a little breath puffed out. Morgan inhaled deeply.

Now he could see the hedge of the sale field, the rough straggled hedge he hoped would provide enough cover for him to approach unseen. Luck was with him: a cattle lorry had parked alongside, presumably to collect the last two pens of ewes. The ones Bethan had been worrying over. He'd watched her. He knew the lorry; the owner would be in the Celyn till closing time.

Davies was alone in the field, sitting in the trampled wet grass, head in hands, shaking. The man was crying.

Without a sound, Morgan lay down, gently lowered Rhodri alongside, then clasping him tightly crawled on his stomach under the lorry. The boy woke immediately. Even in the poor light Morgan could see he was all Elin: dark hair and eyes and creamy skin, nothing of Davies. Halfway under the lorry Morgan stopped and released him.

"There's *Dadi*, go on," he whispered, pointing to Davies. "And shush." He gave him a little shove and squirmed back.

Rhodri squealed like a puppy. He crawled on all fours till he was out from the lorry and tottered to his father, who grabbed him and howled into his little head of black hair.

Morgan ran, blinking fiercely to see. His eyes were wet.

Her father was in his study. There was no smell of hot pies. Her mother often opened the Rayburn door half an inch to remind herself she was cooking. Judging by the pastry, the pies had been ready an hour ago. He came into the kitchen looking pleased.

"I've chopped some leaves and salady bits to go with the pies – well, to eat with them; probably won't go. And I've sorted my sketches. A productive day; a few will make good paintings. How about you, dear?"

Couldn't he notice it was almost dark and she'd been an age?

"Oh, not bad." She squeaked open the jumbled dresser drawer and took cutlery through to the breakfast room.

"Speak to Morgan?" he asked.

"Yep."

"Did he tell you how he's doing up there?" he placed two tumblers of water at the exact tips of their knives. "He didn't say much to me, too busy with his sheep. What do you think?"

"I'm thinking of phoning the police. Report Morgan for abducting a child."

"Good grief!" Her father sat down with a thump.

"The only thing stopping me is that he's probably returned him by now."

He opened the sideboard.

"We need something stronger than Adam's ale."

"Dad, I hate bloody whisky!" She flopped at the table. "And I'm so sick of bloody crying." She had his full attention and not just because the story involved Morgan.

Before she'd finished, he'd changed his shoes and reached for his coat.

"I'll pop to the Celyn, there'll still be plenty there to tell me if anything's happened."

"What about your supper?"

"I may hear more if I eat there. See if you can eat both pies, dear, you're looking a little thin. Get changed and warm yourself up first."

"Thanks, Dad," she said, so relieved to be taken seriously. She was grateful for his prompt, decisive action and the calming toot-toot as he drove away.

His bowl of wilting salad sat too close to the Rayburn. She stabbed a knife into the hardboard pastry and scooped the innards on to a plate from the bottom oven. The meat sizzled as it hit the scorching china: her father was obsessive about heating plates. She flicked the blackened pastry into the

Rayburn fire. One taste of the burnt meat and she was across the garden scraping it into the undergrowth. Supper for some creature and her father wouldn't see it in the bin.

It was completely dark now, but the moon had strengthened and as she turned from the hedge she saw his figure standing in the drive. There was hardly time for him to have returned the boy, but this was Morgan, who could keep up with a lurcher. He reached the back door first.

"I parked up the lane. Can I come in and explain?"

"You'd better," she said. "Why? Why the hell did you take that dear little mite and frighten him half to death?" She sat at the kitchen table.

He stood. "His father was still there in the mart field, waiting. The boy's safe, he'd only been missing for three quarters of an hour."

She got up and stamped about. "Morgan, I want the truth. Dad's gone to the Celyn to make enquiries. He could be back any minute with another side to the story."

"The boy was wandering about alone. I picked him up, rescued him."

"Rubbish, I don't believe you."

"The sale was over, there was no one on the field. I was just about to take him to the pub when I saw you leaving."

"What on earth did I have to do with it?"

"I had this image," he spoke with the same air of bewilderment as when he'd stolen the sheep. "What the three of us would look like, as a family."

"What?" she sat down shivering. The seams her waterproofs had worn thin and her wet jeans had welded to her legs. "What are you talking about?"

"A crazy vision, that's all. Without sounding insulting, it could have been any woman and any child – not for you to think I have serious intentions about you."

"Are you insane? Nothing could be further from my mind, frankly."

"I'm sorry to keep involving you, Bethan."

"That's my stupid fault. I'm keeping my distance from now on. He isn't the son of your friends: he didn't even know you. If my father comes home with a different version, I'll go straight to the police. I mean it."

He half-closed his eyes, an expression she found hard to interpret. Remorse, or a devious squint?

"Here he is now."

"You don't have any pups, do you?" she said, livid he'd heard the car first.

"I will have soon." He stood up and whisked his coat round his long legs, like Mr Gentleman on stage in his black cloak. He opened the back door almost casually, timing it right, knowing Mr Pritchard's preference for entering The Plas through the vestibule. He slipped away across the lawn, leaving the door ajar so she had to get up.

"Morgan here?" said her father. "I saw his van in the lane."

"You've just missed him," said Bethan. "He came to explain some convoluted story, but he's lying. What did you hear?"

"Absolutely nothing. I might go up to Abernant in the next few days and have a chat with him. Something's not right."

"I shouldn't bother. He's mad. By the way, you'll be pleased to know there are no collie pups."

TWELVE

Bethan was in her bedroom. She could hear her father in the loft, sorting. How he had the nerve to go on about her mother's hoarding when the ceiling joists were probably straining under the weight of newspapers, hundreds saved for interesting articles! They spent an inordinate amount of time sorting. Neither knew why; there was no mention of moving house and no one had sorted when her mother was alive.

Bethan was studying her little Fair Isle cardigan Morgan had squirted with lamb's blood all those years ago. The inside was as meticulous as the front; her mother managed this complicated mathematical process with such ease that they'd taken her exquisite knitting for granted. Bethan folded it into tissue paper then polythene to save it from the moths. Her father still wore his sleeveless Fair Isle pullover under his suit jacket, despite three moth holes in the rib.

She heard the thump of the stepladder folding.

"You there, dear?" he called. "May I come in?"

She took a moment to answer. "Okay." She was sitting in front of the window at her desk, fashioned from a door on the base of a treadle sewing machine. She anticipated his usual comment that light should come from the left, but her crumpled mart drawings caught his attention first. She'd spread them out to dry.

"Are you planning to develop any of these, dear?"

"No, too depressing." She was about to say, if only they were photographs, she might have picked out little Rhodri in the confusion of legs and sheep, but thought better of it: she didn't want to refuel her father's interest in Morgan's crackpot life. Nor did she want to revive her resentment; her father was far too concerned for him.

"Think of all those wonderful dark colours," he said. "Indigo, Payne's grey..."

"Where would you be without Payne's grey?"

He chuckled. She was all right with these light interludes, though some area of culture was usually in the offing. Had she been lolling on her bed with a magazine like a normal eighteen-year-old, he'd be running his hands through his wire-brush hair in desperation. He liked her to be 'doing'; maybe it took the onus off him regarding careers, diversions, entertainment even.

Sunday was their most difficult day of the week, with school markings overflowing his study to the breakfast room and his customary pre-school migraine brought on by the dread of Monday morning. Then there was *Dr Finlay's Casebook*, which Bethan couldn't bear to watch without her mother. Her father was sarky about the signature tune and that of *The Archers*. She and her mother had thought both very jolly.

"I'm wondering what to say to Morgan," he said. "This damn business. Did he say anything else last night?"

"Not really. He went on about his image of a family then reassured me it could have been any girl and small child, Rhodri and I just happened to be there."

"Ah, the imagination," he smiled, as if Morgan had excelled himself.

Bethan could feel despair breaking her voice. "It's nonsense, Dad, just bloody nonsense." She stared at one of her drawings, how easily she could slide a little boy into the picture, a small waify soul peering out from the sea of dark wet trousers.

"Don't be too harsh on him, dear. What is he, twenty-five or six? A lot of men are married with children by then. Maybe he sees his friends as…"

"He doesn't have any friends, Dad. And there's no need for you to go up to Abernant."

"And no need for you to get het up, dear. I'll go down and see to dinner. Can't go wrong with chicken – famous last words. And afterwards we'll talk about making a new start next week: tomorrow, in fact."

His stock phrase, making a new start. How or what it was they were going to start remained a mystery to her, but it seemed to act as a sort of solace to him. They'd skirt round a few subjects and agree to deal with them properly the following week when everything might change for the better. Their Sunday night short chats and non-starting Mondays had become such a ludicrous ritual Bethan wondered why they'd never seen the joke. Her mother would die laughing.

Bethan usually washed up after supper. Her father made such a meal of it, trying to prise the washing-up sponge down each individual prong of a fork (he'd say tine), though while drying up, he'd do the same with a tea-towel. Often when putting things away, he'd subtly introduce a topic. If it were on Bethan's future, he'd glance up at the ceiling as if Alice was hovering to offer inspiration or acknowledge he was doing his best with their only child. Tonight, after chicken, mashed potato (they failed at good roasts) and sprouts, he said, "Why don't you visit Veronica, dear? Get away for a few weeks."

"Really?" It was a big thing for him to suggest his only daughter stay with her racy cousin in a city.

"Your mother was always revived by Cecily or Veronica's company."

Bethan remembered her gazing sadly from the sitting-room window whenever they left. He promised faithfully to feed the guinea pigs, Bethan's main concern.

Veronica had arranged little plates of comforting nursery-size food: slivers of smoked salmon, black olives, delicately chopped fruit, dark squares of bitter chocolate. Uncle Bryn had told her on the phone all about Morgan and the boy.

"So, so creepy. How come you got involved?"

"I just did," Bethan didn't bother to describe Rhodri's wet pink face, dark curls, little legs clamped fiercely round her hip, his grim determination to cling on. It would have been wasted on Veronica.

"You can't help it, can you?" Veronica lit two cigarettes and handed one to Bethan. "You're obsessed by him."

"Don't be ridiculous! I can't stand him." Bethan blew the smoke straight out. "I can't even smoke properly."

"Practice. God knows what he's up to, but it's high time you escaped. Country life: please, can't think of anything worse. Your father's always lived the life of a bachelor, he'll be fine. It's your chance. And the boy is back with his parents. Come on, we'll have a nice time."

On the first day, Veronica was busy in her gallery. Bethan wandered the city then made her way up to their old house. Standing on tiptoe she could see the wall of the back garden where the guineas had run free in the daytime. The secret hollow obscured by ferns where she'd hidden sixpences in the end of a drainpipe for the brother and sister next door to discover. The three of them made a village in a disused fox den, with the boy's Corgi cars and plasticine people. Bethan had studied the siblings: the boy cried when his sister squashed his cars into the earth.

At nine she was cutting the grass with a small Atco lawn mower, carefully circling the ugly feet of the papier-mâché women. She imagined her mother alive and the three of them still living there. Veronica was right – her father would survive on his own, though her tummy gave a hot flip at the thought. She'd stay with him until their damaged hearts were repaired a little.

She returned to Veronica's flat and a welcoming committee. Veronica handed her a glass of white wine and bundled her into the middle. "Little drinks party for you to meet my friends and my man."

Bethan had heard about Veronica's man, and here he was: arty and good-looking, kissing Bethan on the cheek, saying he'd heard so much about her and couldn't wait to visit the wilds of Wales and swim in the wonderful raging rivers. He didn't look like a swimmer. He gushed on. Veronica must have portrayed the place in quite a different light from her usual damnation. Bethan's connection to her landscape suddenly felt immensely old-fashioned and a great comfort.

It seemed reasonable to excuse herself after the long walk through the streets. Concrete always got to her. She sidled out, fled to the bathroom and washed her face. Veronica had given her carte blanche to her stuffed make-up bag (the size of a handbag) and she rummaged through tubes and pots, black mascara, pale peach lipstick. If she took an age, they might forget about her. The decision of changing into some sort of outfit was too daunting, her jeans were fine and she unpacked a clean T-shirt. Veronica had made her bed with a folded-down corner of the bedspread like a hotel. Bethan would have given anything to disappear under the blankets.

Back in the spacious sitting room, she tried to sneak into a corner and drink. Swallowing felt weird, that and a churning tummy were all reminiscent of that bloody cheese and wine do. What was wrong with her? Veronica would be the first to tell her: only child, convent educated, living in ghastly isolation.

The following night the two of them went to the little cinema tucked down an alleyway which Veronica thought she'd discovered, and where Bethan had seen *Bambi* at the age of five.

The film was *If.* They walked home in stunned silence, passing old men with stiff dogs on their last constitutionals. At the fountain in the middle of the road, a girl was balancing on the low circular wall, hazy in the mist of splashing water. A tall man with his back to them seemed to be flicking water on his face, carelessly, considering his smart suit. The weather wasn't that hot.

They began their post-mortem of the film on the seventy-two stairs leading up to the flat. It had taken them that long to speak of it. Though set in a boys' school, there were many connections to their convents.

"Christ, what a film," said Veronica, going straight to the fridge for wine. "See if we can get the LP of the music tomorrow, relive our evil visions."

"I'll be gunning down Sister Margaret tonight." Bethan took a mouthful of wine. "I've just realised, that man in the suit looked like Morgan."

"Morgan! In the film? You're joking."

"No, at the fountain, splashing his face. I think he was across the road as you were unlocking the door."

"What on earth would he be doing in Bath?" Veronica swatted the idea away.

Her father rang from his school office the next morning to see how things were.

"Fine," said Bethan. "We went to the pictures last night to see *If*."

"Ah lovely, Rudyard Kipling. Wonderful."

She didn't enlighten him. When the film came to Swansea, she would take Nia and pick out the parts relevant to her torturous convent days.

"Seen anything of Morgan?" she asked her father.

"Once or twice in the distance. Don't worry: I haven't been up there, haven't had time. So you're coming home on Sunday? That's good, we can talk about starting, seriously for once. I have some news."

THIRTEEN

MORGAN SWORE LOUDLY. A lamb born in August and the aged mother wandering away. Seeing Morgan, she picked up speed as if relinquishing all rights to her bleating child dumped at the mountain gate. No point trying to catch her, she'd have no milk by the look of her, too concerned with herself to show interest in her lamb. Accidents happened, but there was no time for bottle-feeding, he was contract fencing some distance away. No one local employed him, they were too wary – yet he was the best fencer around. The lamb lay against the gate, a weakling. Waste of a cartridge. He could walk away and it would be dead in half an hour, or knock it on the head.

He picked up a stone. A figure on the hill brought Bethan to mind. Lately he'd seen her out walking; at a slower pace, head down, shoulders rounded. She never saw him. His own desolation after his father's death hadn't lasted half as long as Bethan's. Mrs Pritchard had died over a year ago. He picked up the lamb. The stable at The Plas was ideal for a *swci*.

He drove there immediately before it died. The Riley was in the drive, but there was no one about. He parked as close to the house as possible and left the van door wide open for Bethan to be swayed by pitiful bleats and was about to ring the doorbell when a grey Mini van came up the drive. He groaned inwardly: Nia. He half-expected her to sweep round and drive away at the sight of him, but Bethan was in the passenger seat and they pulled up behind him. He watched them get out, curbing a giggle, probably about him.

He looked at them anew. Young women, both with a mass of thick shoulder length hair. Nia's was as black as his own. She was surprisingly elegant; essential he supposed, for her peculiar chosen career. Bethan was a little shorter and curvier with reddish chestnut hair. Attractive girls, poles apart and good friends. Some lone men might have felt a stab of envy, but he enjoyed his solitary existence, accountable to no one.

Mr Pritchard opened the front door. "Ah, all of you! Splendid. Come in."

Morgan smiled at Bethan charmingly, wishing he could shoo Nia away.

"I thought you might like to rear an abandoned lamb." There were no accompanying bleats from his van to capture her heart.

"A lamb?" said Bethan. "But it's summer."

"Happens now and then. Rams break out, ewes you think are barren catch late. Damn nuisance. Mother's a broker, no milk, but then I'd no idea she was in lamb. Was going to knock it on the head then thought you might like to have a go at it? I've brought bottles, milk powder and a bale of straw."

"Morgan, honestly," said Nia.

Bethan stuck her head in the van and stayed there.

"Goodness knows where we'd put it," said Mr Pritchard.

"The old stable?" said Morgan. "Move the ladies over, the paper women; just adjust their deckchairs a little." He answered their questioning looks quickly. "I saw them there once when I was looking for you."

A month ago, he'd come to the stable door to find Mr Pritchard slumped in another deckchair alongside those awful paper women. He'd crept away; astonished anyone would bother constructing such useless articles when the result was grotesque. His stepmother could barely make a bed. He didn't believe in souls, but something of Mrs Pritchard must have lingered in her terrible sculptures for her husband and daughter to put such importance on them. They gave him the creeps. He'd never considered an after-life. Bethan had talked about an uncle reincarnated as a seagull and her mother as a cat. What would his father choose? Morgan often held the sepia photograph tight to his face to breathe him in, with the magnificent Welsh Cob.

"What do you think, dear?" asked her father when Bethan emerged from the van, and she beamed and nodded madly. "Righto, well I never."

"Hell of a tie," said Nia. "Have a think about it before you agree, Bethan."

"No time," said Bethan. "Poor thing's practically dead."

"Five bottles a day, but not too much: little and often or it'll get bloated," said Morgan. "Don't name it – for your sake – or pamper it, or it won't move for the dogs."

"If you're that fussy, why ask someone else to do your dirty work?" asked Nia.

"Because Bethan'll do a good job. You might as well start it off in a box in the kitchen. It's not going to go anywhere."

They all trooped inside. Mr Pritchard put the kettle on, while Bethan went in search of a box and old towel. She returned to the kitchen and to her surprise found Morgan feeding the lamb colostrum through a stomach tube. That was always the first course of action: had he done that at Abernant, it wouldn't have arrived at death's door. She didn't know about the protocol of *swci* lambs, whether she was supposed to thank him or vice versa. He obviously expected to have it back.

They all opted for tea. It was a rare sunny day and Bethan suggested they took it out to the garden. She stayed cross-legged on the kitchen floor, cradling the lamb and trying to coax its little head round to a normal position; a neck twisted back on its body was a sure sign of imminent death.

Tea taken alfresco was anathema to all three. Farmers ate inside, Nia worried about strap marks affecting her slinky dresses and Mr Pritchard preferred to take a tray into his study. They pulled wonky chairs up to the peeling table.

"I hope it lives," said Nia. When Mr Pritchard went back to the house for biscuits she lowered her voice. "All that work and Bethan looking like the cat who's swallowed the cream. You know damn well she'll devote herself to reviving that flipping lamb. If it lives, she won't want to give it back. You can be a cruel sod, Morgan."

"When your magician pins you to a revolving board, let me throw the knives."

Mr Pritchard returned carrying a plate, "Only Rich Tea, I'm afraid. The lamb doesn't look too promising."

"Just saying, Nia can work her magic on it," said Morgan. He was never anything but civil in this esteemed company and knew Nia liked and respected Mr Pritchard. The last time the two of them had been at The Plas together was the night their father died, nearly nine years ago.

"Talking of magic," said Mr Pritchard. "Did you tell Morgan about the rabbits, Nia?"

"No."

"Tell him, it's such a coincidence."

"We bought some New Zealand Whites from Elin Davies, Tŷ Newydd."

Morgan narrowed his eyes, "Really? Did you mention me?"

"Hardly." She knew she was preening.

"Good rabbits, you said, Nia," said Mr Pritchard. "Funny though: meat rabbits with no fat on them. Slender and tender, ideal for popping out of top hats."

Morgan had no desire to reveal Elin Davies' compassion for her rabbits, none of their damn business. Had Nia noticed the size of the runs, she'd know there was more concern with the rabbits' welfare than their deaths. He was shocked she had sold to a conjuror.

Bethan was coming across the grass. "Did I hear you talking about the rabbits? Fancy the woman who sold them coming to watch Nia's show."

Morgan turned sharply.

"What? Why on earth would she do that?"

"Check our magic wasn't cruel, apparently," said Nia. "She was reassured."

It was unthinkable: anxiety for her rabbits forcing her to a seedy working men's club. He would have liked to question them on her appearance, whether she was alone, the club, the date, quite forgetting he loathed her. As for Nia, sitting there all smug at his indignation.

"Bit tall for that van, aren't you?" he said. "Whatever made you choose a Mini?"

"For the odd occasion when there's no changing room at a venue. I've become an expert contortionist in confined spaces."

Mr Pritchard blew his nose. Morgan said he'd take the bale of straw from the van to the stable. He moved the women's deckchairs to the wall and built a small pen from boards and planks for the lamb's eventual graduation from the kitchen, then unearthed an old dustbin for the sack of milk powder. The others went inside.

Twenty minutes passed before they heard Morgan's van leave. By then the lamb resembled a sleeping swan, its little neck set rigid. Bethan kept it in her lap, trying to ease its head back and coax it to suck a bottle. Her father emerged from the cold pantry holding a bottle of champagne. She laid the lamb back in its box and stood up. Looking slightly embarrassed he set the bottle firmly on the kitchen table studied it for a moment then took three best glasses from the dresser.

"Bit premature, Mr P," said Nia. "I wouldn't hold out that much hope. I'm so sorry about Morgan bringing it here, he's the limit."

"No, this is for my news," he said shyly. "And it's fine about the lamb."

"Oh. Should I be here?"

"Yes, you should. I'd rather you hear it from the horse's mouth than from gossip. I didn't want to say this in front of Morgan; it could be a big blow for him. But I know you prefer your extraordinary career to farming. You seem settled with your life."

"A good man would be nice," Nia laughed. "Anyhow, I do love champagne."

"Dad, whatever is it?" Bethan couldn't imagine anything in their lives worth celebrating with champagne, an extravagance so unlike her father, who was now casting a tea towel over the cork with the panache of a head waiter. And here was her best friend quite at home admitting to a love for champagne.

"Dad, what?"

The cork popped with a dull thud and he just made it to a glass. He poured an inch of bubbles, waited for the bottle to quieten then, struck by a thought, left the room. The lamb stirred and Bethan rushed to the box. She looked at Nia, who shrugged. Her father was rummaging in the cloakroom. He returned carrying a paper bag, which he handed to Bethan. She pulled out a new metal marker for sheep and placed it on the table next to the bottle, rucking the cloths. The letter B was jigsawed out at the end of the rod.

"Well, that's definitely premature," said Nia. "It's bigger than the lamb."

He gave an awkward laugh, filled the glasses to the rim and handed them round. Twirling his hair into a unicorn horn, he raised his glass. "B for Bethan. If or when you marry, dear, you'll always be the owner of any sheep. Cheers, or chin-chin as your mother said." He took a large mouthful. "I've bought Cwmgwrach."

Bethan froze, then drained her glass in two mouthfuls. Nia was horrified then started yakking on with her usual candour, the Cwmgwrach roof, the track, the terrible cold of the place. Bethan stared at her father, who was twirling his hair for all he was worth and looking equally startled, as if he'd made a colossal mistake. Anguish crossed his face when Bethan remained dumbstruck. "Have I done the right thing, dear?" he asked tentatively, his eyes watery at the enormity of it all.

She felt a pique of joy and began to nod, little, short, unstoppable nods.

"So you'd leave this lovely house for that dump?" Nia looked exasperated.

Mr Pritchard's eyes darted round the kitchen in surprise as if he was seeing it for the first time. "I'm not sure we like it here any more," he said. He topped up everyone's champagne and raised his glass. "A toast to Bethan's farming career and to our dear Alice, who would definitely approve."

"To Bethan and Mrs Pritchard," said Nia.

"Mummy," Bethan began to smile and smile, her mouth stretching to her ears.

Bryn looked happier. Nia stared from one to the other, using every possible facial expression of a magician's apprentice.

Bethan suddenly thought of Veronica, who saw The Plas as lacking comfort. Wait till she saw inside Cwmgwrach. On Bethan's last visit to Bath, Veronica had been so desperate for her to move to civilisation, she'd arranged a river trip so there was no escape: listen to sense or drown.

"I am a sheep farmer," said Bethan. "A sheep farmer. Dad, thank you."

Nia noticed the *swci* lamb was dead, but had no intention of spoiling the moment. She could kill Morgan for bringing it.

PART THREE

ONE

CWMGWRACH STILL STOOD solid, unlike the mountain smallholdings that disintegrated the minute they were abandoned. A few roof slates were missing and a windowpane smashed, but the walls had inherited the indomitable spirit of the Williams family and the stonework was good. The farmhouse seemed injected with resilience, a presence worth preserving.

They'd all returned over the years it stood empty. On their individual pilgrimages: Morgan to fish the river and afterwards sit at the kitchen table with his flask of tea; Nia briefly, to marvel at her spartan upbringing turning to magic; Mrs Williams sat at the table in candlelight, eating fish and chips from her place of work, wrapped in double newspaper to keep hot for the trek from the village; Tomos and Steffan occasionally got drunk in the house and slept slumped untidily across the table, heads on hands. From innate shrewdness or telepathy, not one of their visits coincided.

Mr Pritchard had bought Cwmgwrach for next to nothing with a small nest egg of his wife's, with enough money over after selling The Plas for 130 sheep and a trained sheepdog. They were buying the sheep from the neighbouring lawyer who'd bought the Cwmgwrach flock; being descendants they were hefted to the same part of the hill.

Bethan tried to contain her over-excitement. She knew her father would miss his study and vestibule, but the farmhouse had as many rooms as The Plas. He was ambivalent about taking on the Williamses' kitchen table until she pointed out the extra space it would give them for books and so on. The roofer said it was made in the house and the only way to get it out was as firewood. When he raised his axe to it Bethan screeched "Stop!" She'd rather have chopped up the octagonal table at The Plas, where her mother's pile of stuff had become a shrine to be faced at every mealtime. She didn't have the heart to go through it; every time she changed the cloth she replaced the empty packets, knitting patterns and paper bags, patting them neat in a morose ritual, though an empty space would have been more poignant. In the end her father agreed the table suited The Plas and they would leave it.

Bethan knew Cwmgwrach intimately: the house, barns, doors and gates that needed lifting to close and bolts that need jiggling. As a small girl, the gloom, bare walls and stark passageways had been a gothic fairytale.

The builders scraped the black masticky stuff (Mr Williams swore it cured damp) from the floors and prised crumbling hardboard from bedroom fireplaces and banisters. The house shook itself down with gratitude and began to breathe again.

Nia set to with sugar-soap and manic vigour, scrubbing her family away. "Diesel, dirt, boiling tripe, ugh, I can still taste them," she said in a fury. "Filthy bastards, oops sorry Mr P."

"Not at all, dear – jolly decent of you to help. Any news of Morgan? He hasn't been near us for months. I'd like to see him, know how he is."

"Oh, that'll be all about land, a reminder of the nine-acre feud. Don't you worry, buying Cwmgwrach was out of the question for him anyway, but it'll have stirred up some nonsense in his warped brain. Probably the last straw."

"I'd hate to upset him. And how will it be for you seeing us in your old home?

"Fine. My departure from Cwmgwrach was a magical transition for me," said Nia, always hoping to appeal to his penchant for words.

"Very good." He took an old wallpaper scraper to the soot coating the range chimney. "Yes, to find a gentlemanly magician offering an apprenticeship and pleasant accommodation was a wonderful turn of events for you. Tell me, does your training include ventriloquism?"

"Dad," said Bethan. "That's not magic." She filled a kettle and lit the little primus stove; if he got a move on they could use the old Rayburn. "Tea or coffee?"

"Coffee, please," said Nia. "Actually, the thought of my words coming from another being, even made of wood, does sound appealing. I could reinvent my awful family, sit them on my knee and question them – magic them into civilised human beings."

"You'd have to stick your hand up their bottoms and through their innards," said Bethan and they got the giggles and made a show of retching.

Her father went to the window and stared outside.

"Alice and I were great movers. Interesting business reinventing oneself."

Bethan was scratching at flagstones with wire-wool. "The Plas was my fourth home. I was ten." She readjusted her mother's wrecked gardening gloves.

"Morgan probably can't trust himself to visit you at the moment," said Nia. "However vile he is, he wouldn't want to blight your excitement. He thinks too much of you both. Let's have this coffee and slap some emulsion on the walls. By the time we stick up all your paintings, we won't recognise the place. Where will the paper ladies live, in the cowshed?"

Mr Pritchard smiled, grateful for her assumption that his wife's mad women were even making the move. The last three had virtually fallen apart. "Probably."

Bethan knew her father was as enamoured by Nia as he was by Morgan and she often felt superfluous to their conversations. Not that she minded. Nia brought out a lighter side of her father and her visits were a godsend, especially since her mother's death. She arrived on the morning of the move, her usual chatterbox self, with a chocolate cake and bottles of cider. Bethan couldn't have wished for more. The trauma of moving had hit her the minute she woke.

The Cwmgwrach track was too narrow and precarious for anything like the removal lorry that transported their Bath household. They'd hired two smaller vans that travelled up and down all day.

Nia showed Bethan a pile of thin sticks. "My mother grew raspberries. She snapped these canes into pieces the morning we left here, so no one else could use them; cut her hand on one. That's what I mean about my family." She threw the bits into the air.

"Talking of your mother, shall we have fish and chips for supper later?"

"We'll make up three beds first, and I'll stay and help tomorrow, if you like."

"Definitely. Thanks so much, Nia,"

Bethan had vivid memories of her first evening at The Plas. Their largest house yet, she'd run up and down the red-carpeted stairs and along the landing till she could barely breathe. Her parents seemed lost. They placed the octagonal table against the north-facing breakfast room window with the big old wireless at the furthest edge and the three of them ate a cobbled-together supper like strangers, their awkwardness palpable. All was fine once they'd nested. Her father chose a small reception room for a study and her mother took up residence in front of the breakfast room fire. Each end of the fender was a coal box with a padded top where she'd sat reading and knitting, swapping ends when she remembered, to even up the mottled scorch marks on her legs.

Now her father sat in the Cwmgwrach kitchen, staring at the mantelpiece. Bethan had been quietly obsessing about the layout of their stuff; everything from The Plas apart from the octagonal table had come with them, as it had from Bath and their previous homes. She was about to ask Nia what she'd taken to her flat, then remembered she hardly owned anything. She asked about the bowl of marbles on her mantelpiece.

"Morgan gave them to my younger brother, would you believe? I found them buried in ash in my mother's bonfire and scrubbed them up for memory's sake. He probably nicked them from somewhere."

"Nia!" Mr Pritchard frowned with smiley eyes.

When he left to collect the fish and chips, Bethan went outside on the pretence of checking the guinea pigs. On the face of it, apart from their immediate view, nothing in their lives would have changed, but she needed a few minutes alone. The upheaval of moving to The Plas – in a different country, where many of their neighbours spoke a different language – paled into insignificance against this move. She crossed the yard then ran with a new energy up through two fields to the top track, stopped and turned then stood for five minutes surveying the land below: a glint of river in woodland and acres of rough grass.

When she returned, Nia had laid the table, opened the cider, and poured it into three glasses.

"Talking about those marbles, I keep them to remind myself what an evil old cow my mother was, trying to burn them, and just how unpredictable Morgan is. I can still see my little brother's face when Morgan poured them out of his coat sleeves into his dirty little hands. There must have been fifty. At least."

TWO

THE TŶ NEWYDD sale was to start at ten. When Morgan first saw the advertisement, he imagined divorce for the Davieses and a farm dispersal. However, it was merely a reduction sale.

He was going for several reasons: to sneak a look at Elin, and Rhodri maybe, and for the chance of bumping into the Pritchards on neutral ground; they could be there for some sort of agricultural equipment for their new venture. On hearing they were buying Cwmgwrach, he'd gone to ground. His feelings were too complex to even visit The Plas on the pretence of borrowing a book. Now they were installed in Cwmgwrach, he hadn't spoken to them in six months. He'd seen them; they hadn't seen him.

He went outside to feed the dogs. Ready for work, they devoured the bread and tripe in seconds and swung round for attention. He was watching the grey mist smoking over the horizon. He returned to the kitchen, finished the cold toast then changed into clean working clothes.

Money next, in case he saw something worth buying at the sale. He edged furtively along the crumbling wall to the fireplace as if keeping a lookout for spies, laughing out loud at the likelihood. Most of the village people had only heard of Abernant. He took his knife to the crumbling wall and scraped out a stone. As always, his heart raced, preparing for the sight of the scrunched-up paper bag, but equally the possibility of its absence. The latter could mean an intruder as devious as himself, instigating a mystery that (perversely) he might enjoy, almost worth losing his stash. But the brown bag never failed to appear, tissue thin, sticky with damp cobwebs and fat with cash. He took out a wad of twenty-pound notes, gauged the rough amount by its thickness, stuffed them into his overalls and rammed the rest back into its niche.

Boots on, he went outside. Ness trotted to the gate and whinnied with surprise when he ignored her and walked straight on, flattening a dark path through the dew-wet grass. It was a fair distance up across the mountain, past the lake, even if he strode out with a good pace.

Tŷ Newydd was partly hidden under a floating haze with the watery sun doing its best to filter through the silhouetted trees. He could make out the toy-sized buildings with lorries creeping in round them and, when closer, vague outlines of livestock sardined into rows of pens huffing out steamy breath. When he arrived, it was from the opposite direction to everyone else and he was probably the only buyer on foot. Familiar with every inch of the farm he climbed a low fence into a back field and merged with the crowd before too many noticed him. Those who did discreetly stepped aside and those who acknowledged him scanned the crowd to make sure they hadn't been seen. He was well aware of all that.

This would be the third time he and Davies had met since their one-sided fight on the mountain. The first was in the farm stores, both buying work boots, and they'd conversed for a few minutes as though nothing untoward had happened. Davies seemed more concerned over the appalling sheep prices than his wife's adultery, leaving Morgan astonished and indignant on her behalf.

That day at the mart they'd exchanged no more than a curt hello. Morgan had watched Davies earlier in the day, carrying his exhausted child back to the parking field, presumably for a sleep while the sheep were being loaded. The old Land Rover was never locked: it wasn't worth pinching. The boy was though. Morgan had lifted him from his seat and walked a little way with him still sound asleep. God knows what would have happened if he hadn't had the good fortune to see Bethan. Seconds after Rhodri woke it was her face that greeted him.

If only Davies knew Morgan had witnessed him weeping.

Morgan had half-expected the mart field to be swarming with police, but then realised it suited Davies to keep quiet. With publicity in the newspapers, the boy's mother would have killed him for such negligence. Perhaps he'd never owned up to her precious son going missing, albeit for less than an hour. She was essential to the running of Tŷ Newydd.

These days Davies was reputed to barely leave the farm and hadn't been seen at any mart since. He'd certainly no time for idle chat today. He actually looked as though he'd been expecting Morgan. They nodded. Morgan crossed the grass to the auctioneers' caravan for a catalogue. Fortunately no rabbits were listed: he'd no wish to see Nia and her magician.

Half the farmers and neighbours gathered round the refreshment van would be here from nosiness. Ignoring the smell of sizzling bacon he moved on. He shied from queues and his stomach recoiled at the sight of heavily-paunched farmers stuffing faces already scarlet from whisky and ketchup. At least the walk had cleared his head. He worked through the pens: they were good sheep.

Then he saw the mare. In a vain attempt to quieten her, she was penned next to six Welsh Black cattle, her companions on the hill. Davies had done nothing to prepare her for the sale; Morgan couldn't understand the man. The sun caught the shine in her coat, but her mane and tail hung in stiff matted locks. Wild-eyed, she crashed round the tiny pen, hitting her hocks against the galvanised bars. The imprisoned cows were no calmer. Brought from the hills at first light, they bellowed in confusion, rolled their eyes and barged each other. Morgan thought of Elin Davies' Guernseys standing patiently in the milking parlour – although they could have their moments.

He was thumbing through the catalogue when something knocked his boot. An old collie was stumbling past; her dull coat as matted as the mare's mane, dusty clumps of grey fur that had once been black and white.

"Interested?"

Morgan looked round. Davies inclined his head towards the old dog. At the sound of his voice she slumped to the ground, her gaze fixed to her master. "She's still got a bit of work in her, round the yard and that. Another year or so." He poked his boot under the dog's stomach and lifted her clumsily to her feet. "This old bitch I mean." The dog gazed at Davies with devotion. Davies scrutinised Morgan, who took a step back.

"You're selling her?" Morgan said incredulously. "How old is she?"

"Coming up fourteen. Putting her in at the end of the sale if you're interested."

"When she's worked her guts out for you? You bastard."

Davies took a second to react. He lurched forward, hand bunched into a fist, then instantly – aware of onlookers – dropped his arm. "Someone will have her."

Morgan turned away. He wasn't sentimental, but there were limits. Surely she deserved to end her days in her own home after a lifetime of gathering the mountain. Davies moved through the crowd, the dog tight to his heels.

Morgan looked up at the farmhouse; every window shone black and the upstairs curtains were closed. No sign of movement. He hadn't set eyes on her for an age, perhaps she and the boy had finally left. He turned his attention to the catalogue; the mare was number 56. Now the refreshments van was deserted, he bought a mug of tea.

"Nice little mare for you now, boys," announced the auctioneer. "Shown in hand today, but she is broken. Just been running on the mountain for a while," he gave Davies a cursory glance, "Ever since Mr Davies invested in a quad."

Davies grimaced. He'd led the pony into the ring on too long a rope, doing his utmost to display her properly. She pranced and twisted round him.

"Good and lively, do you well," said the auctioneer. "Who'll start me? There were a few imperceptible nods and winks before they'd completed a circuit of the ring, the mare fussing and messing around. Morgan's subtle eyebrow movement came in and the gavel fell. "Sold to Mr Morgan Williams. Thank you, everyone."

"Come on, man, she hasn't reached the reserve," Davies shouted on hearing the name. "That's not even meat price."

"No reserve on her, Mr Davies, I'm afraid."

A drover took the pony and handed Davies another rope. His old collie gazed up at the livid face and shuffled into the ring, close to his side.

"Right, gentlemen." The auctioneer made no effort to disguise the disgust in his voice. "Now we have Mr Davies' elderly bitch, who apparently still has plenty of work left in her, round a yard. Nice kind old dog. She could sit by your fire in her retirement. Who'll start me?"

More than half the crowd left the ring.

When all monies had changed hands and men began to load lorries and trailers, a group of farmers paused to watch Morgan slip a doubled length of baler twine through the mare's head-collar.

"Daniel to the lion's den."

"Out of the frying pan into the fire."

The mare whirled one circular dance round Morgan as he led her from the pen, then settled as they came through the crowd. He walked in long even strides; she jogged alongside, facing him with her rear end outwards. Coming to the farmhouse, he leapt on to her back, expecting her to rear in protest and together they could put on a show in case she was looking. Either the pony didn't dare or had decided to behave. It moved forward in quiet imitation of a dressage horse performing under an elaborate bridle rather than tatty head-collar and bareback rider. An upstairs curtain twitched. The mare was too small for him, though he sensed they made a handsome couple.

He thought about her less these days. He still loathed her for ending their affair, but was secretly grateful for her lascivious initiation. Every rendezvous had thrilled him. But he'd lived without sex before her and since. He'd no interest in casual relationships. Occasionally he reflected on the gallery launch, locking eyes with Veronica at the piano, singing for all he was worth and the seductive looks she cast his way.

He and the mare crossed the mountain with ease and joint knowledge of the terrain. They passed below Craig Siglo, where she'd grazed next to Ness while Davies punched him, then sat and calmly lit his pipe.

This mare was a whim, an unnecessary purchase, but it had felt more and more vital to have something of Elin's. If he couldn't have the boy then the mare.

He could ride out with Veronica; he needed to set his sights on something. He'd followed her and her boyfriend on a boat trip, stalked them from Pulteney Bridge all along the riverbank from tree to tree, then squirming through people's gardens. The ignorant pair chugged past ducks and swans, Veronica and whatever his name was. Or he could sell the mare to the Pritchards for gathering – maybe give her as a peace offering. Money didn't interest him, as long as there was enough for rent and sheep feed.

The Pritchards hadn't turned up today. He so regretted his withdrawal from the most significant people in his life. His reappearance had become more and more difficult with time and would soon be out of the question.

He'd kept an eye on their building work, creeping to Cwmgwrach after the builders had left, but there was never any sign of them. Their renovations were basic, which surprised and confused him further. One day he'd feel pleased to see little change, the next he'd rather the whole lot flattened and no one inhabit the place.

Spying on the exhausted father and daughter on their moving day, he was fuming to see Nia involved. The small removal vans continued for most of the day, when he could have offered his tractor, trailer and himself.

Ness whinnied her disapproval when Morgan arrived in the yard on the new mare. Betrayal.

"You grazed together," he spoke to them both. "Remember, while I received my hiding?" He'd keep them in adjoining fields for a while; mares could be funny sometimes.

The auctioneer hadn't said her name and he hadn't thought to ask. She had a tiny white star on her brow. He'd call her Seren.

THREE

Bethan was looking out of the kitchen window vaguely thinking about supper. She'd fallen into her mother's role of producing some sort of haphazard evening meal and trying not to resent it. It wasn't that arduous for her to rustle something up during her farming day, and if it weren't for her father, she wouldn't have a farming day. Fortunately, he wasn't too bothered about food and once whisked a salad off to his painting shed to "capture the wonderful design and colours": nasturtium leaves, flowers, orange slices and mint sprigs. Bethan had droned on about the new potatoes congealing in crystallised butter and going cold.

The ewes were in the field above the house. She was watching them saunter through the trees when something closer caught the corner of her eye, a flash of movement on the footpath circling the yard. She ran to the window over the sink.

A pony and rider were slithering down the bank. The rider was flat on his back to help the pony's steep descent. They bounced on to the track and the rider sat up. Morgan, but he wasn't on Ness. He was tying the pony to the gatepost and coming in. Bethan called out to her father. She'd opened the back door before Morgan came round the corner. "Well, stranger," she said, and saw him mistake this for hostility.

The door opened straight into the kitchen. No one used the front door.

"Morgan, how the devil are you?" said Mr Pritchard, almost hopping with delight, desperate to shake hands and usher their unexpected visitor inside. "Come in, have a drink. I was hoping we hadn't upset you, taking on your childhood home."

As Morgan began to shake his head the phone rang.

"I'll get that," said Bethan, relieved. By her father's effusive welcome, Morgan might well enough have risen from the dead. With the back door still open, the outside telephone bell her father insisted on installing doubled the noise of the ring. She'd barely finished her hello before Veronica started.

"Bethan. Morgan was loitering outside my flat last night. You were right: it must have been him the night we saw *If*. Have you seen him yet?"

"Yes, just," said Bethan.

"He's there now, is he?"

"That's right. Are you okay?"

"It was so bloody spooky, him standing across the road staring up at my windows, for what seemed like hours. I know this sounds awful:" she gave a short bitter laugh, "I was about to finish with Simon, but I might wait for a bit. Look, I can't bear to think of you with a loopy neighbour. How long have you been in that ghastly place now?"

"A month. You know I have a dog."

"I do, just keep talking about him. If Morgan comes again, I'll call the police."

"So good to have my dog at last, I know you're not keen, but he's great, dead sharp and handsome."

"How I once thought of Morgan. Is he in the house? Morgan, not the dog."

"Both are actually. He's tri-coloured, lovely tan eyebrows."

"Say my name and look at him. Morgan, not the dog."

Morgan was sitting at his old table, staring down at the surrounding clutter.

"Well, glad the gallery's going well, Veronica," said Bethan. "Yes, come and stay when you get a chance."

Mr Pritchard grimaced and sent his regards to his niece. There was an almost imperceptible movement in Morgan's hands, resting on the table.

"Did he flinch?" asked Veronica. "Blush, anything at all?"

"Very slightly. But it might clear up later. Bye then." She made a point of peering out at the drizzle as she went to the dresser for cups.

Mr Pritchard had set the percolator going on the stove. The Rayburn was out. Bethan had been busy outside and her father was no good with fires; he'd always praised her mother's "black fingers", and now hers. Her mother had relished the compliment; Bethan was more cynical. He'd never liked tending the fire.

"Veronica well, dear?" he asked. "Still going out with what's-his-name?"

Bethan stared hard at Morgan as she replied.

"Simon. Yes, she is. And she's fine."

Morgan's eyes flashed, he fiddled with a stray envelope, sliding it back and forth on the table.

"The dog living inside then?" he said. "Working alright?"

"Yes. Considering he was trained by a man, he's getting used to my voice." Glen looked up at her and flipped his tail.

"He already adores you, dear," said her father.

"Looks like it," said Morgan.

Bethan beamed.

Her father moved to the stove as the percolator bubbled. "How are you for reading matter, Morgan? I'm two-thirds through *War and Peace*. Have you tried it?"

"Yes, I have."

A glow flooded Mr Pritchard's face. The percolator showered coffee over the stove.

"Dad, the coffee!" said Bethan. "Think I'll leave you both to it." Glen rose the minute she walked to the door and nudged her boots over in excitement, already a habit. She shut him outside while she put them on.

Morgan might have thought she'd left. She could hear him saying he'd actually been reading *War and Peace* over the last few months. What better reason for his absence? He might not be lying. Her father would be bursting for a lengthy analytical discussion and Morgan would expect nothing less.

Bethan went straight to the pony, who was tied too high to snatch the bit of growth round the gatepost. She picked some grass and stroked its neck while it ate. Considering its connection with Morgan, it seemed relatively calm. She had her back to the house in sight of the kitchen window, not that they'd look out. Her father would be heaping books onto the table for Morgan to choose and sign the notebook to acknowledge the loan.

She knew she'd seen him in Bath that time. They were entertaining a peeping tom. Her father was the most animated she'd seen him for months, obviously gladdened by Morgan's reappearance.

Veronica knew Bethan had wanted a dog since she could walk. On hearing they'd bonded, Veronica laughed: surely dogs were devoted to whoever feeds them. Bethan said Glen would die for her, nothing to do with food. And now this:

Morgan suffering from the same fanatical devotion. Bethan wondered how often and how long he'd been keeping watch, the insidious creep. That damn gallery launch, Veronica flirting away.

She gave the pony a final pat and climbed the bank, Glen at her heels. They'd check the sheep and by then Morgan should have left; he couldn't carry more than a couple of books on the pony. She hoped to God her father didn't invite him to stay for a meal. He was so pleased to see him she decided not to mention Bath and Veronica. She'd kept most of Morgan's misdemeanours secret from him, apart from the boy.

By the time she returned, an hour had passed and the pony was still there. A water bucket had been placed at the gate. It was still unfair. If the front door weren't jammed, she'd have tiptoed through the house to eavesdrop on whatever Morgan was finding more important. Passing the kitchen window with the briefest glance inside, she had the feeling the room was empty. She opened the back door and switched on the light. Her father's were the only boots by the door, cups and coffee pot next to the sink and, apart from his usual pile, not a book in sight. She found him in the study in front of his typewriter, one hand propping his head, the other corkscrewing his hair.

"Honestly, Morgan's the bloody limit," she started. "He's gone without the pony, how the hell could he forget her?"

"Bethan. Ah." He pushed his typewriter away and turned to face her. The corkscrew was perfect: Nia could have magicked it into metal and opened a bottle. "She's still tied to the gate because I hadn't a clue what to do with her. Morgan insisted you needed a pony to gather the mountain; he actually wanted to give her to us." He looked more anxious than when he'd broken the news of buying Cwmgwrach.

"What?" Bethan flopped into the armchair.

"I've bought her. We have hay and straw, don't we, and buckets – that sort of thing? He said she should be the right size for you."

"Dad!" She hugged him, kissing his emery-board cheek with a surge of tenderness that shocked her. He rubbed her kiss in for posterity, not to be hurtful. They were hopeless at touching. "She's perfect."

"Get the poor thing untied and installed somewhere comfortable. She's called Seren, the Welsh for 'star' – rather nice, isn't it?" He smiled thankfully as if relieved of some dreadful burden. He often wore a look of confusion, as if he'd mislaid the rulebook on rearing motherless daughters. He'd joked about sending her to finishing school. Auntie Cecily had packed Veronica off to Switzerland for valuable lessons like how not to tread on a ballgown while descending a staircase. Finished. Like a lamb. It was impossible to finish a lamb on a poor hill farm – she could just hear Veronica's triumphant "Exactly!" But then a finished lamb was ready for slaughter.

The pleasure of slitting and spreading a bale of straw for her own pony was overwhelming, however dilapidated the barn. Bethan stabbed the pitchfork into the wads, flung them around and pictured her mother's joy as she led the mare into fresh knee-deep bedding. Being an atheist, her father never came out with inane platitudes like "Mum's looking down on you." Bethan made exceptions.

She phoned Nia, not expecting much enthusiasm. Bethan's new life was Nia's idea of drudgery, one she couldn't wait to escape; though she did sound genuinely pleased. Once she knew where Seren had come from, her attitude changed immediately. She talked about Morgan re-entering their lives with a vengeance and that any pony of his would have a savage temperament and no doubt kick or bite, or both.

Bethan couldn't begin to think of Seren as a rogue pony.

She didn't bother phoning Veronica, though she was fond of horses. It was only a matter of time before she would ring again to discuss Morgan. She was obviously stirred-up and curious, agitated by a sly man she barely knew. The phone rang soon after supper. "I thought you said he'd all but disappeared from your lives, but he's there again. Did he mention me at all, give any hints?"

"No. Believe it or not, he came to give us a pony. Give! But Dad paid him."

"What! I hope it doesn't have his devious character."

"Just what Nia said."

They talked about the mare, her size and colour until Veronica lost interest. Bethan suspected she would soon be paying a visit, if only to sneak up the mountain and lurk round Abernant. She thought about the implications of Seren being a gift. Maybe Morgan was trying to impress Veronica with his generosity.

On the opposite wall her bookcase leaned slightly to one side with the weight, exactly as it had at The Plas. Her childhood animal books still filled two shelves. *Black's Veterinary Dictionary* stood out, recently acquired in a second-hand bookshop in Swansea.

FOUR

A HINT OF nervousness began to creep in. Her father asked if she was all right on her own all day. Nia rang one evening and said, "Don't be frightened to…" and Bethan said she wasn't frightened and what was wrong with everyone.

"I was going to say don't be frightened to ask for help at lambing time, even though I hate bloody sheep. And don't forget the first Cwmgwrach lamb is always born on St David's Day, whatever date the rams went in. Pens ready?"

"Yes, and I've cleaned the shed."

"Anything wrong, Bethan?"

"No." Nothing she could put her finger on. It was probably all in her mind, but there were a few times since speaking to Veronica when she'd seen movement in the woods on the opposite side of the river. Long sessions of concentrated staring from her bedroom window had given her intimate knowledge of every boulder, tree and branch. Whenever she spotted a slightly different shape to a tree trunk then looked back to find it vanished, she convinced herself it was a flap of Morgan's coat or one of his lean limbs jutting out and he was spying on Cwmgwrach. He should know Veronica would hardly visit so close to lambing, risk getting her hands dirty.

After they'd hung up, Bethan noticed the thin triangle of blood seeping round her nail. She bit off the peeled skin and sucked her stinging finger. At school, the whole class had threaded needle and cotton through the fleshiest part of their thumbs. They put it down to nerves. Miserable convent girls with thumbs like pincushions.

It was after ten when Bethan heard the chug of the engine. Morgan had bought an old Land Rover when his post office van died. There were no headlights, to prove he could see in the dark – not until he swung round the last bend, when they flashed on and off in case he hit a cat in the yard, maybe. Glen barked. Bryn was engrossed in school stuff in his study. Bethan had found a lame Abernant ewe on their side of the river. Morgan was coming to collect it.

She squeezed her bloody finger and stepped out into the night. He'd parked next to her Land Rover. Hers was even older, with no first gear and she had to thump the driver's door open with her shoulder. Even so, it completed her dream.

"It's in the cowshed." She pointed needlessly and retreated embarrassed into the lamp-lit kitchen, leaving the door ajar. Through the gap she watched him move swiftly across the uneven stones, disappear into the cowshed and emerge with the small ewe clasped to his chest. He gave the door that lift and extra jiggle it took for the latch to drop, as he must have done a million times. When he'd shut the ewe into the back of the Land Rover, he turned towards the house.

Bethan ducked back and willed him to go. Just go. He couldn't expect to come in now and it was late enough to reasonably not invite him. Then her father was stretching round her to open the door and snap on the main light.

"Why are you in the dark, dear? Ah Morgan, collecting your ewe? Bethan found it down by the river."

She nodded and stepped back. "Last year's lamb."

"Do you fancy a drink of something, Morgan, warm you up?" asked Mr Pritchard.

"Thank you," Morgan kicked his boots off and came inside. "How's the mare going, well behaved enough for you?"

"She's good, thank you." Maybe he was spying from the woods to check her progress with the mare. She could hear the young ewe crashing round the bare Land Rover, anyone else would be keen to get it home. He sat down at his old table and before she'd closed the back door, the ewe had given up and gone quiet. Mr Pritchard offered tea, whisky or cocoa and they agreed on whisky.

Bethan thought of going to bed, but apart from her own curiosity, she'd promised Veronica to report back on any news or contact with Morgan. To occupy herself, she set up the ironing board, expecting a comment from her father, but he didn't notice. She folded clothes onto the Rayburn lid, never ironed. Her arm swept back and forth across blouses, even sheets and towels, as she listened to their conversation and threw in the odd comment. At midnight she found herself making ham sandwiches. Eventually their discussion veered from literature to fencing.

"I hear you're the expert," said Mr Pritchard. "Would you be willing to fence for us?"

"No, no," Bethan said quickly. The thought of him working in her fields was too much. The only half-decent fence on Cwmgwrach was the perimeter; to redo every field would take months. "We don't need it yet."

"I thought we were desperate?" He looked at her in surprise. "You were saying that gathering will be a nightmare."

"My father kept the walls intact in his days here," said Morgan.

"We've barely started," she said. Her hot glare met his black eagle eyes. She was well aware they followed her every move: up and down to the fridge, the ironing, cutting bread, pouring drinks. Most times she wouldn't have waited on them, tonight she just wanted to keep on the move. He'd hardly changed since she first met him. Few lines round his mouth or cheeks; but then his smiles were like the sun, rare, fleeting and equally powerful on the odd occasions they appeared.

"Oh, it'll come," he murmured, annoying her further.

"Perhaps we'll sort out what exactly we need, then contact you," said her father, seeing her face. "The new people at The Plas, have you met them yet? Charming family, North Walian. We're invited to dinner once they're settled, apparently. Is that why you're ironing, dear?"

"Of course he's met them," said Bethan. And if he hadn't, he'd know everything about them; in between jaunts to Bath.

"Jolly keen gardeners," continued her father, undeterred. "That would please Alice."

"I hope that ewe's alright," she said. "No straw, no water to drink." She looked at the whisky bottle three-quarters empty. Morgan had forgotten all about the little lame ewe, he'd crash home and probably leave it in the Land Rover overnight. She grabbed the bottle as though about to whack somebody.

"*Iesu mawr*, I've just noticed the time," he said. "I'm sorry to keep you up."

"Not at all," said Mr Pritchard. "Excellent to see you again. Now don't stay away."

She took the glasses and plates to the sink. Her father accompanied Morgan to the back door and she stopped clattering the washing-up to listen. Morgan was in the yard when she heard him say he could start the fencing whenever they liked. The Land Rover started up. No headlights flashed through the kitchen, maybe it was more from his feral instinct to lie low than a statement of bravado. She imagined his mother hissing "Lie low" in his baby ear before abandoning him, words not understood at the time but forever ingrained.

The engine of the invisible Land Rover faded. His stealthy ways intrigued her. He couldn't bear anyone knowing his movements, but who and why would anyone be keeping watch in the early hours to see him drive away from Cwmgwrach? It was an arrogance; as if anyone was remotely interested.

Her father closed the back door. "Fancy, he's definitely read *War and Peace*."

"Really, Dad, I'd rather we asked someone else to fence."

"I thought he was the best fencer around – even those who don't like him say so."

"No one likes him."

"I prefer to make up my own mind, dear. He hasn't done anything against me."

"Yet."

The wind got up about two. She hadn't slept. Her book had been riveting before tonight, now the same paragraph blurred as her eyes finally drooped to a slit and closed. The book fell to the floor and alerted her. She found her place and bookmark, but the minute she switched off the lamp and curled back down, she was wide awake. The sound of rain joined the wind and she remembered the Williamses' dread of cold rain during lambing, those endless weeks drifting into a couple of months. The ramshackle sheds at Cwmgwrach were all but useless. Morgan was quite right; they had a lifetime's work rebuilding the farm.

She tightened the bedding around her. The rain tapped the window like birds' beaks. She considered getting up and making a drink but pulled the blankets over her head and stuck her fingers in her ears. With the tapping on the glass came another noise. She slipped out of bed, tweaked open an inch of curtain and shot back. She didn't think the tree in the yard was close enough to reach the window, yet a branch was thrashing across the glass like a windscreen wiper. She opened the curtains another inch. The branch appeared to retract a little and slowed until just the tips of the leaves were tickling the glass in arched wand-like movements. She crawled back into bed and lay perfectly still.

It was three when the wind picked up again. Leaves faster and louder, hitting the window, movements too regular for the wildness of any wind. Downstairs one of the cats was meowing: they must have forgotten to put him out and he sounded desperate. She slid out of bed. Her father's bedroom was at the far end of the landing, but so as not to wake him she crept along in the dark. The old Bakelite light switches snapped on and off like fire-crackers.

In the kitchen, she opened the back door and the cat strolled through, now totally blasé about being in or out. Bethan stood on the back step to inhale the smouldering bonfire she'd lit earlier, tempted to sneak through the kissing gate and poke the hot cinders back into flames. She shared Mrs Williams' passion for a good fire, using the circle of black stones where the widow had burnt her husband's clothes. Her eyes adjusted to the dark. She saw a thin, straight plume of blue smoke. The night was as calm as the day, and the branch bashing her bedroom window as still as the rest of the tree.

FIVE

ORGAN ACQUIRED A telephone and a bathroom in the
same week. He felt immensely pleased with himself.
The phone was paid for by a fencing job on a large farm where
the farmer was ripping out a white cast-iron bath in favour
of a primrose bathroom suite for a new wife. Beyond belief
to Morgan. A Swansea plumber turned the fourth bedroom
at Abernant into a bathroom, creating an extraordinary
surprise in a virtually derelict house. Morgan made countless
unnecessary visits to admire his new luxury.

Improving a rented farmhouse wouldn't have occurred
to him, but aside from his own fastidiousness, a bathroom
offered other possibilities. He played out scenes. Veronica,
after several gins, asking for the lavatory and expecting an
outside *tŷ bach* only to be led through the dark, shabby hall, up
uncarpeted stairs and along bare floorboards, where he would
throw open the bathroom door. Or he could merely direct her
and wait downstairs for the shriek of amazement.

The new black telephone sat on a pristine directory on the
kitchen windowsill. On his next out-of-the-village shopping
spree he purchased bath oil specifically for relaxing tired
muscles and a telephone book. He made the vet his first entry.
Once he knew their numbers, the Pritchards and Veronica
would be added next.

He was no drinker, but the only way he could think of celebrating his achievements was to call at the Celyn. He'd done little more than hang around outside as a teenager, had occasionally been inside as an adult, but usually went straight home after the mart, leaving the other farmers to drink to success or drown sorrows.

Tonight, a wet Monday, the place was too quiet to employ the barmaid. He'd never liked the idea of perching at the bar like most lone drinkers, but despite him moving to a table, the bored landlady still managed to target him for a chat. She flattened her glittery bosom half across the bar and spoke with a familiarity and accommodating smile that might have set him on edge had he not been emboldened by two pints of his father's favourite beer.

Gradually he obliged and half-heartedly fell in with her conversation. She brought him over another pint – her treat, she laughed, to encourage him to become a regular. When she joined him at the small circular table, he realised with a jolt she was talking about the woman who'd given birth to him, his real mother. He bought her a gin and orange. Satisfied with his full attention, she wiggled back in her chair and folded her arms, now content with her lot for a dreary Monday night.

"The previous landlady found you, my predecessor," she said. "She was a bit of a witch, brought you back to life with her potions. Then somehow, years later, she caught up with her runaway barmaid – your mother."

He leant forward. "Is she dead?"

"No. Your mother went a bit loopy and was whisked off to a nursing home on the outskirts of Cardiff. Apparently she's by far the youngest resident, but there's nowhere else for her to go. It's all wrong." She flapped back to the bar for another gin, making no attempt to disguise her enjoyment in telling the tale.

He nodded. His mother's madness was the first shock, then her age. According to this landlady, she'd given birth to him in her forties. He'd never imagined anything other than a slip of a girl turning his father's head. Maybe he'd inherited his taste for older women: Elin was ten years his senior and Veronica three.

Without asking whether he'd like them, the landlady had already written the nursing home details on the back of an envelope and pushed it across the table. He slid it into his pocket, refused another pint and left the pub.

His Land Rover was the only vehicle in the rough old car park. He sat there, stunned. Then with a blunt pencil he made the third entry in his new telephone book, then a fourth and fifth and so on, flipping the pages, writing at random: 'Abandonment' in A, 'Runaway' in R, 'Bitch', 'Heartless' and so on. At P he felt slightly calmed by the sight of Bryn and Bethan Pritchard. Before adding his mother's name, he wrote 'Purgatory', a word unknown to him until Bethan had introduced it, but it seemed appropriate for his situation. Finally he wrote 'Megan Price'.

He went as soon as he could, before lambing occupied every hour of the day. The nursing home was an impressive manor house on the edge of a village outside Cardiff. He tucked the empty box, gift wrapped in gold paper, under his arm and rang the bell. He still had time to change his mind. It felt like a full minute before a haze of pale blue uniform wafted slowly to unlock the frosted glass door. A pale woman asked the name of the person he was visiting.

"Sign the book, name and time. She'll be flipping about round the back sitting-room or in the garden – can't keep her still," she looked at him properly. "Are you a relative?"

"I haven't seen her for a long time," he said.

"She won't know you," she said and walked off.

He stood in the stale heat. The visitors' book lay open beneath a plastic clock, gilt mirror and dried flowers. A mist of newly sprayed air-freshener fell on his hair as he wrote 'Megan Price' under Patient and 'Jenkins' under Visitor.

In the front sitting-room a man was thumping a black piano to a group of blue-rinsed old women staring at giant song sheets. Morgan kept walking. The back room held the comatose and troublemakers and made him think of certain farmers grazing their best ewes in the front fields on show. The view of lawns, bursting spring flowerbeds and a small lake was sadly wasted. The only man in the room had slumped sideways in his wheelchair, the remnants of his last meal splattered over a tartan bib. A television was on at the highest volume. The few women who were awake droned, hummed, sang or talked to themselves. A wispy-haired woman stood by a door, cradling two alarm clocks. "Can someone tell me when it's half past five? My daughter will be here from America."

"Isn't it time we stopped doing nothing?" began a cacophony of questions. "Will you take me with you?" "What are we doing here?" "When are we going home?"

Morgan turned to escape and bumped into the nurse.

"She didn't recognise you then?" she called to a slightly younger woman standing by the window, barefoot with a tremor. "Megan!"

A woman turned her head and Morgan flinched. Her movements were quick and darting like his and she had the posture of a dancer. Dark eyes, face framed by short silver hair with six or seven cowlicks; comic hair, reminding him of Mr Pritchard's twirled corkscrew, except these were dead straight for four inches then bent at right angles. Her earlobes were elongated by the weight of chunky silver, her lips were painted scarlet. She was tall, upright, dressed in two cardigans and a floor length skirt rimmed with mud.

"Come and sit down, Megan," said the nurse. "It's almost teatime and you have a visitor."

The crazy-looking woman wrenched at the locked handle on the glass door, walked swiftly to each corner of the room then swivelled her top half round. "Are you from the television?" she asked him, eyebrows raised and wide-eyed.

"No. I've come to see you, see how you are."

The nurse nodded to a chair and left. He sat down.

Megan Price came towards him, dragging a wooden side table from someone's chair. She took time positioning it then sat down bang in front of him. She glared and began to simper, dragging her skirt up and down, revealing glimpses of blue and white thigh. Her noise changed pitch and rose and fell like the whinny of something lost.

Morgan looked round. No one was stirring.

She tugged at her skirt, stretching and rubbing the fabric as if doing the washing. Gradually her simper died. She began to sing 'Daisy Daisy' very softly, reminding him of someone, he couldn't think who. He leaned back in the chair, tempted to request some operatic aria and put her repertoire to the test. She continued sweetly but blankly until he extended a hand.

She leapt back. "Go away, you're freezing cold."

"Do you remember Williams Cwmgwrach?" he asked, as gently as he could.

"They starve you in here. And look at the nurses, they're all fat lumps."

"Do you remember a farmer on the Black Mountain? He drank in the Llwyn Celyn. You were a barmaid."

She tilted her head back, shook her silver spikes and stared at the ceiling.

It was then he saw her uncanny resemblance to Mrs Pritchard's papier-mâché women. "You had a baby with him, didn't you?" he said. "A boy."

She looked out of the window. A black cat strolled into the room. She resumed her simpering. The cat curled round a chair leg then scarpered at the clatter of china.

"You left him to starve. Then a black cat, just like that one, licked the baby boy and kept him alive."

Her noise grew louder and louder: up and down, practising her scales. The man in the wheelchair banged his spoon on the tray; his "Shut her up" came out a growl. His eyes rolled, he had no escape. How Morgan empathised: day in day out – he could have throttled her after ten minutes. But then there was the repetition of the banging spoon. The woman waiting for her daughter from America was there winding and winding her alarm clocks. His mother wrenched her skirt up again. He felt sick. She launched into 'We'll Gather Lilacs' and the old man began to weep. She had the most beautiful voice and knew every word. The minute she finished, she was back to her low moany ranting. Morgan tried to stay calm.

The nurse appeared.

"Now now, my love, stop that nonsense." She eased the skirt from his mother's iron grip and tucked it tightly under her legs. "Your visitor doesn't want to hear that awful noise, especially when you have such a wonderful voice." She smiled at Morgan. "She keeps us entertained." She trotted off again and he wondered how on earth she could work here.

His mother stopped. "What would my visitor like to hear then?" she said, with spooky lucidity.

"About your baby," Morgan shuddered. "Are you sorry for abandoning him?"

"I had no baby." She shook her head violently and resumed her ghastly noise.

A girl wheeled in a tea trolley. "Quiet now, Megan. Goodness, is this your son?" she said pleasantly. *"Duw, Duw*, he's you on his two legs." She handed him a cup of tea, trapping him for at least another five minutes.

"I was about to leave," he said. "It's no good."

"Is there anything you'd like me to tell her later? Some evenings she'll talk to me and occasionally she'll listen."

"Yes. Please." He fixed his eyes firmly on his mother. "She knows well enough I'm her son, but can you tell her she also has a grandson? He's about three, handsome little boy. He has our black eyes. His name is Rhodri."

"Oh Megan, did you hear that? There's lovely, Mamgu Megan."

Megan gave a hideous laugh and swiped her cup off the table. Morgan put down his tea and for a second their eyes locked. She wasn't that unhinged. Her laughter followed him to the front door. He should have strangled her, if only for the sanity of the man in the wheelchair. As the blue overalled woman unlocked the front door, he heard Megan singing.

He drove away in a blinding rage, fingers still itching for her scraggy throat. He'd never go again, she could rot.

In less than a mile he was forced to pull into a field gateway. He had the shakes. Shuddering uncontrollably, he stumbled out of the Land Rover and walked the length of the field, snapping off sticks to beat hell out of the hedge and sobbing all the way round like a bloody baby. He straddled a stile, struck by a chilling thought: if he'd inherited her singing voice, why not her insanity?

Drained of all colour and emotion, he headed for home. No wonder he loathed women.

SIX

DURING HER LENGTHY search for Seren, Bethan became conscious of being watched. It was unusual for the mare not to come at first calling. She found her at the farthest end of the farm, where Cwmgwrach land met the mountain, standing mournfully by the river, her head almost touching the ground. She didn't stir as Morgan appeared through the trees. Neither did Bethan.

He was on to the situation immediately, quickly spotting a nasty little gash in Seren's neck, and suggested they take her through the river and up to Abernant. "I have Battles cream. Looks like she's caught herself on rusty barbed wire. This fencing needs doing. Why don't you want me to do it?"

"I didn't say that."

"I'd only charge for materials. Your family have been good to me." He took the head-collar and slid it over Seren's head.

"I have Battles at home, thanks," said Bethan firmly, taking the rope.

He stepped in front of her. "We'd be up to Abernant in ten minutes – it's much nearer than Cwmgwrach. Don't be silly. And we're at the shallowest part of the river."

He was right. Seren was far closer to Abernant.

"I'd rather go home," said Bethan calmly. "It's not that much further." She began to lead Seren up the slope. Her back tingled with expectation, that childlike fear of being grabbed in a game of chase and the memory of him lifting her onto that horrendous zip wire in the trees. The bogeyman. She kept moving and when he called out, "Think about the fencing," she knew he'd stayed put. Her breathing slowed to normal.

Seren's cut opened and closed very slightly and oozed a little blood as they walked at an even pace. The small clean split was too straight and neat to have been caused by barbed wire and she wondered about a stitch. That would mean her first vet's visit.

When they arrived, Nia was waiting for her in the yard, "Come on, coffee time."

Bethan was always pleased to see Nia, but today she was tearful with relief. "Look at this first – do you think I should get the vet?"

"Good God no, we'll bathe it, put something on it. Please don't say you're enjoying all this? I know I lived here but it's a bloody lonely place on your own."

"I'm fine."

After they'd seen to the cut and settled Seren in the barn, they walked quietly round the heavily pregnant ewes.

"Morgan wanted to see to her," said Bethan. "She was right down by the river, and he was keen to get us up to Abernant. I had to stand my ground."

"Good, ignore him. And don't forget, I'll come and help with lambing whenever I can. Let's hope you have the weather. How you feeling about it?"

"Don't know really. Dread, anticipation, the thrill of seeing my first lamb."

"Let's have a meal before it all starts. My gentleman's been teaching me to cook. It's my birthday next Sunday."

"I'd love that." Just as Bethan tended her sheep, so Nia tended her. They were both aware of the gruelling time ahead.

Back at the house, the phone was ringing. Bethan wasn't surprised to hear Veronica's voice; Morgan had definitely disturbed her cousin's equilibrium.

Nia mouthed, "Ask her." Bethan looked blank. "To my birthday supper!"

Bethan made a face; she couldn't entertain Veronica so close to lambing. Nia grabbed an envelope and wrote "She'll have to go straight back for the gallery!"

Veronica needed no persuading; she'd catch the train to Swansea.

"Why not drive?" asked Bethan.

"I don't want him seeing my car at Cwmgwrach."

Bethan told Nia Veronica's car was playing up.

Bethan arranged to meet Veronica at the railway station on Sunday evening and they'd drive straight to Nia's. The gallery was closed every Monday; a friend could work on Tuesday and feed the tortoises, who didn't seem to hibernate, allowing Veronica two nights at Cwmgwrach.

In the week before the birthday supper it rained every day. Bethan slithered through mud to feed. Filling the hayracks was a battle with the heavy lids before the wind wrenched them from her numb hands and slammed them down. If Morgan was spying on Cwmgwrach, he didn't rush to help her. She didn't care.

She devoured her farming books and replayed knowledge she'd gleaned from the Williams family: overfeed and lambs grow too large in the womb; too little and the ewes will have no milk. A good stockman is one who stands and watches.

And so on. She hardly left the farm: the effort of peeling off sodden waterproofs, getting washed and changed grew more onerous. She was in danger of becoming a recluse.

The birthday do, however, began to loom as a welcome indulgence and by the end of the week was uppermost in her mind. She trod the wet fields picturing the three of them in their finery. There was the added pleasure of Morgan's ignorance; he knew nothing of their planned celebration.

Sitting at Nia's exquisitely laid table the following evening, that thought struck her again. Her smile broadened. If he could see them now. Pearly white tablecloth and candles, the aromas of cinnamon and cigarettes, every vegetable freshly pulled from Mr Gentleman's garden and apples over-wintered in his attic. Bethan was pleased to see Veronica looking so impressed. In the car she'd eulogised about Welsh lamb, but Bethan knew there was little chance of that. For her and Nia the smell was a sharp reminder of weak lambs being revived in the bottom oven and the taste was too close to that smell. Neither of them could stand lamb.

Nia produced a delicious meal of pork tenderloin, red cabbage cooked with apple, new potatoes and leeks in a creamy sauce. They were admiring her apple pie deluxe when there was a tap on the front door. "Ah," she said. "The man responsible for conjuring up this recipe."

"I do apologise for disturbing you," said Mr Gentleman. "We have a visitor."

Bethan's stomach flipped.

"It won't take a minute and I'd like you to be in on the decision, Nia. It's Elin, Elin Davies. She's giving up rabbits and would like to know if we need more."

"Elin! Lovely," said Nia. "Come in, just in time for dessert."

Bethan breathed out and looked at Veronica to see if she'd also expected Morgan. It was difficult to tell.

Mr Gentleman drew Elin in front of him and gave her a polite little nudge. She came in like one of her rabbits about to thump the floor for danger. He followed.

"I'm so sorry, I wasn't going to stay." She looked round at him. She was wearing her farming clothes and would clearly rather be anywhere else in the world. Bethan just stopped herself saying, don't worry, I usually look like that.

"Nonsense, the more the merrier," said Nia.

Having drunk Veronica's champagne, most of Nia's red wine and Bethan's white, the three of them were already squiffy. Talk of rabbits would be welcome.

After introductions, Mr Gentleman returned their attention to the apple pie. "Pastry made with freshly squeezed orange juice, apples cooked in cream with grated orange rind." He pointed to orange flecks. "Zest!" With that he swept from the room and returned with two bottles of Sauternes to complement the dessert and brandy for afterwards. He filled their wine glasses. "Here's to zest."

Bethan imagined him wafting his wand over the pie. They remained at the table with Mr Gentleman playing court jester. A man in his fifties, enjoying the unexpected company of four young women, pulling playing cards from Veronica's beehive hairdo, swapping full wine glasses and turning them upside-down. He plucked a warm egg from Elin's ear to make her feel at home – she squealed and caught their mood so rapidly Bethan suspected she was also a little worse for drink, especially when they grew louder and she had no trouble keeping up.

When it became obvious no one could drive home. Nia invited everyone to stay. Elin phoned Davies. Bethan rang her father, picturing him in his study, bogged down with schoolwork, his Sunday night migraine preparing to attack. She wondered what he'd make of Mr Gentleman. They'd probably take to each other.

There was no suggestion of retiring to loll on the sofas and armchairs, so no stultifying break in atmosphere or conversation. They stayed on the hardback dining chairs with the table an essential prop for glasses, bottles and elbows. Suddenly it was two in the morning and five goblets were still swirling with amber brandy.

Veronica threw back her last mouthful, turned to Nia and said, "Your brother is stalking me."

There was a split second of sobriety.

"If you mean Morgan, he's my half-brother," Nia said coolly. "He's nothing to do with me."

Elin sat up straight. "You're Morgan Williams's sister?"

"Half."

"I think it's time for bed," said Bethan diplomatically, furious with Veronica.

Mr Gentleman, still sprightly and upright, stood up and offered spare beds in his house, then hastily conceded they'd probably prefer to stay together. He reversed out, bowing. Veronica was quickly installed in the spare bedroom. Nia offered to give up her bedroom, but Bethan took one sofa and Elin the other.

It was only to be expected that the two farmers woke before the others. It was seven, late for them. Bethan found herself on the floor, her head pounding.

Elin sat up on her sofa. "You fell off," she said. "I pulled the cushions down and rolled you onto them."

"That was kind. God, my head. How's yours?"

"Fine. I drink all the time."

"I'll go and make us a cup of tea." Bethan dragged herself up. Neither of them had undressed. She crept to the kitchen past a loud purring noise from the spare bedroom. She smiled as she found cups and filled the kettle; Veronica would die if she knew she snored.

"Good strong tea and Rich Tea biscuits." She balanced a small tray in one hand and closed the door quietly with the other. "I must go straight after. Due to start lambing. I just hope nothing's happened."

"I remember you. From that awful working men's club when I came to check my rabbits. I didn't say last night."

"Oh yes, your rabbits. Why are you giving up?"

"Divorce. Long overdue. So you know Morgan."

"He farms above me on the opposite side of the river. A mile or so, but my closest neighbour."

"Poor you." Elin downed her cup, though it was boiling. She stood up. "I must go, our lambing's started too. He'll be out in the sheds and I have a little boy."

"What, he'll leave him on his own?"

"No no, he'll take him with him. If he's willing to go – he has his father's temper. But my husband will be tamping if I don't get back soon. I go out too often these days, frequenting those terrible clubs, to watch the rabbits and on the off-chance Morgan might be singing. He never is, of course."

And Bethan knew. "And see half-aunt Nia?"

Elin raised her eyebrows and, wide-eyed, nodded towards the door. "What a turn of events, my little Rhodri's father becoming that Veronica's stalker," she laughed bitterly. "He's obviously moved on to greater heights."

SEVEN

THERE WAS A tree down. They'd passed through the green tunnel. Dark even in daylight, it was Bethan's favourite part of the track and Veronica's least. At the end a large ash completely blocked their way. A strong wind was whipping the thinner branches off the ground and the tips were flapping out over the drop to the river. Bethan drove through a couple of potholes and stopped an inch from the trunk. Veronica's head hit the passenger window and she sat up.

Apart from the usual rattling from the old Land Rover, they'd travelled home in heavy silence, Bethan's mind on Elin and Veronica slumped against the window, pretending to nurse a hangover when she was more used to alcohol than any of them.

Elin had sworn Bethan to secrecy. Rhodri's parentage must be kept quiet until the time was right. Her husband was fooling himself and might try for custody, but you only had to look at the boy's eyes. Bethan had just stopped herself crying out in agreement. Crossing the river, his small legs clamped round her waist, black eyes glued to hers in fright. Concentration had addled her brain. But it was only his eyes, his skin was a peachy cream.

She bashed open the Land Rover door with her shoulder. "Damn, we'll have to walk."

"Can't you ram it out of the way with this wreck?"

Bethan jumped down. "Are you mad? It's a tractor job. Come on, the ground's a bit wet but at least it's not raining."

Veronica had insisted on coming back to Cwmgwrach to see her uncle, who stayed late at school every Monday. She knew. She slid from her seat, her feet squelching into a pothole. The wind took several Kirby grips and made electrified candyfloss of her hair. She swore. If Bethan hadn't still been livid with her, she'd have laughed at the sight.

They struggled over the waving leafy barricade and on to the straight stretch, kept gloomy by overgrown hedges on both sides. Bethan's sign to keep dogs on leads had been splattered with more lead shot. Beyond the gate, the rutted track opened up onto the flattish acres of rough grass with the first glimpse of mountain. They walked in silence some distance apart: Veronica teetering in her ruined shoes, clutching her overnight bag to her front. Bethan preparing for the sight of an early lamber. The ewes she could see appeared peaceful with the heaviest recumbent against the walls and banks.

"So what are you going to get up to today?" said Bethan.

"I might confront him," said Veronica archly.

They fell back to silence. The track dipped down to the farmhouse. Bethan opened the final gate into the yard and saw the tail-end of a figure skulking through the garden.

"Here's your chance."

"What?"

"To confront him."

They came round the corner of the house and caught Morgan on the opposite side of the yard, supposedly leaving by the kissing gate. He showed no surprise at seeing Veronica or their state of dress.

"Ah," he said. "I thought I'd come to discuss the fencing, but no one was here."

"It's Monday – Dad will have left early for school," said Bethan. She told him about the tree. Veronica stood there, haughty, shoulders back.

"If it's too big to move, I'll fetch the tractor," he said.

"It is."

Veronica made a leap forward.

"I've something to say to you."

"Oh yes? Come with me, then." He looked down. "What about your shoes?"

"I'll lend you some boots and a coat," said Bethan, glad to be shot of her.

Veronica didn't speak after that. Acting weirdly, as if there were no option, she pulled on the socks and wellies with childlike obedience, straightened her little black dress, grabbed the coat and set off after Morgan at his pace.

Bethan ran upstairs to watch from her bedroom window. He held the gate open for her then overtook and they walked apart, past the pigsty and down the hill towards the bridge. Halfway down the slope they disappeared from view. By the time Bethan had changed into her working clothes and cleaned her teeth, they were reduced to black grubs crawling up through the undergrowth on the opposite side. If Veronica actually made it to Abernant, she would realise the ordeal of delivering that bloody launch invitation.

She went downstairs, put on her boots, locked the back door and dropped the key into her pocket. If Veronica was back before her, she could damn well sit on the wall and wait.

The majority of in-lamb ewes were slowly grazing across the bottom fields. Seren whinnied to her from a distance.

The mare was quiet enough to keep with the sheep and they were company for her. The ewes were relaxed around Bethan. She'd left Glen behind: though he could walk through them discreetly enough, his presence put them on alert. They gave her the odd glance as they snuffled up wisps of hay from the racks; there was little grass to speak of yet. Some lay down nearby. Nothing was amiss. Filled with relief, she vowed not to leave the farm again until after lambing.

Had the birthday evening ended differently, calmly with a little less drink, they could have driven back to Cwmgwrach with their usual banter: Veronica complaining about Bethan's cronky Land Rover. She settled on the large mossy tump Mr Williams had favoured for observing his flock. She'd watched him from the other side of the river, messing with his pipe more than he smoked it, just like her father.

She wondered if Morgan knew he was a father, Elin hadn't said. He was aware of most things. Bethan tried to remember the details of that mart day: the boy's fear (and hers), with Morgan showing off crossing the river and the devious way he'd discovered Rhodri's name, insisting it would cure the boy's shyness if he told Bethan himself.

She left the fields and went to the cowshed to count the sacks of feed. She jumped. The papier-mâché women were still in their special corner at the far end, but their deckchairs were closer and one was missing her head. An arm and two feet were half buried in clumps of daggings left over from years of shearing – she hadn't started clearing the cowshed. The head had fallen into a box like a public decapitation and there was a caving-in under one eye, the colour of a bruise. She lined up the dismembered limbs; it was time to let the women go. She'd discuss them with her father.

She was making cheese on toast and a pot of tea when Veronica came into the kitchen.

"Bet you were worried about me!" she said, flushed.

"No." Bethan's only fleeting thought was that Morgan could seduce or kill her, and either would do. They deserved each other.

"You won't believe this, Bethan, he has a bathroom, an immaculate bathroom. I went along a dark peeling landing, creaked open an ancient door to an overwhelming scent of soaps, lotions, expensive stuff. A Narnia wardrobe moment, astonishing. And sparkling white towels, good towels: I read the labels."

"Heavens. And what about the stalking?"

Veronica blushed.

"Oh, that wasn't him. He laughed, said I must have been mistaken; if he stalked someone, they would never see him."

God, thought Bethan, she believes him.

"He'd arranged the soaps in bowls. Where would he have seen that? Honestly Bethan, it's worth the horrendous journey to see the bathroom."

"Tea?"

"Better not, he's waiting by the tree for your Land Rover key to reverse it out of the way. I came back with him in the tractor, his road's as hellish as yours."

Bethan put on her boots and whistled to Glen.

"I'll move my Land Rover."

"I'll come and show you where he is."

"By the fallen tree, I presume?"

"Oh, of course." Veronica blushed again.

Not yet he won't be, thought Bethan. He'll have raced close enough to the house to eavesdrop – and Veronica had unwittingly left the back door open to make that easier. Now he had to run back. He was too fit to be caught out of breath.

When they arrived at the scene, he was languishing against the Land Rover bonnet.

"If you reverse, I'll bring the tractor up from the lane. I've got the chainsaw for logs, but leave them to season."

"Thank you," said Bethan.

"I checked your ewes – are you feeding enough? High protein? They look well now because they're in lamb. Don't be fooled."

They swapped the vehicles over and he started the chainsaw. They left him to it and drove to the railway station. Veronica had a change of plan; she would see her uncle another time. Bethan returned to find most of the tree stacked in logs and space to drive through. No Morgan.

She seemed to be continually buying sheep cake from the small allowance her father had put aside for her first year of farming. After that, he'd said the farm must pay for itself. She took inordinate pleasure in writing out figures and seasons, doing her sums. She couldn't remember Mr Williams taking out feed at all.

There was no lamb born on St David's Day. She was pleased to break the Williams tradition. She would form her own.

It started quietly as if to fool her. She thought her first lamb was an illusion from Mr Gentleman, who preferred to be called an illusionist rather than magician or conjuror. The ewe stood up, proving the small white mound clamped to her side was indeed a lamb. Bethan clapped her hands to her heart. It looked to be a few hours old, licked spotless and up on its feet, tail wiggling as it drank in earnest, shoving at the ewe's udder. She caught it and dabbed the navel with iodine; she'd carried the little pot around for weeks. The mother circled Bethan's legs, bleating till her child was safely back on the ground and bashing at the milk bar. A ewe lamb, to Bethan's delight: a good start.

According to Nia, Mr Williams had once said (after ten pints) that the sight of every new lamb gave him a stab of joy.

A couple of weeks into lambing a relentless rain began. There were few barns or outbuildings sufficiently intact for pens and shelter. The bales of last year's hay that came with the farm ran out. Instead of bringing home sacks of feed in the Land Rover, Bethan ordered it in bulk with the hay, then worried over the frequency of the deliveries. The driver assured her the narrow track dictated the size of the lorry hence the loads were little and often. Her farming notebook lay unopened.

Every day she was up at first light and on with her waterproofs for endless trudging, scouring the land for ewes in difficulty. Her weight dropped drastically. Her father insisted from his study it would soon be over. The rain had to stop. The constant downpour and biting wind swept through the flock standing eerily motionless, backs to the wind like sodden statues. Ewes were lambing and walking away disinterested. If two or three had lambed in the night she was incapable of matching the lamb to its mother. She carried the lambs round, searching for freshly lambed ewes, peering for fresh blood under every matted tail. Finding two frail lambs hunched together giving little feeble bleats, she began to cry.

And Morgan was there, vaulting the gate with the agility of a deer. No doubt waiting till she was properly sobbing.

"I can't do this." She held a limp lamb by its front legs. A ewe stood a few yards away, placenta dangling in blood beads.

"They're too hungry to mother-up," he said.

"What?" She looked at him in horror. "But I'm buying feed all the time."

Morgan rugby-tackled the nearest ewe and offered her a fading lamb, she responded with a sharp stamp then stretched to sniff it.

"I'd turn the lot to the hill if I were you." He spoke without condemnation. "You can feed them from your Land Rover. My father always did it. Gathered all the sheep down with everyone else and once they were sorted, he'd turn his back to the hill. It was a sort of unspoken race, no one managed to beat him to it. There's always a bite coming through on the mountain and you're only feeding your own."

A little white leg lay in a patch of rushes. He saw it before she did.

"Fox," he said, hurling it into the air. "Come on, we'll pair these up, then I'll get my dogs and we'll move them."

"I've been cruel, then?" She looked down to hide the heat flooding her face.

"Inexperienced," he said. "That's all it is. No farmer ever stops learning."

"Please don't tell my father."

"You can have some of my hay. And I'll teach you to shoot and lend you my spare gun. Foxes seem to pinpoint different farms each year. Let's hope that was a one-off. I'll start the fencing for when the ewes come back down. We should exchange phone numbers too."

She began to shake. Her face was on fire with cold rain, tears and shame.

EIGHT

THEY MOVED HER sheep quietly to the hill. Twice a day she drove up with feed, aware the terrain would finish off her old Land Rover. She'd already had to bring nine weakly ewes back down for intensive care, which made her question the sense of the move.

Morgan crept into the barn and found her bent over a ewe, legs splayed apart, her left knee wedged into its neck, right knee in the groin and shoving a lamb to the udder.

"You shouldn't stand like that," he said, bringing a wad of hay to the pen.

She jumped, unsure of his meaning. She was worn down by the horror of failing her flock and exhausted by bottle feeding twelve *swcis* four times a day. She had too few pens. It was soul-destroying.

Occasionally she heard his whistle, sending his dogs out on the hill; sometimes she strained in the hope of hearing it come closer. There was no need; he appeared at the precise moment of every potential disaster. When she struggled to knee a poorly ewe up into the Land Rover, he materialised at the side of the vehicle. At the final cases of mis-mothering he came through the rushes and had them paired up in minutes. Some days he'd work his magic then vanish, other days he'd linger. She was grateful but uneasy. However low her profile, he saw her and she imagined him a hare flat in his form, lying in wait for her to falter. How he found the time, what with his own lambing, contract work and Veronica to stalk. She longed for the end of lambing, but wondered how she'd be without him around so often.

He was always clean-shaven with a clean shirt, incredible he should evolve from such an unsavoury father. Like hers, his waterproofs and boots were filthy and stained with all sorts – rancid milk, lamb gunge, antiseptic, iodine – nevertheless, there was an underlying fragrance about him. She presumed he smoothed on aftershave or cologne, always prepared for a visit from Veronica.

Because of the influx of foxes, he became obsessive that Bethan should learn to handle a twelve bore. Her first lesson was on a weekday when her father was at school. He brought two shotguns. His mood was intense, though he joked about a secret arsenal at Abernant no one could possibly find. He gave her a firm talk on safety, and how a gun should always be carried broken. She'd never seen him that serious, but it was good. He scared her.

He turned her towards some steak and kidney pie tins dangling from a tree and handed her the lighter gun she would have on loan. It was heavy. He stood at her side showing her how to shoulder the butt and take the weight on her left hand, then moved behind and put his arms round her to explain the way to aim: cheek close on the butt, look along the barrel and line up the bead with the target. She liked both the closeness with the gun and the feel of his lean solid form against her. She breathed in his strange aromatic scent.

"Handle her gently," he said quietly. "Caress her as you would your love."

His warning about the recoil didn't prepare her and she'd lost so much weight the gun drove into her shoulder and almost sent her flying. She turned to him.

"Watch out," he said sharply. "You've got a second cartridge. And never wave the gun about."

She aimed at another tin. It bounced and she beamed. The tone of his "Well done" implied beginners' luck.

That night she told her father.

"Goodness dear, whatever next," he said, without lifting his head from his newspaper.

The following afternoon an elderly fisherman came panting up the bank.

"Bloody dog running havoc through your ewes. He's had one, needs putting out of her misery if she isn't already dead. Up by your mountain gate."

He left. Bethan was alone. She looked at the end of the barrel sticking out from the dresser and felt sick. The rain was fine, but more than drizzle. The ewe lay in mud on the other side of the gate as if she were trying to get home. Glazed eyes already filmy and part of her throat ripped open, wool plastered in soil and blood.

Bethan approached quietly, hoping to God she was dead, but the body rose and fell gently with its last breaths. Hands trembling, she loaded the gun as Morgan had instructed and pointed it at the ewe's brow, between her eyes. She braced herself and fired. The crack reverberated through the valley and the ewe, from her shoulders up, bounced into the air and fell. She fired again and watched the blood spill from beneath the head. She fell to her knees and dropped the gun to the ground. Apart from the entry point, there was no damage to the ewe's face.

When Bethan could stand, she tilted the head with her foot, the underside was a mashed tangle of blood, brains and shattered bones. She recognised the black tip of the tail; it was the soprano, the ewe with the highest baa in the flock. She flipped open the gate and, shaking uncontrollably, walked home. She'd deal with the body later.

Apart from cider, the only alcohol in the house was whisky. Always whisky. She added a few drops to a strong coffee with sugar for the shock and sank into a chair at the kitchen table. The mug jittered and slopped. She hadn't checked the other ewes; she should go back. If only her legs worked.

Morgan appeared. He'd heard the shots. If he was shocked by her direct action, he did well to conceal it and went straight off to bury the ewe. She stayed at the table and waited with anticipation for his praise – indeed expected it. Gradually her shakes subsided. This was an achievement, another step forward in her farming career, though she was struck by the irony: only learning to shoot the previous day.

He stormed in enraged, crossing the kitchen in boots clogged with wet earth. *"Iesu*, you idiot, you're damn lucky to be alive. How close were you?"

"What?" She pointed. "From here to the sink."

"You never shoot a target at such close range. If you'd touched the skull with the end of the gun, you could have burst the barrel and I'd be burying you. Nothing else was attacked – I had a good look round."

"Thank you."

He left. She'd craved his praise. She was shaking all over.

He stayed away for a while, then came through the bluish haze early one morning. Bethan was on the hill with Glen. They discussed weather and hay then he asked why her mother made the papier-mâché women. He was always catching her off guard.

"I've no idea really," she said, having lived with glue, ripped newspaper, plaster of Paris dust and cupboards of wool all through her childhood. "Maybe they were her alter-egos."

She suspected he was responsible for their final destruction. Maybe it was better than finding them rotted down to wire skeletons. She'd stamped on a dismembered leg and the chicken wire had folded and clamped her foot.

"Full moon tonight: I'll be as loopy as her." He saw anguish cross her face. "Sorry, Bethan, I didn't mean it like that. I was very fond of her." He quickly began to extol her eccentric mother's virtues and how he'd never met anyone like her.

To talk about her mother brought great comfort to Bethan. Both Morgan and Nia were important links with her parents. When they parted, she headed down the hill and could think of nothing else.

Last night's supper dishes were soaking in hot water. Her father must have only just left for work. The window over the sink overlooked the start of the track and further on a ramshackle barn. Glen went to sit at the gate next to two faded Daz daffodils. Bethan wiped the windowsill, climbed on a chair and opened the fanlight to talk to him. Without changing position he twisted to look up at her and flip his tail against the ground. The next minute he was barking. It was too early for the postman. He shot round the side of the house to the yard, snarling. She jumped down and heard a yelp as though he'd been kicked. "Glen!"

It was less than an hour since she and Morgan had parted company, and he was there tying Ness to the wicket gate. He had an old army rucksack on his back. Bethan had never seen him with any sort of bag yet he always managed to produce things from somewhere on his person: antiseptic spray, hoof clippers. Naturally they both carried knives.

Glen was acting completely out of character: hackles stiff, a low growling. As Morgan came through the gate, he leapt at his trousers and split the outer seam, which unravelled down to his boot. Glen ran back to Bethan. The open trouser leg flapped and she saw a trickle of blood on Morgan's thigh.

"*Iesu mawr*, what's the matter with your bloody dog? He knows me."

"Maybe it's the rucksack."

"I'm checking for stragglers your side of the river. Do you need to come?"

"No, I'm cleaning the house." She turned away.

Glen shuffled a short reverse on his bottom, his eyes pinned to Morgan. She cajoled him into the house, closed the back door and very quietly slid the bolt across. Glen's low growl persisted. She stroked his head. His ears were pricked straight up like furry antennae. He stared at the far door which led to the sitting-room then trotted over to press his nose to the inch gap at the bottom. He gave one bark and ran back to Bethan. The door opened and Morgan strolled from the sitting room into the kitchen.

"You should lock the front door," he said, grinning. "Never know who's about."

Glen sat at her feet, rumbling. Anyone else would fear his sudden aggression. He barked again as the post van came hurtling down the track. Now, she could dash out to the postman if only her legs weren't paralysed. He'd save her. From what, a madman, a joker or a fellow farmer to whom she seemed inexplicably attached? For life? Neither of them was going anywhere.

He was sitting at the kitchen table, looking for all the world as if he'd merely entered his own home. He had. This was his territory. For a split second her heart went out to him: she wouldn't leave Cwmgwrach after mere months, let alone a lifetime. She could only imagine her face.

"*Duw* Bethan, I didn't frighten you?" he said.

"Nope," She was tempted to say a dog was an excellent judge of character.

The postman threw a couple of brown envelopes into the box by the gate and instead of circling the yard as he did every day, he reversed at a stupid speed to turn at the barn. She watched dust engulf the van.

"I'm sorry, I didn't mean to, but you should keep the front door locked, especially here alone."

"I will from now on."

"Come with me – when did you last go high on the hill?"

"I'm due to." She'd noticed before how their moods sometimes calmed and settled simultaneously.

She locked both doors and tacked up Seren. They rode straight up the mountain, picking their way through the derelict smallholdings, over ring fences embedded in brambles and the rubble from river-stone buildings. Seren's hoof snapped a roof slate in the grass and several ewes shot out, big lambs tight to their heels, crashing through the chipped enamel dishes and pans Bethan and Nia had used to play house.

An elderly ewe baaed patiently, waiting alongside a pile of tin sheets for her bleating lamb to summon the intelligence to reverse out. Morgan dismounted a second before Bethan. As he lifted the sheets, the startled ewe jumped away from her pile of black droppings, high stepping a few yards, head up. Bethan crawled through his legs and freed the lamb, who shot to its mother and the two took off. At a safe distance the ewe stopped and turned to view them with suspicion while the huge lamb shoved at her udder. Bethan looked for Morgan to share her pleasure. He was already riding on.

For once sunshine highlighted the mountain in bright violet blocks and stripes. The landscape was changing from turf to rock and once or twice Seren stumbled. It was the roar of water Bethan could hear and they came to the place where three streams entered a pool high above the river.

"We'll watch from here," he said, dismounting.

Anyone would be drawn to such a spectacle. The water circled the pool quietly then flowed over the lip and changed character and colour. From calm grey it gathered speed into a white curtain of froth surging down the rocks, crashing into the churning brown river. She slid off Seren. There was nowhere to tie the mares, so he looped the reins with baler twine to the saddles so they wouldn't stand on them then took her hand and led her to the edge of the ravine.

"They'll wander off," she said. "There's nothing to eat."

"They won't. Now. Watch the same piece of water."

"You can't have a piece of water," she said, instantly cursing her father's obsession with language.

"Follow its journey from the top to the bottom." He kept hold of her hand.

She held her gaze to a pattern of crystal droplets as it left the pool and smashed down the rocks with a speed as phenomenal as the thunderous roar.

"Watch again." He squeezed her mother's wedding ring into her fingers.

Her eyes darted back to the top for the next white shower.

"That's how suicides happen," he said. "You're transfixed. Mesmerised."

She was. So much so she was unaware he'd let go of her hand. He'd slipped behind her to grasp her by the shoulders. He gave her the slightest push forwards and immediately back; for a better view, he said afterwards. Two moves in less seconds, no time to scream, just a massive intake of breath. He let go and she swayed. She'd only heard of palpitations, never experienced them. She stamped to bring strength back to her legs, reclaim her footing and breathe out.

He laughed. That was him all over. She shouldn't be here.

"We'll climb down," he said and set off in front, zigzagging down the steep sheep walk, an impossibly narrow path above the vertical drop to the river.

She focused on the khaki rucksack bobbing against his back, no doubt sneaked from an SAS soldier sleeping on exercise. The path began to peter out and flatten into marsh then river. He began to cross on smooth stepping stones,

"Wait," she shouted at his black hair, whihc was glistening silver in the spray.

Miraculously he heard over the deafening boom and made a show of holding his hands out to her, practically bowing. She thought of little Rhodri. How they hadn't drowned that day.

She tried to work out his expression, as if she ever could – 'gleeful' was closest. He was pointing behind the waterfall. He skidded her over the wet stones, in places wading in to ensure she kept her balance. Then, most extraordinary, a plateau of blue rock and a dark cavern and there they were, standing behind the waterfall with foam cascading over them into the swollen river.

She gripped his hand tightly. Water sequins sparkled on their soaked skin. Suddenly he leapt away, no trouble keeping his footing. She wobbled; the surface of their platform was smooth as glass. Her feet began to slide and her arms shot out as she struggled to stay upright. He was smiling and shouting. "What?" She couldn't hear. Water rose over her feet as if the plateau was on the move. She cried out. He caught her, whirled her round like an ice-skater. His shouting was singing.

"No," she shrieked. "We'll go in."

He threw back his head, twirled her faster over the stones, his voice straining to its limits to beat the waterfall. "You are..." now a delirious yelling, "...you are my heart's delight..." The song he'd sung at Veronica's launch. Her mother's favourite.

"Stop!" She was scarlet.

"And where you go, I'll always be."

"I can't swim!" She expected another line, a joking push or astonished sneer.

The manic serenade stopped instantly, he clasped her quivering hand and led her out from behind the crescendo of white water and across the stepping stones. Back on land he hugged her to him tightly, just for a moment.

"I'm having a shower fitted," he said.

She was dizzy. He was quite mad. She played along.

"Don't you have a bath?"

"A shower's quicker, especially at lambing and haymaking. And more hygienic." He looked sideways at her as if questioning her standard of cleanliness. "The plumber's installing it at the end of the bath."

He walked her to a small oasis of closely cropped grass, like a private beach, and leant the rucksack against a boulder. She sat and dipped her feet at the water's edge, waiting for a sarcastic comment about swimming, but he didn't go in for sarcasm. There was no conversation.

He was concentrating on setting the stage. To her astonishment, he was billowing a white tablecloth over the sun-dried grass then delving in and out of the rucksack till the cloth was covered in a variety of containers and foil parcels. He handed her a heavy crystal glass as if it were the most normal thing in the world, a cork shot through the air and he was pouring cold champagne. Two sips and he was unwrapping salmon with sprigs of dill and spooning tiny warm potatoes onto white china plates. They ate with heavy silver cutlery. He refilled her glass.

"To your first lambing. It was hard for you."

Hard enough for suicide? she wondered. Had he introduced her to the waterfall as the ideal location, before next year? She was tempted to ask him, but it seemed ungracious after all the trouble he'd gone to with the picnic. Her head bubbled with fizz – she hadn't eaten since last night. Fizz and shame over her hungry ewes.

"This picnic is incredible," she said, full of tears.

After their first course he took a bowl to the river, which had been in full spate for weeks. It had slowed slightly with the sunshine, but still stole six strawberries as he bent to wash them. She watched them speed away on the froth, small red hearts in whisked egg white. He dipped the rest in a tiny pot of caster sugar then stretched across and held one close to her mouth. Thinking it churlish to take it with her hand she bit neatly, leaving the little green stem in his fingers, then coloured with embarrassment.

"Oh God, the horses," she said, pretending to just remember them, which was partly true.

He looked up.

"They're fine. Time to go."

She stood up too quickly on rag doll legs. He was tipping the champagne bottle vertical, his dark lips on green glass.

Apparently, Veronica's boyfriend decanted warm brandy from his mouth to hers, which sent her crazy.

Kneeling on the white cloth to gather things, Bethan took all this to be a successful practice-run for Veronica.

PART FOUR

ONE

THE UNHEATED CINEMA took up the third floor of a huge square old building owned by an eccentric baker. A library was on the second floor and the baker lived on the first, with his bakery on the ground floor. Being a film fanatic, he drove to Cardiff twice a week to pick up the latest releases: popular ones for Saturdays, arty for mid-week. He had been running the cinema and baking bread simultaneously for years.

It was the night before Bethan's first sheep sale as a vendor and she was meeting Nia. The enthusiastic baker was showing *If* for one night only. The little cinema, two villages away, had been one of her mother's favourite haunts so they knew to take hot water bottles, expect the trill of a phone from under the stage, ignore the odd mouse and be grateful when the sound matched the picture. They sat at the back.

Nia chain-smoked throughout the film, continually turning wide-eyed to Bethan to mouth "Whaaat?"

Bethan hugged her hot water bottle and swayed imperceptibly. Watching it for the second time, it seemed even more outrageous.

When they came out, the rain was strange and sleety, though it was only late September. They emptied their hot water bottles at the kerb.

"My lambs will be all bedraggled for tomorrow," said Bethan, mournfully.

"Everyone's will," said Nia. "Bloody hell, how can you think of sheep after all that? Let's go for a drink. If the Celyn's on lock-in, we'll go round the back." She lit another cigarette.

The landlady had called time, but let them in. She was still serving men who'd spent all day unloading hurdles and building sheep pens for the sale. Nia bought Dubonnets and lemonade and they sat in a corner analysing every dark scene of the film.

"So it's all true, then?" asked Nia. "It really reflects your convent days?"

"Except the finale. I only managed to punch a nun, not gun her down."

"I could never really picture your school life. I was a bit envious, especially after reading *Malory Towers*. But you never said much, just always seemed glad to be home."

"Glad to come up to Cwmgwrach."

"I never understood that. Why you craved my life. I was half-starved, responsible for all the *swcis* at five, with a nasty father and evil brother to avoid."

"He's helping me gather tomorrow morning."

"I've guessed he helps you more than you let on. Be careful. Don't mention this film, not that he ever goes to the pictures. He doesn't need any more wicked ideas."

They were the last to leave the pub. Nia was deeply shocked by the film. In a strange way, Bethan felt it put them on an even keel. They both carried the burdens of their past. Nia wished her good luck for the sale.

The night was particularly black. Bethan turned off the lane and thought of Morgan driving without lights. She often did the same now, testing her knowledge of the hazardous track. Tonight that seemed tame.

Fortunately her headlights were on when she saw the tree. She skidded sideways and stopped at the trunk. This tree was larger than the last and had fallen closer to the first gate, but again the track was completely blocked. She groaned and sat there for a moment. She usually thought nothing of getting in and out of the Land Rover to do the gates, in pitch dark and all weathers, but tonight she didn't feel like walking the last quarter of a mile home. Other than sleeping in the Land Rover, there was little choice. She got out, locked the doors and scrambled through the horizontal branches.

Once in winter, not long after moving to Cwmgwrach, she'd been dropped off at the end of the track. The blackness was so dense she'd had to cling to the bank to literally keep on track. That was six o'clock at night. Midnight was no different – she was fine with darkness. There were two minutes of trees to negotiate, then on to the open fields. She walked fast, turning in a 'What's the time, Mr Wolf?' circle every few yards. Rushes swished in the ditch running alongside the track, in places she could hear the river, a screech owl made her jump. Footsteps? She circled again: nothing. She ran for the last slope and, passing the dilapidated sheep shed, saw the kitchen light.

"Why would anyone in their right mind see that film twice?" He'd come out from the trees.

She jumped sideways, but something kept her running for the kitchen light.

"*Nos da*," he called.

"I thought it was great," she called back. Her feet and heart were racing, despite a painful stitch, round the side of the house and into the kitchen. He hadn't followed. How could he talk about right minds? The doors were locked, curtains tightly closed. Her father was in bed. She dropped to a chair and caught her breath.

Her sleep was fitful, what with the film, him and apprehension about the sale. The village would turn out in force to see how the headmaster's daughter fared as a sheep farmer. At least her father would be at school.

The sheep had been down off the hill for a few days. With Morgan's fencing complete, she no longer had to rely on a dilapidated perimeter fence and river as the boundary. Following old landmarks, collapsed walls and memory, he'd divided Cwmgwrach into the original fields, installing new five-bar gates in solid wood that shut with precision and swung open without having to be lifted. Bethan was quietly thrilled.

They were gathering the fields together. She and Glen were bringing sheep up from the river and Morgan worked his dog along the top, to meet somewhere in the middle. Glen's behaviour was still a little peculiar round Morgan. The dog didn't seem to trust himself and Bethan had him on a long rope until Morgan was out of sight. As the sheep began to cluster together and head up through the woods, she had to flip the rope awkwardly up over bracken and brambles. Slip-sliding behind, she hauled Glen back, released him and he shot from her grasp like an arrow, all his training seemingly forgotten.

As the two groups of sheep were about to meet, Glen's bunch was going at such a pace that Morgan's dog panicked, ignored the whistles and sent them back, fanning out towards Bethan. Glen flew round, some ewes stopped dead in confusion, the front ones hurled round in fright and one fell. Way above her, Morgan held his arms out like a preacher and yelled.

"What the…?"

Glen swept from left to right, deaf to her commands. She watched with mounting horror until eventually Morgan's dog took control. A ewe lay panting at her side. Bethan threw herself to the ground, catching her hand on a boulder. With the sharp pain, she could have wept about everything.

"You're supposed to be with that lot." She squashed her smarting fingers tightly together with her good hand and held back tears of frustration.

Morgan came down to her, trailing Glen behind him on a piece of baler twine.

"Did that performance give you goosebumps?" He knew the sight of dogs gathering sheep on the hills sent a shiver through her; she went on about it enough. To him it was work.

"What? Oh. I hope you didn't hit him, that was my fault."

"I should have beaten the shit out of you then."

She quickly got up.

"You better not have touched him." She grabbed the twine.

"I didn't. But the dog's turned; you could do with another to bring on. I've got two up there now; a young bitch that would suit you."

"Glen's fine with me. He's only tricky if you're around."

"Well, I am around," he snapped, then flashed his charming smile. "Come up tomorrow; see if you like the little bitch. You could breed some pups, they're no relation. You'd love that."

He knew the ins and out of her.

"I don't need another dog, thanks."

For the next two hours they sorted out batches of lambs and brokers. The mood was tense. She shut Glen in the old railway carriage. She'd cleaned it out, removed the partitions and made a good-sized kennel but still he looked dismayed: he lived in the house.

Morgan had already picked out his best lambs. Anything remotely second rate was off to the abattoir. Why he needed to impress people he hated, she never understood. He loaded his trailer with her sheep first, drove them to the mart field then returned to Abernant for his own.

As usual she was unaware of him until he was in her face. She was busy sorting her pens, putting the same stamp of lamb together, to be auctioned in even lots. Everyone was doing the same. A farmer lifting a hefty ram lamb over an adjoining hurdle didn't notice it kick out and catch Bethan just under her eye. From nowhere, Morgan was at her side. She climbed out of her pen and sat on the grass.

"Damn it," he said. "Let me take you into the Celyn for a brandy for the shock."

"I'm fine," she said. "I must get on. They're about to start."

He pulled her up to take a look. She smelled aftershave.

Fortunately her lambs were sold in the middle of the afternoon, better than first or last. If you were first, buyers hadn't got into the swing and if you were last, everyone had already bought. She took her crook into the ring to move her lambs around and look the part as they leapt about. She even said "Slowly, slowly" when the auctioneer asked her how the price was faring. They all sold.

Morgan had higher prices, but hers were reasonable. After her traumatic first lambing, she considered them excellent. When he suggested her black eye might have helped her bids, her spirits sank. In her Land Rover mirror she saw her purple eye socket looked just like Terramycin and her pleasure resurfaced. They'd sold on merit. Having no lambs to take back to the farm, she could extricate herself from him and drive home independently.

Her father gave all his attention to her account of her day. She didn't mention the possibility of another dog, but then he left all farm business to her discretion. The seed was planted and overnight she considered the connotations: she'd be saving a dog from a miserable life on a chain, training one had always appealed and the very idea of puppies gave her goosebumps.

"Want a friend?" she asked Glen in the morning and the eager flip of his tail decided her.

It was afternoon when she began the climb to Abernant, dressed for the rain they lived with day-in day-out without comment. In the yard she caught her breath and waited, assuming he'd have seen her a mile off. His dog was tied to the kennel. There was no sign of other dogs. Probably in some dingy barn, taken out occasionally to put through their paces.

He called out to her from the sheep shed. He'd sectioned off a square at the end with old planks for Ness, who stood there now as he rubbed her lathered back with a handful of straw, his expression preoccupied, solemn, the mare's expression knackered.

"Just back from the waterfall," he said, without looking round. He dropped an empty hay-net over the partition into a pile of tangled string, then stepped out of the pen. The exhausted mare lifted her head to whinny as he crammed the net full.

"I've come to see the bitch," said Bethan. "I've been thinking about it." She watched his fingers secure the net to the wall.

"Thought you might," he said, running a hand down the mare's neck as she pulled at the hay.

His soaked wax coat was pushed on to a cobwebbed nail, stiffened by rain and protruding from the wall as though still occupied. He turned to take hers, which was equally wet, removed it by the collar and hung it next to his. Their rigid sleeves knocked together then settled to lightly touching, against the grimy limestone wall, like they'd shed their husks. Two fat coats like wax doppelgangers hovering above them.

"Where are they, then?" she asked. "The dogs?"

"Your cardigan's wet too."

"Not really," she shrugged.

His thick damp fingers were at her throat, working at the tiny buttons. Scrubbed hands stained with iodine, blemished with bruises, disproportionate fingers always surprising her with their nimbleness. She felt them travel at speed down through her buttons and saw his sloe-black eyes following to her waist. He removed the cardigan and hung it on a separate nail away from the coats.

The shed was filthy. Years of impacted sheep shit, yet a slight heady perfume of good green hay wafted over them. One hay-net managing to outdo the smell of soiled straw and diesel, just as his cologne or aftershave, or whatever it was, overshadowed his dirty overalls.

"The dogs? Are there any?"

"I have to take the mare's shoes off first," he said abruptly. "Now she's quiet."

Bethan's teeth began to chatter. She felt she'd stepped out of her body; she'd been warmer in her wet things.

"You go inside," he said. "Throw some logs on the fire, warm up and I'll be about twenty minutes. Then we'll look at the dogs."

She lifted her coat and cardigan from the beam.

He'd done little to the house since her last visit. The shotgun was propped in the same place against the old kitchen cabinet and the dusty mantelpiece still only boasted Mr Williams' photograph, dead centre. The one difference was the back wall where rows of rough shelves had been built and jammed with books. There was no clock to time him. She dragged a chair to the range.

It could have been twenty minutes when the front door opened. Boots clicked up the bare wooden stairs, a door opened and closed and he came back down and along the hallway. He pulled up a chair, she shunted hers along and they sat like bookends either side of the fire, just like perching on the coal-boxes with her mother, swapping ends when their legs scorched. Her mother's purple blotches had been permanent, but she never seemed to mind. That upset Bethan.

"I'm thinking there are no dogs," she said. "This fiasco has shades of that day with little Rhodri, enticing him here with an imaginary litter of pups. Why trick me?"

"They'll be here tomorrow. I'll keep the bitch for you," he said, with a smile.

"You're beyond! You know that." She scraped her chair back, rolled her cardigan into a ball and stuffed it into her coat pocket. "I should know by now, your eyes squint when you lie and when you flirt. Christ, it's hard to sift through the rubbish your face comes up with. I think I know you, then you fool me again." Her coat was like damp hardboard. She tugged the unyielding sleeves over her arms and yanked up the back. It felt like someone was in there with her. She marched to the door. "My God, I feel sorry for little Rhodri."

"What do you mean?" Morgan sat ramrod straight.

His violent moods could erupt from nothing and no one knew she was at Abernant, but she was in a bloody fury.

"Having a bastard like you for a father!"

His body slumped.

"That day at the mart was the first time I'd ever seen the boy. I knew straight away – I'm surprised you didn't. I only wanted to talk to him, bring him here for a while. He wasn't willing."

"Willing? Of course he wasn't willing, he didn't even know you! No, I can't think why I didn't guess then – those black, moony, calf eyes."

The slow-motion slide from his chair was cartoonish. He collapsed in the hearth inches from the fire.

"I'm going," she said. She slammed the front door then crept round to the kitchen window to peer in, expecting him to be up and doing, making tea. He was on his knees in the hearth even closer to the flames. She walked away and returned. Twice. From her awkward position at the window, flames seemed to be coming from his hair. She burst back in. He wasn't on fire. She gave him her hand and she pulled. He was a deadweight. "Morgan, for heaven's sake. Help me."

He turned to face her. The front of his hair was singed and his bony cheeks plastered in grey ash. A pitiful mess, he came to life, stood up and stepped from the hearth. Keeping firm hold of her hand, he led her along the brown hallway. "I want to show you my bathroom," he said. "You can have a shower, if you like."

They went upstairs and he opened a door to a dismal bedroom, saved only from utter gloom by a well-established fire burning in a small black fireplace. It was spartanly furnished: a mattress, wardrobe and chair. Drooping cobwebs heavy with flies clung to the beams, the bare floorboards were split in places and balls of straw, hay, sock fluff and dead leaves had welded together and been blown into the corners by the draughts from a rotting window frame. The chair was overflowing with clothes. The mattress was wedged against the window wall and made up with dazzling white sheets, like an immaculate sailing boat docked in the wrong port.

Bethan saw only the fire and the sheets. The ambush was set. He'd come in and gone straight upstairs to check the fire.

She let him undress her, shivering shyly as he rubbed her body with a soft towel. She wouldn't have minded straw. She started to untie her scarf but he placed his large hands over hers and insisted she stood before him, naked apart from the thin strip of black silk around her neck. He studied her as though she was unexpected. His eyes rested on the small glass beads sewn along the edge of the scarf, glittering in the firelight.

"And there's something about that, again," he smiled.

There were no pillows on their white boat. Their bodies slid round the crisp sheets, he slipping his arm under her back to lift her effortlessly to different places, pulling chunks of her hair to bring her head to his. Exquisite pain, brief and thrilling. Squeezing her nipples so hard, she tensed to stifle a yelp. Red hot poker pain and long breathy sighs.

He made love as he lived life, everything a contradiction: his good aftershave against an aroma of sheep; a smile, a scowl; a lingering kiss, a peck; passion, disinterest; tender, animalistic. His black eyes held hers lovingly then, glazed and deadpan, stared past her into the grey sky. It was primitive love-making, shameless and raw. He whispered *"Cariad"* and dragged her to him by the silk scarf. She'd always laughed when he'd used *Iesu mawr* as an expletive, Big Jesus? Now he was groaning *Iesu mawr* over and over with passion, it seemed totally appropriate. She was drowning in a mad euphoria. It hurt. He was kind, handling her with the confidence he would his livestock.

Afterwards he got up and stretched. A sign of good health in an animal, she was always relieved to see a new lamb stretch. His body was strong, hard and spare; she'd seen his top half at shearing. Staying naked, he stoked up the little fire then ran downstairs to fetch brandy.

He called from the landing, "Come and have a shower."

Veronica had not exaggerated. The bathroom was pristine, a palace in which Morgan instantly became king. The shower had been installed over the bath at the opposite end to the taps and plughole. He pulled a cord, tested the temperature of the water and leapt in. His eyes lit up as he soaped his olive skin, she expected to be invited in, but he seemed to have forgotten all about her. He soaped and rinsed himself all over three or four times, raising his arms, twisting and turning with the fluid moves of a dancer. Just when she thought he'd finished his peculiar performance he lunged forward and positioned his hands either side of the taps. He put his head right down, stuck his bottom in the air, spread his legs and stood on tiptoes. The water surged over his bottom and between his legs. He looked round and up at her and grinned. She left the bathroom.

He joined her in minutes and, hopping into a pair of trousers tugged from the heaped chair, said, "Davies doesn't deserve that little lad, leaving him alone like that in his Land Rover."

She didn't shower. Minutes of silence elapsed as they finished dressing. The pile of clothes had fallen to the floor and among them she saw a corner of black silk. Her hand went up to her bare neck and she slowed down in her own dressing.

"Have you anything to eat?" she asked. "I'm starving."

"Don't most people smoke afterwards?" he smiled.

Once she heard him clattering downstairs, she rooted around in the jumble of clothes. In between shirts, jeans, overalls and socks she unearthed six silk scarves. In length, quality and colour practically identical to her own; all her scarves were black or navy. She threw back the crumpled bedclothes to search for the one she'd been wearing; felt under the mattress then scoured the dusty corners of the terrible bedroom. She touched her bare neck in case it had reappeared as mysteriously as it had vanished.

He'd gone outside, but had left a triangular jam sandwich and white serviette on the table. Bethan took one bite and threw the rest on to the fire. She picked up her jacket, now stiff as wood. He was waiting in the yard. It was pitch dark.

"I'll drive you home," he said, gripping her shoulders. "I never think of Elin Davies. It's you I think of constantly."

"Well, don't." How weak she sounded.

He kissed her, long and hard.

TWO

HE KISSED HER again at the end of the drive, then dropped her at the house and drove away. The outside telephone bell was on its last two rings and the house in darkness, though her father always left the kitchen light on if she was out. She'd no idea of the time. The phone began again as she opened the gate, so she ran to the back door, took the key from the split stone in the wall and burst into the kitchen in her boots.

It was the school secretary. Bethan blushed as if she knew. She was ringing from her home to say Mr Pritchard had been taken to hospital that afternoon with bad chest pains.

Bethan was completely taken aback; she'd never known her father ill. Without moving from the spot, she wrote down the number and dialled the hospital. A woman's voice told her he'd suffered a mild heart attack, but no need to come now, it was late and he was settled, far better to come first thing in the morning. The mellow voice was asking if she was alright and telling her to get some sleep. Bethan would have liked to keep talking, but they said goodnight and she put the phone down. She should have asked her to check they had the right person; her father had walked ten miles on Sunday. Surely overweight people had heart attacks?

She looked at the kitchen clock. Five minutes to midnight. She stared down at the state of herself: wax coat thick and slimy from a second dose of rain, her jeans were wet when she put them back on, her boots coated in mud. She'd been with Morgan for nine hours. What timing: her father rushed off in an ambulance as she lost her virginity.

She arrived at the hospital at 8 a.m. On the seventh floor she forgot her directions and stopped to ask a young nurse in the corridor.

"Mr Pritchard? Ah yes," she nodded and smiled as if they'd become best friends overnight and was about to relate some jolly incident. "Mr Pritchard died at seven-thirty this morning."

Bethan felt her body sinking. Arms enfolded her from behind, walked her to a side room and lowered her into a chair. All she could remember afterwards was dropping the book she'd grabbed from her father's bedside table, the bookmark falling out and a loud voice from the next room severely reprimanding the thoughtless nurse. Someone handed her a cup of sweet tea. She took it carefully, expecting the cup to rattle in the saucer as she shook, but the thick heavy china was built for purpose.

He lay neatly on a high trolley, fully dressed in his suit and shoes, hands by his side, feet together and face in calm repose. Another heart attack that morning, with his slight angina, had been enough to kill him. Bethan had never heard of his angina.

Other than his skin turning yellow, he looked quite well. She didn't really want to touch his face, but felt obliged, though alone in the room. She laid the palm of her hand very lightly on his cheek. It felt like an emery-board: he was in need of a shave. She lifted the spectacles perched on his thin nose and immediately replaced them. When she was little, she'd hated him removing them, his pink squinty eyes made him a completely different person. Better to remember him as he was, through thick glass.

Seeing the bar of his watch chain fastened to the slit in his lapel, she assumed his silver watch to be in his top pocket and was about to check, then imagined being spied on through a two-way mirror, like they did in police stations. They'd think she didn't trust them. His shoes, good brogues, needed a polish. Funny, he was obsessional about correct fittings, but never worried about the state of shoes, however expensive. She thought the hospital could have given them a bit of a buff. Someone had obviously tried to brush his mad hair.

The sister had said to take as long as she liked. Bethan sat on a hard plastic chair at the side of the trolley and watched him for an age, waiting for him to sit up and say lovely things about her. All that unfinished business. She suppressed an urge to grab him by the collar and shake him – she still had masses to say, even if he didn't. When she came from the room, she was given a plastic bag with the contents of his pockets: watch, wallet, fountain pen, pencils, sketch pad, notebook, handkerchief and diary.

Nia was waiting in the corridor. Bethan vaguely remembered someone asking if anyone could be with her, she must have given them Nia's phone number. She didn't live far from the hospital. She looked shivery and came towards Bethan almost accusatorily, to outward appearances more upset than the daughter of the deceased.

"I had no idea, Bethan," she said. "Absolutely no idea at all that he was ill."

"Nor did I," said Bethan. They flung their arms round each other and sobbed.

They drove back to Cwmgwrach, drank themselves into a stupor and Nia stayed over. Glen barked a few times during the evening and ran to the kitchen door, but neither heard him go crazy in the early hours or noticed the scratch marks on the door. Nia left first thing to feed and water the rabbits as Mr Gentleman was away. She would return before lunchtime.

Bethan's morning felt out of order. She went into the sitting room and sat on the sofa, upright and feet together, as if it were a hardback chair, at a loss as to what to do next. Images of yesterday paralysed her with shame. Morgan would be devastated; her father was the most significant person in his life. She couldn't tell him over the phone. The thought of him appearing today spooked her and she locked herself in.

She telephoned Auntie Cecily. Her father was an only child; there was no one on his side of the family. She felt she ought to look for papers, his important documents could be anywhere; there were crammed cupboards and shelves in every room of the house. His study might be devoted to school stuff. He was weird about his things. His precious long-case clock had stopped; she didn't wind it and was uneasy about opening his bureau. Every pigeonhole was stuffed with paperwork. A white envelope protruded from the rest with "Bethan" in his flamboyant handwriting, written diagonally across one corner and underlined. This was it, she sighed with relief, fully expecting to read her instructions on his death.

The envelope was stuck down; she used his paper knife to open it tidily. A wad of papers had been folded singly in chronological order: receipt for a second-hand fairy bike, bills for school fees and uniform, shoes and more second-hand bikes. It was the cost of her upbringing, a comprehensive account or financial drain, of rearing a small daughter. She packed the papers back into the envelope, glad to be alone. It shouldn't have been a shock; that was her father, everything accounted for in writing, but the discovery left her deeply disturbed. The last invoice was for a second-hand Raleigh bike, her thirteenth birthday present.

She took the envelope to her bedroom and put it at the bottom of a drawer, a damning little collection to be stored away and brought out as proof for whenever she felt crazy. She lay on her bed and considered throwing the whole bureau into the bonfire circle and putting a match to it. But her father had bought her dream. Perhaps there was another envelope somewhere: farm, sheep, Land Rover, dog, pony.

In the drawn-out ten days before the funeral she was never alone; Nia and Auntie Cecily took it in turns to come and stay. Glen barked in the night. The phone rang a couple of times and no one spoke.

She already missed her father. However separate their lives, she had been happier with him in the house, even ensconced in his study for hours. She'd also felt safer. Morgan's respect for her father gave her sanctuary; he'd never have caused an upset with Mr Pritchard at home.

The morning her aunt left, Bethan drove to Swansea to meet Nia and register the death. Afterwards, they split up for an hour and Bethan found a smart clothes shop to buy something for the funeral. She immediately felt uncomfortable; the shop smelled of wooden floors and perfume and was virtually empty. Two glamorous assistants leaned against a marble counter and watched her quickly gather an armful of dresses without really looking at them. She turned towards the changing room and walked into a wall of black wool and the smell of lanolin.

"Try this," Morgan laid a black dress on top of her pile.

Heat spread through her and her knees weakened under the feather-light armful of clothes. He was at a row of scarves, untangling a long silk one with tiny beads sewn on with silver thread. He wound it round her neck, his rough fingers catching the fabric.

The assistants whose help she'd politely refused edged closer. It was easier to disappear into the changing rooms than speak and cause a scene. She hardly ever wore dresses. She started with his choice as it was on top and the right size. The satiny lining under the soft thin wool fell over her head and slithered down her legs. A swirly full skirt – Veronica would approve. Just as she was about to take it off, the changing room door opened.

"I wish to God I'd known your father was ill." His tone was slightly aggressive, just as Nia's had been initially, as if Bethan had deliberately withheld information.

"So do I," she said quietly.

He took her firmly by the hand to a full-length mirror. "This suits you; I'd like to buy it. You look lovely." The shop girls came closer. He had dressed thoughtfully, but still they looked an unlikely couple.

"No. No, thank you." She shot back to the changing room, ripped off the dress and caught the exorbitant price tag fluttering from the neck. She sat on a small padded bench under the dresses to gather her thoughts. Had there been a window, she'd have climbed out. When she eventually came out into the shop, he'd gone. An assistant handed her a bag: he'd paid for an identical dress and sparkly scarf. Crimson-faced, she walked briskly through the crowds, carrying the bag; he'd be spying on her from somewhere.

Nia had suggested meeting at a restaurant. She was already there, waving from a window table. Bethan rushed inside. Once again she decided against confiding in her. It would change everything about their friendship and she couldn't bear that. They had a good lunch to save cooking that evening and then parted for another hour. Nia had forgotten to go to the bank and Bethan needed shoes or boots. The minute Nia was out of sight, he came edging round one of the pillars outside the post office.

"Didn't you see me from the window?" he said. "How could you not have seen me? I'd see you anywhere."

"No."

"Oh, I think you did."

"Morgan, I didn't and I must get on now; I've got more shopping to do."

"I've waited nearly two hours for you to come out of that restaurant. I've been standing across the road. You must have sensed my presence."

His face in hers seemed more angular, his voice snarly and she was relieved to be in busy streets. He repeated his last sentence in a loud voice. Behind him, a shabby bear-like man in a checked suit and hat with a flower mouthed to Bethan, "You okay?" and she nodded. The man walked on a few yards.

"You have an hour before you meet Nia," said Morgan.

Bethan hadn't mentioned a time, just called out "See you later" as they left the restaurant.

"I want to talk to you properly," he said. "To say how sorry I am about your father. He was very important to me – he changed my life. I would have liked one last conversation with him, that's all." He opened his arms and moved forward to embrace her.

She stepped back. "So would I. I've had vivid dreams, nightmares," she lied – they were wide-awake thoughts. "That our pain happened simultaneously, a cruel coincidence: the pain penetrated my father's heart as you penetrated me."

"Bethan!"

"It's been a huge shock. We were both denied a goodbye. Let's leave it there, Morgan. Anyhow, I've just seen a friend." The man in the checked suit hadn't moved far. Bethan walked up to him.

"Could we pretend to be friends for a moment?"

"I'd be delighted, care for a coffee?" He took her arm.

She didn't look round, but made an excuse when they came to a café, thanked him profusely and ran off to a shoe shop. She tried on shoe after shoe, thinking about what she'd said and Morgan's look of mortification. He didn't appear. She chose and paid for a pair of black high heels, then forgot to buy food. Driving back to Cwmgwrach she blamed her erratic behaviour on the circumstances. She'd find something for their supper.

This time they were blocked barely halfway along the track.

"Damn, not again!" She slammed on the brakes.

"What do you mean, again?" asked Nia.

"It's happened before. You can leave your stuff here if you like and I'll lock it," Bethan started gathering her bags. "I'll take mine, they're not heavy. Just as well I forgot to buy food. At least it's daylight."

"Nothing like this happened when I lived here."

"The trees are older, I suppose. I need to get my own tractor so I can move them myself."

They crawled through the branches and were home ten minutes later.

"Tea?" asked Bethan. "Have to be black, there's no milk."

"Coffee then. I'll make it."

"There's no coffee, I meant to buy that too. Actually, there's not that much for supper, sorry."

"Bethan," Nia was holding the fridge door wide open.

Bethan's hand went to her throat. The phone rang. She jumped. It stopped. Clasping her neck, she stared into the fridge: two steaks bleeding on a pink plate, two frosty pints of milk, a cheese-shaped greaseproof package, orange juice, potatoes, yoghurts, sausages, two cream cakes.

"God, I'm stupid, I went shopping yesterday."

"Bethan, you hate steak." Nia closed the fridge and opened a cupboard. "And is this the coffee you don't have?"

Bethan gave a little shriek as Nia took out a large jar of coffee and peeled back the unbroken foil. The phone rang again. Bethan jumped again, answered it and, leaving no time for anyone to speak, said, "Wrong number."

"You leapt a mile when the phone rang. And most villains break in to steal, not stock up fridges! What's going on?"

"Nothing."

"Okay, well think up a story while I get some long screws to fasten down the windows. Just as well winter's coming. I take it the tools are in the same barn?"

Bethan nodded. With Nia outside, she opened the fridge again. It was packed so full the little light was practically obliterated. She closed the door and went to wash her hands; concentrating on the gush of hot water, her trembling went unnoticed.

Nia returned, shaking an old tobacco tin. "Do you know where he's getting in? A rat can flatten itself to squeeze through an inch gap."

Bethan shook her head. She followed Nia from room to room as she expertly jammed and secured each window. Back in the kitchen, Bethan asked for a cigarette.

"You don't smoke. Have you done it, Bethan? Have you succumbed? You don't need to tell me, but the state you're in, you can't live here alone. I'm here again tonight and tomorrow night – well, I can't get out. I suppose we'll have to ask him to move the bloody tree." She opened her packet and lit two.

"There's no one else."

"Tell me when you're ready, Bethan."

"Maybe."

They ate biscuits and cheese and a cream cake, then Nia switched on the television and Bethan sat at the other end of the sitting room with more death-related paperwork. It was raining as usual, late afternoon, not yet dark enough to close the curtains.

There had been no movement or shadows at the window to catch her eye. His face materialised like the Cheshire cat, only it wasn't grinning. A cattle coat with an oversized hood gave him the ghostly appearance of a pale-faced monk. As she reached for the curtains he shook back the hood, flicking more raindrops onto the glass. His drenched hair was stuck to his forehead in jagged spikes. He jerked his head towards the back door. She shook her head and wrenched the curtains across. Four steps for him, round the rain-butt and onto the cobbles and he was at the smaller window. Had Nia turned, she would have seen him immediately. Bethan rushed to pull those curtains. Then came a faint galloping of fingernails, tip-tapping impatiently. She made a mouth-size opening in the curtains and hissed "Go away".

"What did you say?" called Nia.

"It's bloody freezing in here." She ran through to close the sitting-room curtains. "Have to start lighting the fire and drawing the curtains earlier, keep the warmth in. Think I'll have a hot bath, then bed." She climbed the stairs in the dark and edged round her bedroom wall to close the curtains before switching on the lamp. In the bathroom, she lowered the blind before pulling the light cord.

Peat-coloured water flowed from the taps. After days of rain, she'd had no choice but to pump up their supply with the river in full spate. She held a little bottle under the hot tap till blue bubbles turned the water a darker brown, then stepped into the bath and kept the tap running until only her head showed. A brief moment of security: buried in rusty water with Nia downstairs and the doors locked. She washed then lay still until the water had cooled.

The tree started against the window the minute she crawled into bed, leaves swishing across the glass just like before. Realising how stupid she'd been, about so many things, she dragged the duvet over her head and curled into a ball. Even the tree danced to his tune.

THREE

THE CHAPEL WASN'T large enough for the friends and colleagues of a popular headmaster and the funeral was held in a Swansea church. Morgan sang his heart out as he had for Mrs Pritchard, his amazing voice resonating way above the others. Again, Bethan couldn't see him.

They brought her father back to the mountain chapel and lowered him into the barren earth alongside her mother. In the two years separating their deaths only three others had been buried in the graveyard. In the bramble hedge along the black railings, blackberries were beaten to purple slime by the rain. Despite the grey sky, the little jagged stones sparkled on the graves. A fierce wind was ever present. Her father would also have the expansive views he'd recommended for her mother. On the slow, winding drive back down the mountain she asked Nia if it was melodramatic to call herself an orphan at the age of twenty.

"A bit." Nia squeezed her hand. "But I suppose you are."

Bethan hadn't been able to face putting on the spread for afterwards and had opted for the Celyn. Whether or not the teachers had been forewarned about the grim pub she didn't know, but they all had to return to school. Auntie Cecily and Veronica looked a little taken aback by the place, but rose to the occasion.

Bethan and Nia sneaked past the function room to the bar and ordered two large gins and a tonic to share.

"Doesn't seem a minute since mum's funeral," said Bethan. "Saying she was a funny one. And now Dad. Don't know who was the funnier, or should I say weirder?"

"Wonderfully eccentric," said Nia. "Your parents were such an influence on my life. I adored them both."

"Morgan said much the same. I may well not see him now Dad's dead."

"Don't be ridiculous. Whether it's you he's after or Cwmgwrach, he won't stop. And I know you won't move from there."

"No, I won't!" She couldn't think which was worse: Morgan seducing her to get the farm, or moving. "Of course I won't, why should I?" She took a big slug of gin.

"Quite right."

They drank two more, discussed her batty parents then thought they should probably show their faces in the function room for a soggy sandwich and cold quiche. Nia went in front, mimicking Mr Pritchard's Groucho Marx walk.

"I should be flopping about in wellies three sizes too big."

Bethan smiled. "Nia, I'll never leave Cwmgwrach. I have to make a success of farming and get the approval of my father, dead or not. And Mum."

"I know that." She opened the door.

They entered a fug of cigarette and pipe smoke and women fussing with leftovers and clearing plates. People were deep in conversation. Veronica and Auntie Cecily looked less snooty, trapped in a corner with flushed farmers and miners.

"Spirit me away, please," said Bethan. "Honestly, call yourself a magician."

"I'm not that advanced yet. Don't worry, it's all but over."

"I'd like to be invisible and eavesdrop, hear opinions on my father." Unless their talk had already reverted to sheep. Somehow, she thought not.

Nia had assured her he was well liked and held in high regard. Some had been a little in awe of him, but friendly cultured eccentrics were few and far between locally. Boring mad farmers were ten a penny.

"I mean," she'd said, "an artist coming to mart to draw!"

In Bethan's mind, speculation would be rife. The headmaster who'd bought his young daughter a farm.

Auntie Cecily and Veronica came home with her, Veronica to stay one night, her aunt two. Nia would return again the minute her aunt left. That first night, the three kept up their intake of gin, didn't eat again and staggered to bed before ten, a huge relief to an exhausted Bethan. She wasn't quite sure what Auntie Cecily had made of her sister's odd husband.

After breakfast, Veronica left for Bath. She'd made no enquiries about Morgan, but then it wasn't the moment. Bethan waved her off then took a wheelbarrow to the cowshed. The papier-mâché women were no more. She shovelled their remains into the barrow, crunched limbs, chunks of stiff clothing and hats, and tipped it onto the bonfire patch. She set a match to the pile then threw on the rotting deckchairs. Once they were ablaze she swept out the cowshed.

Back in the kitchen Auntie Cecily asked about the evil-smelling blue smoke.

"Glue and old paint," said Bethan. "Mum's paper women."

"Goodness. I didn't know they were still with us. I suppose they were bound to fall apart sooner or later." She was making coffee and slicing the fruit cake she'd brought.

Bethan couldn't stay inside.

"Do you mind if I take my mare to the farrier? She's slightly lame; I'll have to lead her to the village."

"Course not, dear, you must get on."

Bethan drank her coffee and ate her cake standing at the back door, twisting a head collar, hoping her aunt wouldn't tidy the house.

Seren needed cajoling up the track. Bethan wondered if she'd overheard Nia's advice to lie low, and stroked her neck and spoke encouragement. If Morgan was around, he wouldn't appear until there was more cover, assuming he wanted his usual privacy. He hated to be discovered doing anything. She passed the top gate. Seren walked with more comfort along the flat.

A troubled bleat came from the ditch. Bethan stopped dead. She'd moved the sheep to the lower fields, so there shouldn't be any up here. The next bleat sounded more anxious. She tied Seren to a fence post and went to investigate, peering through the spiked wet reeds that edged the mossy trench. There was nothing to be seen. The noise rose to a frenetic warbling then weakened to short high bursts. She tripped, half-fell and brown slime seeped up the sleeves of her jacket. She squelched the length of the ditch. Morgan climbed from the other end, gave another pathetic bleat and ran past her. He untied Seren, threw himself across her back and twisted her round.

"You've no right here." He looked and sounded demented. "Go back to your precious Bath."

"She's lame," she shouted, pleading. "Morgan, stop. I said she's lame."

He laughed and kicked the mare on towards the next gate, sending up yellow dust from the track. Bethan stood there. She couldn't run home and involve Auntie Cecily. She made for the dilapidated barn in the trees, held together by ivy and interwoven saplings and managed to reach it before there was any sign of him returning. She grabbed a stick and squeezed through a small gap in the stone wall. The barn was windowless, but a few missing roof slates gave her enough light to scramble over a pile of rubble in the far corner and sink down behind it.

Her hand gripped the stick with her knuckles pinched white. She suddenly saw herself as ludicrous, preparing to brandish a length of hazel at a madman, and flung it across the building. Her insides burned at the thought of poor Seren. The mare was a sweetheart and he'd ridden her away like a bloody cowboy. His horsemanship usually sent a buzz through her. Now, she felt sick.

She steeled herself for the cracking of twigs or disturbance of stones, but there was enough mud to move around in silence. Whatever the terrain, he'd arrive as quiet as a mouse and easily slide through the gap. Expecting his face to appear felt more nerve-racking – whatever the next part of his plan, it was only a question of time. Nia was right, though her insight had stung Bethan at the time: Morgan's obsession with Cwmgwrach was driving him to desperate measures. When the dark shadow obliterated the slit of light, she scrunched her body into a tighter ball, unwilling to speak and reveal the slightest tremor in her voice.

"Where is she?" she whispered at last. Silence had got her into this mess.

"Come on, I'll see you at Abernant," he said. "Walk fast, we need to talk."

"I can't. I'm taking her to the farrier."

"I'll see to her feet."

The shaft of light returned and he was gone. She scrabbled over the rubble and peered through the hole. He was running like a deer across the field. She could only think he'd hidden Seren in the woods, to ride down through the river and up to Abernant. She crawled out of the ruin like a rabbit from its burrow. She had no choice. Nia would be livid. The quickest way to Abernant on foot was back to the house, down over the bridge and up through the trees. She'd collect Glen for moral support and protection: he hated Morgan.

She opened the back door to the clatter of vacuum bits.

"Cooey, just come back for Glen." she called.

"Okay, dear," Auntie Cecily called back. "I'll get lunch."

"Don't worry about me: I might be a couple of hours."

Halfway up the hill a piercing stitch made her double up. She pressed hard into her side and, surprised by her prominent ribs, saw her mother's skeletal body.

"Bethan!" A desperate shout disorientated her. She spun round. A female voice and coming from home. "Bethan! Bethan!" Then she saw Nia across the valley, her small incensed figure leaping up and down by the pigsty, waving both arms. Bethan waved. Nia made huge beckoning motions, yelling for her to come back. They slithered down and met at the bridge.

"What the hell are you thinking?" said Nia. "Going up there? Alone!"

"He took Seren. Galloped off on her, and she's lame. He's doing her feet."

"Never! I'll ring him and say if he doesn't bring her back immediately, we'll phone the police. Your aunt needn't know the ins and outs, if you calm down."

Bethan darted looks all round her.

"How did you know where I was?"

"Your aunt said you'd only just left and I didn't see you on the track."

As they crossed the yard to the house, Bethan heard the vacuum being crashed round the spare bedroom. "I'll ring him now quickly while Auntie Cecily's occupied." She was into the kitchen and dialling before Nia had shaken off her boots. He had an outside bell. She pictured him running across his yard; his phone probably didn't ring that often and he was innately nosey, maybe a little lonely. Ten rings, and he answered.

"I can't come up to Abernant," she said coolly. "Nia and my aunt are here. Please bring Seren back. Carefully." She put the phone down. "He didn't speak." She took off her boots.

"We'll give him an hour. Look Bethan, I don't mean to sound disrespectful or hurtful, but whether he's after you or the farm, the coast's clear with your dear father gone."

The vacuum moved into Bethan's bedroom above the kitchen. Just like her mother, her aunt bashed into the skirting boards with contempt, either for the work involved or the house itself, or both. Bethan sat in the old sofa and told Nia about Morgan's skilful impression of a ewe in distress and his berserk behaviour.

"Bastard," Nia threw her cigarettes across the kitchen. "Have one and keep the packet. I won't say it again, you cannot live here alone."

"I couldn't agree more," said Auntie Cecily. She'd left the vacuum running. "God, what a place. Far too big for one." She poured a glass of water and trotted back upstairs.

"Funny she didn't ask about Seren," said Bethan, lighting a cigarette with shaky fingers.

"Wouldn't occur to her. Listen, what about taking a lodger? Elin's looking for somewhere to live. She's cut right down on her rabbits."

"I don't think so. Anyway, she has a son."

"Well, you have enough bedrooms."

"It wouldn't work," Bethan stood up. "I'm going to phone him again."

The sofa faced the window over the sink. Seren was tied to the gate in the same position as when she'd very first seen her.

"She's back." She ran outside. The mare whinnied. She wasn't in the state Bethan had feared. Not sweating or even breathing heavily. Her unshod feet were trimmed and shining. Bethan checked every inch of her then spoke loudly to the trees above the bank. "I know you're in there watching. Keep away from here."

FOUR

SHE'D NO NEED to shout, he was only on the path at the side of the house. She muttered a few expletives to herself. Shocked by her language and venom, he crept forward for a glimpse. Her arms were clasped around the mare, her body heaving against the animal's neck in rhythm with her sobs.

He'd unearthed some old engine oil for the mare's hooves, thinking the sight of them neat and polished would please Bethan, take her mind off things. Like Veronica the day after his father's funeral, appearing unannounced all tarted up. That's all he'd intended for Bethan, to distract her from any morbid thoughts.

He left quietly, tramping the couch grass that had been his father's vegetable patch. At Abernant the two cats were sniffing round the back door, forever trying to sneak inside. His usual harsh "Pssst" sent them flying; just as well Bethan couldn't hear. He watched them scoot under a barn door then went into the house. He wouldn't hound her. People took death in different ways.

When the posh aunt left, Nia was there all the damn time.

He spent a few weeks of intense surveillance then one morning, through binoculars, he followed a white vehicle along the Cwmgwrach track. It turned to reverse as close to the house as possible then disappeared from his vision.

He ran. In less than ten minutes he was down from his hill to the trees above the Cwmgwrach farmhouse, looking down on a small removal van. Two men were carrying boxes and furniture inside.

Morgan could only presume Nia was moving in, though he couldn't believe that she'd give up her home at that daft old magician's mansion, especially after producing such a successful dinner party – albeit for her own birthday. As fortune would have it that night, Bethan had tugged the curtains together too vigorously and left a small gap at one end, enough for him to watch his glamorous half-sister sashaying round the room. He'd stayed for less than twenty minutes, long enough to see she was a new person.

He compared his own move from Cwmgwrach, his drab possessions stuffed in the old post office van. His stepmother had departed by tractor and trailer. Yet here was Nia with enough belongings and funds to hire a removal firm.

He couldn't see either girl. From behind the thickest tree he watched the calm efficiency of the removal men. It was only a slight movement that drew his attention to the far corner of the yard. He moved closer and almost forgot to be discreet. *Iesu*, boys grew fast. It had to be Rhodri; his mother had come out of the house. The boy was kneeling on the ground with his arms around Glen, who was sitting stiffly, his head turned away with the angst of being hugged.

"Rhodri," she said. "Please come away from the dog."

Rhodri didn't move. The men came from the house carrying steaming cups, followed by Bethan with a tray of what looked like sandwiches and cake. They all sat on the wall in the sunshine. Completely taken aback, Morgan almost came out into the open.

He could join this party. He'd been trying to concoct excuses to approach Bethan since her father's death; he could walk straight down there now and ask whether she'd like her father's books returned.

"Get away from the dog," Elin repeated.

Self-consciously, Glen shuffled his bottom an inch or two, too kind to make the first move. When he looked back to find the boy's face still glued to him adoringly, he lengthened his neck, raised his head and turned away with false nonchalance. It reminded Morgan of the bull at Tŷ Newydd. The times he'd watched Elin Davies trying to hook the ring, only for the bull to avert his gaze, calmly lift and turn his head just out of her reach then lower it between his front legs. The bull was anticipating her taking control of him. The dog was wary of his own temperament.

The girls had their backs to him. Elin's tangle of black hair was tucked up under a stiff crimson scarf, triangling out on the back of her head. He thought about her dark silk scarves, the redness caught him out as much as anything. He moved slightly to see the inside of the van. It was half-empty. There was time. He began the run home.

His precious tools were stored in the parlour, one room in the house not quite fallen into decay. Traditionally it was kept for best: high teas and laying out dead relatives.

His father had shown no regard for tools or machinery and they soon became junk, but Morgan bought good quality and treasured them. Scythes, saws, dagging shears: everything cleaned after use. He removed the square of blanket and guard from the orange chainsaw, topped up the fuel tank and chain oil. Every link was weapon sharp and spotless, he'd bought it new. He didn't rush – the two men were taking their time, maybe carrying everything to its correct position in each room, and no doubt there'd be more tea breaks. Those girls were obviously keeping their strength to themselves.

The chainsaw fitted snugly between the tractor seat and the wheel arch, though he kept one hand on it as he drove from Abernant. He knew every inch of Cwmgwrach land and the track was a second home to him. The hours he'd spent crouched among tree roots watching wildlife, the rain falling into the leaves and the leaves falling to the ground, and now surveying Bethan's life. The leaves were rusting over; it wouldn't be long before the trees were skeletal again and their bony trunks offered no decent cover. Snow defeated him, apart from the time he walked backwards in boots too big for him. He got that idea from Mr Pritchard, who liked air to circulate his feet, nothing to do with stalking. He didn't know what he was going to do without Mr Pritchard.

He was about to turn right when the white van came bumping down the last steep stretch of the Cwmgwrach track. He cursed and waved it out into the lane in front of the tractor. The man in the passenger seat raised his hand and the van drove off towards the village. They couldn't have emptied the van in that time, not in the mannerly way they'd carried in the first half.

He sat there seething, his simple plan scuppered. It would have given some satisfaction to bar the van's exit and increase the hire costs for her. He was still reeling from the shock of seeing her and the boy, let alone the thought of them moving in with Bethan. Maybe the remaining contents of the van didn't belong to her and the men were going elsewhere, like a livestock lorry after a mart, delivering batches of sheep here and there, the farmers sharing transport costs.

He turned up on to the Cwmgwrach track and drove to his chosen spot. After felling one tree he always picked out the next, his ritual. He'd inconvenience the girls as consolation. Apart from their shopping, Rhodri might go to a nursery or playgroup; he was too young for school.

Each tree was expendable: dead, dying or blocking the light from younger trees. He valued trees, believed you had to have a bloody good reason for cutting one down. This might be the last; he had wood for this winter and maybe the next two, allowing for seasoning.

He tugged the cord. The noise felt too powerful for the size of the engine. Bethan was fanatical about preserving trees; she froze at the sound of a chainsaw. A few of the cracked lower branches had split and already brushed the ground. He knew how to make a tree fall exactly right; this one wasn't huge but enough to block the track. The trunk wheezed, creaked and crashed to the ground. He put the saw back on the tractor, took a sack and shovel and scraped up the woodchips and sawdust. Then trod the remaining dust into the mud and camouflaged the exposed white cut with branches, dirt and leaves, as best he could.

He couldn't believe Nia hadn't sniffed a rat, although she was probably too young to remember the palaver of that fallen tree, years ago. He and his father were setting off for mart with a trailer of brokers and one of the largest dead oaks had come down naturally and blocked the track. They'd missed the sale. The disruption and vivid memory of his father's apoplexy had stayed with Morgan and had, in fact, planted this whole idea in his head. Even better: towing away the offending trees had helped him ingratiate himself with Bethan. She never asked what he did with them or mentioned firewood. Then there was that pleasure of watching Veronica teeter the last half-mile in stupid shoes.

He climbed into the tractor and drove home, smug and slightly demented. His vigil wait for Bethan's phone call lasted in vain. The following morning, still nothing.

He was fencing within earshot of the outside telephone bell when he heard the distant burr of a chainsaw. His binoculars flashed across the valley and pinpointed a flash of blue on the Cwmgwrach track. He set off in a smooth swift run. Someone had stepped into his shoes.

The old man's beard was coming into new growth. He sneaked up through furry thickets like balls of rabbit fluff. Mrs Pritchard had called the pale mushroom green the colour of raw linen; he'd barely noticed the stuff till then. Whatever the colour, the feathery bushes gave good cover.

He saw Rhodri first. Perched in the driving seat of Bethan's stationary Land Rover trying to wrench the steering wheel round. It was Elin: wielding the chainsaw, driving it through the trunk, pausing to take a cloth from her belt and mop her face, like him at shearing. The possibility of the girls dealing with the tree themselves hadn't occurred to him and there they were: red-faced, formidable, sleeves rolled up, Bethan hurling the wood into the back of the Land Rover and blinking madly as if afflicted by a nervous tic. He knew that smarting pain well enough; salty sweat streaming down his forehead, eyes stinging. Her neck glistened. His mind blistered with crazy thoughts; he imagined the slimy feel of throttling her.

Half the tree had already gone. He'd been awake all night; they'd obviously started early this morning when he'd fallen into a short deep sleep and dreamed of his mad mother. The size of the tree would mean at least five journeys with Bethan's

Land Rover. Just one for his tractor and trailer. Judging by the amount of wood Bethan had chucked in the Land Rover, he had about an hour.

He weighed more now. Heavier with muscle, sturdier, like the ivy gripping the same black drainpipe. His feet found the same jutting-out stones. The tree alongside the house had matured to a stable support for his braced legs. Finding the window nailed up, he fiddled the fanlight open with his knife, breathed his body flat to its bones and squeezed through the miniscule space into his half-sisters' old bedroom. Landing on the floor, he was eight with the girls snoring and snuffling in a jumble of old clothes, a couple of squabbled-over battered dolls and one or two books.

The dark walls were now white. This was the bedroom he'd imagined her having, with enough space for the boy, unless Bethan had suggested the box room for him to sleep alone. A single bed was encased by a floor length white quilt with a symmetrical pattern of red tulips. It looked antique. He threw himself across it, expecting to inhale the fustiness of an old seamstress, but it smelled of clean river water as if wafted over the bridge every day.

He'd bought his bed linen in Swansea.

"I want a pure white bed," he'd announced, and the assistants had run round gathering packets of sheets and pillowcases, looking back at him, so out of place. Back in the dingy Abernant bedroom, he'd wiped his knife clean on his jeans, split open the cellophane packets and proudly made up his mattress on the floor with the crisp white bedding.

There had been four beds in this room when he was a child. It was impossible to pick out her furniture, not knowing what was here before she arrived. He hadn't paid much attention to the pieces coming off the van. There was a canvas camp bed with a pile of bedding. Bookshelves crammed with orange and white Penguins and a full box of books on the floor. He took one from the box, flicked through and read a few pages about two lively girls in a similar landscape, but Ireland. One was describing her mother spreading her long skirts to pee then watch it trickle down the road. He placed the book next to the bedside lamp, open at that page.

He climbed back out and crossed the yard to the cowshed. Against the back wall, replacing the papier-mâché women, were half a dozen hutches of unsettled rabbits lolloping round their new surroundings. He kicked the door in temper. A few rabbits thumped their back legs. He'd actually made room for them by destroying those grotesque paper women.

That evening he sat outside his house for a while and studied the stars. Later he was tempted to light a fire, though the brief Indian summer had warmed the kitchen. He fed the dogs. He fed the cats only because healthy cats made the best ratters, but he preferred them feral. The pair had come from the same wealthy farmer as the white bathroom and gave him the creeps more than rats. After a cheese sandwich and a coffee, he opened the whisky he kept for the visitors he never had. He sat in the dark, squirming from the taste of each tot, revisiting his women.

He felt little for Elin. Her invasion into Cwmgwrach was a shock, but a setback he'd overcome. Veronica could go to hell. He thought back: all that loitering opposite her flat, until she turned the tables and matched his bravado. Parading in her window in something skimpy, smoking coloured cigarettes in her tortoiseshell holder, knowing how he loathed smoking. Haloed gold in the lamplight, throwing herself at her boyfriend, playing to the gallery, testing the resilience of her audience. It was then he hired different cars and sank back into the shadows. She must have put herself on display most nights; he only drove to Bath every ten days or so and never kept to the same day. It was always the boyfriend who hastily drew the curtains and Morgan wondered whether he was in on Veronica's sordid tease.

Whenever the couple left the house, wrapped round each other, she'd scan the street with a snooty disdain and dismissive little snort. Morgan could have taken one step out of the darkness and touched her, those were the best times. Driving home, he sometimes wondered what, in all seriousness, he was hoping for.

He had many spying positions around Cwmgwrach. From his favourite spot he could watch Bethan cross the kitchen, back and forth to the fridge. The journey seemed constant, yet she was only drinking tea and could have left the milk bottle on the table. She'd yank open the fridge door, peer in with her bottom in the air, squat down for a proper look and get up in one nimble jerk from her haunches. Not at all dreamy like her mother, drifting vaguely round The Plas kitchen. Bethan was neatly made, robust, with definite, economic movements and strong for her size. He liked the way she'd dealt with weakly lambs last spring. He'd taught her, but she'd adapted his method to suit herself. She'd catch the ewe, squash it into a wall with one knee then spread her legs to hold it there vice-like, while she bent sideways to push the lamb to the udder. It wasn't difficult to imagine her legs clamping his, pulling him into her. She always worked the same way round: her left leg rammed deep into the wool just behind the ewe's shoulder.

He put on the light and fetched his unused writing pad, Basildon Bond, like Mr Pritchard's (duck-egg blue according to Mrs Pritchard), and wrote in a mixture of upper and lower case without realising why it looked a disjointed mess. Like most farmers, he rarely had cause to write. He said how impossible it would be to approach her with that bloody rabbit woman in residence. How he felt usurped, redundant. How deeply he cared for her. How he missed her father. How he couldn't hope to match his intellect, but how he'd promised him he'd look after her.

The last part was a lie. No one, least of all Morgan, had been prepared for Mr Pritchard's sudden death. He tried to write the word 'love' with a flourish, but his fingers froze claw-like round the pen – a fountain pen like Mr Pritchard's. He smudged the wet ink until the duck-egg blue was black and screwed the paper into a ball.

Dizzy from whisky, he had a shower, twisting and turning under the water, his head full of monkey chatter. That night he dreamed of twitching rabbits and a fluttery-faced creature who became Bethan, blinking nineteen to the dozen from her salty sweat and doing her best to keep up with the wood.

FIVE

IT WAS ELIN's idea to deal with the tree. She'd always had her own chainsaw.

"Someone's desperate for firewood," she said.

Having expected to come to a jagged splintered stump they found the base of the trunk had been freshly sawn.

Bethan thought of the other fallen trees. Fallen or felled?

Between resting the chainsaw and driving each load down to the farm they took a breather and scuffed in the leaves for missed logs. At each break Glen rushed to the edge of the track and stared unwaveringly at the same point in the trees below, ears pricked, his jaw juddering in a soft growl. At the last load Bethan strolled over to him and, when Elin wasn't looking, took a big stretch and casually waved two fingers into the ether. She'd never given the V-sign. The thought of her father that time in Aber, tuppence short for his *New Statesman*, gesticulating to her mother across the street, completely oblivious of a gang of boys in fits. Bethan could have died.

The evenings were drawing in. Her paying guests had been installed for ten days. At Nia's suggestion, Mr Gentleman had kindly written out a proper rental agreement. Everyone liked Elin, but Nia thought, and he agreed, that knowing someone solely through rabbits wasn't good enough. A two-month trial would take them to Christmas. Before Elin signed the document Bethan took out her father's Ordnance Survey map to warn her of the exact location of Abernant.

Occasionally Bethan tried to continue her life as if a new family had not taken residence. After her mother's death, she and her father had fallen into a haphazard regime. When he died, she realised she'd inherited many of his pernickety ways. Her tea had to be made from a kettle on the boil, drunk from the same thin bone china cup, coffee from a mug, cereal in a rustic pottery bowl and she always used the silver fork engraved with his initials. She fed the dog and cats before herself. Glen ate by the back door. The cats ate in the kitchen or on the yard wall – nothing to do with the weather, more their mood. Now a boy was here, they chose the wall.

She tried to have breakfast before the new arrivals came downstairs. Every morning Rhodri placed his farm animals round his bowl while his mother rummaged in the cupboard in case a different cereal had appeared overnight.

"There are oats for porridge," said Bethan.

"He doesn't like porridge," said Elin.

"Toast?"

Rhodri banged a carthorse into his spoon and said, "Jam."

"I don't like the idea of toast and jam round his teeth so early in the morning."

Bethan had noticed their toothbrushes before anything else, slotted into her tooth mug on her bathroom shelf on the day of the move.

Elin rummaged again. "Just seeing if there's anything else he might like."

Rhodri threw a cow and sheep across the kitchen.

Bethan brandished the fruit knife. "They sell other cereal in the village shop."

He was small, skinny and strong with a massive mop of ebony hair that didn't match his body, a lollipop head on a scrawny torso. Eyes so dark it was almost impossible to distinguish the pupils and luxuriant curling eyelashes that must impede his sight; the roots dense as eyeliner. Veronica had once glued false lashes on Bethan and she'd had to lift her head to see out.

As an only child, she could identify with him. He was fiercely independent, never tugged at his mother's sleeve or appeared to need her and took no notice of the rabbits, but then they were his dinner. To Bethan's astonishment, he seemed to have immediate knowledge of Cwmgwrach land. She thought he roamed too far for one so young, but he was stoic, surviving like a wild creature.

Over and over she tried to pluck up the courage to tell Elin about his brief kidnap. One evening after supper she would, maybe; Rhodri in bed, good fire, bottle of wine. But Elin seemed to do nothing but sort her stuff upstairs and suddenly too much time had elapsed to say a word. Bethan imagined the horror of a dark winter teatime and no Rhodri. "Oh, Morgan did lure him away once, but not for long. Yes, I was involved. I meant to tell you when you moved in."

Most of the time she was grateful for their presence. Like Veronica's tortoises: 'something else breathing in the house'.

Late one evening after the news Elin turned to Bethan, "I do watch Rhodri. I know you think he's running wild, but I have my eye on him all the time. I'm not neglecting him."

"I didn't think you were," said Bethan.

"I've been deluding myself. I had this ridiculous idea that if Morgan saw him playing in the fields, he'd be overcome with paternal feelings. That he wouldn't be able to resist him."

"Would you want Morgan to be a father to your son?"

"I've watched him without him knowing. Wouldn't he just hate that?"

"Definitely." Bethan hadn't set eyes on him.

"The day Rhodri bashed his head on a rock, Morgan was within arm's length of my poor little chap. I was about to run down, but I waited a second. Nothing."

"I wouldn't hold out much hope. I'm glad you watch Rhodri, he's very little," said Bethan. She was glad; the kidnap could remain her guilty secret if he was that closely watched.

Rhodri had started to give Bethan the creeps, those black eyes following her round the kitchen. She often stayed up late or got up early, just to be alone. Made tea in her special pot for one, rearranged food in the pantry, moved pans to different cupboards and ran silently up and down the stairs six times in bare feet. Reclaiming her house. One night, sitting on the bottom stair catching her breath, she watched the boy pad across the landing to the bathroom. Once he came down to the kitchen and stood and stared at her. He was sleepwalking. She wondered if Morgan had orchestrated Elin's move to Cwmgwrach, with Rhodri as his stooge.

As time went on, she saw the sense of Mr Gentleman's rental agreement, especially when Elin talked about her divorce settlement being sufficient to buy half Cwmgwrach and divide it into two nice houses. Bethan's horrified reaction would have jolted most people into house-hunting elsewhere.

Then just as it seemed things would never change, Rhodri began at a playgroup near Swansea. With time and petrol costs, it wasn't worth Elin coming home so she walked about, then sat in an Italian café to read and drink coffee for the two hours, five mornings a week. Bethan felt such a sense of relief that when Elin asked if she'd be alright on her own, Morgan actually slipped her mind for a moment.

She hadn't seen him since he'd abducted Seren.

There were rams to raddle and put in with the ewes. She told Elin she was quite capable of managing them.

The makeshift handling pens were in view from his hill. Her hands barely trembled as she secured extra hurdles with baler twine. It was still sensible to loathe him with a vengeance but she would get on. Damned if she was nervous. She was sort of ready for him. The rams looked nifty, ready for action, with their top lips peeled back into a sneer at the scent of ewes. She wanted to fix at least one harness before Morgan appeared, but keeping hold of a ram and securing the leather straps proved impossible. One sensed her jittery mood; his sharp horn caught her arm then just missed her eye. She pushed him away, chucked the harness and abandoned the battle.

This was the precise moment he'd normally materialise. Minutes passed.

She could put the raddle straight on to their wool, as many farmers did. She couldn't see the Williamses forking out on leather harnesses. She hung the tin on a post and eased through the pen, wedging each ram into a tight corner. Not attempting to tip them, she stuck a stick in the red gunge and, with some difficulty, plastered their chests with them standing. They moved off with intent in fast high-stepping trots; heads up, sniffing, and lips still curled. In minutes, three ewes boasted red rumps.

Bethan watched, puffed up with pride. Her accomplishment gave her courage. She could cope with Morgan now – in fact, some admiration wouldn't go amiss. To see her rams working and her ewes at last looking well, was not a time for solitude.

He'd probably discovered Elin's morning routine and was drinking coffee with her in the Italian café.

In November it snowed unexpectedly and heavily as Bethan was returning from Nia's. The track of wet orange leaves was obliterated by a white sugar coating. The tyres crunched as she drove under black branches topped in crystals, inching her way carefully round bends she could usually have driven blindfolded. Not so easy in snow.

Whenever she went out alone at night, she left the main gate in the wooded part of the track unbolted. Occasionally she'd talked herself into a state and become too spooked to get out of the Land Rover to open and close it. Despite a few dents and shattered headlight, she'd almost perfected her manoeuvre. First a gentle push with the bumper to open the gate halfway, drive through slowly, brief bash as the gate swung back, then accelerate at speed before it crashed back with more force.

Tonight the bumper touched the gate. Her heart flipped. Nothing moved: the bolt was fastened. She sat for a moment. She could reverse and risk going over the edge. She peered for footprints in the snow and saw nothing. It would take seconds to jump out, run and pull back the bolt.

She did it. He must have expected her to open the gate wide and loop the baler twine over the other post, but she was back inside and locked in when his distorted face appeared. His fingers flattened to white blobs on the glass as he tried to prise the side window open. He was mouthing something inaudible over the noise of the diesel engine. She stared at his snow-white shirt and revved the engine.

She was about to outwit him. Had he thought to slide the bolt across, he'd have trapped her. The gate was ajar, swinging slightly. With no first gear, she had to pull away in second, but it worked, she smashed into the gate and shot through before it flew back.

The entire landscape was masked pure white and empty. She had to guess where the ditch bordered the track. She aimed for the ruin, the only landmark. Safely past and she was bumping carefully down the incline to the house.

"Jesus Christ!" She gripped the steering wheel.

He was an upside-down face on the windscreen, his grimace reversed to a grotesque smile. She slammed on the brakes, the Land Rover slid sideways and came to a halt, and he slithered down from the roof on to the bonnet.

"I can't hear you," he shouted through the windscreen.

"Get off, you lunatic, for Christ's sake!" She felt her face burning.

The headlights and snow illuminated the house. Morgan leapt from the bonnet like a cat and was at the driver's door, wrenching the handle up and down.

"Go, just bloody go," she hiss-screeched through her teeth then slid the window open an inch and held on to it. "For Christ's sake, the dog will wake Rhodri. Elin will still be up. God, to think I was worrying about a tree on the track."

His thick fingers came in, clamped hers and pushed the window wide. She dodged the arm that followed, but he reached to stroke her hair then withdrew.

"I never do the trees when you're alone," he said, with surprise. "Hadn't you realised? It's only when you're in company and I've no idea where you're going or what you're up to." His expression was a poor attempt at lovesick, more of sly satisfaction. "It drives me mad, I can't bear it."

Stunned, she put her face to the glass. "Fuck off."

He flashed a look of disgust then a charming smile and began to jog down the hill. She straightened the Land Rover and drove slowly down. He disappeared through the gap at the side of the house. She slumped over the steering wheel. He would either be creeping down through the garden and back up to Abernant, or lying in wait.

She grabbed her bag and ran to the back door. As she turned to lock it, Glen leapt at her back with such enthusiasm that he knocked her against the door. The house was in darkness. Elin must have gone to bed. Not even a lamp on in the kitchen.

Still shaky, she knelt to stroke Glen and wondered if Elin had thought to let him out before she went to bed. She filled the kettle. If she opened the door now, he would pick up Morgan's scent and tear round the side of the house, barking and growling and wake them. He leant against her legs while she drank a cup of hot chocolate at the kitchen table, anticipating a tap on the window.

When all had been quiet for half an hour, she opened the back door and whispered, "Go and do something." He looked at her and sat down to wait; she always walked across the yard with him last thing at night. "Go on." She held the door open at a dog-sized gap, knowing exactly how fast she could slam and bolt it and how quickly Morgan could move. "Go on." At last Glen caught her anxiety and realised what was required of him. She was not leaving the house. He walked to the hedge, peed and came straight back.

She locked the door, left the kitchen light on and felt her way upstairs in the dark. There was no light showing under Elin's bedroom door. She tiptoed back along the landing and closed her curtains, determined not to put on another light. She reached the bathroom in the dark, hearing her mother's warning to always be careful at the top of the stairs. She had lived in constant fear of falling down stairs and escalators. Whatever would she make of all this? Bethan flushed with shame at the thought.

The thick curtains were as effective as her parents' old blackout curtains, though he knew her bedroom, damn him. She sat at her dressing table and switched on the lamp. The pink bulb was little more than a child's nightlight and left the rest of the room in deep shadow. She grimaced at her hazy reflection through the worn-out silvering of the mirror. Did she look mad?

Veronica's gift of body lotion sat on *Middlemarch*, the book her father had insisted she read before she died. She could turn the key in the door and read for a month. She began to massage her neck as per Veronica's instructions, but couldn't remember whether to smooth up round her chin or down to her heart. She spread the excess from her slimy throat over her arms and when her hands were ready, she picked up the book, hoping her bookmark had miraculously moved forward from chapter two. She went over to the bed and sat down on the edge. The room was cold; she'd find her nightie before she undressed. She never made her bed and the duvet was in a mound. She turned to pull it straight. Had she not rearranged her room, her bed would have been in full view in the spotted dressing-table mirror and she might have noticed the duvet rising and falling.

A large hand shot out and clamped her mouth. His rough palm killed the scream that would have penetrated the house and had Elin bursting through the door. He pulled her down beside him, shoving her head deep into the feather pillow. The shock was so great she almost vomited into his hand.

"Don't speak," he whispered; his lips brushing her ear. He removed his hand.

Her eyes sprang wide and she felt hot enough to burst. Though smiling, his expression was insolent as if an ear-piercing scream wouldn't have bothered him in the slightest. Her speech returned.

"Get out, before Elin hears."

"But I'm spending the night with you, what's left of it."

"I said get out. How the bloody hell did you get in?"

"The front door was unlocked. I thought you were never coming home. We won't speak above a whisper. We won't move. I'll leave before daylight. She won't hear a thing. Would you rather get undressed?"

"My God, what possesses you? You're insane."

He dragged the duvet from under her to cover her and she saw he was fully clothed. The pink lamp barely lit their locked faces. She lay rigid. Her little travelling clock ticked for its life, the duvet crackled like paper, her heart thumped. He stayed on his side, propped on one elbow, watching her. She stared wide-eyed at the ceiling. He stroked her cheek then lay back. They stayed there, side by side, not touching.

She'd no idea what to do for the best. Eventually she turned her back on him, rolled over and curled up. He eased up to her back, put his arm round her and searched for her hand to hold under the duvet. Her face was a few inches from her clock. It was 3 a.m. For an hour he did nothing more than tweak her hair from his face, squeeze her hand and whisper flurries of unfinished sentences softly into her right ear. When he wanted her to hear he spoke clearly, but quietly.

As the minute hand reached 4.30, he peeled his hand away from hers and slid it down between her legs. Holding her there firmly, he heaved her body back against his so they were curled tightly together again. She tried to stay cold. He squeezed her there, squeezed and pushed hard against her jeans, then slid his hand back up.

"Willpower and self-discipline interest me," he said. "Elin Davies teased me for five years."

She didn't move or speak. His hot hand had gone. She'd die. How clever he was to stay dressed. Lying together, fully clothed. Three hours of stroking and murmurings to stay in her head as the most fearful, sensuous night ever. When the clock said six, he flung back the duvet and leapt from the bed, assuring her she'd sleep the minute he'd gone.

"Be quiet,"she said, in her loudest whisper. "After all that, don't wake them now."

"They're not here."

She threw back the duvet, sat up and still whispered. "What do you mean?"

"They left last night."

She jumped out of bed, ran down the landing and flung open Elin's bedroom door. It was tidier than before.

"She said you'd deceived her," he shouted from halfway down the stairs. "She didn't know you were my girlfriend, or about that time we took the boy."

Bethan closed the bedroom door and turned the key. She lay down on Elin's bed, exhausted. He could break down the door and attack her or bring her breakfast on a tray. Either was possible and she no longer cared.

When daylight came, she crept to the window. It was cold and the glass was wet. There was a ghostly haze over everything, like the clouds had connived to descend in a line and stop just short of the earth. In the gap between land and mist, a red dog fox was picking his way across the garden. She thought about the rabbits and must have made a noise against the window because he looked up, straight at her, his brazen stare unnerving her even further. Sneering at her gullibility. If she'd had the gun at hand, he'd be dead.

SIX

SHE MUST HAVE finally fallen asleep on Elin's bed only to be woken by an insistent knocking on the front door. She sat up. Either he'd lost his ability to walk through doors or was changing tactics; he knew exactly where she'd incarcerated herself. She waited for footsteps on the stairs, but the knocking continued at a polite level, not getting heated and not giving up. She unlocked the bedroom door and crept to the bathroom window. A black beast of a car was parked nose to the gate. She flew downstairs.

Mr Gentleman stood at the back door, his tall frame haloed in a golden glow. "Ah, thank goodness," he said with a long out-breath. "You're here." He stepped forward. "And safe."

She would have liked his arms round her, but he wasn't a demonstrative man and they didn't know each other well.

"Are you alright, my dear?" His face screwed with concern. "I've come for you. Nia asked you to bring clothes and Glen: she wants you to come and stay."

Could she say she'd been taken hostage and it was impossible to leave? Her eyes darted round the kitchen, out across the empty yard, past the old Morris Oxford then back to Mr Gentleman.

"I can't go from the farm," she said, though the notion of staying felt doom-laden. "But thank you."

"I promised Nia I wouldn't leave without you. Lock up everything, though I've heard it makes little difference."

"I don't know..." She looked at him properly. The neat brown moustache moved gently with his lovely smile. He was overflowing with kindness yet as un-huggable as her father. A man of decorum whom Morgan would hold in similar esteem to her father, whose presence at Cwmgwrach would scupper any further monstrous moves.

She looked towards her father's study. How she wished she could still call him for supper then press her ear against the door, daring his typewriter to ping again at the end of another line. She ran back upstairs and stopped dead at her own bedroom door. The bed had been made – the pillows plumped up and duvet straightened.

She hadn't invited Mr Gentleman inside. Her guardian angel with his beautiful voice and manners, and she'd left him standing at the door. She threw a few things in a bag, grabbed her toothbrush from the bathroom and ran back down.

"I'll come, thank you." She locked everything she could think of and they were walking to the car. "I'll have to come back and feed the sheep – oh, and the rabbits. I'll just see to them, if they're there."

"They will be," said Mr Gentleman.

They came to the wire at the sight of her, noses twitching. She filled their dishes and water bottles then put out two large bowls of cat food and biscuits on the wall. She scanned the yard and only then remembered last night's snowfall. There was not a dollop of snow on the stones or a splodge of slush. She looked up; the mountain tops were iced white.

He carried her bag to the car and opened the passenger door for her.

"Elin and Rhodri are with Nia, they arrived last night in a state. Morgan had thrown them out."

"What, out of my house?" She got in and Glen squeezed in at her feet. As they pulled away, she slithered down in the seat and curled up with her face to the door until the car had passed through the village and started over the mountain. Then she sat up.

"You and Elin must have passed each other last night," he said. He took the endless bends with care, avoiding the old ewes who stepped out without warning.

It was the first time she'd ignored the huge views.

"She probably had the sense to keep to the main road."

They were passing the castle ruins on the pointy hill her mother called the coconut pyramid. Bethan remembered a sunny picnic with Auntie Cecily and Veronica and almost cried. She closed her eyes.

"You don't have to tell me," said Mr Gentleman. "But I suspect Morgan was waiting for your return last night," he changed down for the hairpin bends as the road began its descent. "Nia's told me a little of her childhood. I believe he's certifiable."

"Definitely."

"I just hope nothing untoward happened to you last night, my dear."

She shook her head. He was too kind. They drove a few miles in silence before she caved in and described their night of whispers, lying side by side fully clothed, and how he hadn't hurt her. She said nothing of their past. She shuddered.

Mr Gentleman had inclined his head, not to miss a word. "Extraordinary way to behave, with the two of you there alone. We're dealing with a disturbed mind."

The 'we' warmed her entire being. Just for a moment she imagined a tap-tap-tap to be her heart pumping relief.

The tap developed into a knock, and he slowed down. It grew louder. Mr Gentleman said he'd never experienced a big end going, but could imagine this is exactly how it would sound. Her father was always talking about the "bally big end" going, but she'd never experienced one either.

"We'll stop at the bottom of the hill," he said. "There's a telephone box."

On the next sharp bend, the steering wheel whipped through his hands and the back of the car collapsed. There was a screech of metal scraping the road and a shower of sparks. He swerved in and out of the hedge and on and off the opposite bank. Bethan held on to Glen and clung to the seat. As he struggled to brake and remain on the road something overtook them. The rear wheel was bouncing down the hill in huge leaps past a row of cottages, a couple of parked cars and finally hitting the wall of the pub. At impact it soared into the air, twirled, and landed on its side. The dismembered car skidded sideways to a halt.

Bethan stared at the stone wall. Someone was opening the car door and helping her out. Then she and Mr Gentleman were seated by the pub's log fire sipping brandy, shocked but unhurt, with Glen nuzzling into her clenched hand for comfort. She looked round the faces. Their bizarre arrival would be the talk of the pub forever. When an elderly couple burst in and accused Mr Gentleman of smashing up their new car, he almost laughed, quite positive he hadn't crashed into anything. It was the wheel, they said. He followed them outside to be shown the stoved-in bonnet of their Hillman Hunter. He calmly gave them his name and address.

The mechanic from the local garage suggested Bethan walk back up the hill to look for the wheel nuts on the side of the road. She kicked three from the dusty grass.

"How many enemies do you have, then?" he asked Mr Gentleman, while lifting on the wheel. "Wheels don't work loose round here; they're usually stuck fast with muck." He tightened the wheel nuts. "You can drive like this, but get the rest of the nuts soon as possible." He straightened up and wiped his greasy hands across the front of his stained overalls like a child. "You'll get wheel nuts in a scrapyard," he grinned, heaved himself up into the truck, lit a cigarette and drove off, the exhaust belting out black fumes.

Bethan wanted to shout after him to ask if he was serious about someone tampering with the wheel nuts and whether they should be ringing the police. She looked at Mr Gentleman's refined white face and tried to imagine him rooting round a scrapyard.

It was afternoon by the time they reached his house. Nia was pacing the drive with Rhodri circling her on a tricycle.

"We'll be eating in the main house this evening, Bethan, my dear," said Mr Gentleman before pulling up. "I've prepared the old nursery for little Rhodri, so he'll be with us. Now, I must get on with my cooking, after our irritating little hold-up."

"I will tell everyone about last night, but in time. Thank you for rescuing me."

"Mum's the word." He smiled and pulled on the handbrake just like her father always had, careful to press in the button.

Nia ran to open the passenger door.

"You alright? Come on in." She put her arm round Bethan. Glen, still on alert, opened and closed his mouth in what might have been a little snap had he not recognised Nia in time.

Bethan slumped forward and laid her head on his.

"Please don't change your character because of that bastard. I couldn't bear it." She began to weep silently.

"Bethan should have a rest, Nia," said Mr Gentleman. "We'll eat at eight."

Bethan woke to a note with her instructions: 'Borrow a frock and come to the big house at 7.45'. She had a bath, chose a long black dress and made up her face.

Though the annexe was adjoined, she was unable to find a door through – not that she tried very hard. She wanted to enter the mansion by the pillared porch. She went out and round to the drive with Glen at her heels.

Mr Gentleman was too genteel to stagnate in one room, yet standing in the moonlight she counted eighteen sash windows over the three floors. It was a house to boast a ballroom. She pictured endless white dust sheets protecting the Gentleman family furniture. Lamplight glowed from the ground floor.

Nia met her at the door. She ushered her through a grand hallway into a vast dining room and returned to assist Mr Gentleman in the kitchen. Elin was upstairs settling Rhodri in his unfamiliar surroundings.

There was no sign of electric lighting, no chandeliers or lamps. The room was lit by nineteen white candles of varying heights on a baronial dining table and half a tree blazing in a fireplace the size of a tool-shed. The candles flickered in an imperceptible draught from the chimney and cast iridescent reflections from crystal vases of anemones. The table was laid for four with weighty silver cutlery and a mile between each place setting. Bethan swept round in Nia's elegant dress, 'taking a turn round the room' with Glen glued to her side. Away from the table, the room fell into gloom. A wall of opulent velvet curtains draped and bunched from floor to ceiling, the deep purple indistinguishable from that of the old wallpaper.

She tried to choose where she'd sit, unless they were told. Five minutes later they were seated. She and Elin had hugged stiffly, noting each other's puffed-up eyes.

"I fed the rabbits," said Bethan.

Nia appeared wearing a long scarlet dress and giant diamante brooch, Mr Gentleman in a black dinner suit with a white rose in the lapel. Dressed to kill – maybe they were going out later to perform.

"We've cooked an early Christmas dinner," he said. "No turkeys ready in November, so we have chicken with the appropriate festive trimmings."

Elin left the table to help bring in the food. The three of them came back and forth with dishes and jugs, casting giant shadows across the room. When the table was full, it was Elin who opened the champagne and filled their glasses.

"Morgan arrived as soon as you left last night, Bethan," she said. "He was vile, threatening – said I had no place at Cwmgwrach, that it belonged to you and him."

"What?"

"He stood in the kitchen while I packed our things. I couldn't stand up to his temper, not in front of poor Rhodri. It was awful – he was so upset."

Mr Gentleman raised his glass. "To our futures. After this afternoon's fracas with the wheel, I think I'm also in his line of fire. *Nadolig Llawen* in advance."

They lifted their glasses and drank.

"I phoned Cwmgwrach when Elin arrived here last night, Bethan," said Nia. "I presumed you'd gone straight to bed."

"I did."

"Which one of you do you think he adores?" asked Mr Gentleman, carving thin slices of chicken breast.

"My mother always said he only loves two people," said Nia. "Him when he's in and him when he's out. The stories I could tell you. Bethan knows my childhood."

"Yes, do share stories. Stalwart girls, none of you afraid to be alone."

"He poisoned one of our father's collies," said Nia. "It had gone for his lurcher. I watched him chuck a lump of red meat into the shed. We kept strychnine for moles – farmers with a licence could buy it over the chemist's counter. We had enough in a jam jar to kill a hundred men."

"Good God," said Mr Gentleman.

Bethan felt uncomfortable seeing him shocked.

"Once he made me balance a heavy metal disc for him to fix to the mower," said Nia. "I was little. Him swearing and cursing, my tiny hands fighting to keep the damn thing in place, then he smashed it on to my foot, no warning. I thought all my toes were broken. I ran to the dog sheds, shoved my foot in a water bowl."

"A true sadist," said Mr Gentleman. "Do dig in, everyone. There's bread sauce and cranberry, chestnut stuffing and gravy with red wine."

Bethan swallowed. How could her throat be dry after three glasses of champagne and faced with a sumptuous meal?

As they ate, Mr Gentleman's interjections grew more random, as if he were grasping at straws for diversions. Nia told more childhood stories: most Bethan knew, others were horribly disturbing. At the end of the main course, Elin excused herself to go upstairs and check on Rhodri, Bethan quickly following to be shown the lavatory. The hefty dining room door closed and they started up the curving staircase.

"Elin, do they know Rhodri is Morgan's?" asked Bethan.

"He's not." She stopped so abruptly that Bethan bumped into her. "He's mine. All mine." She turned to face Bethan. "That bastard's forfeited all rights. He's had every opportunity to speak to Rhodri; he's spied on us constantly since we moved in with you."

"Why didn't you say? Are you sure?"

Elin shrugged. "Positive. Yesterday a ewe shot past a tree in one of those startled trit-trots, and a corner of his coat was poking out from the trunk. If I heard him whistle his dogs way up on the mountain, I could relax for a while."

They carried on up the stairs.

"Tonight feels like a circus," said Bethan. "With Mr Gentleman encouraging our 'turns', the table lit for centre stage and us in virtual darkness."

"Yes, though if he wasn't the ringmaster, we'd all be letting rip with our gorier details, outdoing each other's horrors. Even plastered, we're restrained because of him, dear man."

They parted on the first landing. When Bethan returned to the dining room, Mr Gentleman was actually talking about the difficulty of restraint. How he must stop tricking his little niece who now believed all pennies came from ears.

Elin came back in.

"Another thing, he loathed moisturiser," she said. "'Whatever are you thinking using that slimy muck, knowing I can't stand anything unnatural or false?' I'd have asked about his cologne if he hadn't been so furious."

"Goodness, the man's deranged," said Mr Gentleman, putting a little silver lighter to the Christmas pudding. The brandy flared into orange and purple stripes in the candlelight. Nia opened another bottle.

"Next minute," said Elin, "It's *'rwy'n dy garu di'* all over again and him acting as if nothing's happened, face the picture of innocence."

Bethan wanted to ask when exactly he had last professed his love for her. She felt she should add to the venomous tales, but her mind was on the groaning shelves in the Cwmgwrach barns: the gunked-up paint pots, creosote, Jeyes Fluid, all abandoned by the Williamses. Unlabelled jam jars of strychnine? She kept quiet. The night was a muddle.

While refilling Mr Gentleman's glass, Nia put her hand on his shoulder. "Could we saw him in half, please, and not as an illusion?"

"Possibly. No one to miss a friendless man when he vanishes into thin air."

I'd have missed him at lambing, thought Bethan. At last she spoke. "The first day I saw him was at the school railings, staring in at me. His hands were round a cat's throat, pretending he was going to chop its neck, how you kill a rabbit."

Elin nodded.

"The day I 'swallowed' a worm," said Nia. "We were ten."

"Ah," said Mr Gentleman. "So young to be drawn to the wonders of illusion."

"And me in their spell," said Bethan.

"Then me," said Elin. "And I really was old enough to know better."

"We are where we are," said Mr Gentleman. "Let's raise our glasses again. Elin has agreed to work for me and she and Rhodri are going to live here. I'm so hopeless at housekeeping and appointments and bookings, all that sort of thing."

SEVEN

CHRISTMAS DREW CLOSER. It was a frenetic time for magic shows and Bethan was subjected to every miners' welfare hall and social club for miles. Her dear friends wouldn't let her out of their sight. She watched the rowdiest audience heckle crude comedians then settle in awed silence to be mesmerised by the fine illusionists. If she didn't go home with them after performances, Nia came to Cwmgwrach. She and Nia always drove to the mountain together to feed and check the sheep. Bethan never went alone.

The rabbits were staying there until after Christmas. Bethan insisted on seeing to them alone: the cowshed was across the cobbles just yards from the kitchen, well within shouting distance. At first Nia glanced at the clock whenever Bethan went out to them, until it was agreed they were becoming totally paranoid.

A week before Christmas, Bethan was pouring rabbit pellets from the glass sweet jar when a tiny package fell out into a feed bowl. A scrawled label had been tied on with thin red ribbon: 'Nadolig Llawen, cariad. You have a lovely time.' For a moment she could only stare at it. Then she imagined his face an inch from hers, saying it aloud with the emphasis on 'you': "You have a lovely time while I rot in hell." She quickly put it in her pocket. Five minutes later she opened it in her bedroom.

White tissue round a black box with a pair of delicate silver earrings pinned to a square of grey velvet.

Veronica rang the next day. "Remember that time you saved my letter as a treat to read with your supper after you'd finished doing revolting sheep things, and nearly didn't pick me up? I was standing in the station for two hours."

Bethan cringed. "Yes, our phone was out of order."

"I've done exactly the same thing: saved what I thought was a birthday card and when I opened it this morning I …"

"Oh, Veronica! I'm so sorry, I forgot it was your birthday."

"Never mind that, it's too near Christmas anyway. No, it's a message from your lunatic on the mountain."

"What! What a Christmas card?"

"A letter no less – well, scribbled note. Said he couldn't write to you because Nia's there permanently and she might recognise his writing and rip it up."

"She was here all the time, but it was getting ridiculous. I've just insisted she went home for some show rehearsal."

"He's seriously ill, he says. If you believe that, you'll believe anything. Probably wants you to go up there. Don't."

It was after lunch, not that she'd had any. His dogs went berserk as she reached the Abernant yard, charging to the end of their chains and, regardless of the pressure on their necks, leapt about on their hind legs and barked themselves into a frenzy. Then they recognised her and went quiet. She pushed open the warped front door of the farmhouse, stepped into icy gloom then made her way down the dark hall into a stench of rancid butter and bacon and the lazy winter buzz of flies around meat.

Morgan was flat on the kitchen floor; face down on the flagstones with the knife he used for sheep's feet open at his side. The shock was greater as she never ever saw him still. She watched for breath. If he was alive, the dogs' madness would have alerted him and he'd know she was standing there. He'd hear a pin drop. She stayed still, cold to the bone, brittle as a frozen bird.

He lifted his head in slow motion and turned it to look at her. "I'm dying," he said feebly in an old man's voice.

His repertoire knew no bounds. His half-closed eyes had sunk deeper in darker bonier sockets and the lines either side of his down-turned mouth were more prominent. His skin bore such a deathly pallor of jaundice her first thought was stage-paint, but the whites of his eyes were also yellow. She stayed at the kitchen door. Such a dramatic decline in a man such as him was impossible.

"I have a tumour at the base of my spine," he croaked, twisting his arm back to point.

She assumed the new voice was his attempt at anguish. He put his finger on to a lump beneath his overalls. This was ridiculous. She waited for him to jump to his feet, whizz her round and laugh at her gullibility.

"Feel it."

She shook her head, "I can see it."

"It's going to kill me." He now sounded slightly tearful. "I thought you cared for me. Feel it, close your eyes and feel it." He gave a squirm.

"I don't want to, I believe you."

"I said feel it." His voice was resuming its odious tone.

If this was a trick and she turned and ran, he'd catch her immediately. If he leapt up and stabbed her, her blood would drain out pale pink like the watery juices of an undercooked chicken. Keeping an eye on his other hand and the penknife, she slowly knelt down at his side. On her knees, arms wrapped round herself, her ribs taut as new fencing.

He grabbed her right arm just below the elbow, pulled it from her body and took her hand. "Unclench it," he ordered. He peeled her fingers open and dragged her right down.

Her stomach tightened. He slid her hand across his overalls, prised her fingers straight and laid them on the lump. He pressed them hard down on a peppering of nodules and what felt like a thick stem. The whole lot squidged and moved.

"Now then," he said. "Sorry for me now?"

She tried to pull her hand away but he played her fingers over and round the strange protrusion. Then a fast manoeuvre: his body snaked round, coiled upright and in seconds their positions were reversed. Bethan lay in his place on the flagstones, face down, hands tied behind her back with a silk scarf. He stepped across her, sat on her waist and began to rise and fall as if trotting out a horse. The pressure increased with each landing, flattening her into the cold stone and squeezing the breath out of her. She held her bottom lip in her teeth, determined not to cry out or plead.

He stopped and stood up. Leaving her hands tied, he flipped her over and hovered directly above her. He began to rub his hands together and what looked like a shower of breadcrumbs rained down on her face. Her reactions were razor sharp, but several fell into her eyes before she'd screwed them shut. She cried out then.

He slid a leaf into her mouth. "Eat."

She could tell he was smiling from the shape of his voice. She spat. There was a stink of school dinners. Her eyes were stinging; she forced them open to a slit, saw his hands rubbing more of the creamy-coloured nuggets and slammed them shut again. Now he was squeezing them between her lips, scooping up the bits he'd dropped and ramming them into her mouth along with bits of dirt and hay from the floor. The texture and putrid taste – she realised it was cauliflower, tiny florets of old cauliflower.

She choked and spluttered. He was laughing maniacally until she began to retch. He stepped back. He could slice ears off live sheep, blast foxes and rabbits to smithereens and live in conditions most down and outs would sniff at, but he couldn't stomach vomit. Vomit and moisturiser.

Sick was filling her mouth, but not fast enough. She struggled with her hands, a finger down her throat would do it, but they were too tightly tied. She retched as loudly and disgustingly as she could, it was coming. Please make her spew cauliflower and filth over him. He picked up his knife, tipped her enough to reach her wrists and sliced through the silk scarf. Then dragged her, heaving, across the kitchen. She recognised a large old whelping box from a barn. Pain shot through her as he tried to bend her body.

"Get in," he said. "Have a sleep, like a dog."

"I'm going to be sick," she mumbled, mouth full.

"Filthy bitch!" He ran from the kitchen as muck showered from her mouth.

She waited in the silence, her eyes closed and smarting, back throbbing. She slid the scarf back and forth through her hands. Was that why he'd suggested her wearing it when they made love, so if the fancy took him, it was on hand for bondage or strangulation? It had felt so erotic, being naked but for a black silk scarf.

Eyes still shut, she pulled herself up and tried to sit with her arms clasping her knees, but her back was too painful. She leant against the kitchen wall and rocked her top half backwards and forwards, that repetitive rock of someone deranged. She'd lost the run of herself. She presumed the show was over, the extravaganza – the feel and stench of his gnarled cauliflower tumour, its thick stem and warty surface.

His gun came to mind and she rocked faster. He could shoot her for vomiting. She forced her eyes open wide, circled her eyeballs then wiped them with a damp tissue from her pocket. Her vision and thinking blurred, she stood up using the wall for support and eased herself along to the kitchen cabinet. The gun was in its usual place. She almost breathed normally. Tentatively she crossed to the window. There was no sign of him in the yard. A cold blow hit her face, the east wind was forcing through the patchwork of glass and hardboard, along with the sound of a distant whistle. She staggered outside, heard a shout then "Away".

He was in the far field, standing on a rock whistling his dogs. Moving sheep. The two dogs had gathered a small bunch of his in-lamb ewes, maybe thirty or forty, quietly weaving them across the bare land. Was this his idea of reparation, appeal to her love of working dogs and all would be well again? She remembered telling him how that first sight of a thousand sheep coming down off the hills had made her tingle with goosebumps. Gone on and on about how awe-inspiring she found it – romantic, even.

With her back steeped in pain, she left the yard and made for the woods, circling awkwardly to check he wasn't following, an agonising waltz down through the trees. At the end, she climbed a five-bar gate he'd chained to its posts to keep it from collapsing. Back throbbing, she was astride it when the only hinge came out, the gate dropped a foot and she fell on to the top rung of heavy rusted iron. She made no noise even though she felt split in two. She wiggled off the gate and forced herself on, didn't look back and didn't cry until the river was in sight. Once across the bridge, she clamped her hand hard between her legs, flung herself into the coarse yellow grass and wailed.

"What the hell's he done now?" Elin was skidding to her knees at her side.

"I fell," said Bethan. Glen was fussing at her face, tail circling with joy. "The gate dropped as I was climbing it. How are you here, where's Rhodri?"

"He's with Nia. I've just spoken to Veronica on your phone. It was ringing and ringing and the back door was unlocked. What's happened, Bethan? Tell me!"

"The hinge fell out of the gate posts."

"Okay." Elin pulled Bethan to her feet. "Let's get you up to the house. Not far now. Christ, your eyes are red raw."

The grass was sopping. Bethan slid, one step forward, two back, overtaken by her new pain. Clinging to Elin, she focused on the pigsty ruin then the kissing gate, the cowshed and, at last, the farmhouse. "Why are you here, Elin?"

"I borrowed a van and came for the rabbits. I thought it was weird, seeing Glen scratching at the door, not being with you. I wouldn't have gone inside if the phone hadn't gone on and on. It was Veronica, desperate to talk to you."

"Oh." Once inside, Bethan stared at the black windows.

Elin hurried to close every curtain tightly then revive the fire. She made sweet tea, ran a bath with drops of lavender then phoned Veronica and Nia.

Bethan lowered her aching body into the steamy water. She'd examined herself for bruises: none on her front, probably some on her back. She slid gently up and down, breathing in lavender fumes. Never had hot water felt so wonderful. The bath had become her sanctuary. No doubt he'd gone sprinting to his precious shower the minute he saw her leave, cleanse his body and mind of her vomit. She was pleased to have messed his floor.

Elin sat halfway up the stairs, on guard. "Bethan, you cannot live here alone."

"I can." She took a dripping leg from the bath, stretched across and closed the door with her foot.

Elin came to the top step. "His own father came close to killing him once. Nia told me the other night how he hid in the trees till midnight waiting for him to come home. Morgan got out to open the last gate and his father ended up with the shotgun yards from his head."

"What stopped him? His own son though – surely he wouldn't have told Nia?"

"No, she overheard him telling her mother. He said had it not been for the rain, Morgan would have heard his heart hammering and, for a split second, it seemed worth a life sentence. Morgan had poisoned his best collie." Elin moved to the landing and leaned against the bathroom door. "Please Bethan, see sense. When Rhodri and I were living here, you were a complete nervous wreck. Look at the weight you've lost. Please think about moving from here."

Bethan sank her ears under water. Elin could continue, she would hear no more than an echo of disconnected words. The amount of her face left showing was all one saw of a nun: eyes, nose and mouth exposed by the wimple. Brain drowning with her ears. She came back up in tepid water with the taste of putrid cauliflower coating the roof of her mouth and Elin banging on the bathroom door.

"Veronica's on her way."

Bethan shot upright; a bow wave hit the bathroom floor and she screamed as pain knifed her in the spine.

Elin burst through the door behing her. "Christ almighty, Bethan, your back's covered in marks! You'll be black and blue. What the hell's happened?"

"You go on, I'll be down in a minute," said Bethan. She could no longer remember who knew what.

The sitting room was beautifully warm; Elin had built up the fire. She'd given Bethan two Anadin, sat her in an armchair and tucked a hot water bottle down her back. The first bottle of wine had taken effect.

Veronica was opening a second. "Strange, how things come to you," she said. "A while ago I was coming home in thick fog, a man stopped me and asked if I knew where a Mr Thompson lived. I said no and he started telling where he thought he might live and asked how long I'd lived in Bath. I didn't realise it was him till he moved on – he'd tried to disguise his accent. I called after him, 'That's Morgan, isn't it?' He kept walking."

"He was made a different way," said Elin.

Bethan pressed her back against the hot water bottle and listened to them drip-feed their hideous experiences, barely hearing each other. She was grateful to Elin for her concerned glances and no questioning.

She couldn't have lambed without him, but then it was second nature to him, mere instinct how expertly he'd paired up the ewes and lambs. His pursuit of her was calculated.

There was an incident during lambing not worth relating to Elin and Veronica, but for her a significant intimacy. She was in a pen trying to get a lamb to suck; Morgan kept staring at her then quickly looking away. She'd asked what was wrong, he said nothing. She asked again. Nothing. Tell me. He said if he told her, she'd be thinking about it all the time. Eventually he explained that whenever she was anxious, a slight red mark came up just above the bridge of her nose, but he hadn't wanted to say anything because he 'knew what she was like'. She was vaguely aware of the mark, but the fact he'd noticed and "knew what she was like" had caused her to blush with pleasure. She'd lived on that for a while. She couldn't tell them now – it was pathetic.

Veronica pulled a bottle of brandy from her bag.

"We need a nightcap, funny how we're all stone-cold sober. That's another funny thing: he doesn't really drink. If his mood swings were based on alcohol, you could predict them."

"Exactly," said Elin.

Veronica poured brandy into their wine glasses, which wasn't at all like her.

"I really thought he was going to strangle me once," said Elin. "With my own scarf! One minute we were... okay, then he suddenly went mad. Scared me to death."

"Bastard. He asked me if I wore scarves," said Veronica.

Bethan sat up straight: it was her turn. She eased out of the chair with difficulty, stood with her back to the fire and stared down at the rug, watching her fingers tremble as she spoke. Nothing spared, she'd kept her own counsel for too long. They listened stunned, with the odd gasp. By the end her whole body was shaking. "Why the hell I mentioned his help at lambing time. I'd rather him dead than appear next year."

"Who but a madman would have thought of cauliflower?" said Elin.

"I'm calling the police," said Veronica quietly.

"No," said Elin. She led Bethan to the sofa. "Totally pointless with a man like that. Fine if they took him away immediately, but they wouldn't and he'd go berserk."

"Would we be talking like this if Nia was here?" said Veronica. "Blood thicker than water and all that."

"Course," said Bethan. "She detests him and they're only half-blood. It was Nia who asked Mr Gentleman to saw him in half. Properly!"

"And straight away he said there's no one to miss a friendless man when he vanishes," said Elin. "He's dead right; there wouldn't be a single enquiry."

"That bloody letter," said Veronica, eyes filling, black mascara smudged. "I should have screwed it up immediately, not told you. If only he was tortured by his own awfulness. I've always been curious about him, how perverse is that?"

"He is a curiosity," said Bethan.

They glazed over and fell into silence, nursing their evil thoughts. No one moved from the sitting room. Veronica and Elin stayed curled uncomfortably in armchairs and slept fitfully. Bethan tossed and turned on the sofa desperate to stretch out on her bed, but too nervy to go upstairs alone. Until she remembered the shotgun he'd lent her. No one stirred as she rolled slowly off the sofa, crept from the room and tiptoed upstairs. The gun and box of cartridges were hidden behind her clothes in the wardrobe. She returned with them to the sitting room, slid them under the sofa and felt a speck of comfort. They woke at dawn with headaches. Bethan was stiff and her back ached.

"Coffee, everyone?" asked Veronica, fishing for a mirror in her handbag. "Bloody hell, I can't remember the last time I slept in my make-up." She filled the kettle, stirred three cups at speed and drank hers standing at the kitchen window, staring up the track.

"I must get home to Rhodri," said Elin after two cups. "Then Nia can come here and you can get back to Bath, Veronica."

"I'll be okay," said Bethan. She'd have rather died than be left alone, and as a bodyguard Nia was preferable to Veronica.

"Don't be ridiculous."

Elin had told Nia everything over the phone. When she arrived at Cwmgwrach all Bethan wanted to do was feed the ewes on the hill. They wedged Glen in the back of her old Land Rover with the bales and Nia drove. Bethan's bruised back jarred with every bump. At least the weather was improving, still bitterly cold, but that relentless rain had ceased for a while. They filled the racks and walked round the ewes as they came to the hay.

Coming down, Nia steered towards the river. Below the treeline, large patches of frost still lay intact under the scrub oaks, thick white glitter weighing the grasses and bracken down to the ground. The river came into view: black water on white rocks. Neither mentioned the beauty of the winter landscape and before they reached the precipice above the whirlpool, Nia changed direction.

"How do you feel, Nia, really?" said Bethan. There were times she had disliked her own father, but if someone else said anything against him... "About Morgan."

Nia slowed to a standstill and narrowed her eyes to slits. "He's the only person I've ever wanted dead."

They both looked across to the Abernant hills as if he were in earshot.

"And you are never to be alone again, never. Cauliflower, Bethan? It's insane. If you aren't willing to move from Cwmgwrach – and why the hell should you? – you'll just have to suffer our shows and come to me for Christmas."

Bethan felt the trembling begin in her fingers. Her whole-body shakes were lost in the juddering of the Land Rover as Nia drove on.

EIGHT

The rock was a damn nuisance when it came to mowing his usual meagre crop of hay, but it gave him a good view. He swayed forward to watch her reach the trees. His father's crook felt unbearably slimy from the vile brown juice of rotting cauliflower. The dogs were looking up at him in confusion, driving a small bunch of ewes round and round the same field for no purpose.

As soon as she disappeared into the woods, he'd jump down and wipe his hands in the wet grass, then go to the house and wash properly. He waited two or three minutes. Even walking in that stilted manner, Bethan would be halfway down the hill. He slid to the ground, looking forward to the hottest shower he could stand.

He let the dogs in to clean up the vomit. She'd sprayed it right across the kitchen floor; she disgusted him. He couldn't go inside, but watched them through the window wolfing it down voraciously and found that equally disgusting. He whistled them back outside the minute they finished, before they started sniffing round and maybe cocked a leg on the table. They'd never been in the house.

One of Elin Davies' scarves served as a mask. Tied tightly up over his nose he caught a slight scent of rabbit and lemon soap, after months on his bedroom chair. He swept up bits of cauliflower the dogs had missed then flung Jeyes Fluid over the flagstones.

She wouldn't have vomited. She was made of sterner stuff. In fact it was a wonder he'd succeeded in putting her off her unsavoury husband. He was duty bound to bring the man's extraordinarily filthy habits to her attention. He'd seen Davies hold valve caps in his mouth while he changed a tyre, when car wheels drove through every kind of muck. He touched his face and wiped his eyes no matter what was on his hands, sheep dip, silage, shit, no thought of disease passed by livestock. He carried things in his mouth like a terrier, a rag or scrap of old cardboard with a scribbled reminder. Morgan couldn't have continued to succumb to her charms if he thought she was having anything to do with her repulsive husband.

His own father had been as bad. His big hands stank long after he'd trimmed and gouged out sheep's feet with his dirty old knife. All sorts were ingrained in his skin and nails. Then the doctor had had the nerve to tell Morgan to keep to his own towel, when it was the vet who'd diagnosed orf on his finger. He'd never shared a towel in his life.

If only Bethan hadn't vomited. It took him right back to that cheese and wine do at the Celyn, with Mrs Pritchard trying to keep Bethan's drunken state from her father.

He missed her parents far more than she did. Whenever Mr Pritchard came to mind, Morgan was racked with despair. And guilt. For the man to die as he was taking his only daughter's virginity. And the way she looked at him afterwards, as if he had forced her to choose tempestuous sex over her father's life.

NINE

Nia sat at the kitchen table in Cwmgwrach, flicking through the first newspaper of the new year and trying to maintain a sense of normality.

"This paper's wet."

"I forgot to pick it up," said Bethan. "It was outside for quite a while."

"Don't know why you still have it delivered."

"My father wanted to keep the paperboy in a job."

The paperboy was 85. The more considerate farmers with appalling tracks fixed containers by the road. He rolled their papers and gift-wrapped them in the previous weeks' papers to leave in old breadbins or toolboxes. Bethan's was deposited inside a section of drainpipe in the undergrowth and often sat there for days. Veronica was so taken by the quaint rural arrangement that she always remembered.

"Says here, at the last commoners' meeting that farmer with one arm pulled a knife on someone across the mountain," said Nia. "Over grazing rights, the idiot. You should start going to them for entertainment."

"I'd really like to ride Seren to the hill today. Don't worry, I won't. Coffee?" Even fussing the mare was a great solace. Seren and Glen looked her in the eye with undying devotion. "Nia, tea or coffee? Nia!"

"You can ride to the hill anytime."

"I'm not going to, I was only saying I'd like to. I feel a bit trapped here. I'm making coffee, would you like some? Nia – what is it?"

Nia looked up, her face drained of colour.

"No, you can, seriously. You can ride to the hill, you can ride anywhere you like." She slid the paper round, pushed her chair back and straightened her arms; her knuckles were white on the edge of the table. "At any time."

"What are you talking about?" Bethan leaned over to take the paper.

"He's never going to bother you or any of us ever again."

Bethan read the headline and a few words and sank into a chair, hand clamped to her throat, where a weight lodged.

"Wouldn't he have adored the drama of it all?" said Nia. He's excelled himself this time."

Bethan covered her eyes.

"Not the cat. He'd hate the cat bit. This isn't true."

"Abernant! It's there in black and white." Nia tipped her chair and stared at the ceiling. "*Young man found dead in bathroom of isolated farmhouse, black cat purring at his side*'. When I was little, I was convinced I could magic him dead," she smiled. "I always thought Mr Gentleman was deluded about magic being in my blood, but maybe it's taken this long. '*Discovered on the bathroom floor, deep gash across his forehead, a bizarre inexplicable accident*'. I hope he suffered."

When Bethan took her hands from her eyes Nia was standing in front of her, arms outstretched, eyes black as Morgan's, hair as lustrous. Bethan ran past her out into the yard and threw up bile from her empty stomach. Nia came out and handed her a hot flannel. They sat on the wall.

"Can we believe it?" said Bethan.

"Of course. Accidental death, according to the paper."

Bethan covered her face with the flannel and waited for a portion of her heart to go out to him, but he'd already torn it out. They looked towards the woods. Abernant land began behind the trees, the spying trees. Nia jumped down from the wall and they held each other in a crush that hurt their cheek bones. They swayed inside on trembling legs and collapsed into the big old armchair, squashed in a heap with their arms round each other, faces lost in each other's hair. When Bethan's hysteria began, Nia squeezed her tighter. When she sensed no end to it, she prised herself from the chair and held Bethan by the shoulders.

"Stop now, or he's won." But no slap, just a shake.

"But why hadn't we heard?"

"We haven't seen anyone," said Nia.

Seren preened with pleasure at having the bridle slipped on and the saddle eased across her portly back, her redundancy lifted. She aimed instinctively for the hill, but Bethan turned her for the track. On reaching the lane, they skirted the village and headed for the hills beyond. Bethan swivelled round to see her bleak mountain shrouded in cloud with Cwmgwrach lost in the trees and Abernant a small black dot.

Seren had carried her to the top of the world. The narrow road curled ahead like a satin ribbon tying the plump hills into a gift. Sheep picked their way through dead heather and yellow grass. Force of habit kept Seren to the spongy turf at the edge of the road to save her hooves. A single bark came from a farm somewhere below and for the first time she thought of his dogs. They weren't mentioned in the newspaper. She imagined them chained to their windswept kennels with no food or water. She'd drive to Abernant and take them, if they were still there. The cats had no wish to be feral so they'd probably sneaked into the house. He never bothered to close the flap on the kitchen cabinet; there was always a block of cheese and a loaf among cartridges and her father's poetry books. She'd take the cats too.

'*Found dead in bathroom*' seemed ludicrously mundane for such a histrionic character. When she thought of his possible endings: he'd rolled his tractor on the hill and jumped clear, survived beatings by his half-brothers and Davies Tŷ Newydd. He was too good a swimmer to be swallowed by the whirlpool, too sure-footed to slip into a ravine and too arrogant for suicide. She thought of the 'hanged man' in his sheep shed and shivered, the brown coat and hat no doubt carefully arranged. Maybe he'd tempted providence with his fake tumour and a real one had grown.

No longer condemned, she surveyed the desolate landscape. Her feet quivered in the stirrups and her spirits rose as the chapel appeared on the horizon, the tall austere building with the crumbling chimney and stone ruin clinging to the side, set alone in a thousand acres of mountain. A car came into view, maybe from a farm in a valley below. The first vehicle she'd seen, it was moving away slowly in the opposite direction. She watched it twist and turn round the endless bends, dipping in and out of sight, in no hurry. The brake lights sparkled for the descent on the far side of the mountain and the car disappeared.

Rain was turning to sleet. She tied Seren to the most sheltered part of the railings and walked through the soggy rushes. The two bent trees still stood at the gate, one at each post, whipped to submission by relentless gales. Neither had grown or changed shape since her mother's dreadful funeral nearly ten years ago. She weaved her way through the rows of tilting headstones and weathered angels leaning at dangerous angles. One or two were practically horizontal, as if those beneath were pushing up from the depths. A few local dignitaries lay forgotten in their cages of spiked iron railings and carpets of matted brown grass, though a recent arrival boasted opulent black marble, gold lettering and plastic carnations.

All her mother's Daz daffodils had weathered into grey and black stripes. Bethan couldn't bring herself to remove them.

The small metal vases were missing from her parents' modest headstones. She should have planted bulbs. She'd come empty-handed, for once not thinking of them. Usually she brought cut flowers and whenever the bunch was an odd number, she gave her mother the extra flower then asked a pertinent question. As it dropped or fell against the others she interpreted the movement as the answer she needed. She hadn't received a lot more guidance on her behaviour when the mismatched couple were alive. She heard her father's "Not now, dear." How little she had to go on.

She'd ridden here on a whim with no idea if the funeral had come and gone or was yet to happen. She could have invited his other victims to her celebration, but she wished to be alone, however eerie. Concoct some sort of mad personal ritual to help heal her fractured life.

There were two new unmarked graves against the back wall that separated the graveyard from the mountain, one roughly filled in with an uneven topping of stony soil and the other a freshly dug hole covered with a sheet of black plastic held down by stones. No wreaths for clues. She made for the heavy door. It needed a kick of encouragement to open. She climbed the stairs, listening out for ghosts and peering through the keyhole of the old schoolroom for a glimpse of Shoni Blacktooth, the hideous old teacher who craved for nothing but tobacco. Maybe those who'd learnt to sing here had crawled from the woodwork to give Morgan a suitable send-off. A rousing service led by the mad preacher, who conducted with bread in one hand and cheese in the other then travelled miles home across the mountain singing tenor. Like him. The chapel was ice cold.

She stepped down into the gloom, sat at the end of a pew and only made out the rat by his horrible pink hands fussing round his whiskers. The size of a cat and colour of the polished organ, he sat upright on his haunches washing his beaten-up face, studying her with the nonchalance of a prize-fighter boasting a prominent cauliflower ear. Her stomach churned at the word. A surreal encounter with him so confident she almost spoke aloud and dared him to sit there glaring at her. He grew bored and sauntered off. What could he live on up here, crumbs from the dead preacher's bread and cheese?

She breathed again. She sat neatly, knees and heels together (the Virgin Mary in mind), hands twisting anxiously in her lap. A band of cold air circulated her head. Her boots had leaked but the brooding stillness prevented her stamping her wet feet. The iron grille on the high window was almost as dense as the priest's spyhole in the confessional box and barred most of the daylight. But not the sound of wind, and her thoughts turned to Seren.

She tiptoed to the window, stepped up on to a pew and saw the sleet had turned to snow, the settling kind of snow. The sheet of plastic had sunk into the open grave. She crept back out into the weather. Before she started round to Seren, a noise lured her in the opposite direction. A man was at the freshly filled grave, slapping down the soil with a spade. He was unkempt and earth-coloured in skin, hair, overcoat, trousers and boots, the archetypal gravedigger. He obviously hadn't seen Seren at the side railings, and at the sight of Bethan he leapt round, bringing the spade across his body like a gun.

She nodded towards the rectangle of mud.

"Can you tell me who this is, please?"

He stared at her in alarm, then back and forth at the mound. His gawping mouth revealed two black teeth and, in her madness, she saw Shoni Blacktooth.

"Do you know whose grave this is?" she asked. "Or who came to the funeral?"

He raised the spade.

She took a step back. "Can you tell me? Please."

He flung the spade into the brambles and scuttled away in a limping hobble. Shackled ankles and clanking chains would have completed the archaic scene. He was out of sight when she heard his growly shout: "No one." She ran round the chapel to see him closing a little gate and heading off across the mountain. He disappeared into the snow, now falling in large flakes.

She kicked off her boots, peeled off sopping socks and stepped onto the unfinished grave. She squelched her cold toes in between the chopped rushes poking from the peaty soil and lifted her face to the grey sky. Snowflakes brushed her flushed cheeks. When she'd oozed over every inch she went up on her mud-caked toes and twirled around the perimeter. Faster and faster. How good this would have looked had she worn the divine black dress with the satin lining and ridden here side-saddle. On she went, a pause for breath, heart banging, the snow thickening.

When she eventually collapsed against the peeling chapel wall, the mountain was white and the thread of road barely visible. Her jacket was saturated. She rubbed at her feet with a damp handkerchief and pushed them back into her soaking boots with difficulty. She had danced and stamped him into the freezing ground.

It had to be him.

Seren whinnied with relief, seeing Bethan come back through the graves. The snow was not dissolving on her back and she looked like a horse cake with a generous sprinkling of icing sugar. A single magpie perched on the railings, disproving the old saying. Bethan was euphoric. She scanned the thick sky to check the weather, not to see a second bird. Snowflakes landed gently in her eyes and she slammed them shut, reminded of putrid cauliflower.

There was a difference at the chapel entrance. Snow changed everything. Approaching the gate, she stopped dead. Just one of the skeletal trees was standing, the other lay splayed across the path. Her eye sockets burned. Both trees were such pathetic specimens that the wind could wrench either from the ground like a weed. A child could have uprooted it. Snow had already built thick ridges along the sparse branches, half-covering the white mound of a grave. Stiff with cold, she bunched her small rough hands into fists and shoved them into her jacket pockets.

The lone magpie flew from the railing to the tree left standing and landed on a thin white branch. He gave a croak and flipped his head from side to side, his attention taken by something. Bethan took a step closer. Her insides dissolved.

A scarf was fluttering in the middle of the tree. A narrow length of black silk sparkling against the white background, shunning the snow, each flake melting instantly on the glossy surface. A crow landed on a higher branch, sending down a shower of snow. The scarf flapped and the magpie dived to attack the glittering glass beads sewn along each end.

The crow flew off. She remembered Nia reporting Mrs Williams' scathing opinion of Morgan: "That one could live where crows would die."

She couldn't run, not with feet frozen like chunks of wood. Quaking but sedate, she passed through the gate, took one more look at her shredded scarf, then untied Seren. The mare could turn on a sixpence. Ecstatic to be on the move, she set off at a pace as though aware of the severity of the situation, her mane clinking together with hard little balls of ice. Unfamiliar with the terrain this side of the mountain, she crashed through dips concealed by snow, but was born sure-footed. It was Bethan's riding skills called to task.

They reached Cwmgwrach without the ghost of a madman leaping out in front of them and not a single vehicle passing. Bethan slid from Seren's back, her teeth clattering like a football rattle and Nia was there, waiting to wrap her in a blanket.

When the snow stopped, they drove up to Abernant and found the two dogs chained to their kennels. Their straw bedding was clean, as were their full water bowls and there were dog biscuits and tins of food stacked in with the gas canisters. They recognised Bethan and leapt into the Land Rover, desperate for human companionship. Driving them to Cwmgwrach she presumed they'd never left the mountain or travelled in a vehicle. No sign of the cats – she'd return.

A few days later the friends gathered for their private wake. Mr Gentleman brought champagne and a large casserole to Cwmgwrach; he thought Bethan had better things to do than cook. She and Nia returned from feeding the sheep to find the kitchen warm and the table beautifully set with serviettes and candles. Never had she seen the place look so welcoming and her eyes filled with tears

"The least I can do," said Mr Gentleman.

"I've put Rhodri to bed, Bethan – hope that's okay," said Elin. "Sheep alright?"

Bethan blinked hard and nodded. They'd arrived at the hayracks on the flattish plateau to see her flock wandering around amiably with no one barging. They'd obviously had their fill. Usually every wisp of hay had disappeared and they charged the Land Rover.

"They look good, mainly because his have gone."

"God knows where," said Nia. "And who was it suggested Bethan turn her ewes to the hill? Well worth him lugging her hayracks up there, he knew his damn sheep would cross the river at the sight of food."

"Yes, I must be simple," said Bethan.

"Quite." Nia handed her an envelope. "Here's what he owes you for hay, among other things. My father stashed money in weird places and Morgan did the same. This was in a screwed-up paper bag in the wall at Abernant. You're all simple – and you, Veronica, acting like a bitch on heat at your gallery do."

"Nia," said Mr Gentleman. "Please."

Veronica bristled, "A country term, I take it. But you're probably right."

"Sorry, Veronica," said Nia. "But I don't know what it was with you all."

"A somewhat mediocre death for such a wild fellow," said Mr Gentleman. "I don't suppose we'll ever know what really happened. Dessert everyone?"

"I might know," said Veronica. "The first time he stayed with me in Bath I assumed we'd shower together, but he preferred to have space."

No one spoke or moved an inch.

"He plastered himself with my gorgeous soap then began to twist and turn like a bloody dance, then he put his hands next to the taps, head down, bottom in the air and splayed his legs for the water to gush between them. Quite a sight, as you can imagine. I think I was too shocked to move. Admittedly, we'd had a few drinks."

Bethan smarted. The thought of those two together.

"He slipped on the soap and went flying, just missed the taps then. He was beside himself, livid, and vile to me for the next hour or so. You're all gawping. I'd say he died through his own fastidiousness."

Bethan knew exactly how he was with alcohol; just one or two Christmas drinks out of loneliness would probably have unsteadied him.

"I'll just take Glen outside," she said, with a sudden need for fresh air. "Last look round, shut the gates and things."

The bracingly cold night was clear with a forest of silver stars. Why was she shocked? He and Veronica had always fascinated each other.

His dogs had been made comfortable in a barn behind the cowshed. She slipped inside to check them while Glen sniffed round the door. Walking past the cowshed to close the yard gate, she heard a faint noise, an owl woo-ed and Glen looked up towards the mountain. She returned to the house calmly.

They were still at the table. She sat down. Mr Gentleman was offering cheese and biscuits when there was a cry from the landing. The women jumped.

"Mami?" Rhodri was at the banisters.

"Coming, *cariad*," called Elin.

"Here, Elin." Nia handed over another envelope. "For Rhodri. Not half enough. I don't suppose Morgan paid his dues there."

"At least the dear little chap will never have to meet his father," said Veronica.

Bethan bent to stroke Glen. She thought she might be sick. In a rush of heat, she was crossing the river, Rhodri's little legs clamped round her hip.

"It has to be said, he was extremely dedicated to hunt you all with such tenacity," said Mr Gentleman. "I don't mean that as any sort of accolade, of course, just a fact."

"His insanity was contagious," said Bethan quietly.

"Well and truly," said Elin. "How the hell you rode up to that terrible old chapel, Bethan, on that creepy deserted road, with a few bony ewes crossing over."

Bethan stared at her.

"I saw you in my mirror as I was driving away," said Elin. "Your fiery mop flying about, till you pulled your hood up. You should wear a riding hat. And I'd recognize my lovely mare a mile off."

"Why were you there?"

"We should compete, see who's the maddest. To tie a scarf in a tree, an ironic farewell. My best gold silk scarf with sequins, would you believe? Not one he liked."

"How extraordinary you both had the same thought," said Mr Gentleman.

"Did you notice it, Bethan?" said Elin. "In one of those bare trees at the gate."

"One tree was down." Bethan looked at Nia, barely able to remember who knew what. "Not gold silk, no."

"Maybe it was under snow."

"There was one magpie. I watched him. He was attacking the glass beads on a black silk scarf."

She stirred before the dawn chorus drowned out the sound of the barn door, swinging back and forth on its creaking hinges. Morgan's dogs had gone.